INTO THE FIRE

Rafe stepped inside and walked on, turning around as the three came in: all women, Ky could see now, shivering as their wet clothes clung to them. All were bald, scalps and faces completely hairless. Were these the escaped criminals? They didn't look like it. Their legs were bare from well above the knees, their feet in thin, now-sodden cloth slippers. Stella shut the outside doors and pulled heavy linen curtains over them.

All three knelt, dripping on the floor. The one who had led them in said, "Admiral, please help us. You're the only one who can."

The voice gave Ky the name. "Inyatta?"

"Yes, sir. Please—don't turn us in—"

Ky fought to keep her expression calm despite a surge of rage at what had been done to them. They did not need her rage; they needed her help.

By Elizabeth Moon

The Serrano Legacy
Hunting Party
Sporting Chance
Winning Colors
Once a Hero
Rules of Engagement
Change of Command
Against the Odds

The Serrano Legacy: Omnibus One
The Serrano Connection: Omnibus Two
The Serrano Succession: Omnibus Three

The Legacy of Gird
Surrender None
Liar's Oath

A Legacy of Honour: The Legacy of Gird Omnibus

The Deed of Paksenarrion
Sheepfarmer's Daughter
Divided Allegiance
Oath of Gold

The Deed of Paksenarrion Omnibus

Paladin's Legacy
Oath of Fealty
Kings of the North
Echoes of Betrayal
Limits of Power
Crown of Renewal

Remnant Population

Speed of Dark

The Vatta's War series
Trading in Danger
Moving Target
Engaging the Enemy
Command Decision
Victory Conditions

Vatta's Peace
Cold Welcome
Into the Fire

with Anne McCaffrey
Sassinak (The Planet Pirataes Volume 2)
Generation Warriors (The Planet Pirataes Volume 3)

INTO THE FIRE

ELIZABETH MOON

orbit

www.orbitbooks.net

ORBIT

First published in Great Britain in 2018 by Orbit

1 3 5 7 9 10 8 6 4 2

A CIP catalogue record for this book
is available from the British Library.

ISBN 978-0-356-50630-2

Printed and bound in Great Britain by Clays Ltd, St Ives plc

Papers used by Orbit are from well-managed forests
and other responsible sources.

Orbit
An imprint of
Little, Brown Book Group
Carmelite House
50 Victoria Embankment
London EC4Y 0DZ

An Hachette UK Company
www.hachette.co.uk

www.orbitbooks.net

For all "the helpers" Mr. Rogers spoke of, who in times of crisis show up to help those who need it—from those who commit heroic lifesaving acts to those whose words spoken at the right moment, whose hug, or hand on the shoulder, save spirits

CHAPTER ONE

SLOTTER KEY, PORT MAJOR
DAY 1

Ky Vatta stood looking out the upper-floor window of the Vatta home in Port Major, just above the entrance. Below, she could see the brick walk bordered by low shrubs pruned into balls, the perfect green lawn, the white-painted palings and gate through which she and Rafe had entered a few hours before.

A chill draft came off the window, reminding her that she was still in the beach clothes she'd put on before leaving Corleigh just that morning. If Stella and Helen hadn't arrived on Corleigh yesterday, if she and Rafe had gotten back to the mainland when they planned, it would have been warm here, too. She could almost feel the elation of the previous morning as they packed to leave the island, planning to buy their own ship and leave Slotter Key together. Her fortune, they'd thought—her back pay, her savings banked on Cascadia, and the money Stella owed her for the shares Ky had given up—combined with Rafe's personal fortune and the stipend he had from ISC, would be enough to buy a spaceship, hire some crew, and go wherever their interests took them.

But then . . . it had all fallen apart. Stella and Helen arrived because the house—this house—had been attacked, a door kicked in, and Helen had feared for the children. They'd brought the news that the money Ky had counted on to help buy a ship—her back pay from Space Defense Force and money owed her for the sale of her shares of Vatta Transport and Vatta Enterprises—had been sequestered by the government of Cascadia, because she was being blamed for the death of her former aide Jen, whose father was on the Grand Council of the Moscoe Confederation. Stella's position on Cascadia, Vatta's secondary headquarters, was threatened, as well. Ky's own accounts here on Slotter Key were also frozen because of the deaths on Miksland. The evidence she'd collected so carefully from the crashed shuttle and from Miksland had gone missing—the evidence that could clear her of suspicion that she'd murdered those who died. So much had gone wrong; probably more would.

The gray sky outside matched her mood. She felt alienated from the house, the city, the entire planet; eight years of physical separation, the attack—she wasn't even sure exactly how long after she'd left—that killed her parents, her brothers, her uncle, Stella's sister and brothers. It was too different—no, *she* was too different. She didn't fit into the Vatta family structure anymore. She didn't have a place in Slotter Key's military; she no longer had her own fleet, the fleet she had built from one old battered tradeship. The men and women she'd commanded—those who knew her best—were either dead or far away, in the Space Defense Force. Her throat tightened; her stomach churned.

She took a deep breath, forcing herself to think forward and not back. She had things she *could* do, things that might—though it was hard to believe—be as interesting, as worthwhile, as what she'd already done. First she needed to find out what had happened to the evidence she'd brought back from Miksland, evidence that would clear her of charges of murder for every death that had occurred.

Then find a way to convince the Moscoe Confederation that she had not killed Jen Bentik, so they would release the lien on her funds. And she needed to know how the other survivors from Miksland were doing. By now, they should be almost through the home leave she'd been told about, ready to return to duty. Grace, as Rector of Defense, would be able to get their addresses for her.

And—if she was stuck here long enough, all the way to the next southern summer, she might even return to Miksland, explore the deep levels, those mysterious laboratories, maybe even figure out who had built them. Rafe didn't have enough money for a spaceship, but he certainly had enough for a charter flight. Scientists were probably down there now. It would be safe, with Greyhaus's people far away and the mercenaries dead. Whoever had first claimed it surely wouldn't dare do anything now that it was public knowledge.

She looked across the street to another front garden as formal as the one below, and the white brick house behind it with its flagstone walk, its rows of shrubs pruned into little pyramids. The second floor was built out over a rounded portico, forming a curved row of windows. Handy for neighborhood snoops, if there were any.

Rain spattered the window, a swift rattle that broke into her thoughts. Across the street she saw a curtain twitch, opening a dark gap, but she couldn't see anyone. So there was a neighborhood snoop. Below, a black car pulled up in front of the house. Stella got out, accepted her travel case and two white containers from the driver, then tapped the code onto the front gatepost. It opened for her. Ky saw someone step out between the portico columns of the house across the street, and then disappear again. Stella waved the driver away.

Ky went back to the stairs and down in time to see Rafe open the door. A gust of cold wet air swirled in when he pulled it back.

"I brought supper," Stella said. She handed the containers to Ky. "Take these into the kitchen, please. I'll be back when I've changed into something warmer."

Stella came into the kitchen a few minutes later, dressed in slacks and a pullover, looking elegant as usual. Ky wished she had asked for her own clothes to be picked up that afternoon. She set out plates on the kitchen table, opened the boxes and made a guess at who wanted which. Stella pushed the opened containers to the middle of the small table and said, "Whatever you want."

After supper, eaten quickly and almost silently, they made the rounds of checking doors and windows. As Stella looked out the double glass doors into the back garden, she shook her head. "I should have checked before supper. There's that miserable stuffed pony, getting wet on a swing. Justin loves it. It'll mildew if I don't get it in the dryer. And the ball looks tacky out there." She turned on an outside light, opened the door and went out, crossing the terrace and then the grass; Ky stayed back, away from the cold wind and rain, watching. Stella came back, raindrops in her hair sparkling in the light, the wet stuffed toy in one hand and the ball in the other. Just as she came into the house, the door chime rang and someone knocked on the front door.

"Take these," Stella said, handing off the wet toys to Ky. She shut and locked the garden doors and headed toward the front. "Dryer's just off the kitchen."

Ky had no desire to visit with company; she ducked into the short passage to the kitchen as whoever it was pounded harder on the door. Rafe, she noticed, had followed Stella. Ky found the dryer, tossed the stuffed toy into it, and stared at the dials, finally deciding on GENTLE. She dried the wet ball with a kitchen towel, then sat down at the kitchen table. She could just hear Stella speaking, though she could not distinguish the words. The tone made it clear Stella was upset. In a minute or so Stella was back in the kitchen, color in her pale cheeks. "The utter nerve—" she was saying to Rafe, who followed her.

"What's the problem?"

"Oh, some military police or something—not Port Major police— said they suspected there were dangerous fugitives in the neighborhood. They wanted to search the house and grounds. I said no, that there'd been a watchman at the house day and night. They thought the damage to the kitchen door meant someone might be hiding inside. I had to show my ID, even. Do I look like a fugitive?"

"Of course not," Ky said.

"I told them to check with Port Major police about the break-in— maybe it was the same gang they were chasing—asked if they knew who the fugitives were, but they didn't answer. Just said to be careful and lock everything up. Oh, and they're going to be doing aerial surveillance tonight."

"We should see what's on the newsvids," Rafe said. "Surely there'd be something about a prison breakout." He led the way to the security office next to the lift and turned on another screen. A serious-faced man was explaining what cut of cattlelope to choose for braising. A streamer at the bottom carried ads for cookware shops. Rafe changed selections. Two women and three men were arguing about a recent election on Dorland and what it meant for the balance of power in the planetary legislature. Here the streamer carried what Ky recognized as financial news. Another try gave them an obvious drama vid, with a stationary block giving time, temperature, wind speed, and wave height.

"Wrong time," Stella said. "Slotter Key's media laws are different from Nexus or Cascadia. Much more tightly controlled."

Rafe switched off the screen. "I'll go on out, then, and repel lurkers, if any."

"It's cold and wet," Stella said. "You should change."

"I have nothing with me. I'll be fine."

"Backup?" Ky said.

"No. Stay here with Stella."

"That's his *I'm up to something* voice," Stella said. "If only they hadn't been so rude—"

"It upset him?" Ky leaned on the wall, out of the draft coming in the door Stella held half open.

"Yes." Stella looked outside again, where Rafe was a vague blur in the dark.

"Why military police?" Ky asked.

"I don't know," Stella said. She glanced at the kitchen door, slightly crooked in its frame and braced with a couple of boards nailed across it. "But I hope they're wrong about any escaped military criminals. That boarded-up door does look like an easy place to break in." They watched Rafe move along the front of the shrubbery and waited for him to turn back toward the house when he reached the garage wall. Instead, he stood still.

"Found something," Stella said. "I wonder what."

"Or someone," Ky said. She moved her pistol from her shoulder holster to the pocket of her shorts. Then Rafe turned back toward the house, walking steadily, not looking back, and behind him the first figure came out of the shrubbery. Then another. And another. They were hard to see in the rain and poor light. Ky heard Stella's indrawn breath, Rafe's sandals scuffing in the damp grass, and behind him, other footfalls, softer. He stepped onto the terrace, walked across it, his sandals slapping lightly on the bricks. He quirked an eyebrow at her. Behind him, just visible in the dim scattered glow of his hand-light, she could see the first of the three following him: short and slight, a bald head paler than the brown face, wearing some kind of thin garment—a robe?

Rafe stepped inside and walked on, turning around as the three came in: all women, Ky could see now, shivering as their wet clothes clung to them. All were bald, scalps and faces completely hairless. Were these the escaped criminals? They didn't look like it. Their legs were bare from well above the knees, their feet in thin, now-sodden cloth slippers. Stella shut the outside doors and pulled heavy linen curtains over them.

All three knelt, dripping on the floor. The one who had led them in said, "Admiral, please help us. You're the only one who can."

The voice gave Ky the name. "Inyatta?"

"Yes, sir. Please—don't turn us in—"

Ky fought to keep her expression calm despite a surge of rage at what had been done to them. They did not need her rage; they needed her help.

"Stella, lock us down," Rafe said.

Stella looked at Ky, at Rafe, at the three wet women who'd been hiding in the shrubbery. "No one can see in now. And lockdown will seal off the kitchen annex."

"Do it," Ky said. She held out her hands; Inyatta grasped them. "Inyatta—all of you, get up; the floor's cold." She reholstered her pistol. "These must be who those men were hunting." She had not looked away from Inyatta; she heard Stella walk to the master panel and key in the code. "Corporal, what's happened to you? Are the others all right?"

"No—and we don't know what, or why—they separated us—they changed our implants—" Inyatta's voice was shaky as she clambered up; she was shivering.

The house lights brightened and a current of warmer air moved across the room. "Internal power and environmental confirmed," Stella said. "Now what? You know these people?"

"Yes. This is Corporal Inyatta; she was with me on Miksland." She still didn't recognize the other two. Ky glanced at Rafe, then back at Stella. "We need to get them dry, warm, and fed. Then find out what's been going on."

"You won't send us back?" Again, the voice gave her the identity: Corporal Barash. "Please!" The third had not spoken at all, and Ky hadn't figured out who she was yet. She had a fresh scar, a raised red-purple ridge, on her head, and puffy swelling that changed whatever her face had been.

"Of course I won't. Come on upstairs. Hot baths, towels, clothes—Stella, have you got some extra warm things? All I have is a change of shirts." Ky headed for the stairs. "I trust you left nothing behind that could be noticed in the morning?"

"No, sir. We ate the paper off the fruit bars." That was the third, and again the voice gave Ky the identification. Kamat—*that* was Durga Kamat? The shaved head, scar, and puffiness obscured what had been an unusual beauty. What had happened to her—to them—and what about all the others? Questions erupted in her mind, but right now these three needed care.

Ky led them to the first of the two bedrooms on the right of the landing. "I'm guessing you'd like to stay together?"

"Yes, please." They were clustered in the doorway, staring at all the flowered chintz.

"The sofa will make another bed. The bath's back here—" She led the way. "This should be a linen closet—yes. Towels, robes—ready for guests."

They looked worse in the brighter light, bruises and puncture marks as if they'd had many injections, marks on wrists and ankles from restraints. Ky said nothing about that. "Stella's my cousin. She and I will be looking for clothes for you, but feel free to wrap up in blankets or anything you find to get warm."

She kept her voice level and calm, for their sake, but when she went back into the hall, her anger shot up like a geyser, dimming her vision for an instant. *All* of them must have been taken, drugged, held. Separated, Inyatta had said. Probably early on, perhaps even at Pingat Base while she had been on a flight to the mainland. Who had done this to her people? And how? Why hadn't Great-Aunt Grace made sure the other survivors were properly taken care of? She should not have agreed to fly back separately—she should have thought—but too late for that. First things: take care of these three. She crossed the head of the stairs and met Stella coming back with a stack of folded clothes.

"I'm taller than any of them, and I have no idea what size underwear they need—but this is what I've got."

"Thank you," Ky said. "I thought I'd be going back to Grace's when we flew back, where my box from *Vanguard II* is. I'd use it, but—"

"It's all right," Stella said. "Plans change, that's all. I've gotten used to it." Stella's lips twitched. "Tomorrow you can order in."

"I don't have any money, remember?" Ky said. Her voice had an edge to it; she wished she'd softened it.

"Vatta tab." Short and flat.

Ky shook her head. "I meant for them. No one can know they're here. I know they aren't criminals, and if they're the ones those men were hunting, something's very wrong."

"That's all right. You need clothes, too, I'm sure. Just order extra. Two of them are near your size."

"And Kamat?"

"Toss hers in with the rest."

"Maybe. Can we receive deliveries while the house is locked down?"

"The front door can be opened; it's just a little slower. The ship armor slides sideways first, then the door opens as usual. And we really should unlock everything daily, if we can, to access the kitchen stores and air it out."

Ky found the three women perched on the couch, wrapped in blankets, when she returned with a pile of Stella's clothes. She set the clothes on the end of one bed and explained the plan for tomorrow.

"What if they come here looking for us?" asked Inyatta. Barash nodded. Kamat stared at her own lap.

"Someone did, earlier. But they didn't say it was you; they just said escaped criminals. And they left after Stella told them only family was here. If they come back, they won't make it inside. You don't have tags in, do you?"

"I don't know," Inyatta said. "They drugged us, and my implant's different—doesn't hold everything it did. They might have changed it out. I couldn't walk well most of the time; they'd give us a shot to wake up more if they wanted us to walk and take a shower. But if I had a tracker tag, they should have caught us sooner, shouldn't they?"

Ky had no idea what the range was on whatever kind of tag might have been used. "They didn't catch you; that's all we know. We'll work on that tomorrow. This house is shielded, and some parts double-shielded. If we unlock it tomorrow, we'll put you in one of the inner offices." She paused; they said nothing. "When you've dressed, turn left out the door, follow the passage past the head of the stairs, and take the first right. There's a small kitchen at that end; Stella's heating up soup."

After soup and toasted cheese sandwiches, they all looked better, though Stella's clothes were too big for all of them. Stella returned, holding a single bedraggled black wig and shaking her head. "This was all I could find in the old playroom storage closet. We had costumes up there, you remember, Ky? We used to have more wigs, but apparently Mother threw them out. I'm afraid it won't be very comfortable—they were cheap wigs for children's games—but you're welcome to try it out. We might be able to trim it so it looks better."

The three passed it around, each one trying it on. It looked entirely fake, and didn't fit two of them, but Corporal Barash wanted to keep it on. Kamat asked if there was a scarf she could wrap around her head; Stella ducked into her room and brought out a tray of them. Kamat and Inyatta each chose one and put it on—one green, one orange. With the baldness covered, they did look more like themselves.

"How did you escape?" Ky asked.

"Remembered what you said," Inyatta said, with a shy smile. "*Figure out the next thing to do, and do it.* When we got the chance—even though you'd said to stick together and we had no idea where the others were."

"You weren't all in the same building?"

"No—I don't know. Where we were was big, many sections, and each was separately locked, besides each cell. All three of us were together because they didn't want us to mix with any of the others that weren't our people."

"They had you in a *prison*?"

"Yes," Inyatta said. "Not far from here, in fact. We walked to the city."

"They said they were taking us to be checked out medically, and then we'd get home leave," Kamat said. "But the first place they took us to—it did look like a hospital—they gave us shots. To take care of any infections, they said."

"And we woke up in that prison," Inyatta said. "There was a lot of yelling we couldn't hear clearly when we arrived—"

"I could hear 'quarantine,'" Barash said. "And 'thirty days to be sure.'"

"They'd taken away our comunits right away, back at the start—"

"The mercs?"

"No, when we got to the base, before we flew here for debriefing. Our own troops."

Ky nodded but didn't interrupt. As she'd thought . . . they were all taken, and now she would have to find them, somehow, and get them released.

"And then we woke up, our heads shaved like this, and—well, I'm the only one of the three with a prepaid skullphone account, but they'd operated on us all, and disabled all our implant communications. And forced Kamat to have an implant."

"Which doesn't do anything I can't do myself," Kamat said. "It's disgusting."

"They said you were really sick, in a hospital, and maybe would die, Admiral," Barash said. "Were you sick?"

Ky shook her head. "Not at all. I had meetings, interviews—and legal stuff to do inside the family. And the news media—Stella, what did they have on newsvids about the Slotter Key personnel who were rescued?"

Stella shook her head. "I'm sorry—I didn't pay attention. I was absorbed in the transfer of command inside Vatta. Mother had left a lot of loose ends. I glanced at one of the interviews you did, Ky, but I didn't read beyond that."

"Nobody said anything to me about infections or disease related to Miksland," Ky said. "You had arranged a medical appointment for me through Vatta—"

"I wasn't about to turn you over to Slotter Key military," Stella said. "Even with Aunt Grace as Rector. Their shuttle failed and lost you—"

Ky noticed the others' heads turning back and forth, like spectators at a tennis game, and held up her hand. "Wait, Stella. Inyatta, do you know where the others are? Still in prison? All in the same prison?"

"All I know for sure is what happened to the three of us. Except that the senior NCOs were taken by a separate flight from Pingats."

"Staff sergeants? Sergeants?"

"Both. Gossin, Kurin, Cosper, Chok, and McLenard. I'm sure, because I recited the names over and over so I wouldn't forget. In case— I don't know what I was thinking, really . . ."

"That was good thinking, Corporal. A smart thing to do."

"And we don't know what they told our families. What if they were told we died of some horrible disease?" Kamat's voice trembled. "What if they planned to kill us all, and the rest are already dead?"

"You're safe here," Ky said. "So get some sleep—we're all on the same floor—and in the morning we'll start figuring out how to help all of you." She yawned; she couldn't help it.

"Were you here in Port Major the whole time?" asked Barash as she stood up and put her soup bowl in the little sink.

"No, I just got back to the mainland today. I was on Corleigh, the island where I grew up. I hadn't been back since the house was destroyed, after I left the Academy."

"Come on," Inyatta said as Barash opened her mouth to speak. "Everyone needs rest." She turned to Ky. "Admiral, thank you for taking us in. And you, Sera Vatta," to Stella. "And you, Ser."

The others followed her down the passage toward the other wing. "Bad," Rafe murmured, shaking his head. "Something's rotten—"

"It's all bad," Ky said. The anger she'd been controlling flared again, white hot. "Aunt Grace *let* them be thrown in prison? Or did she plan it? Is she part—"

"You can't believe that," Stella said.

"I can," Ky said. "And right now I want the truth! Stella, did you know anything about this? Anything at all? What did Grace say about the Slotter Key personnel?"

"Don't bristle at me, Ky. I don't recall her saying anything about them. We didn't have that much time. I met her at Hautvidor; she and Mac and Rafe and Teague. They were all talking about the mercs— whether the Mac-something—"

"Mackensee," Ky said.

"Could land their force on Miksland quick enough to keep the others from killing you all. Then Grace got a call from someone in the military—Slotter Key's, that is—and shooed us all out. Someone's head would roll was the last I heard from her."

"I don't think she's involved in what happened to your people," Rafe said to Ky. "Teague and I overheard enough while in her house to know she was concerned about the others as well as you. But there's division in the Slotter Key military, which she thinks might go back to that civil war."

"Civil war?" Stella wrinkled her nose. "You mean that little insurrection thing she got caught in?"

Rafe cocked his head. "You don't know more than that?"

"She told me about it," Stella said. "Back when I was in trouble—you know, Ky, with the gardener's son. She got involved with someone and ended up in some kind of violent mess. It barely shows up in our history books at all. Something happened to her; she was in a psych hospital for a while."

"She didn't give the details?"

"Not exactly. She did tell me she'd killed some people, that she'd been scared a lot." Stella's voice was cool, calm, as if whatever had happened to Grace didn't matter in the slightest.

"I suspect it was a lot more than that," Rafe said. "She's a very complex woman, and she's—she reminds me of someone I knew."

"Well, it's a hard job."

Rafe looked at Ky. "We'd better get some rest, too, Ky."

"I want to talk to her *now*—" Ky could feel the anger boiling up again.

"It's late," Stella said. "There's nothing she could do tonight anyway."

Ky stiffened. "If she's involved, she certainly *could* do something tonight! Others are still in prison—or somewhere—being mistreated like these."

"I know you're upset," Stella said, "but be reasonable, Ky. They aren't really your troops; you don't have any authority. Grace does, but she's got a lot on her plate."

The tone ripped the last shreds of Ky's control. In just that calm, almost syrupy voice Stella had insisted Ky's earlier enthusiasms and angers were unreasonable overreactions. Older to younger, senior to junior.

"You do not get to tell me who my people are or aren't!" Ky said. "You weren't there, you don't—" Someone had hold of her arm; she spun, freeing herself, and struck before she realized who it was. Rafe, who had slipped the worst of the force and now stood just out of reach, poised in case she attacked.

"Ky!" Stella said, now roused and angry.

"Don't," Rafe said to Stella. She stepped back, frowning.

Ky turned slowly to face Stella. "He's right. Don't. Don't lecture me in that tone, Stella. Ever again."

For a long instant the three of them did not move. Ky stood rigid with the control she exerted not to strike again. Then Stella shrugged. "You're right, Ky. You're not a shareholder anymore, you're not living on Slotter Key, what you do is your own business and not any concern of mine." Her voice was cool, level. "Except that you *are* in my house, and you *are* the one who decided to bring strangers into it, fugitives, and then give *me* orders. And I am your cousin; your actions do affect me; I was attacked in my own apartment on Cascadia because of you. You might remember *that* when your temper cools."

Ky felt the rage subsiding as if it were a column of boiling water leaking out of a pipe.

"I do," she said, her voice still colored by it, but quieter. "I didn't know about the attack."

"Would it have made a difference?"

"Yes. Some." She felt sore, as the tension dropped, sore and tired inside and out.

*   *   *

Stella made it to her own suite, closed the door behind her, and let loose a streak of language that Ky probably did not suspect she knew. How *dare* Ky treat her that way! Ky hadn't even spoken to her on the flight back from Corleigh, had just sat there sulking, as if Stella were responsible for the bad news about her money and missing out on a longer vacation with Rafe.

The problem wasn't just money. Ky didn't have a ship to boss around anymore, a crew that hung on her every word and thought she was wonderful. She was feeling sorry for herself and probably believed Stella had it easier because Stella still had both the homes she'd grown up in, a mother alive, and Jo's children as a promise of the future.

"Easier!" she said aloud, surprising herself with the venom in her voice. "Ha! I have *nothing*. My mother—my real mother—is someone I never met and never will, and my real father was a monster. My so-called family lied about my birth, Jo wasn't any relation to me, and her children—how can I love them as if they were my real niece and nephew when I will never have children of my own?"

Not that she'd really wanted children. But still. The things she might have said to Ky, wanted to say to Ky, boiled through her head, vicious and potent as vitriol. *Ky* was the lucky one. Ky's parents had been her real parents; yes, they were dead, but she was not being hassled by a live "mother" who wasn't, a woman riven by grief and fear, whose only real grip on life was the twins she clung to. And yet Ky, as always, had grabbed the moral high ground, eager to play rescuer to those three peculiar-looking women, no doubt eager to have them kneel at her feet again, bask in their adulation of the great, wonderful Admiral Vatta who had saved everyone.

"Gah!" Stella said aloud. "And ordering me around like one of her soldiers!"

She was sweating now, pure fury hot as summer sun. All the quarrels in their past rose up, all the times she'd been told Ky was smarter or more sensible.

Her daysetter chimed, reminding her it was time for bed. She took a shower instead, letting the familiar beat of hot water on her shoulders relax them, inhaling the fragrances designed to calm, until she could think more clearly. She was the elder. And she was CEO of Vatta, all of it, responsible for the businesses, the employees, their families. That was where her energy should go, not on trying to fix her stormy younger cousin that no one else had ever been able to fix, either.

She had the shares now. She had the support of the corporate Board. Ky couldn't touch any of that. She would show everybody that—monster's bastard or not—she deserved to be where she was: in the big corner office. She drifted into sleep imagining that office and herself in charge . . . She hated the thought of her birth father, the family traitor, the criminal—but it was amusing to realize that he would be proud to see one of his own in charge. More than her adoptive father, the father of her childhood, who had never trusted her ability, who had preferred Jo, "the smart one," to "that idiot Stella."

CHAPTER TWO

SLOTTER KEY MILITARY ACADEMY
DAY 1

At last. Iskin Kvannis, Commandant of the Academy, had changed from his stark white uniform into more comfortable clothes in the Commandant's quarters. He settled into the comfortable chair behind his desk and ran through the messages waiting for him. His wife reminded him about his daughters' birthdays coming up in a couple of tendays—as if he needed a reminder. Their presents were already wrapped and stowed in the desk in front of him. Three minor infractions by cadets were now on his schedule for Commandant's Hours the next day. And the fugitives from the military prison at the nearby base were *still* on the run. His focus sharpened; he checked the time and called the officer who was supposed to have found and taken them back to prison days ago.

"They must have found a place to hide, Commandant," Major Sherman said. "There's no trace of them—"

"Surely someone's reported something—three bald women in military hospital garb can't be that hard to spot."

"We think they got clothes from somewhere."

"They'd be trying to find Admiral Vatta," he said, not for the first time. "You should be looking at every place they might think to find her." Luckily, she was far away, on Corleigh, and expected to stay there another two tendays at least. By the time she returned, the survivors wouldn't be a problem anymore—at least, all but these three. And three—even if they couldn't find and dispose of them before they went public—could be explained away. The injections that would finish their treatment and pass a postmortem examination by any military forensics had finally passed their clinical trial.

"Commandant, a team did go to the Vatta city residence. They spoke to Sera Stella Vatta, who assured them that no one had been to the house or entered the property. A Vatta watchman was resident there for the days the family was gone, patrolling the house and grounds regularly. But she did say that Admiral Ky Vatta was back in the city, at the house."

"What? I should have been told that at once! How long has she been there?"

"It's in the memo I sent." Sherman sounded whiny, as usual; Kvannis clenched his teeth. "She returned just today. That break-in is why she came back. If only you'd let us contact the city police, put out a bulletin. Civilians don't even know about the fugitives, let alone a description."

"I was sure your people would have them back in custody by now, Major. We did not want to start a panic among the populace. But now, I suppose, since your team failed, we'll have to take that risk. I will see that the police are notified. Perhaps your team can keep some kind of watch on the Vatta residence, just in case they show up there."

He sat thinking awhile after that conversation. The break-in . . . had that been one of the over-eager civilian allies? It didn't really matter now; what mattered was Ky Vatta in Port Major. He had already reminded Immigration that Ky Vatta, like Stella Vatta, had violated the law requiring absent citizens to renew their citizenship regularly. He'd been told that Admiral Vatta was a hero, for whom allowances would be made, of course, but now that she wasn't an admiral—now that he'd made sure his friends on the legal side of Slotter Key's military had opened an investigation of Master Sergeant Marek's death at her hand—a few more "facts" might persuade Immigration to do more than sit around with their thumbs in, warbling about the glory she'd brought to Slotter Key in the Battle of Nexus.

He spent a quarter hour drafting a report to the Port Major police about the fugitives, careful to couch it in terms that would both flatter the police and deflect attention from the delay in informing them. Then he settled down to the more pleasant task of blackening Ky Vatta's reputation and questioning her right to be at large on Slotter Key. When he finally went to bed in the Commandant's ornate bed, he was more satisfied with what he had accomplished than worried the fugitives would ever make contact with Ky Vatta.

DAY 2

The next morning, Ky woke from a nightmare with Rafe holding her. She relaxed slowly, concentrating on one muscle after another. "Did I make a lot of noise?"

"No. It doesn't take noise for me to know when you're in a bad place. Teeth grinding and jerky movements are enough. I've done that, you remember."

"Yes." She took a long breath, another. "We are two weird people, aren't we?"

"I prefer to think of us as two experienced adventurers, and all experienced adventurers have memories that give them bad dreams at times."

Ky laughed unexpectedly. "What time is it?"

"A little past dawn. Still cloudy. I think it's safe to unlock the house long enough to retrieve supplies from the kitchen."

"Is Stella up?"

"If she is, she's very quiet. Probably doesn't want to rouse the wild-cat."

"I'm not—"

"Ky, love, you have no idea what you're like when you go full killer. In retrospect, that's what Stella's going to remember."

"I wouldn't—"

"But you could. And she doesn't know the level of control you have. Did you ever physically attack her?"

"She pulled my hair when I was four and she was seven. I punched her back, but not hard enough to leave a mark. We both got in trouble; I heard about it for years. I threw a bracelet at her once when we were teenagers. No—actually I threw it on the floor."

"Well, *that's* a gracious difference." Rafe's mouth twitched; Ky knew he was trying not to grin.

Ky said nothing, heading for the shower.

Stella seemed perfectly calm at breakfast; she led their guests into a discussion of clothes they might need. They were deep in that discussion when the doorbell rang. Stella switched on the remote, waving everyone to silence. The screen showed uniformed men in riot gear standing in front of the house, with a van parked in the street.

"This is Stella Vatta," Stella said. "What is the problem?"

"Why is the house secured like that?" The speaker, in a helmet with its visor down, all in black, had the body language of an angry man.

"Please identify yourself," Stella said.

"Open this door!"

"Please identify yourself," Stella said again. "Name and organization; verification will be obtained to determine the legality of your demand."

"You—! All right, though your attitude will do you no good." The visor flipped up; the man looked into the ID scan by the front door. "Captain Hansed Bontier, Spaceforce Security, 429–772–5187–04. I can have my boss call you—"

"Verification ongoing," Stella said and closed the com. To Ky, she said, "Same man I talked to through the door last night. He wasn't that rude then. Wonder what twisted his tail. Take them into the office; there's a triple-shielded closet. Use the old code. That should be safe enough if nobody talks. The word *anywhere* twice is the key."

Ky got up; the visitors were already standing.

"And use the toilet now, not later. I'll be running my shower; it'll cover the noise. Quickly."

Ky took them all into Stella's home office and shut the door, setting the latch to maximum. "Toilet's that way," she said, pointing. Barash went first, and while the others waited, Ky tapped the code for the security closet and opened the door. They came back into the office, silent and looking scared. "We can talk softly, one at a time for now," she said. "I'm going to use the screen with the volume down."

In front of the house, several black-clad men gathered, one gesturing and the others listening. Visors were up; Ky grabbed and stored images of every face she could. "Recognize anyone?" she asked Inyatta.

"No, sir," Inyatta said. "Wait—that one." She pointed at the man who had identified himself as Captain Bontier.

"If they're trying to keep this secret, they'll control the number of people who see you," Ky said. "They should use the same security personnel at every stage—but if you've been drugged, then you won't know their faces."

Ky tapped the control for a view of the front door from inside, then backed it through the house—and there was Stella coming down the passage. Barefoot, a thick house robe belted around her, obviously wet hair wrapped in a towel turban, she went down the stairs briskly and strode to the front door. There she spoke into the door com. "I have contacted the Rector of Defense; she says you must tell me what it is you want."

Ky switched back to the outside view, then arranged both on the screen.

"I *want* you to open this door. There are dangerous fugitives in this neighborhood; we are searching every house. You were told last night—and then you locked the house down so we could not search—"

"So that no intruders could get in," Stella corrected. "Yes, you said that last night, and I informed you that we had been in the house and there were no fugitives. As I said, the house was broken into recently; a guard was stationed in it when we were gone."

"Then open the damned door and quit stalling."

"I wasn't stalling; I was in the shower." Stella opened the door. Ky grinned at the captain's expression; Stella needed no makeup to have that effect. "We had a long day yesterday and I overslept. I am not in the habit of lying, and neither are my guests."

"You have guests? The fugitives—"

"The *guests* are my cousin and her fiancé. As I said last night. I don't believe you can have forgotten." Stella stepped back and waved dramatically. "Come on in, since you are determined to insult my family and my personal honesty. Any breakage or pilfering will be documented by the house system. I am going upstairs to dress for work, and I trust you will not try to sneak into my private quarters and watch while I do so."

The man's face was red, but he led his squad in. Stella went to the stairs and started up; half the squad turned their heads to watch her, including the captain. When she reached the head of the stairs, Stella called, "Ky, I let them in the house. Are you anywhere up here?"

Ky looked at her three. "Through that door, now. I have to stay out here and be seen; they know I'm here. Once you're in, I'll close it. You'll be safe. It may take several hours, but as long as you don't make noise, you'll be fine."

They looked shaken but she nodded, and they went in. "There's light and air circulation," Ky added as she pulled the inner door closed. Then she pushed the outer door, faced with a bookcase, back into place, and pulled the office door partway open. She sat down in the green leather chair behind the desk, raising it to suit her height, picked up the top two folders on the desk, and opened both, side by side.

Stella, coming along the passage, looked in. "There you are," she said brightly. "Did you find those reports?"

"I found"—Ky read the title off the folder—"last year's P&L, but I'm confused by the coding on page seventeen."

"I'll explain later; I've got to get dressed before the search party comes up here. You haven't seen any strangers, have you?"

"Of course not. Are they still looking for the same ones as last night?"

"Apparently. Be back in a few." Stella left. Ky checked the house security. Two searchers in the living room, with sniffers. Two in the dining room. Four on the stairs now, including the captain at the top, looking both ways and carrying an audio booster. He had probably heard Stella talking to her. Good. She turned back to the folders, frowning and looking from one to the other.

She was reaching for a third when a voice in the doorway said, "*Stop!* Drop that! Hands up!"

She looked up to see the captain glaring at her, weapon in hand. "Oh, good grief," Ky said, still holding the folder. "Who are you?"

"Drop that and put your hands on your head."

"I am in the middle of a complicated analysis," Ky said. She opened the folder and laid it, open, above the two already open. "And besides, you're supposed to identify yourself, aren't you? Are you police? You don't look like police. If you're not police, then I'm not obliged to obey you."

"You—all right. I'm with Slotter Key Spaceforce Security."

"And I'm not in Slotter Key's military," Ky said. "You have no jurisdiction here. So kindly put away that weapon and explain yourself."

He slammed the pistol into his holster, still glaring. "We are seeking three Slotter Key Spaceforce personnel, dangerous fugitives."

"Not here," Ky said, looking down and turning over a page in one of the open folders.

"Our sniffers detected female persons in the back garden here."

"That would be my cousin and myself. We went outside when it started raining because the children had left some toys out."

"What children?"

Ky heaved an obvious sigh and looked up. "About seven years ago my cousin Jo was killed; she had two children. My aunt Helen, who owns this house, adopted them. After the break-in several days ago, she took the children to Corleigh, another family property, because she didn't feel safe in this house with the kitchen door so damaged. My fiancé and I were staying on Corleigh; she asked us to come here and keep an eye on the house until repairs were done. Not that any of that has anything to do with the fugitives you're after, or is any of your business. You say they're women?"

He flushed. "I didn't say that—"

"But you seemed to find sniffer traces of females in the yard suspicious. That suggests that you're after women."

"I didn't—damn it, *I* ask the questions!"

From behind him, Stella said. "No, Captain, you do not. You have demanded entrance to a civilian home in your search for military personnel, after being assured last night that no such were here."

"The house was shielded—"

"As I told you, and as the Port Major police are aware, that is because we had a break-in and chose to engage the full security capability. Which is neither illegal nor suspicious. If you had bothered to check with them, you'd know that—"

He turned to face Stella. Stella, Ky could see, had changed into a lavender suit, and looked every centimeter the wealthy, elegant, powerful woman she was.

"My men have found two bedrooms occupied in that other wing, both with traces of male and female occupation!"

Ky laughed. "You're going to question a couple, both over legal age, on where they choose to sleep or lounge or . . . whatever . . . in a house this size? Once again: you do not have jurisdiction here."

He turned his head to glance at her. "Is that man your fiancé?"

"Yes, he is. And we have been in multiple bedrooms, because we chose to. Why not? Some beds are too hard, some beds are too soft—"

He stared at her. "You—!"

"It's none of your business what we do, or don't do, anywhere—and certainly not in this house."

"You've had time to look under all the beds," Stella added. He swung around to look at Stella again. "I must get to the office; you will withdraw your team and leave my cousin and her fiancé in peace."

"We need to scan this house."

"No, you need to find your fugitives and not waste my time and annoy my family." When he didn't move, she looked past him to Ky. "Call Grace. I want this settled before I leave. I have appointments."

Ky didn't bother with the desk phone; she used her skullphone, direct to Grace's private number.

"Ky—what's wrong?"

"A man who says he's with Slotter Key military has insisted on searching Helen's house for some fugitives. We told him last night there were none here; he came back this morning and is acting like we're guilty for turning on the security overnight. Stella wants him out before she goes to headquarters and he won't leave."

"Name?" Grace said. Ky told her. "Do you have a house phone where you are?"

"Yes, I'm in Stavros's home office; there's a secure line."

"Call me on that, put it on speaker; I'll talk to him."

Ky leaned back in the chair as soon as Grace's voice came over the speaker. The captain jerked around at the sound of his name. "Who?"

"This is Rector Vatta. You will personally report to my office at once and explain yourself; I expect you within the next ten minutes."

"But I—but Rector, that's not—"

"Ten minutes. That's not a suggestion, Captain; that's an order. Do I have to send a team to bring you in?"

"N-no, Rector. I'll—"

"Hurry," Grace finished for him. "Nine minutes forty seconds."

He looked two shades paler, and with a muttered "Sorry" turned away; Ky could hear the quick sound of his boots hurrying to the stairs. His team emerged from the various rooms they were searching, and within two minutes they were all outside, jogging down the front walk to their vans.

Stella raised her brows. "It never ceases to amaze me how the sound of Aunt Grace in a snit gets people moving."

"Including you!" came from the speaker.

Stella jumped. "You're still online!"

"Ky didn't close the connection. How secure is this line?"

"Secure as we can make it," Stella said.

"Who is that man looking for?"

"The people who were with me in Miksland," Ky said. "Spaceforce personnel. Did you know they'd been drugged, shaved bare, and thrown in prison?"

"*What?*" Grace's tone mixed surprise and anger; Ky's own anger retreated a little.

"Yes. Including implant surgery on a Miznarii woman without her consent, while she was unconscious—which is a crime—and tampering with others' implants, and not allowing them contact with their families—or any outside contact at all."

"I don't—"

"You didn't know? You didn't think to find out what happened to personnel you, as Rector, were responsible for?"

"I'm leaving for the office," Stella said. "You two can waste time fighting if you want to, but—"

"*Go!*" Ky and Grace spoke at the same moment. Stella retreated. Ky wished she hadn't; she had intended to apologize this morning, but things happened too fast.

"Ky, I did *not* know," Grace said. "I was told they were evacuated from Miksland to Pingats, given a medical evaluation there that suggested they might need quarantine for fourteen days because of something in the tunnels. Then they were to be sent home for thirty days' home leave with their families. That's where I thought they were."

"That didn't happen," Ky said.

"To all of them? Are you sure? And how do you know?"

"A reliable source," Ky said. She'd expected Grace to realize she must have the fugitives there, but she wasn't going to say so, no matter how secure the line was supposed to be. "I suggest you start calling before that man arrives at your door. Contact the families if you don't believe me. Oh, and they overheard someone say *I* was in the hospital and expected to die of something caught down there."

"But you were checked out—you're fine."

"Yes. Checked out by Helen's own physician, not Spaceforce."

"I'll call you within two hours," Grace said, and cut off the connection.

Ky sat back. The security panel on the desk informed her that the house was locked down, all entrances secure, no indication of attempts to breach, and no new sensors in place. Her concern that the team might have placed bugs faded, but she pulled out the portable scanner and checked that room carefully. Nothing.

When she opened the secure closet, she found the three women huddled in one corner.

"We didn't know who would come—"

"They've left. The house is fully secure again. They didn't discover anything and the captain should be just about arriving at the Rector's office to have a very uncomfortable hour or so with my aunt Grace. She didn't know anything about your situation."

"So we can—come out?"

"Yes. Might be best to stay upstairs in case someone else shows up."

"Can we call our families?" Kamat asked.

"No," Ky said. "Whoever's responsible is undoubtedly watching your families, expecting you to make contact. It might risk them, and all you survivors, to call them now. But we do need their names and addresses, to work out some way of letting them know without alerting the other side. The Rector's going to call them, probably today, but that can be presented as just ordinary courtesy. *I* think she should've done that before." Before more questions could be asked, Ky went on. "Do you have any objection to a short-term DNA adjustment? It'll confuse scans, if you run across a roadblock or something."

Kamat raised her hand. "I know I'm already contaminated with an implant, but I really don't want any change in DNA. It's against my religion."

Ky nodded. "Of course. And we'll find a way to get that implant out, too."

"But the—the connectors—would still be in my brain—"

"You said you weren't getting anything from it; it may be they just put in something to make you think it was an implant. And even if it is, the connector interface won't operate without the implant itself."

Kamat blinked back tears. "I'm afraid my family will think I'm damaged. They'll see the scar; they'll ask why I cooperated."

"They won't believe you were drugged unconscious?"

"My mother, maybe. My father—he's very strict; he says people are so tempted by the ease of implants that they pretend they were drugged."

That was a complication Ky hadn't anticipated. "Well, I think the best thing is to get it removed as soon as possible, and hope for the best. Surely it will be better if it's out than in."

"That's true," Kamat said, but she didn't look much happier.

"For now, clothes for you—and me." Ky called the store Stella had suggested and asked for the concierge shopping department. Since she had the sizes in hand, thanks to Stella's questions at breakfast, it didn't take long to order several outfits for all of them. She asked for delivery, and—offered a choice of times—selected late morning.

She looked up to find Rafe watching her. "You didn't order *me* any new clothes," he said. "You like this shirt on me that much?"

"I like that shirt *off* you," Ky said, grinning. "But you can call Grace's house and ask Teague to bring you something more suited to the weather. And my box, as well."

"I'll do that," Rafe said. "And if he hurries, I can change and one of us can pose as the house butler when that delivery arrives. Does your aunt have a butler?"

"Not since Stavros died."

"We should have someone on the door," Rafe said.

Ky went down the passage to tell the others their new clothes were on the way. They stood up when she came into the room as if expecting an inspection. "Relax," Ky said. She looked around. "Are you all comfortable enough? Need anything besides new clothes?"

"No, sir."

"Rafe's called in an associate of his, to bring our things from my aunt Grace's house. He may be staying; I've met him and he's safe. Don't ask him questions about his past."

"No, sir, we wouldn't," Inyatta said. "Isn't there something useful we can do? Cleaning or laundry or something?"

"Well . . . yes, if you want to." Keeping busy might be therapeutic. "All the equipment—"

"We found some," Kamat said. "Laundry?"

"There's an upstairs laundry on the other end; downstairs is just off the kitchen. And I expect it's only an hour or two until your new clothes are here."

"Yes, sir. We'll get busy." They all looked happier.

"When we've all changed clothes, I'll want to hear all the details you remember about what happened to you." Their faces tightened. "I want to find the others, get them to safety. You're the only people I know who know anything."

Inyatta nodded. "I understand, sir, but we don't know much."

"You may know more than you think you do," Ky said. "You recognized that man—Bontier—as someone you'd seen before. I'm thinking those who kept the base on Miksland a secret may be the same as those who abducted you."

"What did the newsvids say about us?" Barash asked.

Ky shook her head. "I didn't hear anything—though I didn't pay much attention. Like the Rector, I thought you'd been given leave and were home with your families. The lack of interviews—I thought you just didn't want to be bothered."

"Come to think of it," Rafe said, leaning on the doorframe, "I don't recall any airing of those interviews *you* did, Ky. I didn't watch every day, but—did you ever get notice of when they'd be on?"

"No. I didn't really think about it."

"Do they have censorship here?" he asked. The other three edged past him, carrying cleaning tools, and headed for the big suite where Ky and Rafe had slept. "I did notice, while I was staying with Grace, that your news shows are bland compared with those on Nexus. Cascadia's are drenched in politeness, but even they show more sides to questions."

"Censorship?" Ky thought for a moment. "I don't think so—at least, when I was kicked out of the Academy, it was for creating a public embarrassment for the government—but after I left, it would've died down fast."

"Or been suppressed," Rafe said. "That war Grace was involved in—Stella seems to think of it as some minor little thing, but wasn't that two continents rebelling against the planetary government? And didn't it go on for years?"

"That's not what I was taught in school," Ky said. "*A minor uprising generated by a disagreement over fishing rights and a tax on shipping* or something like that. Just some riots, some criminal elements taking advantage of disagreements."

"Sounds like a cover-up to me," Rafe said. "You should ask Grace about it. Because if whoever kept Miksland a secret for so long was involved in it—and part of Slotter Key's military was involved, as well—then it's not really over."

Ky tried, and failed, to imagine Great-Aunt Grace in the middle of an actual war. As a young woman, of course; it was a long time ago and she would have been . . . maybe twenty? Younger? But surely she would have been the same upright, prim, proper girl that she'd been as an old woman in Ky's youth. If she'd been involved, it would have been as a—a secretary or something. Someone in an office, organizing the files.

"Maybe," she said to Rafe. "I'll ask her. But right now I need to look over those files in the office here."

And think. She needed to think what had happened to the other survivors, and why, and what she could do about it.

CHAPTER THREE

DAY 2

Instead, she stared for a moment at the files on the desk and then pulled them closer. Whatever this was—whatever she needed to do to protect the survivors—would cost money. Yes, she'd handed over her shares to Stella, and Stella claimed she lacked the money to pay Ky what was due, but that was exactly why she felt entitled to go through the reports on Stella's desk. She was going to need *some* money—undoubtedly less than those shares had been worth—and something might have slipped her cousin's attention.

Stella, she realized, had revised some of the procedures Helen had used; Ky nodded as she read. Helen, the former CEO's wife, whose own background was in science, not business, had run the business as simply as possible, and as a result skimped on in-depth analysis from the business viewpoint. She hadn't done anything bad, exactly, but she had missed opportunities that Stella clearly did not intend to miss. Ky, who had seen Stella as the secondary headquarters CEO, was well aware of Stella's gift for corporate leadership, and the uptick in profits from Helen's resignation to the present proved how much better Vatta would do under Stella's command. If, that is, the fines levied on Vatta could be overturned.

In the silence of that hour, Ky remembered the quarrel of the previous night again and felt a twinge of remorse. Stella still rubbed her the wrong way, but she'd been at fault. And perhaps, as Rafe had suggested on Corleigh, she herself was in need of a consultation and analysis of the effects of that more than half year in Miksland. She queried the medical app in her implant and found a recommendation there for a tune-up by a specialist. Well. Maybe. Maybe she could take care of it herself. Moray was a long way away and right now she wasn't sure which local specialists she could trust.

The house system flashed an alert: someone was opening the front door. The speaker came on. Rafe's voice. "Teague. Thank you. Come on in."

Ky relaxed, realizing only then that she was halfway out of the chair, her pistol in her hand. The medical app, still active, recommended a touch of neuroactive. She set it back on passive, holstered her pistol, and went to the head of the stairs. Below, Rafe and Teague were chatting; the door was closed and secured. Rafe looked up.

"He's going to answer when the delivery comes. I'll change down here, and back him up if anything happens."

"Thanks," Ky said. "I'll come down now and get my box; we'll stay upstairs after."

"Full brief?" Rafe asked.

"Go ahead," Ky said. "We'll need him later."

"Right."

Ky went down to the suite to tell the others that another man was in the house. They were through with the cleaning, and stood gathered around the spiral stairs up to the top level. The hatch that sealed the lockdown looked ridiculous protruding through the ice-blue ceiling.

"What's up there?"

"Two more bedrooms, from when this was the children's wing. Can't get there now with the house locked down, but this, where we are, used to be the playroom and common study space. The older ones could retreat from the noise up there; there are two bedrooms with dormer windows." Ky set her box on the sofa, took off the float pins, and unzipped the seal. "This is stuff from my ship; they sent it down when they left. Should be some clothes in here you can wear until the store delivery comes."

"It's the fanciest house I've ever been in," Barash said.

"Same here," Inyatta said. "Was yours like this?"

"No," Ky said. "Ours was on Corleigh, near the tik plantation, on the east coast. One story, sprawling out a bit. I could walk to the beach, though we also had a pool. My father had offices there in a separate building—mirroring the data here, so he could work from there much of the time. Coming to the mainland was a big deal."

"Is that where you were until yesterday?"

"The island, yes, but not that house. It was destroyed—along with the offices—in the attack after I left the Academy. I was in space, then. In fact, this visit was the first time I've been on Slotter Key since . . . I left." They were all looking at her, waiting for more. She could feel herself growing hot. "Actually, I was on an ansible call back here, to talk to my uncle Stavros, when it happened. The call cut off; I didn't know why until later." She looked away, staring at the wall. "Everyone there—and in the headquarters here—was killed. Why they didn't target this house we don't know, but that's why Aunt Helen, Stella, and Jo's twins survived."

No one spoke for a long moment, then Inyatta said, "I'm sorry, Admiral." The others murmured something.

Ky shook her head. "It's—not something one can forget. Even when not directly witnessed." As she spoke, her fingers brushed the familiar case, the case that held the family-related files sequestered from her father's implant. The files that recorded what her father had seen that day, before he died, that she had watched, seeing it as he had, engulfed in his recorded emotions.

She pushed that memory down and lifted out the top layer of clothes. These women had their own more recent trauma to deal with. She would not impose any more of her own on them. "Here—see if any of these fit." Inyatta and Barash could wear the exercise pants and tops; Kamat was too tall, even though she had to roll up the slacks Stella had lent her.

Not long after, new clothes arrived in the store's own delivery van. Rafe brought the boxes and bags upstairs. Ky pulled out her own choices from the boxes and left the rest for the others. They all came down to lunch in new clothes, including Ky. With scarves wrapped around their heads, socks and shoes on their feet, with the five of them around the larger table in the downstairs kitchen, eating off the yellow-and-green-striped plates, the three fugitives looked less like refugees. While they ate, Ky continued her mental list. Wigs, or time for the women to grow out their hair. She had no idea how long it would take. And Kamat needed surgery. Possibly they all did, depending on how badly their implants had been damaged. New implants, then. But the rest of them—how much time did they have to find the rest of the survivors? How long would it take to organize a rescue? With the military obviously complicit—or some of it—who could she ask for help?

Her skullphone pinged. "Grace," said the familiar voice. "Secure call. Now."

Ky slipped her feet into the new ship boots she'd ordered out of habit and headed back upstairs to Stella's office. Rafe, coming out of the living room, looked a question and she gestured: *urgent call.*

"Ky, where's Stella?" Grace asked before Ky could do more than identify herself.

"At the office, I suppose."

"Are those persons with you?"

She must mean the survivors. "Yes."

"Don't let them leave, for any reason, and don't lower the house security. The situation is far worse than I thought. I have been stupid and careless; the danger is extreme. Do you know where Teague is? He's not answering at my house."

"He's here. What—"

"Tell him to go back to my house and remove all of his and Rafe's equipment. Quickly."

"Aunt Grace, what is it?"

"That man—that captain—tried to kill me. His second yielded to interrogation. Tell Teague, Ky; keep Rafe with you. I must contact Stella immediately. I'll call again."

The contact ended. Ky glared at the com set. "Dammit, Grace," she said in the silent office. "I am not your baby niece anymore. And I'm not going to sit here doing nothing."

Out in the passage, she saw Rafe and Teague lounging near the head of the stairs, heads together. Before she could speak, Rafe's gaze sharpened. "Trouble?"

"According to Aunt Grace, yes. Teague, she wants you—just you—to go to her house immediately and remove all of your and Rafe's 'equipment,' whatever that is. She wants Rafe to stay here, and me to await further instructions." She could hear the impatience in her own voice. "That nosy officer with the search team tried to kill her, she said."

"Was she hurt?" Rafe asked.

"She didn't say, but I got the distinct impression the captain is dead, since she mentioned interrogating his second."

Rafe grimaced, then nodded. "Teague, you'd better go."

"Pull everything? Even the internal house surveillance?"

"Yes. We don't want any of that available to whoever this is."

"But that will leave—"

"Just her stuff. Yes. But it's good."

"What about placing an external nearby?"

"Better not since she wants all our equipment gone."

"And bring your clothes, too," Ky said. "You'll be staying here for a while."

"I need the combination to the back gate," Teague said. Ky gave it to him. Teague smiled, his rare and rather sweet smile. "This will be fun. I'm gone." And he was running down the stairs. Ky and Rafe followed more slowly.

"What does she think it is?" Rafe asked.

"She didn't explain. Just gave me orders. Stay inside. Don't let our friends out. Don't let the house security lapse. Send Teague. Keep you here. And wait for her next call."

"You're still annoyed with her."

"Well, yes. You'd think I was twelve years old again and Missy Bancroft had just fallen off the roof and broken her arm. Do this, do that, wait, do the other thing. Even at twelve, I knew what to do when someone fell off a roof."

"That really happened?"

"It did." Ky could not help relaxing as she remembered the details. "She climbed the tree in our front yard and then jumped down onto the porch roof. I knew the roof was slippery. We all yelled at her not to. But she wouldn't listen, and sure enough she slipped. And Aunt Grace heard us yelling and came out just in time to see Missy slide off, taking a length of gutter with her, and land in the flower bed. I jumped out of the tree—"

Rafe grinned. "You were up the tree?"

"Yes, of course." Caught in the memory, Ky went on. "We'd started out racing each other up the tree to where the balloon had gotten stuck—"

Rafe laughed; she glared at him. "I can't help it," he said. "You and some other gangly tomboy clambering around in a tree . . ."

"She was taller than me," Ky said. "Most of them were, the girls in that group. Daughters of my mother's friends."

"And you . . . you instigated that race up the tree, didn't you?"

"Only because Vera Smittanger let go of the balloon string and the package tied to it. Anyway, after Missy fell off the roof, that was the end of the party. Aunt Grace told us all what to do before she even found out if we'd have done it on our own." Ky shook her head. "At the same time lecturing us for not being young ladies now that we were approaching what she called *the gateway to maturity.*"

Rafe laughed again, shaking his head. "It's not funny," Ky said. But it was; she could feel laughter bubbling inside. "All right, it wasn't funny *then*. In hindsight—" She could see them, the group of girls all appalled by Missy's fall, and then smarting under Grace's lecture. "Then all the mothers came out—and we hadn't had time to brush the leaves and dirt off our party clothes. They all got on us." She chuckled.

"Speaking of clothes," Rafe said. "Did you notice that your new outfit is remarkably like a uniform?"

Ky looked down at herself, the dark-blue pullover and slacks. "No, it's not; it's just the dark color."

"Not entirely." He reached out to touch her hair in its snug braid. "Admiral to the core. I like it."

"Good," Ky said. She leaned on him a moment. "I'd better go tell the others we're not going anywhere." And how was she going to plan a rescue, let alone perform one, if she was stuck inside the house?

Stella Vatta answered the call in her office at Vatta headquarters. A chill ran down her back at Grace's first words; she realized an instant later that she had her other hand on the pistol she carried in a concealed holster under her perfectly tailored suit even as she answered the question.

"Yes, Aunt Grace. What's happened?"

"That fellow who was at your house tried to kill me," Grace said. "I've contacted Ky; Teague should be collecting all that equipment from my house and going to yours—"

"You're sending the trouble to *my* house?" A flash of anger she controlled quickly. But still. First Ky, then Grace, assuming that Stella and everything she owned would be at their disposal.

"No, I'm hoping it hits mine first. Stella, I'm serious. What's the security setting at headquarters?"

"Highest. After last night, I called the late shift and had it raised."

"Good. Have someone with you at all times, though I think they'll go after me first."

"Who? Why?"

"Miksland," Grace said, answering the second question. "They're trying to shut down all inquiries, military and civilian. Claiming there are dangerous diseases in a secret laboratory, and that Ky couldn't have gotten in if she hadn't known about the research beforehand. They're trying to pin it on Vatta—claiming that we're all plotting revenge for the earlier attack on us."

"That's crazy! We've never had anything to do with pharma or medical research . . . have we?"

"Not here. There was some research decades ago on using tik extracts, but it went nowhere and your father sold off the company. Doesn't matter what the facts are, though; some people will believe anything. And there's an offplanet Vatta company that produces pharmaceuticals . . . I don't have the files here, but I think it's where that boy you found lives."

"Toby?" Stella's breath caught in her chest. "His family?"

"Maybe. I'm not sure. What I am sure of is that Miksland was an anthill waiting to be kicked, and we kicked it. Ky was there, she saw things, she kept records and reported. The evidence she submitted, though, has gone missing. The other survivors, except for your three, are locked down in multiple facilities on medical grounds— supposedly in quarantine—and I haven't been able to locate all of them yet, let alone get them out."

"I'll check which pharma-related units are where, and warn the managers. And I'll need to open the house briefly at least once every few days, because we need to use the real kitchen."

"No more than three people unshielded at any time," Grace warned. "I'm holding the entire team who showed up at your place for now, but we have no long-term confinement here. What worries me more is the disappearance of the evidence Ky brought back: the flight recorder, the bio samples, and the logbook of that fellow Greyhaus. Was it destroyed, or stored someplace—and if so, where? I should've insisted on making copies in my own office before she handed them over." A pause that Stella did not interrupt. "I'm getting old, Stella, and apparently careless. But if I resign now, or if I'm fired, there's no one to speak for Ky and the others that I trust completely."

"Hang on, then," Stella said.

"I will," Grace said, and cut the connection.

Stella called up the Vatta extended files. Toby's father was indeed employed by a subsidiary, VNR Technology, that manufactured reagents used in pharmaceutical quality control, and had a research section that did something Stella didn't understand.

Vatta had two other subsidiaries, one located on the same planet and another on an orbital platform in the same system, involved with pharma. One was still doing research on tik extracts and had produced several marketable products. As it was then after midnight at Toby's family home, she sent a text warning there, and to the managers of all three subs.

Her skullphone pinged.

"Stella, do you suppose we could hire a cook?" Ky sounded perfectly serious and also completely calm, as if they'd never had a quarrel. And what a ridiculous question, when real danger threatened.

"A cook? Why? We have the programming in the kitchen appliances."

"Yes, but Rafe says he's tired of program-cooked package meals. And so am I, and neither of us really enjoys cooking. You're busy with the business. I thought maybe we could hire a cook—even part-time, or every other day or something—who could do it from scratch. From shopping to cleanup—no extra trouble for you, for instance. I know Aunt Helen likes to cook, but she's off with the kids."

"You have any idea what that would cost? We'll talk about it when I get home."

"Spoilsport," Ky said. "I was hoping not to have to figure out how to defrost those green lumps in the freezer without having them go limp."

"You spacer types," Stella said. "You're entirely too dependent on galley equipment. Cold water, put them in—wait, do you even know what green lumps they are? And how many?"

"Six of them, whatever they are; the label is smeared. They've got frost all over them. I thought we should use them before they got too old."

"Maybe they already are," Stella said. "Cold water for a half hour, until you can see the surface. If it's mushy, discard. If not . . . oh, never mind, I'll come home now and take a look." And she could talk to Ky without fear of anyone listening in.

"Would you?" Now Ky sounded plaintive, a tone never natural to her.

"I can, today, but only for a few minutes. And we'll talk about a cook."

Stella looked at the clock after that conversation. "I'm going home for an early lunch," she said to her secretary. "Cory Dansen won't mind if I cut that appointment by ten minutes; it's just that quarterly report that I've read and will approve and sign for. Ky's trying to cook and she's hopeless. You'd think someone her age would know how to steam broccoli or grill it, but she's hardly been near a kitchen for the past sixteen years, so I suppose she's forgotten. Call Sandy, please, and ask him to meet me at the car at 1145."

"Yes, Sera."

At home, she found the others crowded into the upstairs kitchenette with the makings of cheese sandwiches they'd taken from the pantry before sealing the house again. "That doesn't look like green lumps," Stella said.

"I gave up on them. They smelled funny. What about Barash? She says her mother taught her to cook, and if she has a good wig and a Vatta employee ID she shouldn't trigger any doubts."

"You want me to fake a Vatta Transport ID? All because you can't cook broccoli?" And of course, Ky was giving her orders again. Stella pushed that thought down.

"I have other things to do," Ky said. Stella felt her jaw muscles clench. "And yes, Barash could cook broccoli, but if she can go out, she can acquire things for the others with less suspicion than ordering them in."

"Toasted cheese, with paprika and a pinch of cayenne," Stella said to Barash, who was standing near the kitchenette's mini-oven.

"Yes, Sera," Barash said.

Someone had manners, Stella thought, and sat down at the table. She waited to speak until Ky had a mouthful of sandwich. "And while I'm waiting, more news from Aunt Grace. Serious trouble, she says; she's got that team locked up for now, but can't keep them long—no facilities there. None but the officer have knowledge beyond 'these are fugitives and need to be caught.' The officer knows more but has some resistance to the drugs." Stella accepted a plate from Barash. "Now, your idea about having one of our guests pretend to be house staff— that makes sense, and allows everyone more flexibility, but it will take time to get her an ID. What color wig?"

"Brown, Sera."

"That was your natural color? But I have no reason to be ordering a brown wig. If it was for Ky, it would be black; for me it would be blond. We'll have to try some colors around your face, see what would work. Some people with brown hair have a skin tone that can handle a different color—Thank you," as Barash slid a toasted cheese sandwich onto her plate.

Grace Vatta tapped her fingers on her desk, wondering what else she could do. Mac was on the way up from interrogating the uncooperative captain. The man had a block on the interrogation drugs they had handy. Her own inquiry into the whereabouts of the survivors was on someone's desk—it annoyed her that she didn't know whose. Her inquiry into the lost evidence had been halted at the level of a lieutenant colonel whose general, he said, was unavailable, in transit from Port

Major to Hautvidor. Her new secretary, Pamela, was supposed to be contacting survivors' families. Surely someone was home and available to talk. But not yet.

She had been so happy when Ky was finally out of that mess, showing up healthy and whole, with nothing more complicated than Marek's death to deal with. Or so it had seemed. Instead, she had missed this conspiracy. Enemies had gotten ahead of her—of *her*!

Mac came in and shut the door behind him. "Pam seems fidgety this morning."

"I had to ask her twice to keep going on the list and tell me only when she had a live one." Grace snorted. "I don't think she's bent like Derek, but she's easily alarmed."

"Ah. Well, I managed to pry one name out of Captain Bontier, but it's no joy to us. We already knew that family had something to do with Miksland."

"Quindlan?"

"Yes. A major on a general's staff, in Public Affairs."

"Well. That could be a factor in a cover-up, couldn't it?"

"Indeed. I've pulled his record. Actually, all records of Quindlans, but he comes first." He handed her a datastick. "We need to set up a working group, Grace. And we need a secure way to share information. Ky has those three survivors, you have authority to dig into just about anything—but you're too visible when you do it. We need to find some reliable people inside the military—probably in the ground troops, because that's who was in Miksland, according to that journal Ky found that's now disappeared."

"I wish she'd copied everything before she turned it over."

"So do I, but she didn't. Nor did you."

Shortly before the normal close of business, a dapper figure in a neat gray suit strode up to the door and pressed the bell. Teague opened the door. "Sir?"

"I need to speak with Sera Kylara Vatta."

"May I ask your business?"

"It is confidential. I need to speak with Sera Kylara Vatta."

"I will ascertain if she is available." Teague took advantage of his new greater height and saw the man's expression harden.

"It is necessary that I speak to her."

"Wait here," Teague said and shut the door, leaving the man outside. He closed the inner door carefully and reported the conversation. "I think he's a process server," he said at the end of a detailed description. "He has that unfriendly friendly look, the *hail fellow well met* that goes before *you have been served*."

"She's not available," Rafe said. "She's locked up in Stella's office on an ansible call."

"He's going to wait, I'm guessing."

"Let him. She's not going out anywhere."

"And if he's still there when she comes out?"

"I'll tell her." Rafe scowled. "I don't suppose he's after the three guests and merely acting like a process server . . ."

"I don't think so. No military vibe to him. I will inform him that she is not available at this time, but he may wait outside if he wishes."

"I'll warn the others: silent and invisible."

"Go, then."

Teague waited until Rafe was out of sight in the children's wing before returning to the door. Sure enough, the man in the gray suit was standing on the top step, looking disgruntled.

"Sera Kylara Vatta is not available at this time, sir. And you did not provide your name, affiliation, and suitable identification."

The man looked at him sourly. "Who are you? I didn't know they had a butler."

"No reason you should," Teague said. "Now: your name, affiliation, and identification, please."

"You don't need my name. I'm obviously not a crook—"

Teague tipped his head. "Pardon me, sir, but I do not think a business suit rules out criminal behavior." Did real butlers have this much fun? He had no idea, but if they did maybe he could switch careers. "I must have your name and business identity."

With obvious reluctance, the man pulled out a wallet. "George L. Lewisham," he said. Teague looked at the ID. It said GEORGE L. LEW-ISHAM, and the image matched the man's face. The ID also gave MARKS & GRAVESON, GENERAL LEGAL SERVICES as his employer. "That satisfy you?" the man said.

"Thank you, sir," Teague said. "I appreciate your cooperation, and Sera Vatta will be informed when she is available."

"I'll wait inside," the man said, stepping forward as Teague stepped back, and reaching for the door edge.

"No, sir," Teague said, tapping the man's hand with the short rod he'd concealed in his other hand. The man jerked it back with a grunt of pain. "This house does not belong to Sera Kylara Vatta, and she is not my employer. My orders do not permit me to allow anyone but a family member into the house without the owner's permission." The man was now nursing bruised fingers under his armpit. Teague shut both doors and locked them. He glanced aside at Rafe, who had come downstairs and through the sitting room, ready to help if needed.

"That was a work of art," Rafe said, slipping his gun back in his pocket. "You are the very image of the stuffiest kind of butler."

"Did you ever have one?"

"Oh, yes. For a short time we had a full staff in the city house, then the city grew up around what had been the summer place and we moved there permanently, but we had fewer staff. I remember Soames, the butler, from when I was a small child. It gives one a bad start in life to be addressed as 'Master Rafael' by half the people in the house, and 'Rafe, you little brat' by older sisters. A sort of split personality."

"And now?"

"Now I'm just Rafe. The various roots and forks of the tree all melded together."

Teague looked at him, wondering if someone who had had multiple personas, including temporary DNA mods, could possibly be a single person. For himself, the change he'd gone through, from Pauli Gregson to Edvard Teague, from someone almost ten centimeters shorter with curly hair and dark eyes, to his present above-average height, yellower skin, straight hair, and gray eyes, had affected—and was still affecting—his personality and how he thought of himself. Tall and lanky, rather than medium and medium, made more difference than he'd anticipated when he'd agreed to the changes. He now recognized himself in the mirror, but the ghost of that other face still hovered in front of it, as if painted on a veil.

Rafe, watching Teague watch him, hoped that Teague was having an easier time with his transition from whoever he'd been than he himself had had with his numerous changes. And he hoped he could settle permanently into his own present identity: not ISC's CEO, Ser Rafael Dunbarger, but Rafe the private person, perhaps never using his other identities but always Dunbarger . . . or some other name he'd then stick to. Ky, he was fairly sure, would not easily adapt to new identities the way he had. She was all of a piece, solid as wood or stone all the way through, something he found comforting in its predictability.

Ky came down shortly after that. Rafe positioned himself in one of the front rooms; Teague opened the door. "Ser Lewisham," she said. "Your credentials were verified. I'm Kylara Vatta; I understand you wanted to speak with me?"

"Yes." He handed her a flat, narrow package. "You have been served." He nodded and went down the front walk without a backward glance.

Teague closed the door for her. Ky pulled out the scanner Rafe had given her and ran it over the package. "No explosives we recognize," she said as she handed the package to Teague.

"I'll run a complete scan before I open it. Any other advice from your legal team?"

"Send it to them at once, so they can interpret it. By law, it has to allow me five business days to respond."

"If they pay any attention to the law," Rafe said.

The package proved to hold no toxins, explosives, or spy devices, so Ky took it upstairs and faxed its six pages of dense legalese to Vatta's legal experts. Stella arrived in the next half hour, bearing the translation into plain language, and with several packages. Ky looked at the translation and tried to ignore what Stella was saying to the others. "The intent was to notify you that you must appear before Slotter Key's Twenty-First Special Court—which has jurisdiction over cases involving a foreign citizen—within twenty-two days, as a formal inquiry into the deaths of Slotter Key military personnel under your presumably illegal command over the past half year, specifically the deaths of Master Sergeant Marek and Moscoe Confederation citizen Commander Bentik. Please contact this office if you need further explanation of the serving, or if you require legal representation. Be advised that any request for additional legal assistance must be approved by Stella Vatta, CEO."

It made no sense. She'd expected to testify about the events on Miksland, but to a *military* court. Back on Corleigh, Stella had said the evidence had gone missing and Grace was looking into it. And why a civilian court that handled cases involving foreign citizens? She wasn't a foreigner; she'd been born on Slotter Key. She'd had a Slotter Key passport, until it was blown up in the original *Vanguard* near Moray. She looked at the others, intending to ask Stella's advice.

Stella was handing Barash the wig she'd brought. "This is your wig," she said. "And if you don't mind, I need a different name for you, if you're going to play a cook. What's your first name? Or your middle?"

"Melisandra," Barash said. "Alexandrina Sophronia."

Ky blinked. None of those were common names, as far as she knew. She stuffed the papers Stella had brought back into the envelope. She'd talk to the legal team the next day and let them explain it. She had time. Surely Stella would grant her legal representation.

"My mother read novels from two centuries ago," Barash said. "One of my sisters is Theodosia Francesca Emiliana. My brothers are equally embarrassed by theirs. We all use nicknames."

"Mellie? Allie? Sophie?"

"Allie has more common longer names," Inyatta pointed out. "Allison, Alice, Alexis, Allegra, Alliona—"

"That would be all right," Barash said.

"Then you're Allie the cook, and your new papers will say . . . Allison, I think."

"Yes, Sera. But—" Barash looked at the wig Stella had given her. "It's—nothing like my own hair."

"That's an advantage, actually. But it will go with your skin tone, I'm pretty sure, and if not we can dye it here. Try it on."

With the curly red-gold wig on, Barash did look different; even her bone structure seemed changed.

"It's the curls around her ears," Stella said. "And the height on top. Not at all military and suggests a very different personality. I'll take care of her makeup." Stella pulled out a makeup kit from another bag and went to work. When she was finished, Barash looked not only different but at least five years younger, like someone named Allie.

Stella drove Barash the ten blocks to Minelli & Krimp, the gourmet grocery on Pickamble Street. She already liked the young woman; now, she decided, she'd much rather be driving with "Allie" than with Ky. Allie didn't mind following orders without question.

She introduced "My new cook, Allie," to the manager. "She'll be using the Vatta account to purchase groceries. Go on, Allie, pick up everything on the list while I chat with Ser Vaughn." The girl marched off, list in hand. Stella smiled at Ser Vaughn. "My cousin and her fiancé are staying with me, and Mother and the children may be back anytime. So I decided to get a cook in. And a man for the heavy things; his name's Teague. You probably won't run into him. He's actually my cousin's fiancé's man, but he's lending a hand."

"Wise choice," Vaughn said. "What service did you use for the cook?"

"Actually, a hint from a friend of my mother's. We vetted her through the business, of course. I don't expect we'll need her for more than a half year, maybe a whole year at most, unless Mother takes to entertaining again. She knows that." She smiled at Vaughn. "It's good to have a quality grocer we can trust."

"Of course, Sera," he said. "And of course we're always glad to deliver directly to the house, should you prefer."

"Thank you. She says she's not used to driving in the city and frankly I'd prefer she not try. But I wanted you to meet her in person."

"Certainly; I appreciate that. You do know that our full inventory, including specials of the day, appears on CitiInfo?"

"Yes, thank you. But I actually enjoy coming here."

On the way back to the house, Stella explained the ordering process to Barash. "The manager knows you now. And we have a separate connection from the kitchen that doesn't go through any of the private servers. They'll deliver and bill the house account."

"Do you tip the delivery driver?"

"No. That's included in the delivery charge. So what are we having for dinner?"

"You said fish, so I chose the best-looking white fish." Barash glanced at the row of baskets. "I'm not sure how much will be reasonable for us . . ."

"Not to worry. For all the store knows, I'm stocking up for winter emergencies."

Back in the house, Stella showed everyone where the kitchen computer was, logged Barash on as Allie, Cook, Employee with an ample per-purchase limit.

"Should she order weekly?" Ky asked, looking over Stella's shoulder at the store display.

"Not at all. Every day or so is fine. She knows what to do," Stella said. She was not going to have Ky bossing Allie around on household matters.

CHAPTER FOUR

DAY 3

The next day the new kitchen door and its installation crew arrived early, interrupting breakfast. This involved more people, activity, and mess than Ky had expected: two trucks parked in the driveway and two in the street. Two carpenters, master and apprentice, to repair the door's framing and supervise the door's installation by the installers from the company that had built it. Locksmith to install new multiple locks. Painter to match the color of the former door on the new one, inside and out. Stella had left Ky to supervise and explain the new cook's presence, if needed.

Teague, in the persona of butler, told the various work crew where to park and also stayed in the kitchen while the workmen fitted the new door and a locksmith installed the new locks; Rafe stayed in the security office watching for any sign of official intrusion. Ky sat at the kitchen table, "supervising" Barash, who chopped and sliced busily, packaging the results for storage, while she tried to think her way through organizing some kind of rescue for the others. She left the work crew to Teague. The work crew didn't seem to notice that the rest of the house was shielded heavily, and by the time Stella was due home, they had cleaned up, taken away the broken door and the boards used to secure the opening, and departed.

In the noise and confusion, Ky forgot about the summons locked away in an upstairs safe.

That night Stella gave Barash her new ID, including supporting documents that already looked used. "This should take care of inquiries. I contacted Mother from the office, via the secure link on Corleigh, so she knows I've indulged in a new cook, but not what your real background is. As it happens—and I didn't know this—she *did* speak to a friend of hers about needing a cook since it looked like Rafe and Ky would be staying with us. I thought it was logical enough, but I didn't realize she'd anticipated me."

"It wouldn't be too hard to add more security to the kitchen area," Rafe said when supper was over. They had eaten in the main house's dining room this time, and the three survivors had taken the dishes back to the kitchen, leaving the four to talk alone. "Then we wouldn't have to keep someone in the kitchen all day and evening."

"Father always said they left the kitchen out because of the shape of the house," Stella said.

"I understand that," Rafe said. "But the kitchen addition is a simple one. We can't do ship-hull level, but I'm sure Teague and I could contrive something to block the kind of scans they're using, so there'd be no problem having any number of us anywhere in the house save those upper-level rooms."

"How long?" Stella asked. "And how much material do you need?"

"I'm fairly sure Vatta Transport supply will have what we need, and enough of it."

"Give me a list," Stella said. "I'll check on that tomorrow. Would we still need to turn off the house security to go from the main house to the kitchen?"

"Not once I deal with the door between them," Teague said. "It would be unlocking just that door, as when we open the front door. The French doors to the back garden are a bigger problem, but if we want to use the garden we can always go around by the gate, right?"

"It's going to be a nightmare when the twins come," Stella said. "They're used to running in and out all the time."

"How long is that?"

"A couple of tendays, unless Mother decides it's safer on Corleigh and puts the twins in school there. And they shouldn't see—our other guests. If Grace thinks it's dangerous, I'll tell her."

"We can worry about that later," Rafe said. "For now, the kitchen—"

"Go on," Stella said with a wave of her hands. "It's too complicated for me—trouble at work, trouble at home—" She leaned back in her chair and shut her eyes.

Ky looked at Stella. She wanted to ask about the summons and the Vatta legal department, but clearly this wasn't the time.

"You need to talk to Aunt Grace," Stella said, sitting up again. "She should be able to help you with these—our military guests. It's not that I'm not sympathetic, but they can't stay here indefinitely."

Ky could think of nothing polite to say, but finally managed, "I'll call her tomorrow morning."

Grace Vatta knew her house on Dunkle Street would be empty when she arrived home that evening. Mac was out gathering data; Teague had left to help out at Helen's house. Although she'd finally gotten used to the sounds of houseguests moving around, and found both Teague and Rafe to be pleasant, cooperative guests, she looked forward to a quiet evening alone.

She felt the chill even with her coat on when she stepped out of the car and said goodbye to her driver. At least it wasn't raining. Her security detail wasn't close as usual when she glanced around. There'd been a traffic issue four blocks back. She waved her driver on. They would be here in minutes, she was sure, annoyed if she stood outside waiting for them. She would go straight inside, locking up at once; they would ping her skullphone to check on her.

She took the paper she'd found stuck in the door—some kind of advertising, she supposed, though the neighborhood was posted for no flyers—and stuffed it into her capacious bag. The door's lock mechanisms responded appropriately to her touch and swung open.

She stopped abruptly. The door was supposed to produce a specific sequence of tones when opened, and it hadn't. Instead, a faint hissing came from low to her right; an acrid smell stung her nose. She stepped back, pulling the door closed, fingers automatically finding the panic button on the inside, under the safety bar. That would alert security, though she hadn't taken the time to code in the problem. Already she felt dizzy. She slapped the external door controls to LOCK, grabbed for the rail to her left, and stumbled down the steps to the walk, wondering what it was this time.

Across the street, past the row of trees between sidewalk and curb, Ser Dallony was just going up his own steps. Grace took a breath that burned all the way down her throat, tried to call out, but her voice failed, a weak croak. He didn't look around. Her driver was long gone by now; he'd waited only to see that she'd unlocked the door. She still saw no sign of her security escort's second car. Back down the next block, across Missamy Street, a woman in a scarlet coat walked a white dog. Grace glanced back at her door. Was any of the stuff—whatever it was—seeping out? Was it heavier than air, or lighter? She couldn't see any vapor, but it was getting darker fast, as often on autumn evenings. She felt shaky, her mouth dry. She should move away from the house. No, she should stay there to warn Mac when he arrived. She should call Mac on her skullphone now, and not wait outside—

"Excuse me," said a pleasant voice. "Are you all right? You look tired or ill."

Grace looked up. A woman in a scarlet coat, a white dog. They had been down there and now they stood before her. Had she blacked out for a moment? The dog sat down, tongue lolling. Grace tried to speak again. Her voice came out weak, scratchy. "I . . . something . . . happened. Who are you?"

"Alice Vance," the woman said promptly. She had a pleasant face, carefully made up. She looked to be in her forties, a few gray strands in her medium-brown hair. "I live about a block and a half—well, almost two blocks—that way." She pointed ahead, the way she'd been walking. "You're Rector Vatta, aren't you? I've seen you on the news-vids; I knew you lived somewhere around here. Is this your house? Do you need help up the steps?"

"No," Grace said. She did not know Alice Vance, but her implant informed her that a family named Vance lived in that block. Husband Jaime. Wife Alice. Children Pedar, Chloris, and Vinnie. Grace tried to swallow; her throat was dry. "Do you have . . . water with you?" Her voice sounded weak, shaky.

"Yes," Sera Vance said. "I take it for Polly here. And a collapsible bowl, but you won't need that. Was your water cut off?"

Grace shook her head. It wasn't entirely safe to drink anything a stranger gave her but she needed water badly. Alice handed her a smudged bottle with a screw-on lid.

"The water's clean," Sera Vance said. "I'm sorry about the outside; I just refill it every day because it's for the dog, really."

Grace touched her tongue to the water. Her implant approved and she let a little trickle down her throat. It burned, then soothed. Another swallow that didn't burn at all. "Thank you," she said, screwing on the cap and handing it back. Her voice was still weak, but closer to normal. "There was some kind of bad smell in the house. I didn't think the pest control crew was coming today, but that must be it."

"You should call your doctor," Sera Vance said, her expression now worried. "If you like, I could call for you."

From the corner of her eye, Grace was aware of a vehicle moving very slowly from the corner toward them. Where *was* her security detail? "No thank you," Grace said to Sera Vance. "I'm sure I'll be fine

now. I just needed to wash out my mouth." She had no intention of
going to a doctor or clinic if she could help it; she had avoided doctors
successfully for years.

"Then would you like to come along to our house and clear your
head?" Sera Vance asked. "It's too cold to stand outside this evening.
I'll walk with you, in case you feel ill or need more water—I'm sure
that's better than trying to go back inside."

"Thank you," Grace said. Maybe whoever was in the vehicle
wouldn't attack when another person was there with a dog. The dog,
in fact, had gotten up as the car neared, standing alert, tail and ears up.
"I think I will. As one gets older, I've been told, one's reaction to different chemicals changes." She forced a smile. She felt steadier; her impulse to call Mac on her skullphone faded. He would worry; he would
also tell her to see a doctor. He might even insist on a hospital visit.

Sera Vance laughed. "My mother said the same thing. I'm glad to
help. Why don't you take my arm?" To the dog she said, "Come along,
Polly."

Grace thought of Mac, this time more clearly, but took Sera Vance's
arm; the white dog trotted ahead, the leash not quite taut. The car
went on by, windows up, dark blurs inside it. Grace tried to think of a
way to let Mac know without arousing his protective side. It was hard
to think, but after all she'd had a shock. Finally she thought she had
the right phrasing. "I need to make a call," Grace said, as they walked
along. "If you'll excuse my doing it as we walk."

"Of course."

Mac answered on the second ping. "MacRobert here. Who's calling?" Which meant he was with people, perhaps still in that meeting
he'd mentioned.

"Grace," she said. "I think I forgot the day the exterminators were
coming. Came in the house and there was an awful smell. I'm going
down the block with a neighbor, Sera Vance, but you should plan to
eat somewhere else tonight."

"Oh. Sure. Tomorrow, then?"

"Yes. I'll need to find someone to clean the stuff out of the air, first."

"I'll take care of that. Talk to you later."

Good. He wasn't panicked about her; she would have time to re-cover fully before they met again. Grace brought her full attention back to the street. Quiet, as it usually was when everyone had come home from work. They crossed Missellin Street and went on down the next block. Lights shone from some windows; dead leaves rustled along the gutters. A night bird, overhead, gave a wavering whistle. The length of the block went by. Grace felt better with the fresh air, though her throat was still tight. They crossed Missanna.

"We're the third house on this side of the street," Sera Vance said. "And I see Jaime's home; the light's on in his den."

"You have children?" Grace asked out of politeness.

"Yes, three. Pedar left this morning with his science class on a field trip; they'll be back tomorrow night. Chloris should be practicing her viola, and Vinnie is either doing his homework or pestering his father. We'll find out shortly."

Inside the Vance home everything seemed normal. A small boy, about the same age as the twins, sprawled on the floor reading; the dog trotted over and licked his ear. The sound of a stringed instru-ment played imperfectly came from the back of the house. A door opened, and a tall, thin man said, "Alice—I was starting to worry. Oh—" as he caught sight of Grace. "I'm sorry."

A girl perhaps thirteen came through a swinging door, scowling. "I will *never* get that passage at measure ninety-two. My fingers just will not do it."

"Supper in fifteen minutes," Alice Vance said. "Everyone wash up. And this is Sera Vatta; the exterminators left too much chemical in her house, so I invited her here." To Grace, she said, "Just sit down and I'll bring you more water in a minute. The casserole's in the oven, all that's left is putting in the cheese biscuits."

Grace sat down. It was the girl, Chloris, who brought the water. "Do you like music?"

"I like some music," Grace said. She did not like listening to chil-dren practicing.

Silence descended. Chloris left the room at a call from the kitchen. Delicious smells drifted out into the sitting room, and Grace's memory brought up a reference. It had been decades, most of her life, but she had smelled that food before. In Esterance, as a young girl who thought she was an adult, she had eaten it with friends in a café before . . . things happened.

When Sera Vance—Alice—came to call her in to eat, Grace had mastered her memory, and asked what the casserole was. "It smells like something I had years ago—"

"Yes. My mother-in-law taught me to make it, back when I was on Fulland, doing research. I met Jaime and his family there. His mother saw the way the wind was blowing and decided I had to learn to cook all his favorites."

It tasted the same, down to the exact mix of spices. Grace had ignored the slight dizziness when she stood and walked in favor of dinner, telling herself that dizziness at her age, after a shock, was essentially proof of normalcy. Ignoring minor symptoms had stood her in good stead for years; as long as she could breathe, eat, and walk, she didn't need medical attention.

She ate without concern; the children were eating theirs and her throat felt better anyway. The slight tremor in her hand—she lost that forkful of casserole—was just another aftereffect of being scared. Probably had nothing to do with whatever it had been. She'd been in it only a few seconds, after all. She realized she'd lost track of the conversation around the table, and looked up to find Sera Vance watching her, brow furrowed.

"Sera—Rector—are you feeling unwell again?" Sera Vance's voice sounded unnaturally loud; both children were staring. "Are you sure we should not take you to a clinic? Jaime—" A knock on the door interrupted her, freeing Grace from the need to reply. She wasn't sick—she was just tired and a little shaky. Jaime—as Grace now thought of him—got up to answer it.

"Is Rector Vattá here?" asked a familiar voice. "I'm Master Sergeant

MacRobert, and her office is looking for her. There was some mistake about dates, and her house—"

"Of course, yes." Jaime's voice. "Come in; she's having dinner with us." And something in a lower tone that Grace could not hear.

Mac was in uniform, as he was only rarely these days. "Good evening, Rector," he said, as if they didn't call each other Grace and Mac all the time otherwise. "The department has a crew at your house, decontaminating it. The company apologizes for the error; they thought you had left for the weekend. You have a room reserved, or I can take you to your niece's house, if you prefer."

"Thank you, Master Sergeant. I hate to intrude on my niece—" She turned to Alice Vance. "My niece—great-niece, really—Ky Vatta and her fiancé are staying there, and they've had hardly time to see each other since the rescue."

"You know her?" Chloris sat up straighter. "You know Ky Vatta?"

"I've known her all her life," Grace said.

"But she's famous! She's an admiral! And then—"

"Chloris." Jaime smiled at her and shook his head slightly. "Sera Vatta knows all that."

"But—" Grace could see the effort made to calm down. "Just tell her we—our strings class—admires her most of all. Bela even wrote a little piece about her. If she'd ever like to hear it—"

"Chloris. Later."

"I'll tell her," Grace said. "Master Sergeant?"

"There's also a call from Commandant Kvannis, Rector. It requires a secure line."

Grace sighed, intentionally loud enough to hear. "It was a lovely dinner, Alice, Jaime. Thank you—"

"I'm sorry to have interrupted dinner," MacRobert said. "I didn't mean to—"

"Sit down, join us," Alice said. "Our oldest isn't here, so there's plenty—he's at the two-hollow-legs stage."

"No thank you, Sera," MacRobert said. "I'm sorry; it's very kind of you, but I really should get the Rector to a secure line. She has important calls waiting."

The look on Mac's face convinced Grace not to delay. Kvannis must really have his undies in a knot about something; perhaps it had to do with the personnel from Miksland. She felt much better, she told herself, not just because of Mac's help down the steps. Yet the fragmented memory of Fulland, of Esterance, of the riots and the ... things that had happened ... that she had done ... remained. She struggled to pull them together. Jaime Vance was from Fulland, from Esterance? Which side had his family been on? And had she run into any Vances back then? Mostly the people she'd known used only single names, often not their own—call names, they'd said. But she had been well known, especially postwar, after all the communications were back up. Her trial had been widely publicized.

"You're damn lucky you're alive," Mac said when they were back in the car. "Any symptoms?"

"Pain in my throat and nose, temporary loss of voice—that's why I didn't call you immediately. Some dizziness, weakness—that passed off fairly quickly. I think I'm fine now." She didn't mention the tremor. He would be sure it meant something dire.

"You're going to the hospital. No arguments." He said that last firmly though she hadn't argued. She *had* felt better, but now—as the car moved swiftly through the streets, around turns, bouncing a little over the occasional pothole—she had an uncomfortable feeling that she ought not to have eaten before being checked out. That maybe being checked out was a good idea.

"Did Kvannis really call me?" she asked to take her mind off her uneasy innards.

"Yes. He wants to get hold of Ky and said he couldn't reach her at the Vatta city house. Some questions about the people she knew in Miksland, he said. I didn't give him her skullphone number."

"Good. Nobody should have that but those she chooses." Grace paused. Her stomach really was upset, and she could feel the muscles in her arms and legs twitching now. Surely it wasn't the food; the whole family had eaten from the same dishes. "What was that stuff in the house, anyway?"

"MZT-43. Bad one, Grace. I wouldn't be surprised if you threw up that dinner you just ate; it attacks mucous linings, among other things."

She should know what MZT-43 was, but it was hard to think, harder every minute.

They reached the Marvin J. Peake Military Hospital before the worst happened; staff with a lift chair were waiting at the curb. "Rector—can you make it out of the car?"

"Of course I can," Grace said, but her voice was weak and harsh again. Her legs trembled when she tried to stand. Mac helped her, and she was in the chair, safe, but feeling much worse now. "Call the family," she said as they pushed her inside, and he nodded.

The kitchen had been closed off again, and they were all in the dining room listening to the survivors tell more about their experiences, when the house com warbled from the security office across the entrance hall. Stella went to answer it. "It's probably from Vatta headquarters."

"Go on," Ky said to Inyatta, who had stopped midsentence.

"Then I opened the cell door," Inyatta said. "That loudspeaker was still going about the emergency in Wing B. I gave Barash the door card, and she let Kamat out—we were all kind of shaky, so we raided the food cart and hoped that would help, and it did."

"And Kamat remembered we should be sure the evening dose was missing, so it looked like we'd taken it," Barash said. "That curtain we hadn't been able to see past was actually a kind of changing room— there were more suits like our guards wore hanging in it. We put the booties they wore over our slippers and that helped when we got outside—"

"We almost didn't," Kamat said. She shuddered. Ky nodded encouragement. "But Inyatta just kept going, like she knew—"

"I knew I'd rather die trying to escape than be drugged and helpless in that place," Inyatta said. "It seemed to take hours to get out of the building, though, let alone out of the compound. We'd relocked the doors the card opened, but they had sniffers, if they'd thought to use them."

Stella hurried across the foyer to the dining room. "Ky—that was MacRobert. It's Aunt Grace. She's been poisoned!"

"What?"

"Someone put poison gas canisters in her house! It could have killed her—it should have killed her—and she could still die—" Stella's breath came in gasps; she was trembling. Rafe stood up and went to her.

"Stella—take a deep breath—easy now." He took her arm and guided her to a chair. "Sit down. If Mac's with her, she'll be taken care of. Where is she?"

"That big—that big military hospital in the city. He said stay here, stay safe, don't come, but I—but we're family—" She looked at Ky. "We should go."

"If she's that sick, we can't help," Ky said. "Mac's right; he'll be sure nothing more happens to her." The possibilities ran through her mind as if outlined in light. "We need to call your mother—if this is the start of new attacks on Vatta, she should stay on Corleigh but maybe not in the beach house."

"You don't think anyone would kill the twins—"

"And you need to alert Vatta headquarters," Ky said. "All operations, here and elsewhere."

"Don't you even *care* about Aunt Grace?"

Ky bit back the first response and tried for something less antagonistic. "Stella, I do care about her. I care about the whole family as well. I can call headquarters, if you'd rather, while you call your mother."

"You're not listed anymore," Stella said. "You have no authority there. It's *my* domain." Her eyes glittered with unshed tears, and the warn-off was clear.

Ky could see, from the corner of her eye, the three survivors staring fixedly at the table. "You'll want privacy for that," she said, and stood, beckoning to the others. They followed her out of the room. To them she said, "I'm going down to the gym." Rafe gave a slight nod toward Stella; she knew he would stay with her, try to calm her.

"There's a gym?" Kamat asked.

"Yes," Ky said. "My uncle Stavros put it in. Come see." On the way down she considered explaining more about her background and Stella's, but they didn't need to know—yet, anyway—and she did want to hear more about their escape. Surely they knew something useful.

They had all worked up a sweat on the machines by the time Rafe showed up at the door and beckoned Ky over. "I come in peace," he said. He glanced past her at the others; they had been chatting at the other end of the room.

"Of course," Ky said. "Nobody's mad at you. Has she calmed down yet?" She wiped her face.

"She's gone up to the office and wants to be alone. I suggest that you not bother her tonight."

"Wasn't planning to," Ky said. "Neither of us can do anything for Grace tonight. So I'm focusing on what we can do for the survivors who are being held captive. Our guests have some ideas—we were about to go across the hall to what Uncle Stavros called the bunker."

"Bunker?"

"Situation room, it would be, in military terms."

Rafe gave her a puzzled look and said, "Do you want Teague down here?"

"Yes, both of you. He worked for the guy who got your parents out."

Rafe paused to call Teague on the house com, then followed her across the hall into the bunker. "Stella knows a lot more background on politics than you do—" he began.

"I've been gone for ten years."

"And were busy the whole time. I know. She says Grace isn't popular. Widely believed to be behind the former President's apparent suicide, after the attack on Vatta, even though it was the Commandant with him at the time. Apparently there's a rumor she and the Commandant had a connection in the past. Lovers or something."

"Aunt Grace?" Ky stared at him. "She's at least ten years older than he was, maybe twenty, and she never had any interest in men after her husband died. That's what my father told me."

"Stella said the same—that it was ridiculous, but a rumor nonetheless. And Vatta *did* use her as a corporate spy of some kind. Stella's afraid some enemy—corporate or political or a mix—may be targeting Vatta again, rather than this having anything to do with these three." Rafe smiled at them; they smiled back, a little stiffly. "I'm less sure. If she were just Vatta's master spy, sure, but she's administrative head of the Defense Department—surely an attack on her is more related to that. After all, we know they're interested in this house because of our friends here."

"That man, that officer who was here today—Aunt Grace ordered him to come to her office with his team. Could that have triggered an attack?"

"Possibly. Ky, from what you've told me about Miksland, the evidence you've found—both a civilian and a military component were involved. Maybe they were intentionally involved—maybe there's one enemy with two faces."

"Or three," Teague said, turning around from the map he'd been looking at since he'd arrived downstairs. "Mac wasn't kidnapped by the military or the Quindlans . . . that was a criminal organization, not a legitimate corporation."

"Malines," Rafe said, nodding. "But maybe they're all allies. Ky, were there any military personnel named Quindlan or Malines when you were here before?"

"There was a Cadet Quindlan in the senior class when I entered— I didn't have any problems with him. I don't remember his first name. Dad said the Quindlans weren't friends but weren't all bad—and back then the President was a Quindlan. Dad had voted for him. I think the cadet was his son, or maybe nephew."

Kamat said, "A Lieutenant Varian Quindlan supervised the shop I worked in on my first cruise. Seemed like a good officer. That would have been . . . maybe nine years ago."

"I knew a Malines—Dexter—in Basic, but he washed out, straight into the brig. He stole from our platoon sergeant." Inyatta shook her head. "Really stupid."

"So there is some infiltration of two suspect organizations into the third," Rafe said. "Over time, could have been a lot more."

"I take your point," Ky said. "Not one enemy, but several working together. Still, we need to figure out where the other survivors are being held, and then how to get them out. And quickly."

DAY 4

Stella was pleasant at breakfast before leaving for her office. Rafe gave her a list of equipment they would need to upgrade the house security and include the kitchen in it.

"And we're going to need more people," Teague added. "There're more than a dozen people to locate and rescue, and we don't have Gary's—" He stopped and shook his head.

"If you have someone in Vatta's security section," Rafe said, "someone you trust, with experience in . . . locating missing persons or shipments, a really good hand with electronics—"

"I'll do what I can," Stella said. "I'd usually ask Grace, but—" She picked up her case and edged toward the door.

"But surely there's someone you can ask. Grace ran your security for years; there must be—"

"Most died in the explosion, but I will look." She had her hand on the door.

"Stella, may I continue to use Vatta's legal department about this summons thing?" Ky half stood to get Stella's attention.

"Yes, of course, Ky. I saw that notation on the bottom of the memo and sent word down to give you whatever you needed. Just call them." Stella went out, and Teague followed, turning down the driveway to open the gate and spot for her.

CHAPTER FIVE

MARVIN J. PEAKE MILITARY HOSPITAL
DAY 4

By the next morning, Grace wished she could forget the preceding hours, a string of unpleasant, painful, humiliating moments without any respite between them. The dinner, she was assured, was not the problem at all, though everything she threw up was collected and later analyzed. Her head ached, then the first injection site turned into a row of red lumps before the staff figured out an allergen had been added to the toxic gas. It itched, then burned. She finally fell asleep around 0500, only to be woken at 0530 by a nurse demanding that she take an immediate vision test.

"I can see you perfectly well," Grace said. "Let me sleep."

"First the test."

After the test, it was only fifteen minutes until 0600, when the day staff arrived and the hall lights brightened. Brisk footsteps went up and down; voices in the hall were not muted. A different attendant came in to take vital signs. Grace wondered, not for the first time, if anyone could sleep while having their blood pressure taken. Only in a coma, she was sure. At 0700, the first doctor of the day arrived, closely followed by Commandant Kvannis and his aide, for whom Grace presented an intentionally groggy old-lady persona. She didn't really suspect him of anything, but giving away information went against her principles.

"I don't know," she said in answer to every question about Ky. "I can't remember . . . I hope it's the gas . . ." She hoped she looked as bad as she felt, and apparently she did, or close enough, because Kvannis left, still unsatisfied but convinced the Rector had narrowly escaped death.

At 0915, Dr. Hermann, who had supervised her arm's growth from bud to full functionality, came by. "I'm not lead on this," he said. "But you've got a very good specialist in poisonings; she's a friend of mine, and she flew in overnight from Makkavo. I told her how easy you are to work with, how compliant—" He grinned at her; her noncompliance in the matter of regular checkups once her arm was growing well had been, he once told her, unprecedented. "—so you can expect the same level of gentle pressure from her."

"I'm touched," Grace said. "I feel much better, and I have a lot of work to do. Important work." She lifted her head to glare at him and wished she hadn't. Neck muscles spasmed; she saw his gaze sharpen.

"Yes, of course you have important work. But you also have the residue of a quaternary toxin in your body—the stuff's damned hard to root out. You will not be leaving the hospital today. Or tomorrow. Or the next day. So get your tantrum about that over with before Sylvie arrives, because as I said she's a friend of mine and doesn't deserve the worst side of your tongue."

"I need sleep," Grace said, head back on the inadequate pillow. Her right foot cramped; she ignored it. "They kept me up all night."

"Sometimes it takes that," he said.

"A vision test at 0530?"

"The stuff attacks nerves, including the optic nerve. Once you're blind, it's too late."

"They didn't tell me that."

"Standard procedure. Some people go skewy worrying about it. Ah—here's Sylvie. Doctor Maillard."

Sylvie Maillard was a short, dark woman whose intensity reminded Grace of an older Ky. "Good news or bad news?" she said.

"Bad first," Grace said.

"That hiss you reported wasn't a gas canister *starting* to spread it in your house; it had been open for at least a half hour. It was supposed to be a knockdown dose as you came in the door. So you got more than you would otherwise, even with only a single breath."

"I held my breath—"

"When you heard it, yes. But like most people, you undoubtedly took a relaxing breath as you walked in. Everyone does that when they get home. The Ahhh Reflex, we call it. What that means—in terms Doctor Hermann says are meaningful to you—is that you won't be getting out of this hospital room for at least six days—and quite possibly longer. Given the intake, you have done well so far, but there are possible late complications. Later today, after another battery of tests and if I deem it appropriate, you can have communications equipment moved in here, so you can work from bed for a limited time each day. And I do mean limited. If not, we'll take an alternative tack and you won't be working at all."

Grace met Maillard's gaze, every bit as determined as her own. "I don't like it, but clear. If I'm in that bad shape, why do I feel better? I'm just tired."

"It's not just broken sleep. Typical of this class of poisons, MZT-43 continues to damage systems until you die, but its effects are not immediately lethal with the dose you received. Victims of a light dose typically feel upper-respiratory irritation at first, but that encourages them to drink and eat—which gives some components more time in the gut. You need to be monitored closely until it's all gone, with appropriate treatment for the various complications as they emerge."

"Not *if* they emerge?" Grace scowled. This might be as serious as Hermann looked.

"No. They will. You've already had IV and parenteral medication, the room's getting extra oxygen, and if necessary we'll intubate and put you on a respirator. At this point, if we are alert and don't make mistakes, you'll live and recover, but if you walked out of here and did not receive exemplary treatment somewhere else, you'd be dead by noon tomorrow."

"Oh." Grace had not imagined it being anywhere near that bad.

"So I expect your full cooperation with all procedures," Maillard said. "And full disclosure of all symptoms. Anything, no matter how minor. We're not talking about full functionality in a regrown arm; we're talking about survival."

"I'm in favor of survival," Grace said. She could feel her heart pounding. That couldn't mean the cramp in her foot, could it?

"Excellent," Maillard said. "Then we understand each other. If all goes well, the next two days will be the worst. If not . . . well, let's not go there. Depending on your latest lab results, you may be able to have communication with your office late this afternoon, but I strongly advise you to let your subordinates do the work. You're not young, and this toxin has killed people much younger than yourself."

"Thank you," Grace said.

Maillard raised an eyebrow. Just one.

"For telling me," Grace said. "One likes to be aware of the level of danger."

"Good," Maillard said. "I'll see you again when the next lab results are in. Until then, take it as easy as you can." She left.

"You ratted on me," Grace said to Hermann. "She's a formidable woman, but I doubt she's like that with everyone."

"I didn't want to see two formidable women butting heads," Hermann said. "Now she's gone, I'm going to check your fine-motor control in both hands . . ."

The rest of the morning Grace endured more treatments and tests. Mac showed up around lunchtime with a report from her office and his own activities.

"And Ky?" Grace asked. "How's she? Has she gotten in touch with Kvannis yet?"

"No. I suspect she and Rafe are . . ." His fingers intertwined. "Last person she'd want to talk to is someone official, I guess. You know Teague's over there playing butler—keeping interruptions to a minimum, is my guess."

"Anything else?"

"Something peculiar, actually. Military and civilian police are indeed looking for three fugitives from a military hospital here in Port Major. Thing is, as far as I can find out, they were never here, and this is the only military hospital in the city. There's that psychiatric ward in the Joint Services base hospital, but my police contact told me the search isn't for crazies, but for personnel possibly infected with a dangerous disease and under quarantine."

"Quarantine. That's one way to hide people."

"Hide who?"

"Not sure we should discuss this here."

"Sure thing. I hear your doctor coming. I left minutes ago." Mac ducked into the room's facility and out the far door seconds before Dr. Maillard came in.

"So you've had a visitor, but I don't see piles of work on your bed. That's good." Maillard slapped a fat file down on the bed-table. "Ren says you like data, and don't come apart if it's not all positive, so here you are." She opened the folder. "This is your basic chart. Red lines: level of toxin by organ system. Blue line: temperature. Green line: blood pressure. Yellow: heart rate on top, respirations below. Black dotted line: the average rate at which adults clear the toxin. Notice your clearance is well below that line: you're not clearing it as fast as most, probably because you're much older than the others we've seen."

"Having it around longer isn't good, I gather."

"No. The longer it's in an organ system, the more damage it does." She stopped abruptly and looked closer at Grace's face. "Did you know you have little marks on your face? Have you been poking it with anything?"

"No . . ."

"Let's see." Maillard pulled back the bedcovers and pushed up the gown. "Yes. Petechiae. Not a good sign at all. That confirms my concerns, and here's what we're going to do. We're going to knock you out, chill you—which, yes, slows your metabolism of the toxin, but also its action. Then we're going to use specific chemicals, different for each organ system, to extract the toxin rather than waiting for your body to clear it, using procedures similar to dialysis for kidney failure."

"How long will it take? When will I wake up?" Grace asked.

"If all goes well, we'll be done with the clean-out in eight hours, and you'll be awake, or at least in normal sleep, in another three. These procedures will save as much function as possible, but you'll still have aftereffects and may need rehabilitation for several tendays after. You'll need to have your implant out to avoid damage to it; the neuro treatment could scramble its wits. Since you're a high-ranking government official, you'll need to hand it over to a trusted subordinate with all the proper clearances for secure storage. Who would that be?"

"The visitor I just had, Master Sergeant MacRobert."

Maillard touched the call button. "Maillard. Page a Master Sergeant MacRobert and see if he's left the building. I need him here."

"I notice you have a guard on your door," Maillard continued, turning to Grace. "That's good. You should have a detail with you—outside your door, including during the treatment, with full recording capacity. Can MacRobert arrange that?"

"Yes," Grace said. Her mouth felt dry; she reached for the glass on the bedside tray.

"No more than a sip. And only because you've already had food today, so a little water's not the problem it might be." Maillard leaned both arms on the bed table. "You need to know that there's a chance that you'll die during this procedure. It's never been done on anyone your age, and though your baseline is good, much like someone fifteen years younger, we're still dealing with an aging metabolism. If you were clearing the toxin at the normal rate, we'd take the slower route. But we don't have time for that now. The petechiae indicate that serious damage is already occurring."

"It's done," Grace said. "Mac knows where everything is."

Maillard tipped her head to one side. "Are you two more than co-workers?"

"Friends," Grace said. "Who sometimes—not all the time—comfort each other."

"That's good. Total solitaries die more often, in my experience."

Mac poked his head in the door. "You called?"

"I did," Maillard said. "The Rector needs a fairly radical procedure that will involve general anesthesia, hypothermia, and a series of drugs to yank the toxin out of various organ systems. She'll be on machines similar to, but not the same as, the most advanced medbox technology. She needs her implant removed and properly stored, secure, until she can have it reinserted."

"It's got classified—"

"I understand that. She says you hold a high enough security rating to take charge of it. Is that correct?"

"Yes," Mac said, after a glance at Grace. "But I don't have a proper carrier."

"We do. It'll be bulkier than the usual: full nutrient bath, oxygenator, power supply, so it'll be ready to go back in when she's ready. I would prefer you stay in the room when it comes time to remove it, so there's a chain of control."

"Absolutely," Mac said. "Will you do that right now, or do I have time to inform the Rector's closest relatives?"

Maillard shook her head. "The longer we wait the more chance of irreversible damage that will affect her quality of life. Every fifteen minutes matters. You can call them during the procedures, as long as you do not leave this facility and maintain control of her implant. If things go as planned, it should take no more than eight hours— preferably only five or six—and she'll be ready for reimplantation sometime after midnight."

"Please," Grace said, glancing at Mac.

"I'll be here," Mac said. "And I'll stay. We have that other situation under control, Rector, don't worry about it. I'll have a complete report for you when you're ready."

She was ready now, except that she wasn't; she felt dull, heavy, aware at some merely physical level of something wrong inside. And the fear gnawed at her, fear she did not want to admit.

QUINDLAN INDUSTRIES & CONSULTING HOME OFFICE

Benny Quindlan faced his uncle's senior operations officer over the smaller desk in his uncle's outer office.

"That was the stupidest thing you could have done," he said.

"You're calling your uncle stupid?"

"You're telling me he ordered it?" Benny was almost sure his uncle hadn't.

"Not exactly ordered it." Maxim Furness had started to sweat; Benny could see the shine on his face. "But he wanted her out of the way."

"And she's not. And she knows, and the military knows, and all Vatta knows that someone had access to a quaternary poison gas that is supposed to exist in only two military facilities on the entire planet. Where the inventory can be checked, and probably already has been."

"It could've been Kvannis; he hates her enough."

"It could have been but it wasn't—it was us. You, rather."

"She'll be out of her office for several tendays, if she even survives. And already the confusion there has enabled us to make some inroads in her security. We'll get more—"

"Which will be found and healed by those ISC techs she's got staying with her."

"Ah, but they're illegals now. They overstayed their visa."

"And you know that because—"

"Because we have contacts in Customs & Immigration, just like every other commercial giant on this planet."

"Even so—" Benny began when the outer door opened and his uncle, silver-haired and impressive as always in his perfectly tailored clothes, arrived for the day's business. He and Max both stood.

"Good morning, Max; good morning, Benny." Michael Quindlan gave them each a polite nod. "Ben, my office."

Benny gave Max a look that he hoped was half as commanding as his uncle's, and followed Michael into his office. The desk there was big enough for two men to lie down on. Michael waved him to a chair, the better of the two that sat before the desk.

"Sit down, sit down. I'm glad you're here this morning. We have several situations to discuss that I would prefer not to do over any phone." His uncle pulled out and set up on the desk a security cylinder and thumbed it on. Lights along one side blinked green, one after another. "What were you talking to Max about?"

"Using gas at Rector Vatta's house."

"Ah. And your view on that?"

Now he was on the microscope slide, exposed under his uncle's flinty eye. "I think it was a bad mistake," he said. Michael nodded permission to go on. Benny gave his reasons.

"Good analysis," Michael said, at the end. "I had intended to start this morning by saying much the same to Max, but you have saved me the trouble." He grinned, more feral than humorous. "All I'll need to say is *Benny was right.* And assess him a fine." He paused, opened a drawer, and pulled out a neatly bound folder. "I think it's time you took a look at this." He pushed it across the desk.

Benny picked it up. "Project 43.36?"

"Yes. Do you recognize the code?"

"No, Uncle."

"Good. It's not in any of the usual sequences. Tell me: what do you know about Miksland?"

"What we were taught: a terraforming failure, barren, just rock and ice. Not worth worrying about with all the fertile land we have without it. Until recently, when suddenly it seems there's a military base on it, some question about what else is there, and I've seen a fuzzy image of some kind of big hairy animal with tusks—"

"Where?"

"One of those conspiracy sites you asked me to keep an eye on."

"Right. Well. In fact, it's not a terraforming failure, it's not barren, and—though it's not widely known—it belongs to us."

"Belongs—?"

"To us. The Quindlan family. We . . . managed to tack that claim onto a rather bulky piece of legislation about the time a connection of our family determined that it had potential."

Benny stared at his uncle. "The whole . . . *continent* belongs to us?"

"Yes. In rather convoluted language, and nobody seems to have noticed, but yes. We have . . . er . . . encouraged the belief that it's worthless rock, but in fact there are valuable mineral deposits and . . . you can look at the file for the rest. Now that others have noticed it exists, we need to make our claim public and decide what to do from here on—and I want you to bring me some proposals. We're meeting—all the seniors in the family—the day after tomorrow."

"But sir—Uncle—what about the military presence?"

"Long story; read the file. It's data-dense, and it has keys that will get you into the files stored in our servers at Portmentor. Don't lose it."

"I won't," Benny said. At his uncle's nod, he rose—his knees feeling a bit unsteady—and went to the door. Max was still in the outer office; behind him he heard his uncle's voice calling, "Come on in, Max!"

Benny's own office was down two floors, and his com light was blinking when he arrived. His sister Linny, he noted on the screen. He slid the folder into his office safe and locked it, then sat down at his desk.

"What did he want?" was Linny's first question. "Did he give you the promotion?"

"No. He was annoyed with Max for that operation against Grace Vatta."

"That viper," Linny said. "It should've killed her."

"Lin. It didn't kill her and it could have repercussions on the family. Using a rare weapon isn't the smartest choice. We're not supposed to have that stuff."

"We're not supposed to have a lot of things," Linny said. She was, Benny reflected, the most openly bloodthirsty and action-oriented Quindlan of his immediate family, and he wished she'd been tamed before she'd become his responsibility.

"Lin. You're still fourth tier. Do not start anything."

"Oh, big brother's going to scooold me? I'm so scared."

"Big brother is telling you not to buck first tier unless you want to spend the next two years counting barnacles on the dock on one of the smaller islands."

"Uncle Mike wouldn't do that. He likes me. He likes me better than you."

"That may be, but he doesn't like anyone to cross him."

She closed the call without answering. Typical. Benny looked at his schedule, told his clerk to hold calls from anyone junior to him, unlocked the safe, and opened the file. A day-after-tomorrow meeting meant his uncle would expect an outline of his presentation by noon tomorrow.

Two hours later, a call buzzed through. "How's it going?" asked his uncle. "What page are you on?"

"One oh five," Benny said.

"Good. That chart on one oh three?"

"Yes?"

"New data. I'll send it to your desk, unlabeled. You can figure it out."

And that was all. Benny allowed himself a moment of rubbing his temples and wishing he'd been born into another family before pulling up the new data.

MARVIN J. PEAKE MILITARY HOSPITAL

Mac sat down in the chair beside the bed and took Grace's hand. He could see the tiny red marks on her face, on her arms, and Maillard had told him privately what they meant. Her gaze was hazed, as if she was in pain, or sedated, but she hadn't had the sedative yet. Across the room, two nurses organized a tray of equipment and drugs. He hated seeing her like this, and he knew she hated being here, needing to be here.

"I hope what Maillard does will clear this out," Grace said.

"I'm going to trust that it will, and that your usual hardheaded stubbornness will pull you through anything. Most people your age wouldn't have survived having their arm shot off." He squeezed her hand, but felt her wince and let up his grip.

"I was younger then. Every year counts."

He softened his voice before asking, "Are you really worried, Grace?"

"Not exactly worried. Just . . . taking it seriously."

"Anything else?"

"Past things. Memories floating up. I think the records were all sufficiently slagged, but—"

He put a finger to her lips. "I'll be here. If you start babbling about something you shouldn't, I'll see that nobody hears it, if I have to sing opera at the top of my lungs."

Grace laughed; she couldn't help it. And at that moment, Maillard walked in at the head of a line of assistants, all ready.

"Good to hear you laugh, Rector. This is the team that will be working on you. Jess, give the master sergeant custody of the implant support box. Rector, you will have a sedative and then local anesthesia for the process of removing your implant, because although it is not physically painful, it can be quite disorienting. Then general anesthesia for the chill-down and flush of the toxin."

Grace did not argue. That in itself told Mac she was not anywhere close to being well.

Stella called Ky in early afternoon. "Grace is getting some complicated procedure; Mac is staying with her. I've been told not to come to the hospital, not to send flowers, just to wait. She's our *relative*. I hate waiting."

"And *I* hate being locked out of official channels," Ky said. "There's nothing at all on the news about the other survivors. Plus Rafe and Teague looking at me as if I'm supposed to pull the stuff they want out of the air."

"I can help you with that," Stella said. "I have access to Grace's old Vatta files, so I know now who else she handpicked for Vatta Security. I'm sending someone over within the hour with the equipment Rafe asked for."

"Fine," Ky said. "How will we know he's the right one?"

"You'll know." Stella cut the connection abruptly, and Ky managed not to snarl at her absence.

Stella had been right. Ky recognized the man as family the moment she saw him on the viewscreen. For one horrified instant, she thought it was her brother San, killed in the attack on Corleigh years before, but this man was a little taller. She let Teague open the door while she got her face back under control.

"I'm Rodney Vatta-Stevens," he said. "Sera Stella Vatta sent me with some equipment to upgrade security here, after the trouble at Sera Grace's."

He looked like San in the face, the same build, the same way of moving when he walked in, nodding to Teague and then to Ky. "It's been a long time since we last saw each other, at the country house one year, a birthday party. You may not remember me." His voice was not like San's, more tenor than baritone.

"I don't remember you specifically," Ky said. "The Vatta-Stevenses—didn't you live somewhere south of Port Major?"

"Southwest," he said. "Stevens Crossing. My great-grandfather part-owned a copper mine there." He went on, explaining at more length than Ky cared about how he was related to several branches of the family.

"I never heard of Couray-Vatta," Ky said, then wished she hadn't. Was he about to start a lecture on the ancestral history of the Couray-Vattas? He was.

With a cheerful grin, he shared all he knew about the Vatta-Stevens and Couray-Vattas as he opened his equipment case and lifted out tray after tray of instruments, finishing up with "Anyway, that's my family lineage. My parents live in Port Major now. My father's down in the bowels of the new headquarters building keeping the big servers running. That's where I was when Sera Stella called me up."

"What's your background in surveillance and countersurveillance?" Rafe asked. He sounded grumpy. He would have even less interest in the genealogy of Vattas than Ky.

"Sera Grace in Corporate Security recruited me out of school. My degree's from Thensantos U, right here in Port Major. Then came the attack—I was on a training mission at the time. Put me through the toughest eight weeks of my life, because so many had been lost. When she was tapped for Rector of Defense, she recommended to Sera Helen that I be moved out of Security for a few years, given more background in communications and computer technology, so that's where I've been. But I've kept up my physical training and martial arts, as a hobby, and I've kept reading."

They moved into the front sitting room, following Teague, and Rafe nodded at one of the chairs; Rodney sat down, then they all did.

"What kind of martial arts?" Teague asked.

Rodney named five or six. "Our club rotates, so we don't get stale. Every half year we change instructors, learn something new or ways to combine what we've been doing with what's being taught."

"So . . . what did Stella tell you about this situation?"

"Two jobs. The first, to bring a list of equipment to upgrade the house security. It's all in the case here, plus some adapters in case something doesn't fit. The second . . . she didn't tell me much, because she said you'd tell me if you wanted me for it."

"Briefing time," Ky said. "We'll go down in the basement; the charts are there." She led the way to the lift installed in the house core and punched in the code. Down there he wouldn't be able to see or hear the fugitives.

Rodney's eyes widened when he saw the displays. "This is like a military mission briefing."

"Exactly," Ky said. "And for that reason, we need your agreement that you want to be in on it."

"Without knowing any more?" He looked at Ky, then Rafe and Teague, and shrugged. "I say yes. Could be dangerous, right?"

"Very," Rafe said drily.

"Just the four of us?"

"Maybe. You have someone else to suggest?"

"Depends. But I do know some people, mostly in my martial arts group. And some cousins back home, on the Stevens side mostly."

"Well, then," Ky said. "Here's what we need to do. First we need to find the people who were with me in Miksland. We think they're all locked up in various military psych wards and/or prisons. Then we need to free them."

"How many people, how many locations?"

"We know the number of people, but not the locations. And that's the first task we're working on. Rafe and Teague have both surveillance and computer skills, but they're not from here, and we can't use anything in the Defense Department."

"Not exactly my field," Rodney said. "But you know the origin point of their travels . . . should be possible to track transport patterns using a program developed by Vatta for tracking its shipments. Pretty common sort of program; shouldn't arouse any suspicions."

"Excellent," Rafe said. "I used something similar to track movements when my family was abducted years ago."

Teague shifted but didn't say anything.

"Secure communications here, right?" Rodney asked.

"Yes. And a dedicated line to Vatta's servers." Rafe answered before Ky could.

"Perfect. I'll need the originating site, and any intermediate sites you've identified. Also any information about which people are where." He looked around. "But what did you want first, the house security made more secure, or your people found?"

"House security," Rafe said, Teague a beat behind him.

"Find the people," Ky said. Rodney looked back and forth among them all. "Rafe, you or Teague could upgrade the house security with the supplies Rodney brought, but he's the only one who knows the Vatta program for tracking shipments. We can do both."

"Ky—I just wanted—" Rafe began, but Teague interrupted.

"I can do it, Rafe. I'll call if I need your help. You left the stuff on our list upstairs, Rodney, right?"

"Yes," Rodney said, with a glance back at Ky.

"Rafe and I are both qualified. No putting things in upside down or the wrong order." Teague smiled.

"But if—"

"I've got this," Teague said, sketching a salute to Ky on his way out.

Rafe moved closer to Ky. "All right then—let's find the people. Do your magic, Rodney."

An hour later, with visuals up on three different screens, Rodney had broken through the first problem. "They're supposed to have their locators on—you've cited the military code—but they turned them off to hide from normal tracker activity. But we've got visual as well, and they might as well have painted themselves bright orange. Vehicles without locators traveling from or through the points you defined on the days you defined are now showing up as outliers."

Colored lines now originated at the airfield near where a flight from Miksland could have landed. Rodney pointed to one particular trace. "Four vehicles without locators departed your starting point A on the date you suggested, spaced ninety minutes apart. Three took one route; one took another. That jibes with what you said about the more senior enlisted being separated from the rest early on. Vehicle one, registered to Slotter Key Defense Department, headed southwest on Highway 21W to a destination fifteen kilometers outside Marlotta, with a label of TRANSFER SUPPLY STATION."

"The trace goes beyond that," Ky said.

"Yes, but someone could have been offloaded at that station. Can't be sure. It was there four hours and twenty minutes, at least. Then it ended some twenty-two kilometers past Egger's Crossing, at Clemmander Rehabilitation Center. Not defined anywhere as a military installation. Was there for an hour and a half, then drove back to Egger's Crossing where the locator was turned back on."

"So you think some of them are there?" Ky asked.

"Very good chance," Rafe said before Rodney could. "We need to find out who owns the rehab center and what kinds of patients it takes."

"Did that," Rodney said, pulling up another image. "This is what Clemmander looks like." A brick building set in green lawns, fronted by a paved approach with three vehicles sitting on it. "It's listed as a facility under Rehabilitation Services, Ltd., a subsidiary of Slotter Key Medical Services Incorporated. They have at least one facility on each continent; several here on Arland. Site says they have contracts with 'major employers, private and governmental, to provide residential rehabilitative care for employees suffering from a variety of mental and physical impairments. Not open for uncontracted services.'"

"Very handy," Rafe said. "A way to hide people you want hidden . . . do we have any satellite imagery of the place?"

"Yes, but it's sited in an awkward location, so there's not nearly as much satellite coverage as we'd like. For details, the local planning authority's authorization, eighteen years ago when it was built, may be more useful. Included was the site plan, building plans and elevations, and at least some of the security measures. Here's the only satellite view I could find; the standard mapping image blurs out, like you said it did for Miksland itself. But here's the authorization paperwork."

"Looks exactly like a small prison," Rafe said. "Four pods holding five prisoners each in isolation. Staff security—guards, essentially. Kitchen, exercise area . . . a mini-prison. Except—" Rafe looked at the images of proposed client room décor. "—this is more like a private clinic. Beds, not steel shelves. Chair. Recreation area with tables, chairs, couches, bookshelves."

"Pods aren't equal," Ky said, scowling at the tiny figures in the drawings then back to the descriptive text. "And there's another level. Look—the ground-level rooms have the nice beds and so on . . . the

upper one, the rooms are smaller, thicker-walled, no windows. Described as 'treatment rooms for more severe conditions.'"

"Perfect for isolating problem people," Rodney said.

"What about the other vehicles?" Ky looked at Rodney.

"Traced for two days. The first went north, up the east-coast road,
no locator, then turned west at Sarl Harbor, then north again to a psychiatric residential facility within five kilometers of an AirDefense
base, and a hundred thirty kilometers west of Port Major. Eleven days
after that, a locator-free prison transport left there headed for Port
Major, and arrived at the Joint Services HQ base west of the city. It
lists a military prison sited near the east margin of the base, well away
from any other buildings. That must be where the women here escaped from. The others turned west earlier—look here—" He pointed
to the image. "Almost all the way across the continent, one to another
rehab center a hundred and ten kilometers north of Portmentor, and
the other to a rehab center two hundred thirteen kilometers south of
Portmentor. And yes, all the rehab centers are operated by the self-
same Rehabilitation Services, Ltd." Rodney looked pleased with himself, and Ky thought he had reason.

"We need more people on the team," Rafe said. "Three sites—we'll
never get them all if we start with one: they'll know we're on the
move."

"Four sites. There could still be prisoners incarcerated here in Port
Major." Ky stared at the trace on the screen. "But you're right, Rafe.
We're going to need more personnel."

"There's got to be an equivalent specialist on this planet, if I only
knew—" Rafe said. He stopped as Teague came back into the room.

"I'll check," Teague said. "But how do we know who *they're* working
for? We're not natives here; we don't have the networks. Nor Sera Ky;
she's been gone too long."

"Hostage extrication?" Rodney said. "Sera Grace had a list, but
none she really trusted, she said. Though maybe since then—"

"It would take all of—" Teague paused, clearly editing what he'd been about to say. "That other person's full team, all of it, to pull off multiple extrications involving the same source."

"We've made a start," Ky said. "And you're saying we can't go further without more personnel. So, Teague, how are you coming on the security end?"

"Not done yet—I need Rafe to check results while I test."

"We need to do what can be done now," Ky said. "Let's finish getting the kitchen wing and garage better protected, and talk this over with the others and Stella when she gets home. Which should be in—less than an hour, now."

They looked at her. Then Rafe shrugged. "That's why she's the admiral. Yes, sir, Admiral sir, you're right."

"Start in the kitchen," Ky said. "And fix whatever lets scans count the number of people in there."

Ky gathered her troops, as she thought of them, in Stella's office, for a tactical discussion. Two days of safety and rest had done them all good. Barash, in the disguising wig and cook's outfit, showed a witty side Ky had not seen before; Inyatta was back to her former energetic, serious self, eager for something useful to do. And Kamat, though still distressed about having an "immoral" implant, now seemed focused on rescuing the others.

"Do any of you have any knowledge of these regions?" Ky asked, highlighting the areas Rodney had pointed out on the image.

"I've got some relatives near there," Inyatta said. "An uncle, some cousins. They're out in the country, though. Livestock."

Barash and Kamat shook their heads.

"But shouldn't Slotter Key military be the ones to get them out?" Teague said.

"Except that they haven't."

CHAPTER SIX

DAY 4

Benny Quindlan had read—at least skimmed—the entire file by the time he left the office. But he still did not understand it well enough to present on it the next day. Oralie would be annoyed, but he had to take the work home, and he would have to skip the evening they'd planned. Third time in the past ten days . . . actually, Oralie would be *furious*.

But he knew his uncle too well to risk being unprepared the next day. He'd considered just staying in the office—a space Oralie couldn't reach—but decided against it. She might, being angry, go out with friends and talk about how he was working nights too many times, and that . . . would not please Uncle Michael, either.

A man should manage his household well. One of the twelve rules of the family, the unbreakable ones. When he walked into the foyer, briefcase in hand, she was there, a drink in her own hand, and more challenge than welcome on her face. "You're going to work, then."

No use trying to explain now. "Yes," he said. "And no, we're not going out tonight."

"Then I am," she said, and upended her glass, eyes on him as the liquid flowed down her beautiful throat. She knew he would watch the ripple; she knew him well. He wanted to put his hands on that throat, stroke it, lead her to the bedroom . . . He dragged his mind back to business.

"You are not going out," he said. "There's a reason."

"You got the promotion? We're going to be rich and I can have that necklace you said was too expensive?" Her voice could cut like a knife.

"Not yet; there's a job to do first. But the necklace . . ." It was a small price to pay for her cooperation. "You will have the necklace when I give it to you—very, very soon." Her birthday was coming up; she would think it was that.

Her voice changed with her mood, and she shrugged. "Well, if you have to work, you have to work. What would you like for supper?"

"Simple. That thing you do with rice would be great."

An hour later, she set the plate on the end of his desk. Rice with vegetables and chunks of crab meat in a red sauce. He smiled and thanked her; she went away silently, for which he was grateful. The full scale of the plan was just beginning to emerge from its nest of figures, charts, and documentation. Four hours after that, Benny leaned back in his chair, more frightened than he had ever been in his life. His uncle had trusted him with Quindlan's darkest and longest-laid plans—not just for wealth, but for ultimate political power—which meant his uncle would kill him if he made a hash of it. And the plans were so . . . he hunted for an adjective and gave up. It was too much, too big, and far, far too dangerous. Stealing a continent was one thing—no one had wanted it, at least not then. But plotting to steal several more, all inhabited and thriving under the current government? Was Michael insane? Were all the elders insane?

He looked again at the security cylinder on his desk, the green lights along its side reassuring. But—for such a plan—could his uncle have planted surveillance even here, in his shielded home office inside his shielded home inside the gates and walls of the Quindlan estate? Of course. He dared not even murmur the thought running traitorously through his mind: *I wish I'd been born a Vatta.*

CHAPTER SEVEN

CLEMMANDER REHABILITATION CENTER
DAY 5

Staff Sergeant Gossin, senior surviving NCO from the shuttle crash, said nothing when the morning meal packet slid through the slot. She did not move for another five minutes, as near as she could determine, having no timekeeping device. Her well-stocked implant was gone, replaced by a very basic one that seemed to have, as its main function, dispensing drugs she very much did not want to have in her system.

As she lay there, silent and not quite motionless, she thought over the same miserable string of events. Their escape from the mercs sent to kill them. Their airlift out to what they'd all thought was safety. But had they *all* thought it was safety? Or had Admiral Vatta—who had been determined to get them out safely—betrayed them at the last? Or had she been betrayed by her great-aunt, the Rector? Or was it someone else?

Because betrayed, they certainly had been. It had been reasonable for them to be debriefed separately, that first day, and it had seemed reasonable for them to be in separate compartments on the flight from Pingat Islands Base back to Voruksland, on the way to Port Major. Except she had woken up, more or less, strapped down in a ground transport vehicle carrying not only her, but also Staff Sergeant Kurin and Sergeants Cosper, Chok, and McLenard. She'd scarcely had time to notice that before someone in a green decontamination suit had reached over and tweaked a tube, ending that brief period of consciousness.

There have been two more debriefings—somewhere—somewhen—with never a sense of being clearheaded until she woke up here, in a five-cell pod in some kind of jail, with her head shaved, guarded by people in decontamination suits, whose faces she could not see. They answered no questions, gave only brief orders.

Periodically, she was taken out of the cell and allowed to shower, provided with a clean orange short-legged jumper, clean cloth slippers, and a clean striped robe. Then for an hour she was interrogated by someone behind a window. Every third interrogation was followed by a brief visit with the others confined here, and then by a physical exam and a return to her cell.

She was the senior. She was responsible for the others—all the others, from Staff Sergeant Kurin, next junior, to Ennisay, the most junior—and she did not know where most of them were, or what had happened to them, or even why she and the other senior NCOs were confined here.

Asking had brought little information, and only in the first interrogation. Supposedly they had been exposed to a deadly contaminant, and were in quarantine. Supposedly Admiral Vatta had the same thing and had died. No one would tell her—if they even knew—what the contaminant was, toxin or disease. She didn't feel sick—when she wasn't drugged—but she did feel uneasy, annoyed, and bored.

She sat up when she had counted down what she hoped was about five minutes, and fetched the tray from the door slot. Cereal, hot. A drink that was neither coffee nor tea, but a weak attempt at a brown liquid to drink at breakfast. A packet of sweetener for the cereal, a little container of white liquid for the brown liquid, another little container with a pill she was supposed to take.

And the cell was monitored. Leaving the pill in its container meant she would be given an injection within the hour. That was not a result she wanted, but she knew the pill—blue with a white stripe—was a sedative. It must be the day for moving them from cell to cell. She would be barely conscious for several hours, and then be returned to a cell that smelled strongly of cleansing solutions and also felt "different" from the one she had just left.

Why were they doing this? She ate the cereal with sweetener, because she had to eat something, stirred the white liquid into the brown one, and drank down the pill. The drowsiness came soon after; she was barely aware when she was bundled into a float chair and taken out of the cell.

This time she woke in a larger room, with her companions in their own float chairs to either side. She turned her head. Staff Sergeant Kurin blinked. *I'm aware,* that meant. Sergeant Cosper didn't look at her; he still seemed dazed. Sergeant Chok blinked. Sergeant McLenard stared at the floor. Gossin looked around the room. A transparent screen separated them from a table beyond, with five chairs behind it. A door centered that wall. This was completely new. She tried to turn and look behind her, only then realizing she was strapped into the float chair, unable to turn her body or move her arms.

The door behind the table opened, and three women and two men came in, all in military uniform. Four officers each represented a branch of Slotter Key's military: Spaceforce, AirDefense, Air-Sea Rescue, and Surface Warfare. The fifth represented enlisted personnel, the sergeant major of the entire military, Sonja Tonaya Morrison. They pulled out the chairs and sat down facing the screen, picking up earbuds and putting them in. Gossin could hear the scrape of their chairs, the rustle of their clothing, throats clearing. Someone in a plain gray smock entered with a tray: two water pitchers. Behind him came another, with a tray of glasses, and these were set down on the table, a glass for each of those seated, a pitcher at each end. The two in smocks left. Another man came in, this one in uniform, bearing a stack of folders, which he set down beside the man in the center.

"We'll begin," said the man in the middle. "Is the recording on? Testing?"

Gossin could not hear any response, but he nodded.

"Present at this meeting of the committee tasked with determining the status and prognosis of those individuals who survived the shuttle crash and were recovered from Miksland are myself, Colonel Asimin Nedari, chair, representing Land Forces; Commander Palo Gohran, Spaceforce; Lieutenant Colonel Djuliana Dikar, AirDefense; Lieutenant Commander Howard Buckram, Air-Sea Rescue; and Sergeant Major Sonja Morrison.

"This meeting is being held at the Clemmander Rehabilitation Center, under contract to treat disabled service members, where Staff Sergeant Gossin, Staff Sergeant Kurin, Sergeant Cosper, Sergeant Chok, and Sergeant McLenard have been treated. Circumstances and investigation so far indicate that all such individuals were exposed to dangerous pathogens, and that all exhibit recurrent symptoms of physical and mental degeneration, including loss of physical conditioning, coordination both fine- and gross-motor, memory deficits, and cognitive deficits."

Gossin twitched, all she could do, restrained in the float chair as she was. They weren't sick and they weren't disabled—except for the drugs and the confinement.

"We have been presented with the medical records that document this damage, and the committee as a whole—" Colonel Nedari looked along the table both ways; the others nodded. "—felt it was necessary to see for ourselves the conditions of these cases, before rendering a final decision on their future management. This is our last clinic visit; we have observed all the clinics in which these personnel are being treated. Because of the severity of the condition caused by this unknown pathogen, we have acceded to the medical staff's recommendation to observe from behind a protective barrier, but we will make every effort to communicate with each individual and ascertain their present condition."

A hand went up from the woman on Colonel Nedari's right, the sergeant major. "I'd like it on the record that this restriction of direct contact with the individuals was opposed by the Senior NCO Association on the grounds that no further cases have been detected."

"So noted," Colonel Nedari said. "But of course, the cases have been in complete quarantine so it is highly unlikely that any more cases would have been found—"

"Excuse me," the sergeant major said. "But these individuals had direct contact with Mackensee Military Assistance Corporation personnel immediately after their retrieval, and with our military personnel prior to their arrival at Pingat Base and the Haron Drake Military Hospital, where they were first quarantined. Both Mackensee and Black Torch mercs were in the same underground areas. No cases have been reported by either organization, nor have any shown up from the pre-quarantine contact with Slotter Key troops. The Senior NCO Association considers this reason to question the need for, not the efficacy of, quarantine."

"Noted," the man said again. "Thank you, Sergeant Major Morrison. Nonetheless, this examination will take place under the conditions specified prior to our visit, maintaining quarantine and not endangering unprotected personnel."

A pause, during which no one spoke, and three of the panel sipped water from their glasses. Gossin had a brief time to think about what they'd said about her, about them all, and what it might mean. She felt cold. Their captors could have dosed them differentially; that might be why McLenard's head drooped. She glanced at him again. A line of saliva ran out of his mouth, down his chin, and made a visible wet spot on the bib tied under it. His face had been shaved unevenly, though his head was as hairless as her own. If this was all the committee saw, they would think . . . they would think what they'd been told, that she and the others were impaired.

She wriggled, trying to loosen the straps that held her, but they had no give to them.

"Well, now," the man in the center said. "We will start with . . . um . . . Sergeant McLenard." He opened the folder on top of the stack. "If the rest of you will consult your chips: I will pass this along as we go, so you can see the originals of the clinical notations." He raised his voice a little. "Doctor Hastile, if you will indicate Sergeant McLenard, please, and prepare him for examination."

"Yes, of course. Corpsman—"

Though she could turn her head only partway, Gossin saw two people approach McLenard's chair, one on either side. Both were garbed in full protective gear, bright yellow this time. She could just make out a human face inside the transparent mask—a face partly covered by a second mask over nose and mouth. One touched the chair controls so it lowered to the floor. The other touched a control to the restraints on McLenard's arms and legs; they retracted into the float chair frame. One arm fell into his lap, the hand clenched oddly; the other slid over the side of the float chair and jerked in an uneven rhythm.

"Sergeant McLenard. Can you state your name, rank, and number for this committee?"

McLenard's mouth gaped; his tongue protruded, licked at his lips, but he said nothing. One of the yellow-garbed figures leaned over him. "McLenard! Pay attention! Name!"

"Mmmm. Muh . . . eh . . . luh . . . nuh."

"Rank! Say your rank!"

"Ssss . . . uh . . . ahh . . . juh . . ."

"What day is it?" No answer. Of course, Gossin thought, he could not answer. None of them could. They had been kept isolated, away from sunlight or dark, calendars or clocks. She had no idea how long she'd been here, what day it was, what time of day it was. It wasn't McLenard's fault—and besides, he was drugged. Couldn't the committee tell that?

"Doctor, let's see him walk."

"He doesn't walk without support."

"Let's see, anyway."

The two men levered McLenard up to a standing position; he was clearly unsteady. One took each arm, and the voice Gossin identified as "the doctor" urged him to walk forward. His gait was weak, unsteady; he needed the support of both men to keep him from falling, and after seven or eight steps they half carried him back to the float chair.

"Doctor." That was the sergeant major. "Has he had any medications that would produce this effect?"

"No. He is on a mild sedative to prevent self-injury—" The doctor lifted McLenard's arm, pushed up the sleeve of his robe, and showed a linear scab. "He picks at his arms if we don't either sedate or restrain him. But nothing that would cause ataxia or the kind of mental deficit he shows."

Gossin wanted to scream *Liar* at him, but she was afraid of what they would do to her. She had had drugs that morning; she could feel them fogging her brain, though not as much. She knew the implant they'd put in her head could administer drugs as well.

"And your prognosis, Doctor?"

"Sergeant McLenard will not improve. He will require permanent custodial care for the rest of his life."

"Thank you. When you are ready, we will continue with . . . uh . . . Sergeant Chok."

Chok was able to give his name, rank, and serial number, though in a monotone mumble.

"What is the date, Sergeant Chok?"

"Dun . . . dunno, sir. Don't have calendar. Clock."

"They do," the doctor's voice interrupted. "There's a calendar in the day room. Clocks in their quarters. They don't seem to understand them, though staff try."

"Yes, we've seen the images of their quarters, Doctor. I understand.

Not oriented to time, then. Sergeant Chok, do you know where you are?"

"Where? Can't see out."

"Do you know what kind of facility this is?"

"Issa jail," Chok said.

The committee members looked at one another for a moment. The sergeant major said, "A jail? No, Sergeant, it's a hospital. Because you're sick."

"No windows. No vids—"

"Of course there are vids," the doctor said. "You've just forgotten them." He turned to the other man. "Help me, here. Time to show them how he moves."

Chok, released from the straps, made an attempt to stand but needed help. He took a few tottering steps, tried to shake his arm free of the doctor's firm grip, but then his foot slipped on the floor. Gossin saw a shiny place, as if a smear of grease was left behind.

"He's getting agitated," the doctor said. "Come on, now, Sergeant, let's get you back in your chair before you fall and hurt yourself."

Gossin rubbed her slippers on the footrest of her chair. They were slick, and the floor was polished, gleaming.

"I'd like to talk to him alone," the sergeant major said.

"Now, you know what we were told," the chairman said.

"I know what we were told but that man could as easily be drugged as actually demented. I want to see his actual room."

"Are you prepared to go through both the entrance and exit decontamination, gown up in one of these suits, and spend at least nine days in quarantine?" asked the doctor. "Because that's what it will take to allow you closer contact with any of these cases. We're not going to have you spreading this pathogen—"

"If it is a pathogen." The sergeant major was clearly angry.

Gossin tried to catch her eye, but the sergeant major was focused on Chok, now swaying in his seat as they refastened his restraints. She saw the doctor slip something into the pocket of his yellow suit. Had he already dosed Chok again? And would they dose her again, before it was her turn to be shown off to the committee as a hopeless case? Her stomach roiled, fear and drugs combining.

The chairman turned to the sergeant major, also clearly angry. Both had their hands over the mike pickups, so Gossin heard only muffled phrases that seemed to be an argument about whether the staff might be lying about the "cases" and whether the sergeant major was risking something—probably being ruled out of order.

When that was over, the sergeant major was silent, lips compressed, expression grim then fading to blank. Gossin knew that expression well: the defense of the outranked when the senior was wrong but, for the moment, unstoppable. She had used it herself to escape worse trouble. As the chairman picked up another of the folders, and the others shifted in their chairs, the sergeant major looked at Gossin, a long considering look. Gossin looked back, hoping her face conveyed her fear, her concern. She blinked twice, deliberately.

The sergeant major blinked back, twice. Gossin blinked three times quickly, three times slowly—and twitched as the attendant's hand clamped on her shoulder. "Are you feeling bad, honey?" came the voice she hated. "Need a little pain med, do you?" And a sharp sting in the back of her neck.

Her head was already dipping forward but she was almost sure she had managed the last three quick blinks.

Sergeant Major Sonja Morrison said nothing more during the rest of the presentation. Staff Sergeant Elena Maria Gossin had tried to send her a message. She'd known Gossin before Gossin made staff sergeant, before she herself became sergeant major. Gossin had chosen Space-force; Morrison had chosen Surface Warfare, because she'd had her eye on the position she now held, and everyone knew that nobody made sergeant major unless their duties were firmly tied to the plan-et's surface.

And she, Sonja Morrison of Esterance on Fulland, knew that the current Rector of Defense had been equally tied to the planet's surface, and had actual combat experience in surface warfare. Long ago, and not that far away from Morrison's own background, in the misnamed war that the schoolbooks had whitewashed. The loose strings left behind still acted as fuses to buried political ordnance. Time to look for a string, and yank it as hard as possible, because sure as stingfish were stingfish, her people—*enlisted* people were all her people—were being mistreated by *someone,* and it had better not be the Rector of Defense for some stupid political reason.

She had seen desperation on Gossin's face, seen the quick blinking of her eyes, seen the attendant reach out, grab her shoulder, and put a hand to the back of her neck. They were drugged. They were all drugged, and the demonstration was a sham, the whole thing playacting to excuse this—this hideous injustice perpetuated on innocent personnel. She had thought so on the other clinic visits, but now she was sure.

Her gramma had always said the Vattas were dangerous, but wouldn't say why. Well, a certain Vatta, or several, would find out that a Morrison could be just as dangerous.

If she made it back to Port Major without being drugged herself. She had pulled on the bland face, so often practiced, that gave nothing away, pinged her implant to regulate heart rate, respirations, the levels of stress hormones in her blood so that her sweat wouldn't give her away. When the time came for final comments, she acceded to the suggested verdict with a pleasant little smile, allowing her voice to express only sadness that such a tragedy had occurred.

And after, in the reception prepared for the committee, she ate and drank nothing, while seeming to do so, and entered the same vehicle as the others, who were not in the same danger, she was sure. She hoped.

Nonetheless, she wished she could have been more active—could have walked past that barrier, talked to her people, found out what had really happened and how bad it was for them now. Her imagination insisted on suggesting how bad it could be for her if she didn't convince the right people that she was no threat, just a person who cared about her people, which was both true and normal.

Like the others, she was to co-sign a report to be delivered to the department back in Port Major. She was on the same flight with the rest of the committee. Colonel Nedari invited her to come up to officers' country, where they could work on the report together and sign it. But—fortunately, she thought—six other officers boarded, and if she accepted, one of them would have to be bumped back to NCO seating. She smiled and shook her head. "Sir, I don't think that's appropriate when officers are waiting. Just take it that I'll sign whatever you have ready for me—send someone back for me, and I'll come up but not disturb the others."

"You're sure?" he asked, frowning slightly. "You were unhappy with the clinic staff, it seemed to me. I don't want you to feel that your concerns were not heard, or that you can't share them."

She thought he probably meant that; he had been—barring that one outbreak of annoyance today, which might have been his own discomfort with the entire situation or fatigue from the long journey out here and the early start—what her experience told her was a good officer. Still, she dared not trust too much. She shook her head.

"Colonel, I had not realized how disabled they were; it shocked me, I'll admit. You know my background: my cousin's in care, from a head injury. But what is, is. They're not fit for duty; the service has to do something. We can't keep them on the rolls as active when they can't be. I wish they could be allowed contact with their families, but—" She shrugged. "I agree, we can't risk this thing, whatever it is, getting loose in the population." He would assume she meant the pathogen.

"Thank you, Sergeant Major," he said. "I appreciate that. Word in your ear: I happen to know some of the officers here pushed their way onto the list for this flight, and none of them would be happy to be displaced. You're saving me an awkward conversation; I won't forget it. I'd wanted a dedicated flight back, just the five of us and crew, but—" He spread his hands. "Budget."

"Yes, sir. That's fine, sir; I don't mind at all. The important thing is to see that our veterans get the care they need for the rest of their lives, and hope nobody else gets whatever it is."

The senior NCO compartment on this aircraft included eighteen seats, three abreast either side of the aisle, closed off from the officers in front by a door just past the midship loo, and from lower enlisted behind by a sound-baffling curtain. It was half full, and a long flight to come. Morrison chose a seat and put her duffel on the seat beside her. With luck others would respect her seniority and let her have both seats; then she could stretch out a bit and ease her legs.

At first she thought her ploy had worked. But once they were airborne, the master sergeant across the aisle greeted her by name, and began probing to find out why the sergeant major had been "out here in the sticks." His name tag read UNGOLIT.

"I am like the Ghost of Bailorn," Morrison said, quoting from the intro to a well-known vid-thriller series. "I wander here and there, day and night, on hill and in hollow, all folk to affright." The Ghost, according to the script, was a descendant of Count Dracula who had inherited a vast fortune and a taste for adventure.

Master Sergeant Ungolit laughed, perhaps a little louder than necessary. "But had you ever been to our remote corner before?"

"Oh, yes. Last year I spent half a day at your base, in fact, speaking to the master sergeants—that was just before you were promoted, I think."

"And four tendays before my transfer. I remember wishing I'd been there. So—if you don't mind my asking—does being sergeant major involve a lot of travel?"

"Thinking ahead, are you?" she asked with a smile that had razor wire on its edge. Before he could answer, she relaxed the razor wire just a little. "As a matter of fact, yes. At headquarters probably only half the time; the rest of it is out in the field, visiting as many installations as I can. Certainly I'm on every continent every year, and usually get to all the main bases, and as many smaller ones as we can fit in."

"I'll bet that's tiring."

"That's what fitness work is for," Morrison said, ratcheting the razor wire back into view. Ungolit looked, to her, like someone on the slide. Not flabby yet, but not as fit as he had been. "Sergeant majors must be examples, you know. In case you're thinking in that direction. Hours a day, even during travel."

"How do you—?"

"Creativity," she said. She did not want to talk all the way back to Port Major; she needed to think. "Besides, every base has gyms, and many have terrain that fills the need, just by walking instead of riding."

"That's what I always say." Staff Sergeant Gomes, in the row ahead, had turned around to join the conversation. He was lean and looked well muscled. "If you have the desire, there's always an opportunity."

Ungolit looked unconvinced. He opened his mouth to answer Gomes, then glanced at Morrison and shut it again. Gomes said, "Nice to see you, Sergeant Major; I really enjoyed that talk you gave at the NCO conference on security upgrades."

Morrison nodded at him, not saying what she was thinking—her implant had provided his record, too, and she knew his specialty. "Glad you enjoyed it. I do have some work to do on the flight, though, if you'll excuse me."

"Of course," Gomes said. Ungolit looked as if he wanted to say more, but Morrison turned slightly away and dug into her duffel for her tablet, where paperwork always waited.

After that the trip went as she'd hoped. Two hours before arrival at Port Major, a steward from the officers' cabin came and said she was wanted forward. She checked her shoes—no scuffs—and went forward to the table the chairman shared with the rest of the committee, where the report was laid out. She signed on the designated line, initialing each page below the others.

"Anything else, sir?" she asked.

"No, Sergeant Major, thank you," he said.

And that was it. She returned to her seat, and once more opened her tablet. Her thoughts were far away from the pages she scrolled past. Who might help? Where could she go?

MARVIN J. PEAKE MILITARY HOSPITAL

Grace Vatta woke slowly, confused in the aftermath of the procedures that had saved her life. She heard the voices around her but not yet the sense of their words. She could not remember why she was wherever she was, slipping easily back into sleep and rousing again. When she did finally wake completely, to find MacRobert asleep in a chair beside her bed, she recognized the room as a hospital room, and remembered why she might be in one. Her implant had been reinstalled; it informed her what the date was, the time, and how many calls were waiting to be answered. She had slept through until the next day, as she'd been told she would.

"Mac?" she said. Her voice was weak and scratchy.

"Mmph?" He stirred, opened one eye, and pushed himself up in the chair. "You're awake again. They said you might wake fully in a few hours."

"The implant's in. Or *an* implant's in."

"Yes. It's yours. I had custody of it the whole time and it was definitely yours. I watched." He stood up slowly, listing to one side, and fetched water from the bedside table. "Here. You're supposed to drink some, and I'm supposed to call the nurse now you're awake."

"Wait." Grace sipped the water, which tasted like water only, and sipped again. "How are other things?"

"Complicated. So was your recovery. Let me call the nurse."

Dr. Maillard arrived on the heels of the nurse. "Well, that's a good deal better," she said to Grace. "You'll have noticed your implant's already in. Your arm's fine. And the poison has cleared, though the damage it did hasn't all been healed yet. Now for your mental status exam . . ."

Grace stared at the ceiling while reciting the date, the time, counting backward by sevens, and then naming her physicians. "Not the President?"

"No. I don't like her." Dr. Maillard's face bunched into a scowl. "It's more important that you know *his* name"—she pointed at MacRobert—"and your own name and my name and those of your nearest relatives than the President's. Now: you are feeling much better, and you want out, right?"

"Certainly," Grace said. She didn't feel that much better but she definitely wanted out.

"Can't happen now. Two more days at best, more likely longer. But you can get out of bed, and you can take a shower if you want. I want you up and walking the length of the hall five minutes an hour the first three hours, then a two-hour break, then ten minutes an hour the next four. Report any asymmetrical weakness or pain. Got that?"

"Yes, Doctor," Grace said as meekly as she could.

Maillard reached out and laid a hand on hers. "You're going to be all right, now. Don't worry. But don't hide any symptoms."

She was gone with a swirl of her coat, and was talking to someone else on the way out of the room. "Yes, I'm on the way. Three minutes. Czardany can open for me."

"You want me to fetch food, or do you trust the hospital?" Mac asked.

"I like having you here," Grace said. "Can we send out?"

"I can," he said. "And I have things to tell you. Your concern for those personnel Ky told you about was well founded, but we are going to have a hell of a time mounting a rescue."

"Why?"

"Among other things, because you pissed off Basil Orniakos, remember? Who would ordinarily be on our side. Grace, this is going to be a delicate operation, and you must not lose your temper or go rogue."

"You're serious." Her implant reminded her that Orniakos commanded Region VII AirDefense, and she had jumped the command chain to chew him out the day the shuttle had crashed.

"Very. They could all—well, all but the three who escaped, as you know—be eliminated very easily, and their deaths explained as due to some mysterious disease. We must work quickly and quietly. Ky's begun."

"What about that captain—?"

"He died. Suicided in custody, I'm convinced. The rest of that squad knew only that they were being told to pick up dangerous fugitives. Now, about that family you were having dinner with . . . tell me exactly how you ended up there."

Grace told him, starting with her first glimpse of a woman in a red coat, walking a white dog.

"Conspicuous," Mac said. "Had you ever seen her walking that dog there before?"

Grace shrugged. "Usually I didn't pay much attention to anyone on the street—just went straight into the house."

"It's the coincidence I don't like. And the fact that you weren't suspicious. She shows up right at the critical moment, whisks you off to her house, and invites you to dinner—and you went. And her husband just happens to be from Esterance, where you were during the war."

"Yes. I thought of that when I smelled the casserole. Not before." Now she could recognize how foggy-headed she'd been, trusting the friendly stranger. "But he was too young."

"You know perfectly well that family quarrels last through generations."

"Yes." Grace lay back. "And I did worry about that, but—" But she hadn't been thinking clearly, thanks to the poison already working inside her.

"I ran background on them both. Sera Vance checks out clean. But her husband—he uses the name Vance now—his mother's maiden name—his father's name was Ernesto Arriaga."

Grace nodded. "I know the Arriaga name. But the man I knew would have been Ernesto's father or uncle or something—a generation older at least."

"Felipe Arriaga, by any chance? Active in the Separatist movement? Jaime Vance's great-uncle." His brows went up and he said nothing, waiting. Testing her, she realized.

"Yes." Memories rushed over her: smells, sounds, touch . . . the feel of his hands clamped on her wrists, his weight holding her down. The perfume of citrus flowers following the breeze through the window. The sound of gunfire nearby, which took his attention off her just long enough . . . the sight of his face, anger changing to fear, with the blade of his own knife in his throat. The memories went on: the gush of blood, hot on her face, the noise of a firefight outside, her friends breaking the house door, their voices. "I killed him," she said.

"Well," Mac said. "I thought it might be something like that. Jaime Vance seems clean so far; I'll want to dig deeper, but his father Ernesto was pro-Unionist."

He didn't sound shocked, but then he wouldn't. Grace debated trying to justify what she'd done. Felipe Arriaga had been a monster, delighting in causing pain. That morning he'd come in to beat her again, and threatened to kill the boy Grace had saved, the boy who had, in adulthood, become Commandant of the Academy. But she had explained it all, over and over, during the trial and the endless sessions in prison.

"Was that your first kill?" Mac asked. "You were what—eighteen?"

"I don't know. I'd been in a firefight twice—no, three times, I think—but whether it was my bullet or someone else's, when someone fell . . . I don't know." Hadn't wanted to know, until later. Until after that night when she'd snatched the frightened boy, argued and threatened to keep him alive, had even endured Arriaga's abuse to save the boy worse. Until her kills, starting with Arriaga himself, were for a purpose that made sense to her, keeping her and the boy alive, rather than for a cause she'd never cared about. The group that rescued her, nominally pro-Unification, had cared as little for her or the boy as the Separatists. She had had to fight for their side, again to save the boy, to earn food. Eventually she had fled with him into the scrub, her fragile link to sanity being the trust in his face.

He said nothing more for a moment, then sighed. "All right. I'll send for some food from a trusted source, and then be here if you need help to shower."

She watched him call in an order, wondering if he would be another casualty, if he would leave her now, or in a few days, with a good excuse. She had finally trusted him, but he might not trust her. And perhaps, if he didn't, he was right. He was a soldier, with a soldier's sense of duty and honor. She had had neither, back then. And as she had told Helen shortly before that last firefight, when she had killed and then been wounded to keep Jo's twins alive, she believed she had no morals.

MacRobert wondered when Grace would be fully alert again; he could still see a trace of medication-fog in her eyes. He would not tell her yet about the nurse with a lethal dose of heart stimulant in a syringe who had been intercepted inside Grace's room, about to inject it into the IV bag. Grace would be leaving the hospital for a more secure location sooner than Maillard had wanted, but he could not tell Grace until he was sure she was alert enough to keep that secret.

CHAPTER EIGHT

JOINT SERVICES COMMAND HQ, PORT MAJOR
DAY 5

After landing, Morrison took her duffel from the stack, aware that the officers on the committee were standing nearby.

"Give you a lift, Sergeant Major?" Colonel Nedari asked. "We're all going over to HQ to turn in the report, if you'd like to pick up your file copy."

"No thank you, Colonel," she said. "My vehicle's in the lot here, and I need to pick up my dog from the boarding kennel."

"You don't use the one on base?" Nedari asked.

"No, sir. I have a friend, retired, who runs this one. Petsational, on West Canal Road. Big runs, shade in the summer. Ginger likes it, and Jo-Jo, their kennelman, likes Ginger. By your leave, sir." He nodded, they exchanged salutes, and she went out the gate toward enlisted parking.

She stopped by her quarters on base, locked her briefcase in the safe, and changed to civvies and a leather jacket before driving over to pick up Ginger. It was definitely colder now than when she'd left two days before.

Kris, at the kennel, gave her a hug. "Ginger's fine. She had a good run today, so she won't keep you up all night." After a longer look at Morrison, Kris added, "You look upset about something—and you're already in civvies. Why don't you come along to a party we're having tonight. Nothing fancy—"

"I've got something to do," Morrison said. She heard the tension in her voice, and forced a chuckle. "I know, I always say that."

"You do. And you're just back from a trip, and tomorrow's your day off, so no one will expect you to be in the office at 0700. Don't worry about Ginger; you know I've got a large yard and she and Tigger and Abby get along fine. You can spend the night in our spare room if you get a buzz on. And it would be good for you. Party a little, relax, sleep in . . . and show up at noon looking like everything's fine."

It was tempting. And a party would cover her absence very well . . .

"I still have a couple of chores I can't put off," Morrison said. "But it does sound like fun. Later?"

"Later, but be sure you do show up!" Kris wagged a finger.

"Don't bully her." Irene, Kris's partner in business and life, came out of the back with Ginger on a lead. Ginger let out one delighted woof and lunged at Morrison. Irene tossed her the lead.

"Sit, Ginger." The dog plopped her backside onto the floor. "Were you a good dog?" A whine answered her. "Yes, they say you were. I don't suppose you'd want to go to a party . . ." A yip, this time, and a wiggle from nose to tail. "I guess I'll have to come to your party, Kris; Ginger seems determined." Morrison rumpled Ginger's ears.

"Great. It'll probably run late, so come whenever you're done with your errands. Potluck, but you're exempt."

"I can probably manage something," Morrison said, on the way out of the door.

* * *

Once in the city, with Ginger in the car-crate behind her, Morrison reviewed what she knew about the Rector. Close friends with Master Sergeant not-really-retired MacRobert. Had a house in the city, though Morrison didn't know the address. Another Vatta, Helen, also had a house in the city, in a wealthier neighborhood. What was the best, most discreet, way to contact the Rector? Certainly not by showing up at the department asking to see her, not to mention it was after regular hours. Probably not by going to her house even if the address was listed in a finder. Maybe the other Vatta house? She flicked on the local news to find out about traffic.

"Rector of Defense Grace Vatta remains incommunicado in the Marvin J. Peake Military Hospital, following a mysterious injury. Our reporters have confirmed that a hazmat team showed up at the Rector's residence shortly before the Rector arrived at the hospital yesterday evening, but we have been unable to determine why. Persistent rumors about former admiral Ky Vatta, the Rector's great-niece, who has not been seen in public for more than a tenday, suggest some pathogen was encountered during her long stay on Miksland, but the former admiral is now out of quarantine and resident in one of the family homes in the Harlantown neighborhood. She declined to comment on her own or her great-aunt's condition."

Harlantown. Morrison knew where that was. She was only a kilometer away. But the hospital was closer, in a different direction—should she go there? She looked for a place to stop and spotted an upscale shopping area, its large lot busy with vehicles and shoppers. She pulled in and found a parking spot. Right in the center was a supermarket.

Should she try the Vatta house, to see if she could speak to Ky Vatta, or the hospital, where the Rector was? She didn't know Ky Vatta. She had no reason to go to a civilian Vatta home, and Ky Vatta had no reason to talk to her. But she had met Master Sergeant MacRobert, back in the day. And she had met the Rector at the annual Defense Department reception for NCOs the previous winter. As sergeant major, it could be appropriate for her to hand-carry a get-well card and gift, and perhaps—maybe—run into MacRobert there. She regretted having changed out of uniform, but her visit could be—would have to be—more personal than official.

With that in mind, she decided to do her shopping. "You stay, Ginger," she said to the dog. "I just remembered we're out of dog food at home."

She came out with dog food and groceries, including a tray of vegetable snacks for the party and a small pot of flowers and a card for the Rector, then drove to the military hospital. It served senior government officials as well as the military personnel who lived off-base in Port Major.

Once inside the hospital with the flowers and card, she located the intake desk and asked for the Rector's room.

Even her identification wasn't enough to pry that information out of the clerk. "Sorry, Sergeant Major, but the Rector's location is not available. I can have someone sniffer those and one of her staff will come and take them up."

"I understand," Morrison said. "I was away for a few days, and heard about the attack only while driving into the city. Just wanted to pay my respects and wish the Rector a quick recovery."

"The Rector is lucky to be alive," the clerk said. "Just a sec while I call this in—" He turned away for a moment, murmured into a microphone, then turned back. "Someone'll be right down, if you'd like to wait."

"I can't stay long," Morrison said. "My dog's in the car; I just didn't want to let another day pass without—"

"Sergeant Major!" A colonel, in uniform of course, strode toward her. He paused, looking her up and down. "I don't think I've ever seen you in civvies." His name tag read DIHANN.

"Colonel Dihann." She'd never met him before. Morrison nodded, in lieu of a salute. "I'm just back from TDY, picked up my dog at the kennel, and heard the news about the Rector on the car com. Wanted to pay my respects."

"The gift shop's closed," he said, eyeing the flowers she'd brought.

"Grocery store," Morrison said. "I went along the floral display, sniffing to see which ones didn't smell like dead decaying leaves or that horrible grape drink."

He laughed. "I know what you mean." He leaned over and sniffed the purple and yellow flowers. "Hardly any scent at all. Excellent choice."

"Do you know what happened, sir?"

"Um. Come over here." He led the way to the entry's seating area, now deserted. "Gas," he said. "Quatenary toxin, four levels of attack, as it morphs in the body. She's been very ill; they're now sure she'll live, but she'll be weak for another tenday at least. I'm sure she'll appreciate your concern, Sergeant Major, but I don't think they'll let her have visitors for another day or so. It's not like she's young." He gave Morrison a sharp look. "Meaning no disrespect, of course, but organ system damage is worse in the elderly."

"Yes, sir. Thank you for the information; I'm relieved she's on the road to recovery." Out of the corner of her eye, she had seen someone run a sniffer over the flowers and the card, and then someone else pick them up and turn to go. MacRobert. She stepped back abruptly, a sharp move that might catch his eye, and saw the hesitation before he went on down the passage.

"You said you had your dog with you—what kind of dog? I have dogs myself—love 'em—but it's always a problem if I'm sent somewhere and can't take them." The colonel's continued interest struck Morrison as off in some way, as had his easy recognition of her, even in civvies. After her disturbing surmises earlier in the day, this set bells ringing.

"I used to use the kennels on base," Morrison said, keeping her voice easy, one dog owner to another. "But they were full one time when I had to travel. So I tried out another boarding kennel, only about two klicks from base, toward town, run by a retired senior tech sergeant. They're pricier than the base, but really good, and it's no problem if I'm away longer than expected. Petsational. Tell them I sent you, if you want." She paused. "Excuse me, sir, but Ginger's been in the car long enough. I should be on my way."

"I'll just walk out with you," he said. "Say hello to your dog, if that's all right."

"She'll enjoy it," Morrison said. "She's very friendly." An entire carillon of bells rang now.

Ginger let out a moderate *woof!* at the sound of strange footsteps, but quieted when Morrison unlocked the door. "Hey, Ginger, someone wants to meet you. A moment, sir, while I get her out of the crate." He was looking through the windows at her grocery bags, both his hands on the car. Ginger came out of the crate politely, hopped down to the pavement, and wagged her tail as the colonel turned toward her. "Shake, Ginger." Up came the paw, and the colonel grinned, reaching down to shake it. As he stood he put down a hand as if to brace himself on the doorframe.

Morrison glanced back toward the hospital entrance. Someone came out, moved along the walk beside the building, into the cluster of shrubs that decorated one corner. "Now she's out, I should give her a little walk," Morrison said. "Some of that shrubbery looks like it needs watering."

He gave a conspiratorial dog-owners-all grin and said, "Then good night, Sergeant Major. I'll let you and Ginger get on with your evening." With a nod, he turned away, walked back across the parking area, and Morrison led Ginger toward the nearest shrubbery, connected to that at the front of the building.

"You are one silly bitch," Morrison said. "That goofy act you put on, all grin and tail-wags, someone would think you're nothing but a couch-cuddle." She looked for movement in the shrubbery. There?

Ginger stiffened and gave a barely audible growl.

"What, something in the shrubbery? Probably a cat. Or a bunny."

"Interesting note you wrote, Sergeant Major," came a voice from the shrubbery.

"All I did was sign my name," Morrison said. She laid her hand on Ginger's head, signaling. Ginger squatted.

"On the one hand, yes. On the other, that salutation. Do you have something the Rector needs to know tonight?"

"Something the Rector needs to know as soon as she is able to do something about it," Morrison said. "Someone is mistreating some of my people, and I can't stop it without jumping the chain of command all the way to her."

"Do you recognize my voice? We've met several times over the years."

"Master Sergeant Mac—"

"MacRobert, yes. If this concerns enlisted personnel evacuated from Miksland and claimed to be in quarantine, yes, she needs to know whatever you know. She's aware something's crooked. But she can't have visitors right now, and anyway you're conspicuous. You need to go talk to Admiral Ky Vatta, tonight. She's at the Vatta city residence." His voice sharpened. "Take this, pet your dog, turn and go to your car. Now."

Morrison palmed the paper he handed her, bent down, patted Ginger, and did as he had said, Ginger trotting along happily, tail waving. Inside the glass doors of the hospital entrance, a figure stood, dark against the light. Colonel Dihann? Or another watcher? She opened the car door, leaned in to open the crate, and as Ginger swarmed into the car, raking her claws on the doorframe as usual, then settled in the crate, Morrison saw a glint, as of metallic paint, just below the opening. Without standing up, she touched it. Small, almost flat, and definitely something she didn't want on her car. She slid a fingernail under it and pulled it off. The colonel, no doubt, standing up from petting Ginger. Microphone or locator or both?

"Ginger, how many times do I have to tell you, do not claw the doorframe as you get in? You've scraped the paint again. Good thing I carry touch-up." She rummaged, making noise, under the back of the driver's seat. "Ah. There we are. Still enough to fix this one. Let me see. Sandpaper—" She stuck the tag back down, hard-scrubbing both it and the surrounding paint. That should glitch the signal, at least partly. "That's smooth enough. And now the paint. You know, dog, sometimes you're a serious nuisance. We're going to be late to Kris's party if we don't get a move on."

The Vatta house was not quite in the middle of a long block of expensive-looking houses. A driveway, closed off with decorative metal gates, led around one end. To Morrison's surprise, the gates opened silently as she came near, and her skullphone pinged. "Yes?"

"Take the drive, park beside the garage, facing out." She'd never heard that voice before. And how would a stranger know her skullphone code? Did MacRobert have the same access to service records she did?

She turned into the drive and reversed the car into a space beside the garage, as she'd been directed. "Ginger, stay."

A man in dark slacks and pullover emerged from the shadows. "Sergeant Major, I'm Ky Vatta's fiancé, Rafe Dunbarger. Would you like to bring your dog in the house, or will she be quiet out here?"

That was not what she'd expected to hear. "She will bark only if someone approaches the car. I'd as soon leave her crated."

"Fine. Come with me, please."

Inside, she followed Ser Dunbarger through a dark kitchen into a lighted room where seven people waited around a dining table. Morrison recognized both Admiral and Stella Vatta from newsvids, but not the three other women or the man Ser Dunbarger introduced as "my assistant, Teague."

"Master Sergeant MacRobert told us you were coming." Admiral Vatta's voice and manner convinced Morrison instantly that everything she'd heard about the admiral was true. "Please have a seat. We don't want to keep you long; this house is under surveillance, and your visit here may cause you trouble. You have information about the people with me on Miksland?"

Morrison sat down. The three women across from her had not been introduced. Who were they? Why?—and then it dawned on her. That flash message she'd read while in transit, fugitives escaped from a high-security facility . . . "The information I have," Morrison said, "comes from my participation in a committee whose brief was to make a final disposition of those cases, persons we were told had been exposed to some pathogen or toxin on Miksland, and were now permanently disabled, in need of custodial care for the rest of their lives."

"Do you know where these persons are?"

"Where they are, and where they will be after transport to a single facility, assuming our report is accepted by higher command. I also suspected, but was unable to confirm, that their apparent disability was the intentional result of treatment they received in custody. Since voicing an objection, and a request to meet with the personnel alone, I have been aware of excessive interest directed at me. Veiled threats were made. A tracking device was placed on my car."

"Is it—"

"I dealt with it. With that one, at least." She looked across the table at the three women. "And you are—"

"The three fugitives you've no doubt heard of," Vatta said. "Corporal Inyatta, Corporal Barash, and Specialist Four Kamat. Now, Sergeant Major, we need to know where the others are now, and where they will be moved. And the best way to stay in contact with you."

Fifteen minutes after she'd arrived, Sergeant Major Morrison left the Vatta house in a swirl of emotions. Rage, still, at what was being done to her people. Pride in the courage and determination of the three who had escaped. Astonishment at the technical skills of Rafe Dunbarger, whom she'd thought of as a fat-cat civilian CEO, probably never done a lick of real work in his life. And wholehearted admiration and gratitude for Ky Vatta. Vatta's concern for her people, her determination to rescue the others—Morrison could not imagine how it could be done, but she was sure the admiral would succeed. Morrison had handed over all the information she had: locations, names of prisoners and the staff at Clemmander Rehabilitation.

She arrived at Kris and Irene's place to find the party at full swing. Irene met her at the door. "Hi—you picked a good time." She took the party tray from Morrison's hand. "Oscar and his pack of hounds just left, so there's plenty of room for Ginger out back and less noise. Come on through. I'll drop the party tray in the kitchen." They threaded their way through the crowd in the big living room, mostly people Morrison didn't know, then the crowd in the study, and finally the kitchen. Irene set the tray on the table and led the way to the back of the house. The back porch was occupied by two men hunched over a chess table with three more watching, perched on stools. Irene opened the gate and Morrison turned Ginger loose in the run with three other dogs.

"She's played with all those while boarding; shouldn't be any problems," Irene said. "Come on in and get something to eat. And drink."

Beer and a bowl of Kris's cream of squash soup in hand, Morrison followed Irene into the middle room where there was an open chair. Irene introduced her as "Sunny, owned by Ginger," and then named those already seated: Walter, Arnulf, Bettina, Dot, and Kyuni. Morrison smiled at them and nodded a go-ahead while she set her beer down and applied herself to the soup. She let the conversation go on as she ate, easing herself into the mood to deal with younger civilians. Morrison judged the age range to be thirty to forty-five. Were any of them military? No, she decided after listening to them. Would they have information she might find useful? Maybe. She put down the soup, picked up her beer, and eased back in the chair.

"Are you military?" Walter asked.

"Yes," Morrison said. "Kris and I served together years back."

"Our son's in Spaceforce," Arnulf said. "On a cruiser. He's an environmental tech."

She was used to handling parents. "Congratulations—that's an important job." She glanced around; the others introduced themselves again, with added information. Restaurant owner, farmer, teacher, electrician. All with a love of dogs. Nobody likely to be in the conspiracy or know anything she could take back to Ky Vatta.

CHAPTER NINE

DAY 6

Ky kept an eye on the security videos while Rafe and Teague ate breakfast. Very little traffic on this street in the mornings. When a dark-green van slowed down, and then stopped in front of the house, she used the zoom lens function Rafe had installed to read the lettering on the side. SLOTTER KEY CUSTOMS & IMMIGRATION DEPARTMENT. ENFORCEMENT DIVISION. What now? Four men in uniform got out of the van. She touched the house com. "Rafe! Teague! Would Immigration have any reason to come after you?"

"I don't think so," Rafe said. "Well—I was using an alias, but it passed."

"And later they knew you were here as Rafe Dunbarger—did you have a visa in that name?"

"Yes, and Grace arranged a visa extension for both of us. It might be getting close to running out. But nobody's said anything."

Ky remembered her own summons, with the notation that she was considered a foreigner. She still hadn't called Vatta's legal office again. The men from the van were coming up the walk now.

"Get in Stella's office; get the women into the closet."

"You—"

"I'll be fine; I'm a Slotter Key citizen, even if they don't think so. Send Rodney to the front, with a jacket."

The door buzzed. All four men wore uniforms like those she'd seen at the Customs & Immigration booths. Name tags displayed: COSSEY, MIRBAN, HALAK, and TALLIN. Rodney came out of the lift, up from the basement, wearing a respectable gray jacket.

"Customs & Immigration," Ky said. "My guess is they're going to claim Rafe's and Teague's visas are out of date."

Rodney nodded. "I'm the new butler?"

"Acting, for the moment. You're a Vatta employee, doing electronics installation here."

"Got it." The door buzzed again, longer. Rodney tapped the inside speaker.

"Vatta residence. May I help you?"

"Slotter Key Customs & Immigration; we have information that illegal aliens are residing at this house."

"Please show your identification to the reader," Rodney said.

"You need to open this door. Are you the one called Teague?"

"Teague? No. I am Rodney Vatta-Stevens, a Vatta employee temporarily assigned to this house."

The IDs came through, showing on Ky's tab. She put in a call to Customs & Immigration and linked it to a second call to Vatta Enterprises' legal department. She had just heard one of the Vatta legal staff introduce herself as Deirdre Monteith, legal assistant, when the Customs & Immigration call came through. She spoke first to Immigration, knowing that Monteith would hear the conversation. "This is Ky Vatta; I am sending you imaged IDs claiming to be from Customs & Immigration. Are these valid IDs, and if so, why are they here?" She was aware of Rodney talking to the men outside, but as long as they didn't try to break the door down, she would let him handle it.

"Those are indeed valid IDs, Sera, and the team has come to collect persons who are illegally within Slotter Key jurisdiction," the Customs clerk said.

"*What* persons?"

"Rafe Dunbarger and Edvard Teague have overstayed their visas and made no effort to renew them. They were given an extension at the request of Rector Vatta, on the grounds of essential work for the Defense Department, but as she was told when she applied, such visas cannot be extended again without the persons appearing at the local Immigration Control office."

"You do know that Rector Vatta was hospitalized three days ago, don't you? She may not have turned in the papers before—"

"According to regulations, the responsibility for applying for a visa extension rests on the individuals themselves; they are in violation of Section Eleven, paragraph 3f of the Code. And there is another issue, Admiral."

"Yes?"

"There is no record of *your* having a visa at all."

Ky sighed. "I'm a Slotter Key citizen; I don't need a visa, and no visa was requested at entry."

"Actually, Sera, we know you received a summons explaining that your citizenship has lapsed. Unless you reapply for a half-year visa, and then, in that time, apply and qualify for rehoming, your presence here without a visa is also illegal—you are not a citizen. You left Slotter Key eight local years ago, never returned, never filed any financials, never voted, have not paid any taxes, and appear more recently to have become a citizen of the Moscoe Confederation as commander of . . . uh . . . Space Defense Force." The tone was accusatory. "Your cousin, Sera *Stella* Vatta, when informed that her extended absence and apparent principal residence in the Moscoe Confederation put her citizenship at risk, despite her holding shares in a local business—"

"I hold—held—shares in the same business until recently." Ky was finding it hard to breathe. She had been so sure the summons resulted from a clerical error, something easy to fix. But a new law—when had that come about, and why hadn't she heard about it?

"Yes, but now you don't. And the purpose of your visit here, on our records, was to divest yourself of any claim to the Vatta Transport / Vatta Enterprises stock in order for Stella Vatta to become CEO, with joint headquarters here and in the Moscoe Confederation."

"Yes—" Ky's mouth had gone dry.

"Whereas you yourself showed no further link whatsoever to Slotter Key indicating that you would be a participating citizen. Now, Stella Vatta, as I said, applied for renewal of her citizenship and showed cause why she should be accepted. She is due in court this morning—in fact, she is overdue for check-in, I see here, and if she misses this appointment may also be subject to arrest and fines for failing to appear—"

A gasp from someone on the Vatta line.

"Excuse me?" from the Immigration office line.

"Someone listening in," Ky said. "Not Stella; she left for the court an hour ago." A lie to cover her cousin's forgetfulness was not a lie at all. She was sure Stella was at Vatta headquarters and someone from Legal would be telling her to get herself down to court. Which left the fix she herself was in, and which the Immigration officer continued to tell her about.

"You were supposed to appear at the Immigration office within three days of landing—"

"Nobody told me that when I went through Customs up on the station," Ky said. "And then the shuttle crashed in the Southern Ocean off Miksland; I couldn't *appear* anywhere but in a life raft."

"That is not the point. You could have contacted this office—"

"Surely you know about this from the newsvids," Ky said. "None of the communications devices worked. We could not contact anyone."

Silence. "Then you should have reported in as soon as you were once again in contact. As it is, I have no option but to inform you that you also are in violation of Immigration law. In fact, since you have not responded to the summons—"

"But the court date hasn't come yet—"

"You had three business days to *respond in writing* that you intended to appear; we have received no such notice. If you intend to respond, the written response must be in this office by 1700 today. Otherwise you are subject to seizure and detention."

You'll have to catch me first was Ky's thought. "Thank you for your very helpful advice," she said instead, and closed the contact. "Don't open the door," she said to Rodney. "Not for any reason." And then, "Sera Monteith? Are you still there?"

"Yes, Sera," said Monteith. "You will need to file that intention to appear—and you need to speak with someone senior to me. If you'll come to this office immediately, we can make that deadline—"

"I can't leave the house. Those Immigration agents on the front porch will arrest me," Ky said, trying for a calm tone. "The order's already gone out."

"Well . . . if you'll hold, I'll try to find someone. Or we can call you back."

She bolted up the stairs and down the passage to Stella's office. Rafe sat behind the desk; Teague stood beside it.

"I gather we have a problem?" Rafe said.

"We do. We're all illegals."

"Excuse me?"

"You and Teague for overstaying your visas. They needed renewal; you didn't. I thought that summons thing was based on a clerical error, but apparently I lost my citizenship because I stayed away too long."

"So they'll deport you, too? That gets past the 'no exit visa,' doesn't it?" Rafe leered at her. "Now we can go off and be naughty together."

"No again. I'm to be detained for up to thirty days until an Immigration judge hears the case. You two at least have valid papers."

"So do you," Rafe said. Then his expression changed. "Don't you?"

"Not . . . exactly. I mean, I can prove I was born here, and am who I say I am, if I can get access to the vital records department and also to the Academy database: they stored my DNA, of course. But the papers I had when I left here were lost when *Vanguard* blew up. Nobody worried about it when I was commanding the fleet, but in this mess—I'm sure it will make things worse."

Her skullphone pinged: Vatta's legal department again. "Sorry, Sera Ky," Monteith said. "We have two who handle immigration or customs issues for personnel, Ser Ventoven or Sera Lane. I understood Immigration was explaining why your citizenship lapsed?"

"Yes. When did that start?"

"I believe the first legislation was proposed shortly after the Battle of Nexus, Sera. Finally passed last year. Now there's a stiff residency requirement—maintain a local legal residence, be here one year out of five, and file all paperwork required of constantly resident citizens. Failure to comply creates an assumption of renunciation of citizenship. And it is retroactive."

"And nobody thought to inform citizens who had left before this took effect to let them know?"

"No. There is an automatic grace period for those not resident when it passed; they would be informed when they returned, and if they filed the requisite paperwork they would be automatically reinstated and given new certifications. The grace period varied for those who had maintained a residence through the period and those who had not."

"I wasn't informed when I returned," Ky said. "Customs & Immigration just waved me through; they said nothing about it."

"Can you prove that?"

Of course she couldn't. The Commandant and his aide who had been with her were now dead; unless whoever was on duty remembered . . . Ky tried to think of what to say, but too many conflicting thoughts kept her quiet.

"I believe, Sera, that our legal team should be able to eliminate, or at least shorten, the detention period in your case, because your circumstances are unique: it is not by any act of yours that your residence of record no longer exists. But as you are a citizen of the Moscoe Confederation—"

"I'm not," Ky said, more loudly than necessary.

"Sera, in their complaint against you and their lien on your funds there, they claim you are."

"I made it clear I was from Slotter Key, and commanding a multi-system military force, which—yes—they ended up joining, and helping to support. But I have never claimed to be a Moscoe Confederation citizen, and they never told me they considered me so. My bank accounts always listed Slotter Key citizenship."

"Do you have any ID from them?"

"Yes, with my name and Space Defense Force on it."

"And your original Slotter Key papers?"

"Destroyed in the war," Ky said. She fought the urge to get up from the desk and stride around.

"I see." The silence stretched. Ky said nothing, feeling her teeth grating on one another. Then, "Well. I will have a senior partner contact you very shortly. Do you prefer Ser Ventoven or Sera Lane?"

"I have no preference," Ky said. "But I would like the Customs & Immigration team off our front steps as soon as possible." She ended the call.

"From the look on your face," Rafe said, "that was not good news."

"No." Ky pulled out the desk drawer and slammed it in. That did little to relieve her feelings. "It was not. Let's get our guests out here so we can discuss it. Rodney's guarding the door."

CHAPTER TEN

DAY 6

Sergeant Major Morrison woke early and clearheaded in Kris's guest room and went out to check on Ginger. The day had dawned cloudless and chill; she was glad she had her boots on. Three dogs rushed up to the yard gate. "I'm not here to feed you," Morrison said. "Be patient." She turned back toward the house and saw Kris coming onto the porch with two steaming mugs of coffee.

"I'll feed them," Kris said. She opened a bin and filled a large scoop with kibble. The fence had a feeder section, with access ports that opened to the outside. She poured in kibble, then called the dogs in one at a time to their respective bowls. "What was it you didn't say last night?"

Morrison explained the situation, leaving out the three women she'd met at the Vatta house. What she knew from her committee work was bad enough. "And the Rector is in the hospital—"

"You were going to try to reach the Rector?" Kris sounded genuinely shocked.

"It was made clear to me that trying to go up the regular chain of command would get me sent someplace like that myself."

"You—I can't believe it. They wouldn't—not to the sergeant major."

"Kris, they're watching me. When I heard on the radio the Rector was hospitalized, I realized I could send up a card with flowers—perfectly appropriate in the circumstances. But I ran into this colonel who started asking questions—trying to probe for more—and—a couple of things happened, and I don't want to tell you because you should not know, if someone asks. I heard about the Rector on the car radio; I went to a store and picked up dog food and groceries; I stopped by the hospital with a card and flowers; I came here and stayed overnight. That's all."

"But you told me the worst—didn't you?"

"What's happening to the troops? Yes. And I had to, because I had to involve you and Irene. I may need messages passed; you must not tell anyone else."

Kris frowned, then nodded. "We can do that. But if they come asking—"

"What I just said. We didn't talk about Miksland survivors. We talked about dogs and weather and the Rector's health and you tried to persuade me to let you take cells from Ginger and try to do artificial breeding with them—"

"Which you know I would love to do—she's very healthy, has great conformation, a good disposition, trainable and intelligent—"

"Yes. And I'm still unwilling to subject her to the surgery—"

"It's only a few milliliters of blood—"

"No. But I'm willing to consider it when I retire in a year or so, and can enjoy the puppies. You can tell them that. Are you still thinking of antique Chow DNA for a cross?"

"There's a new strain out from Overholt Beta. It wouldn't take antique DNA; we could order frozen sperm."

"Good. The antique DNA worried me. Frozen sperm sounds more reasonable."

"Cost would be about the same, and not cheap."

"You said puppy buyers would cover it—still think so?"

"Oh, yes. Every time we board her, I get questions about her. Seriously, if you'd consider it—"

"Maybe. Better than no. But for now I need to get out to the base before noon. Work stacks up while I'm gone."

"You take care."

"I will. I do."

On the way to her duplex on base, where she always kept fresh uniforms ready, Morrison hoped Ky Vatta and her crew would soon have some useful information. And would manage not to get caught at it. She had no further reason to contact the Rector unless summoned, and her brief past acquaintance with MacRobert gave her no reason to contact him.

As she entered the senior NCO housing neighborhood, she saw a white van pull away from the curb in the next block. Her duplex was in the next block. She turned into the driveway on her side of the duplex, stopped beside the kitchen entrance, unlocked the door, and sent Ginger inside while she unloaded the groceries and dog food. When she came inside, Ginger had her nose on the kitchen ventilation grate, wagging her tail busily.

"Oh, Ginger," Morrison said. "I haven't been gone that long; there's not a mouse in there. You're such a silly dog." *Silly dog* being a code for "find another." Everyone knew base housing was surveilled: it was the military after all. But the eyes and ears had always been minimal at Morrison's base residence: one eye doubling the normal security camera at each door, one ear in the base-supplied comunit. Anything in the ventilation grate . . . was new.

Ginger wandered into the living room, pointing out another installation in a grate there. And in the bedroom and the second smaller bedroom Morrison used for an office. "Time to go out," Morrison said. "I need to shower, change, and get to the office. I'll be back in time to feed you."

She rumpled Ginger's ears on the way to the back door that opened into the run she'd built within the small backyard. Ginger had a shelter, water, and a feeder much like the one at Kris's. After a shower and a change, she went straight to headquarters admin section and her office. Yes, in only three days her inbox was over half full. Corporal Bannister, her clerk, had them tabbed and ready. Corporal Gorse, on weekend duty, offered to bring her coffee.

"No thanks, Molly. Had a late breakfast with friends."

"I didn't know if you'd be in today, Sergeant Major."

"I'd rather face a clean desk next week," she said, opening the first folder. Routine; she just needed to read and sign. So was the next, and the next. At this rate she'd be done in an hour. She glanced at the clock, and called out the door to Gorse. "Anything in the black box?"

"Yes, Sergeant Major. It came in late yesterday; Corporal Bannister locked it in."

"I should have asked about that first," Morrison said. On an off day, like this, it didn't matter as much, but she usually dealt with higher-level classifications first.

The black box required thumbprints and voiceprint. Morrison went through the usual routine; the box's lock snapped open and she took out the single blue envelope. The box kept a record of every opening, the time every document was taken out and put back in. She went back in her office, locked it, turned on the DO NOT ENTER sign, pulled out the security cylinder, and turned it on. Instead of the usual blue light, a red light flashed repeatedly. "What the—" Morrison turned the cylinder off, unlocked the door, and opened it. "Molly, has anyone been in my office today?"

"No, Sergeant Major. Not while I've been here. I did go down the hall about 0915. Major Pahora asked if you were here and you weren't, and he said then he wanted me to take a box down to Dispatch. I was gone maybe ten minutes. I didn't tarry anywhere."

Ten minutes. A good tech could easily place an illicit eye or ear in ten minutes. Several in fact. "Call Security," Morrison said. "Tell them Sergeant Major Morrison has found a security breach in her office. In the meantime, I'll replace this in the black box; I can't read it until I know my office is clean." Her office had been certified as a secured site for reading classified material, and this was the protocol.

"Yes, Sergeant Major," Molly looked pale. "I didn't—I swear—"

"I don't blame you, Molly. I wasn't here; you didn't know if I'd even be in, and you were asked to run an errand. No harm, no foul. But someone slipped up. We leave it to the Security people. I'll make a formal inquiry to General Visoni once I'm back in my office. Until Security clears it, and us, neither of us goes back in there."

Security arrived, a major Morrison had never met and two techs. "I'm Major Hong. What's the problem, then?" he asked.

Morrison explained. "So I had my clerk call Security and we've both been here, outside, since."

"Had you opened the envelope?"

"No, sir. As per protocol, I brought it into my office, locked the door, and engaged the local scan. At the alarm, I vacated the office and told Corporal Gorse to call Security."

"When were you last in your office?"

"Three—no, four days ago, before I left on assignment."

"And what was that assignment?"

"Sir, that assignment was classified and I cannot discuss it here."

"I see. Who was commanding?"

"Colonel Asimin Nedari, sir. It was a Joint Services mission."

"Do you know if he's on base?"

"No, sir. We got back late yesterday afternoon, and I left right away to pick up my dog from boarding and do some grocery shopping."

"So you didn't stop by the office here?"

"No, sir."

He looked through the open door. "Is that your debugger on the desk?"

"Yes, sir. I turned it off when it signaled a breach."

"Good. What level of security was the document?"

"Level Two."

"Umm. Well, we need to find you a secure place to read it. Unless you're sure it can wait until tomorrow."

"It's most likely one of two things, sir. A copy of the committee report to be filed in this office's safe, or a copy of some courts-martial reports I've been expecting from Dorland. Neither would be urgent. Of course I won't know for sure until I read it."

"When did it arrive?"

"Corporal Bannister logged it in—Molly, what's the time on the log?"

"1730, Sergeant Major."

"And what time did you arrive today?"

He should have seen that on the front desk log. "About 1115; I signed in here at 1117."

A shrill whine came from her office. One of the techs had gone in and turned on the security cylinder. "Sir, it's showing a serious breach."

"How serious?"

"Multiple sources: audio and video."

"Hold where you are; don't touch anything else." He turned to Morrison. "Sergeant Major, I'm going to suggest you leave the area; a serious breach means we have to do a forensic search in your office and in both offices on either side. You'll be out of your office for hours—any personal gear you'll need?"

"Sir, I should secure the routine paperwork that's on my desk. If your tech could bring it out, Corporal Gorse can file it, or we can lock it in the black box."

"That's not a good idea. Someone's seriously interested in your office—and maybe others—and I do not consider this box secure enough for the rest of the weekend. Did you check it with your cylinder?"

"Check the box? No, sir, it never occurred to me."

"Wouldn't have occurred to me without cause, either, Sergeant Major." He turned to the door. "Tim, bring all those papers on the sergeant major's desk, and her security cylinder, out here." To Morrison he added, "If your cylinder and mine find that the box is compromised, we'll have to turn this entire building upside down to find out if others are. And if it's just you, we'll have to find out why." He pulled out his own cylinder and passed it around the classified safe. "Nothing so far. Would you open it please, Sergeant Major?"

"Sir, if you will stand over there."

"Of course."

Morrison opened the safe and removed the blue envelope, still with its seal intact, and left the safe open. The major reached his cylinder into the box; it lit up.

"This is very disturbing," he said. "I'm afraid I'll have to keep you and your corporal awhile longer, Sergeant Major. We need to get that"—he nodded at the blue envelope in her hand—"to a secure location, but if safes are being tapped—I think it's time to call my boss."

"Sir," Morrison said, "with all due respect, is it not likely that the orders to add surveillance to my office—and perhaps others—came from higher up in Security?"

He looked startled for a moment. "That's—no. You're right. Let me think. The safety of that document is paramount. You cannot take it out of the building, but I am certain that the central Administration safe is not bugged, and even if it is, all you're going to do is put that document inside. I will call for an escort; you and your corporal will take it there, sign it in, and you will take the other paperwork to—do you have a safe at your residence?"

"Yes, sir."

"Good. You can take those out of the building to work on at home. We are going to tear your office apart this weekend and hope to have it ready by 0900—what time do you usually come in?"

"0730, sir, but I can call ahead."

"Do that." He held up his hand, accessing his skullphone, murmured his message to the Administration central office. "Someone will be down shortly. If you and Corporal Gorse will clear this area of anything you need—"

"My jacket, sir," Morrison said. Her jacket and Gorse's both hung in the small closet to one side of the office. Gorse also had a sack.

"My galoshes, sir," Gorse said, when Hong's brows lifted. "The forecast said it might rain later, and I'm on duty until 1530 today." She opened the sack and revealed a pair of shiny pink galoshes.

"They're not regulation, Corporal," Morrison said before the major could say anything.

"I know, Sergeant Major. But they're really waterproof and it's a long way from the junior NCO parking area to my quarters, and my service galoshes leak. I do have a coat in the car that covers my uniform . . ."

Stifling an urge to laugh, Morrison said, "You need to learn how to find and mend the holes in your service galoshes. There's some really good sealant—comes in a tube with a blue, red, and yellow label—"

"StickMagic," one of the techs put in.

"Thank you," Morrison said. "I'd forgotten the name. You can get it just about anywhere, and it will hold maybe a half year before you have to replace it. It also works on the shoulder seams of your uniform raincoat."

"Thank you, Sergeant Major . . . Tech Waldstrom."

A half hour later, after depositing the blue envelope in the safe upstairs, Morrison and Gorse headed out the front door. No rain, but the bright morning had clouded over. Down the passage on which Morrison's office was located, techs in white coveralls and bright-yellow gloves were busily doing whatever forensic techs did.

Morrison drove home, let Ginger into the apartment, and talked to her as she might to a person, if she'd been the gabby sort. Her real target was the additional bug Ginger had found. "You would not believe, pup, what happened this morning. It has to be one of the weirdest days in my career, even weirder than the day Corporal Trum got high on whatever that was and came into work carrying a harpoon as a sidearm and wearing nothing but beach shoes and that ridiculous hat. Highlight of my early career for sure." Corporal P. Trum's court-martial transcript had gone the rounds of Land Force III Corps to hysterical laughter and was still read aloud to favored juniors by their sergeants. She grinned as she thought of it. Old Colonel Barringer had included every semi-relevant fact.

"Someone's bugged my office at work. Not the usual, either. Luckily, I'm the steel-rod-up-the-rear sergeant major my reputation suggests— stop, it, Ginger. No dogs surfing the counter! So I always do check my office for bugs, even though there've never been any, and this time the thing lit up and whined. Yes, girlie pup, just like you." She had her late lunch in the skillet by then and bent to ruffle Ginger's ears, then wiped down the counter and washed her hands. "And so, dog, what have you been doing all this time while your mom worked, other than sleeping and pooping? Granted, I'm home early. Got groceries yesterday . . . maybe I should go back over to Kris's and let her stab you for a few cells. Don't worry, you won't have to carry a bunch of pups around. That's what surrogates are for. Or—stay home and do paperwork. Yeah, I'd better do that after lunch."

And think about whether to tell the major about the extra bugs at her house. She finished the remaining paperwork in less than an hour, with Ginger's head weighing her left foot down. "All right, pup. That's done. Want to go for a run?"

Ginger was on her feet in an instant, tail wagging.

"Yeah, you're ready. Let me just put these things away."

Outside, the clouds were thicker but no rain yet. Morrison walked two blocks briskly, then started jogging, waving at other NCOs she knew in the neighborhood. She knew the distances in all directions, and set out on a modest 5K route. She was just past the second kilometer when her skullphone pinged.

"Sergeant Major? This is Major Hong—I tried your residence—"

"Sorry, Major. I finished the other paperwork and went out for a run with my dog. Do I need to come in to the office?"

"No—I'd like to come by your residence and see if there's any . . . uh . . . security problem there. I've got a full team working on the offices near yours as well as yours and—I'd prefer to tell you personally."

"Of course, sir. You have the address."

"Yes. I'll be there in ten."

"Sir. I might still be a block away."

"That's all right."

She looked at Ginger. "We'd better take the shortcut, pup. I promise, I'll give you a longer run later."

A small park—retention pond, grass verge, benches and an exercise set on one side—connected the street she was running on to her own, making dead ends of the street in the middle. She cut through, ignored by the few people in it, though not by one woman's small dog. Ginger ignored the dog, switching to a lope as Morrison increased her pace.

When she reached her own street and turned onto it, she had several blocks more to go. The exercise felt good. She had to stop at one corner for a car on the cross street, but jogged in place. Then on—and ahead she could see a white van that was near, if not at, her duplex. Hong, with his team? She ran on. Another white van passed her and pulled up behind the first. That was odd. Why would it take two sets of techs to check out her residence?

As she came to her own block, she slowed to a walk. Arriving out of breath wasn't a good idea. Now she heard yelling, and a group of men emerged from her driveway, shouting and gesturing. One of them grabbed another's arm; the second man pulled free, swung at the first. Then it was a melee, four—or five?—men yelling and fighting. She had an answer for that. With the full volume and authority of a sergeant major, she bellowed at them. *"Stop that now."*

They paused, looked around, stared in her direction, then two of the men bolted for the first van. Morrison slipped the leash off Ginger and said, "Hush, dog!" Ginger charged, a red-gold streak, and hit one of the men solidly in the side. He staggered and fell. Morrison yelled "How many times?" at Ginger, and the dog swerved after the second man as he dodged around the van. She heard a cry and assumed Ginger had hold of him.

"What is going on here?" she said in a slightly lower tone. Her neighbors had all come outside by now, standing outside their doors.

"That's what I want to know, Sergeant Major." Major Hong, his uniform jacket pulled awry and what looked to be a split lip and a rising bruise on his right cheekbone, limped a little as he walked toward her. "The men in that van"—he pointed to the first one—"were inside your house when we arrived. I asked who they were, what they were doing, and they pushed past us to get out of your quarters. My team and I tried to stop them, but we're cyber security, not a military police riot squad."

"Get *off* me, you brute!" came from the other side of the van.

"Hey, you! Quit hitting the sergeant major's dog!" Master Sergeant Rusty Rustowsky, from across the street, had come as far as the curb. "Need some help over there, Sergeant Major?"

"Please—if you could take that man into custody—" She turned to Major Hong. "Excuse me, sir; I'm going to get my dog back on leash and see that that man does not get away."

"Go ahead." He swiped at his lip. "I think my guys have the other one."

They did, though not in any hold approved by military police. Hong fished out his comunit. "I'm calling the MPs."

When she came to the far side of the van, Rustowsky had his man braced against the side of the van, feet wide, hands spread high. "Good dog," she said to Ginger, and slipped the leash back on. "*Very* good dog."

"She can hit 'em when she wants to," Rustowsky said. "Not just a pretty girl."

"She can indeed," Morrison said. "Major Hong has called the MPs—"

She could just hear the siren in the distance. Ginger pressed against her leg. "I'd better go put Killer here in her run; I don't know what they've done to the place inside."

"I'll keep him here." Rustowsky, not quite as tall as Morrison, was the senior NCO boxing champ and a combatives instructor. Morrison led Ginger back around the van, where one of Major Hong's techs had handed him something to wipe the blood off his chin.

"I'm putting my dog up, Major," Morrison said as she walked past him. He nodded. She found the special snack box for Ginger, put the dog in the run and tossed her two of the treats, then went back down the drive, where the dying howl of the siren indicated the MPs were arriving. By now everyone's front door was open.

The moment the MPs got out of their van, Major Hong, his techs, the other two techs, and Rusty Rustowsky all started talking. Morrison said nothing, but watched carefully. Another MP van pulled up. Morrison's neighbor on the other side called over to her. "Sergeant Major, what did you *do*?"

"Nothing—I took my dog for a run and when I came back this was happening. I knew Major Hong, so when I saw him go down I let Ginger after the others."

"Your dog is a trained guard dog?" one of the MPs from the second van asked.

"And so listed on her license."

Morrison's steady, unemotional tone seemed to be getting through to the MP. "You do know it's illegal to set your dog on someone—"

"Unless they are committing a crime, or resisting arrest. Major Hong had told them to stop. I told them to stop. Apparently Major Hong had reason to believe they might have been committing a crime. So I told my dog to hold them. That one—" She nodded toward the van now holding the first prisoner. "He was kicking and hitting my dog. Master Sergeant Rustowsky saw that and intervened."

"Your dog is tagged?"

"Yes. Her registration number is CD-G-2973."

"I'll need to get that off her collar, or is she chipped?"

"Both. Come on back."

Ginger walked up to the fence, now clearly lame, and whined. "Up, pup, this man needs to read your collar." Ginger started to rear up, then winced and went back down. "Hurt, girl?" Was that blood on the paw that just touched the ground? She turned to the MP. "I'll lead her out, just a moment."

"You can't go in yet," he said as she started for the side door. "Forensics is coming."

"There's no gate," Morrison said. "Regulations."

"I'll read her tag later. Come with me."

Major Hong had straightened his uniform; the bruise on his face was more obvious now, but his split lip had quit bleeding.

By the time Forensics had come and gone, the MPs had turned the investigation over to another officer, a captain, who immediately called his boss. Smart move, Morrison thought, though she didn't say so. She could feel Hong's anger from a meter away, and no captain wanted to "investigate" an angry major with a split lip. Two hours had passed; the light was fading under the clouds, and the temperature had dropped.

"Can we move this inside?" Morrison asked. "It's getting chilly out here."

"I'm sure when Colonel Peleu gets here, he'll do that, Sergeant Major, but he said to stay put."

"Yes, sir," Morrison said. She glanced at Hong and let the shift of her weight from one foot to the other convey sympathy. He relaxed a trifle.

Colonel Peleu wasted no time on the way, and soon seven people were crowded into Morrison's small front room. Peleu turned out to be a quick, efficient analyst. He asked a few pertinent questions the MPs had missed, and then turned to Hong. "Major Hong, what was the purpose of your coming to the sergeant major's quarters? Was the sergeant major under suspicion?"

"No, sir," Hong said. "She had discovered earlier today that her office security had been compromised in her absence, while she was on remote duty." He went on to give the details, including what he'd found was wrong during his team's examination of her office and those on either side. "So I called the sergeant major, who said she was out on a run with her dog, and told her I wanted to check out her residence as well. I don't know why someone would be hacking her security."

"Sergeant Major, do *you* know why someone would be hacking your security?"

"No, sir, not with any certainty. I was on a classified mission, whose results are Level Two classified. It's possible someone wanted to find out what that was about."

"You can't tell me."

"No, sir, not without authorization from Colonel Nedari."

"I think Colonel Nedari needs to be notified of this problem," Peleu said.

"I sent a message to Colonel Nedari, suggesting he have his own security tested," Hong said.

"Excellent. Any response?"

"No, sir."

"I believe the colonel said something about taking his family to Falls Park today," Morrison said.

"Ah." Peleu jotted something down. "He may have turned his personal com off, if he took a day's formal leave. He'll get his message when he comes back, then."

"I still need to go over this house," Hong said. "And Forensics needs to go over that other van—they didn't while they were here."

"It will be towed to the main lab," Peleu said. "If you'd like one of your techs to consult, that's fine."

"If those two were part of the hacking team, they might have tried to remove equipment they put in here," Hong said. "It might be in that van."

"Thank you," Peleu said. A little edge to his voice told Morrison that he'd already thought of that. Hong took the hint, she noticed.

Peleu finished up quickly and turned as he was leaving. "Sergeant Major, I'd appreciate it if you'd stay in contact range; were you planning to leave base in the next twenty-four hours?"

"Sir, my dog's lame; I know that man kicked her and hit her, and I want to take her to the vet when this is over with."

"Oh—of course. Who's your vet?"

"Off base. Kris Stevenson at Petsational. Depending on the diagnosis I might be there several hours."

"Not a problem. In fact, there's no reason to confine you to base; you didn't create this mess. Just let me know if you want to go beyond Port Major, or if you're assigned another trip."

"Yes, sir. If they want me to work downtown—if the work on my office on base takes too long—I do have a downtown apartment. The address is on file, of course, but I could give it to you now."

"On file's fine. I need to get this organized and see if Colonel Nedari has shown up from wherever he went. Good day, Major Hong, Sergeant Major."

Morrison looked at Major Hong. "Sir, I would like to go out and check my dog."

"That's fine. We'll be about a half hour in here, and if you need to take the dog to the vet, we can lock up for you."

Ginger flinched from touches in more than one place. Morrison didn't feel any broken bones, but the right hind paw was swollen and might have been stepped on. "We'll get you fixed up," she said. "You'll probably spend a night or so at the clinic." And she wouldn't have to worry about anything happening to the dog while she was at work.

She called Kris on her skullphone and explained a little of what had happened and her assessment of Ginger's injuries.

"We definitely need to see her," Kris said. "When will you be here?"

"I've got law enforcement in the house," Morrison said. "They're estimating another half hour, and then I'll put her in the car . . ."

"If she's that uncomfortable, I'd put her in her crate now—it's not hot, leave the windows open—and let her rest. How many steps up to your back door?"

"Two."

"Any chance of broken ribs?"

"Maybe, but though she's tender I don't think she's that tender."

"See if she'll accept a sling so you can part-lift her. Call me when you leave. Oh, and nothing to eat or drink. Her, not you." Kris closed the call.

And Ginger had of course wolfed down the treats before Morrison realized she was hurt. She had to remember to tell Kris that when they arrived. Getting Ginger into the house and then out to the car and into her car-crate took much longer than usual. Ginger was clearly in pain now, putting no weight on that swollen hind paw. Morrison had just finished when Major Hong came out with his techs.

"There was intrusion here as well. We believe we've eliminated it. I want to put a warning seal on your doors. It's barely possible your downtown apartment has also been hacked, but frankly I doubt it. You should stay there, or with friends, tonight. Get what you need out of here, and let us seal it."

"Yes, sir," Morrison said. She packed quickly: uniforms, civilian leisure clothes, the papers she'd been working on from the safe, stowed all that in the car, and watched as Major Hong put official NO ENTRY seals on all three doors. Then he and his two techs got back in their van and drove off.

Rusty Rustowsky came across the street. "They're shutting you out? You need a place to stay for a few days?"

"Thanks, Rusty, but I've got that spare downtown, and I may be staying overnight with the vet. I'm taking Ginger there now."

"Think she'll be all right? Brave dog—that scum was really whaling on her."

"I think so. Just as soon nobody knew where I was headed, though. This mess has gotten bigger all day."

"Gotcha. Best of luck, Sergeant Major."

Kris and Irene met her in the clinic driveway with a gurney. "We'll slide the crate right onto it; she won't have to move and we can slide her onto the table. Could be broken toes, and maybe a rib, from what you've said."

Morrison watched through the surgery window. Ginger lay flat on the table, with Kris and Irene both working on her. Irene came out to explain. "A couple of broken toes, all right. We got them aligned; she'll be in a splint for at least four weeks, crated most of that time. Best keep her here, since you'll be on duty."

Morrison nodded. "Whatever she needs." She would see to it that the man who broke her dog paid for the vet bills. Good thing he was in custody. She stayed with Ginger in recovery while Kris and Irene dealt with a string of more ordinary appointments. When Kris came back to see how Ginger was doing, Morrison asked, "Did you ever know a Master Sergeant MacRobert?"

Kris nodded. "Sure. Good guy, but really tough. Had the nickname Mustang-hunter, for picking people out of the ranks to go to the Academy."

Morrison nodded. "Good. I need you to get this to him." She fished a data cube out of her pocket. "I'm going to tell you some of what's happened today—"

CHAPTER ELEVEN

DAY 6

Howard R. Ventoven, of Vatta's legal department, called Ky within the hour, as promised. He had her file, he said. "We have your birth certificate on record here, Sera—or is it Admiral?"

"Sera," Ky said.

"Thank you. We needed it to prove that the transfer of shares was within the family. And your DNA is on file as well, so proving your identity is not a problem. The difficulty—as far as citizenship alone is concerned—is the third leg of the stool. Your absence for so long, your residence in the Moscoe Confederation, and their claim that you are a citizen there, makes this a very touchy issue. I'm assuming you've been paying taxes there?"

"Not really. Part of the support they've pledged to the SDF is docking space and a certain amount of support each fiscal year. Other contributors, including Slotter Key, pledged ships and crew—"

"And the salaries of the crews—I assume they do have salaries?"

"Of course. That's a monetary contribution as well from the major members. It's all pooled together, and then distributed to the personnel and the supply chain." She had waived her own SDF salary, since she had Vatta money coming in.

"Do you have documentation available?" Ventoven asked.

"Not with me, no. Until my ship left I could have downloaded it from there, but now—"

"Now Cascadia is not in the mood to cooperate with you," he said. "Most inconvenient. And they've slapped that lien on your Crown & Spears account, claiming that it's legal to do so because you're their citizen."

"I'm not," Ky said again. "Not at all. Never claimed to be. Crown & Spears knows that, too."

"Can you explain why you chose to base your SDF there instead of here?"

"They had working ansibles," Ky said. "Slotter Key did not, at that time. Communication is essential. Also, the Moscoe Confederation is more central, connected by a single jump to many more worlds, with established trade routes between them all."

"I see. It's good that you had a sensible reason." She heard a muffled voice in the background, and his reply. ("Not now. I'll call him later.") Then he said, "Our best strategy is to lean on the fact that you were not informed, that you had no chance to be informed after you landed, and that you're still due the legal response time allotted, from the time you were informed of your citizenship having lapsed, which was the arrival of that summons, as I understand, in which to reinstate it. In fact, even if you had been told when you finally reached Port Major, you would still have time to make application and stop the clock. I will make that case immediately to an Immigration judge."

"Thank you," Ky said.

"After all, you saved those people on the shuttle. Slotter Key should be grateful, not punitive . . . though in law, such things do not always have the effect they should." Another muffled sound in the background of his office, then "Yes—Nils, get me a list of the Immigration judges in the city and their schedule, please. And the forms someone would need to file for reinstatement of citizenship, and the contact numbers of the relevant officials over in the Department of Immigration."

Ky sat down in the desk chair, the sizzling sensation in her nerves quieting. Maybe it would be over quickly. She needed to focus on her crew, those who had been unfairly imprisoned and mistreated. She needed to be able to travel—

"Sera Kylara? You're still on? Good. I will be working on this, top priority, and will call you again as soon as I have any more information." He cut the circuit before she could ask him about the other issues in the summons.

"Well?" Rafe lounged against the doorframe.

"He's going to work on it," Ky said. "Swears he'll have some news soon. Thinks the fact I wasn't ever officially informed until today means I should be given the allotted time to make application, and then threw in a comment about Slotter Key owing me thanks for those I saved, and hung up before I could remind him my exit visa was rescinded because of the deaths. And that was in the summons, too, at least Marek's and Jen's."

"Do you really want Slotter Key citizenship? I thought you couldn't stand it here and wanted to leave."

"It's my anchor, Rafe, the way Nexus is yours—"

"I was gone from Nexus a lot longer than you were gone from here. And I don't care, really. I care about my family, what's left of it, and I find ISC an interesting set of challenges, but Nexus isn't *home*—as long as Penny doesn't need me, I feel no pull to go back." He tipped his head. "And you—you *do* feel that this is home, don't you?"

"The ocean smelled right, even down there," Ky said softly. "The air—I was afraid to go to Corleigh, those memories hurt—but again, the colors, the smells, the sound of the breeze, even the gravity. It's me. It's . . . right." She looked down at the desk. "I remember this, from before. Uncle Stavros sitting where I'm sitting. Stella glowering at me from the corner over there because we were both in trouble, but she knew she'd get the most blame, being older."

"You had a lot more family than I did," Rafe said. "I had sisters, but no cousins around."

"I didn't expect this reaction," Ky said. She looked at him. "I love being out in space. I love seeing the new places, coming into new space stations, all that . . . but I feel like . . . it's because I have this connection to Slotter Key. That's who I am, a Vatta of Slotter Key. I can't imagine being from somewhere else. Didn't it bother you at all, at least at first, when you used an alias?"

"No," Rafe said. "I thought it was fun. We used to act out plays, when I was a child. Pretending to be somebody else came naturally to me. Didn't you do that?"

"Sometimes . . ." Ky thought a moment. "And in school there were plays. But I liked being on the stage crew more than taking a part."

Rafe struck a pose. "I was the only boy in the family so I got many different parts, sometimes in the same play. Later, playacting had a practical use." He gave her a serious look. "You, Ky—you've always been yourself, haven't you? Just yourself."

"I suppose." Something about that question made her feel restless. "But I've changed—"

"Yes, you grew up, you moved into different social roles. But—when you were first a Vatta captain, did you feel you were playacting?"

"No." Nervous at first, yes. But certain that she could command a ship with practice.

"When we first met, I saw you as younger, inexperienced, but someone completely herself. Solid. It was clear you distrusted me—and I think it's because you detected that role-playing I had been doing. Was doing then, in fact."

Ky said nothing, still mulling over that central difference. Was that really what it came down to? That he was a play-actor and she wasn't? And what did that say about their future?

"The thing is," he said, more slowly, "I had forgotten by then what it felt like to have a solid identity. When I was a small child, I always knew who I was, but when my family sent me away—after what happened in that so-called school—that identity was gone. I had to become whatever it took to survive. And I was proud of it, because I did survive when I wasn't expected to. I laughed at people like you—laughed about them. But you—I couldn't ignore you. I couldn't ignore what your sense of self gave you. When faced with a crisis—when my family was abducted and you were gone—I tried to think more like you, act more like you."

"You saved your family," Ky said. "I didn't save mine."

"Some of them, yes. But I did it by imagining how you would deal with it, if you'd had the chance."

Ky started to speak, but her skullphone pinged again. She held up her hand for Rafe. "Yes?"

It was Ser Ventoven again, the lawyer from Vatta headquarters. "I strongly recommend that you not leave the house until I have further word, Sera Ky. There seems to be some concern that you might be harboring, in order, a dangerous criminal, foreign visitors who have overstayed their visas, and/or fugitives also infected with a dangerous disease. That's in addition to your citizenship issues. I understand from Sera Stella that you are able to secure the house?"

"Yes," Ky said. "The foreign visitors are my fiancé and his assistant. They came to Slotter Key when I was missing, to assist in my rescue."

"I gathered that, but at least one of them—your fiancé—entered under a false name, is that not true?"

"Like many wealthy individuals, he often travels incognito," Ky said. "He gave Immigration his real name when he applied for a visa."

"Yes, but if you are harboring the fugitives I mentioned, who are believed to be affected by this unnamed but dangerous disease picked up on Miksland, then they, as well as you, should be in quarantine. Can you assure me that you are not harboring such individuals, and that you yourself are in good health?"

"No one in this house is sick," Ky said firmly. "Everyone is in good health, mentally sound, and definitely does not need to be in quarantine. I was on Miksland myself, with the other survivors, and nobody was sick."

"But a number died—"

"Those who died after landing on Miksland included two who died of puffer-fish poisoning, after ignoring orders not to eat that kind of fish, and two who died of gunshot wounds in a firefight."

"In which you were not hit."

"I was hit, but not injured: my body armor protected me. Master Sergeant Marek was not wearing armor, nor was Commander Bentik. I shot him, after he shot at me, and one of his stray rounds hit Commander Bentik, as well as another person who wasn't killed."

"You don't think some toxin or bacteria made him go crazy?"

"Not at all," Ky said. "No one got sick. Who claims survivors are sick? And what kind of sickness?"

"Mental problems—sort of like a stroke, they said. Loss of memory, of ability to speak, of coordination. But if you're sure you don't have any such symptoms—"

"None," Ky said. "You're talking to me—you can tell that I can talk clearly, at least."

"Well . . . it would be best, I think, if you were not taken into custody."

"I think so, too, because all the survivors were healthy when they left Miksland. If they aren't now, I suspect they've been drugged. If you can find out where these rumors originate—who precisely—it would be a great help."

"But who would—"

"I don't know—except that by accident of the crash location and ocean currents, we landed on Miksland and realized it was not what everyone thought. Its real nature has been kept secret, even to the point of falsifying satellite data. And whoever spread that lie clearly has an interest in silencing those who know about it. They hired mercenaries to kill all of us survivors before we could be rescued."

"You're sure?"

"I am, and so is my great-aunt, the Rector."

"But she's in the hospital—did she come down with—"

"She was poisoned by a toxic gas," Ky said. Why didn't he know that? Stella knew. Wouldn't she have told Legal? If not, why not? Unless MacRobert told her it was a military secret . . .

"The news said she was very sick."

"Toxic gas," Ky said firmly. "In her house. She nearly died, that's true, but it's not a mysterious disease from Miksland."

"Well, then. We will be working on getting your status clarified. I'm sure we can arrange something; I'm less sure about your fiancé and his assistant. Just don't answer the door."

"I won't," Ky said. When the connection blanked, she shook her head at Rafe. "We're stuck inside until Legal figures something out. It's going to be interesting if Aunt Helen brings the children back to the city."

"When would she do that?"

"I don't know. I don't know if she's talked to Stella. I don't know if Stella's getting her status cleared up in court. I don't know *anything* and it's driving me crazy."

"Did you eat breakfast?"

Ky jerked one shoulder. "Something. Toast, I think."

"You have a cook. Your cook can fix anything you want. You should eat something with protein."

"I sound irritable, you mean."

"Grumpy, I would have said, but yes. Come on down to the kitchen."

Halfway down the stairs, Ky's skullphone pinged again. This time it was Stella.

"I'm cleared," she said. "Pointed out I had already expanded our onplanet investment, with the manufacture of shipboard ansibles here. Cascadia's not going to be thrilled, but business will support both offices at the current level, and I never did take citizenship there. Which means they will get more taxes from a nonresident-owned business—they should be happy about that."

"Good," Ky said. "But why didn't you mention the citizenship thing to me? I nearly got hauled off to jail this morning—"

"You? Why would they go after you? You're the hero. That summons was just a clerical error."

"Apparently not. If you come home, you will find an Immigration van parked out front with some very unhappy agents standing on the step."

"But I thought—when I got the letter and asked about it, they said they were questioning me because I'd set up a business in another system. I asked about you and they said, 'She's different; no one doubts she's loyal.'"

"They certainly doubt it now," Ky said. "That law—it sounds very harsh."

"It's all about the money," Stella said. "Like most things in politics. They worry about citizens setting up businesses elsewhere to avoid local taxes—you'd think they'd look up and find out that people come here to escape high taxes elsewhere. Besides, Vatta's paid taxes on every cent earned on Slotter Key, it's just that we made less after the bombings. So—what did Legal tell you to do?"

"Stay inside with the house buttoned up tight. He's working on it, the one who called me. Named Ventoven."

"I'll check with them as soon as I get back. I'm waiting in line to get my new ID kit. Ah—they just called my number."

By that time Ky was in the kitchen. "You never had breakfast," Barash said. "Omelet?"

"Thanks," Ky said. She sat down at the table and eyed a platter that was almost empty of toast and sausages. "Just so you know, we're *all* fugitives now, except Rodney. Rafe and Teague overstayed their visas, and my citizenship's been rescinded because I was away too long."

"That's ridiculous," Barash said. "You were fighting a war—"

"Tell that to Immigration. Not that they'll listen." Ky picked up a piece of cold toast and wrapped it around one of the sausages. It tasted delicious.

"It's your amazing talent," Rafe said. He had perched on the counter nearest the door. "You've become persona non grata in two systems light-years apart without actually doing anything wrong."

"I know," Ky reached for another sausage just as Barash took the platter away. "Hey!"

"The sausages will go in the omelet," Barash said. "Only a couple of minutes now."

The omelet was delicious. Ky said nothing while eating it, uneasily aware that both Rafe and Barash were watching her. Probably expecting her to have ideas about what to do next. She had none. She felt almost as hollow as when her family was killed and she knew there was nothing left, no home to go back to, no last words of praise or blame. Now: not even a Slotter Key citizen, not an admiral, not . . . anything? She swallowed the last bit—it felt much larger than it should have—and attempted a bright smile. From Rafe's expression it wasn't a success.

"Where are the others?"

"Downstairs, in the war room," Rafe said. "Are all those people you talked to going to call back?"

"Someone will." Ky shoved her hands in her pockets. "Stella, or the lawyer, or possibly Immigration threatening to blow the place up." She glanced at Barash. "Sorry. I know we need to get the others out, but I can't figure out how. It's my fault—"

"It is not," Rafe said firmly. He slid off the counter, bracing against it. "You did not drug anyone. You did not hijack anyone. You are not holding these people . . ."

"But I said I'd get them home safely," Ky said. "Home. To their families. Think of poor Betange—and his brothers and sisters—"

"You didn't know."

"I should have. I should have kept track; I did ask, but—but I believed what I was told. And there was so much to do—"

The misery was too deep, too big. All those she had lost, killed in the war, killed on space stations, on planets, in deep space. She gulped it down, pushing hard against the lump that wanted to eject the delicious omelet. "All right. It's not my fault yet, but it *will* be my fault if I don't see every one of my crew free and reunited with their families. And I can't do that sitting here like a . . . like a bird in a cage."

"You're not going out." Rafe's voice had turned steely, the edge tipped toward her.

"Not right this minute. I'm not stupid. But we have to know where they are—"

"Sergeant Major Morrison—"

"Is probably in danger herself. We'll hear from her when she can, but she has to stay out of trouble, stay free. We can't wait for her."

CHAPTER TWELVE

DAY 6

Ser Ventoven called Ky again an hour later. "Now then. You're familiar with the contents of the summons you received, is that right?"

"Yes," Ky said.

He went on to read it to her again anyway. "You can see how this will interact with the much simpler citizenship issue. As you are not now considered a Slotter Key citizen, but responsible for the deaths of Slotter Key military personnel and a foreign citizen, you are classified as both a foreigner and a potential criminal. Since foreign criminals are not eligible to apply for citizenship, Immigration is insisting that your application for reinstatement of citizenship should be deferred until your responsibility for the deaths is adjudicated. And since you admitted to having killed Master Sergeant Marek, and the witnesses to that event are all now classified as permanently mentally incompetent due to some toxin or disease acquired while in your presence on Miksland . . . I'm sorry, but your situation is very serious indeed."

Ky could think of nothing to say, and Ventoven went on. "Unless you can find a witness who will testify that your shooting Marek was not murder but self-defense—and that the other deaths were accidental, beyond your power to prevent—I'm afraid we have no options. Legally, I must advise you to surrender to law enforcement—"

"I can't," Ky said. "Those people they claim are mentally incompetent have been drugged, kept imprisoned, away from their families . . ."

"How do you know that?"

She hesitated, trying to remember who had been told about that. Stella knew, of course; she had been there when the fugitives appeared. Aunt Grace—she had told Aunt Grace. MacRobert, Morrison, Teague, and Rodney. But could she tell this man? She had the fugitives themselves, and among them was the best possible witness for Marek's death, Inyatta. Inyatta had been in the room—pushed into the room by Marek before he turned and shot at Ky. Inyatta had been wounded by a bullet from Marek's gun, after he dropped it. But revealing these witnesses risked their freedom, if not their lives. "I need you to come here," she said. "I do not trust the security of any communications device anymore."

"What is it you know? Do you know where those fugitives are? I must know, if I'm to defend you."

"Come here," Ky said again.

"I can't just leave now—I have a court appearance in twenty minutes. I could send a clerk—"

Ky's patience snapped. "Come here yourself, or assign another attorney from the legal department to me. I won't say anything to a clerk I wouldn't shout into the open air."

"I'll come. Not until later today; I have other urgent work, you must understand."

"Call ahead," Ky said. "The house will be sealed unless we are expecting a visitor." When she ended that call, she called the hospital and asked for Grace's room.

"I'm sorry, Sera, that room is not available at present from this number. Communications must go through Security."

"Please give me that number."

"I'm sorry, Sera; that number is not available to the general public—"

"I'm not the general public. I'm Rector Vatta's niece. I need to speak to either her or Master Sergeant MacRobert."

"Oh—just a moment; I'll see if you're on the approved list. If you are not, you will need to apply in person through the hospital security desk, hours 0900 to 1700, bringing proof of identity."

Ky waited out the half minute of silence, then the voice came back. "Is this Sera Stella Vatta or Sera Ky Vatta?"

Ky thought about the likelihood of herself being on someone's "good" list and the possible consequences of being caught out in a lie. "This is Sera Ky Vatta calling on behalf of Stella Vatta—it's family concern for a family member."

"I see. Um . . . it's actually Stella Vatta who's approved, Sera, but if you're calling on her behalf—and why would that be?"

"She's very busy herself and I'm taking over some of the family duties for her. She's CEO of Vatta Transport, you know."

"Oh. Yes, I see that notation. Well . . . I'm sure it's all right, but you probably should come in for a screening—"

So the entire rolling doughnut had not yet reached the hospital's communications personnel. Ky yanked at her braid as if that would accomplish something.

"Wait just a moment—I see—" And muffled, Ky heard "Master Sergeant MacRobert—please—I have a question for you." He must have come closer, because she also heard, "Would it be all right to allow Sera Ky Vatta the security code for Rector Vatta's room? She says she's calling on behalf of Sera Stella Vatta."

"Certainly. But let me see if her message is something I can handle without interrupting the Rector's therapy session."

A moment later, Ky heard his voice on the handset. "Admiral— sorry, Sera. The Rector is doing very well now. We expect her to be released in a few more days. Her physicians want her to be steady on her feet and capable of walking at least 300 meters and climbing five steps without any evidence of cardiac strain. Is that what Sera Stella wanted to know?"

He sounded perfectly matter-of-fact, no hint of strain in his voice.

"Part of it," Ky said. "She also wanted to know what to do about her house—she said it wasn't clear to her whether it was safe for occupancy again, and if she should do anything particular with the clothes Aunt Grace might want while still in the hospital. Do they need decontamination, or something?"

"I'm sure the toxins have dissipated by now. Running them through a standard 'fresher unit should be enough," MacRobert said. "But airing them outside for several hours would be better, ridding them of any chemical residue from the counter-treatment. However, her residence does not have any facility for that, and no staff to supervise it."

The open door she'd been hoping for. "Then could you possibly bring some over here? There's a walled back garden where they could be aired, quite private. You could ask what she wants, and bring it here. I'll take care of the airing."

"An excellent idea," he said. "I'll go up and ask her, then bring the items over to—that is the registered address for Helen and Stella Vatta?"

"Yes," Ky said.

"I . . . mmm . . ." His tone was suddenly different, subdued and apologetic. "As it is the Rector's private residence . . . I'm not entirely comfortable rummaging through her . . . through some of her . . . I'm wondering if you might come along and advise me."

"I'm sorry," Ky said. "But I've been strongly advised to stay here. But Stella does have a cook here who would be perfect."

"Um . . . a woman?"

"Oh, yes." And this was even better. Allie could pass on the critical new information to MacRobert, in private. "She'll be fine in Aunt Grace's underwear drawer. When can you pick her up? I need to be sure she's not in the middle of making pastry or something."

"Half hour, about."

"See you then," Ky said. The day looked better already. She had witnesses to what had happened in Miksland, and MacRobert might know how to protect them from being incarcerated and mistreated again. So might Vatta's legal staff. She explained this to Rafe on the way downstairs. Allie was indeed making pastry, but said she'd be done in a few minutes.

Ky intercepted MacRobert when he arrived, before introducing her guests, and gave him a fast précis of her legal situation.

"None of this is the Rector's fault," he said. "She would never do that, any of it."

"I know. But the fact is I *do* have the fugitives under my protection here. They've told me how they were treated once they were back with our military, and we've located the place Sergeant Major Morrison visited, where she saw the supposedly incompetent NCOs. She gave us the other addresses, too. But I'm worried that whoever's behind this will harm the others if too many people know about them. We need to rescue them soon."

"I've got to find a way to communicate with Morrison safely," MacRobert said. "There's that very suspicious Colonel Dihann at the hospital; I know the phones are tapped, but I'm not sure even skull-phones are safe."

"Nor am I," Ky said. "We need a code. But you shouldn't stay here too long. Come meet Allie—Corporal Barash, with a new ID Stella fixed for her."

"You've been busy," he said. Allie, in the kitchen, had taken off her apron and now wore a gray tunic with the Vatta insignia and her name embroidered on the collar over blue slacks.

"Allie, this is Master Sergeant MacRobert; he will take you to the Rector's house and bring you back here to air the clothes before he takes them to the Rector."

"Yes, Sera," Allie said. "There's a pie in the oven; it will be done in just over a half hour—if it takes us longer, can you—"

"I won't let it burn, Allie," Ky said.

When they'd left, Ky called Stella. "MacRobert and our cook have gone to pick up some clothes for Aunt Grace," she said. "MacRobert says she's feeling well enough to get dressed now."

"Oh, good," Stella said. "Is Legal staying in touch with you?"

"Yes. I'm to stay inside. One of them's coming over sometime today."

"I'll be home at the usual time for supper. I'll bring along a couple of presents."

Ky could think of nothing to say to that. "See you tonight, then," she said.

MacRobert dropped Allie and two cases of Grace's clothes off before heading back to the hospital. Allie and Rodney—clearly bemused at being asked to help air clothes—set up the folding drying racks and spread clothes on them. Ky watched out the French doors, wishing she could go out in the garden. It was one thing to spend weeks on a ship going somewhere, with only remote camera views of the exterior, and quite another to be inside when outside was a planet. Her planet. The last time she'd experienced autumn days and nights here, she'd been a cadet, and at this time of day she'd have been in afternoon PT, in the scratchy shorts and jersey, finishing up with ten laps around the playing field.

She sighed and turned away. Plenty of work to do here, now, including deciding how much to tell Ventoven when he came.

"Admiral?" Inyatta came out of the dining room.

"Yes—" Ky said, heading toward her. She'd not broken any of the fugitives of calling her Admiral. She'd quit trying; it seemed to reassure them.

"I think we—all three of us—should write down our statements about what happened in Miksland. In case—in case something bad happens. So it's recorded somewhere. Maybe at Vatta?"

"That's an excellent idea," Ky said. She should have thought of that herself. Or Rafe should have, or Stella. "Or we could record it, downstairs—video and sound—and you could also write something. Or—" The thought hit her suddenly. "A lawyer's coming from Vatta's legal department later today. If he saw the recording being made, he could be a witness."

"Yes, Admiral. It would be better to have both a recording and our written statements, I think."

"Probably. Yes. All right, Allie's working on supper, but you and Kamat can write statements—you shouldn't be working on them together, I know that much. Is she downstairs?"

"Yes, Admiral."

"Then you come upstairs with me; you can use Stella's office, and then I'll go down and tell Kamat. Don't answer the phone, though."

"I won't, Admiral."

Downstairs, Ky found Rodney—back inside from laundry-airing— and Kamat working on aerial scans of the area around the compound where Morrison had told them all the remaining survivors would eventually be held.

"It's remote and rugged," Rodney said when she came in. "Going to be difficult to get a team into."

"It's forested, isn't it?"

"Yes. That makes it hard to detect all the surveillance they've got. I'm sure it's more than what I'm seeing."

"Get Rafe on it, too, Rodney. And start looking at places transport could be stopped on the way in." His expression changed. "Yes, a different approach. If the compound is remote, but has no airfield, that means ground transportation. Roads to remote places usually have remote stretches." He nodded. Ky turned to Kamat. "Meanwhile, Kamat—I want you to write out your version of what happened in Miksland. At least get started on it. Eventually you'll be called to testify, and we need current proof that you're of sound mind. They may have messed up your records—lost them or falsified them—from when you were drugged."

"Yes, Admiral. Should I start now?"

"Yes. Here's paper and pen."

Barash, in her role as Allie the cook, was busily chopping things— a delivery of fresh produce—on the kitchen table. Ky explained the need for a written report, then realized that the records she herself had turned in to the authorities might also have been compromised. She settled in to write her version of events.

The afternoon passed quietly. Shortly before Ky expected Stella home, a woman from Vatta's legal department called to say she was coming: "Sera Lane, another attorney at Vatta, and familiar with your case, Sera. Ser Ventoven cannot leave court at present; the justice has extended the hours. But he said it was vital to see you today."

"Yes. We can open the gates for you and you can park near the garage."

"Excellent. I'm in a small green two-seater."

Sera Lane clambered out of her small car and unfolded into a tall, lanky, slightly stooped woman with steel-gray hair braided around her head. She came in the kitchen door and sniffed appreciatively. "Who's the baker?"

"Our cook, Allie," Ky said. "Let's go through to the dining room—we can spread things out there."

"Howard left me all his notes," Lane said. She set her briefcase on the table, opened it, then sat down. "I've perused them, and the other information we have on you. As he did, I fear this is a very difficult situation, if—as you say—those personnel who might be witnesses on your behalf are in some kind of illicit custody and not free to help your case."

"In Slotter Key law, are attorney–client communications privileged?"

"Yes, with a few exceptions: threats of harm to another person are not privileged and will be communicated. Why do you ask?"

"Because I have scant experience with Slotter Key's legal system— I left here young and very naïve. Within that privilege I can tell you that the best possible witness to my shooting Master Sergeant Marek in self-defense has escaped from custody intended to silence her, and will be available to testify if we can protect her from recapture and the kind of treatment she endured before."

"How do you know this?"

"She is here," Ky said.

"Here? Where?" Lane looked around as if someone might pop out of the dining room paneling.

"In this house, presently writing up her account of what happened. So is another witness, not quite as well placed to testify to everything that happened. We have recording equipment downstairs; I wondered if you would be willing to witness a recording of their accounts."

"I—I had not expected this. Does the military know they are here?"

"No. It would risk their lives. Revealing their location could be fatal to them and to others still in captivity."

"Where are the others?"

"In several remote locations, originally designed for long-term confinement of the criminally insane," Ky said. "So far, they have been drugged and refused contact with anyone outside the facilities. They were carefully dispersed so they could not have contact with one another, or their families, under the guise of their being contaminated by something in Miksland. Their implants were removed and replaced by others with less function; Miznarii personnel had implants forcibly inserted."

"That's—that's against our Constitution!" Lane glared at Ky. "No adult individual can be required to accept any internal electronic device."

"It happened," Ky said. "I don't know who did it, or why, except that Miksland and its base was a huge secret for centuries and someone does not want that secret to come out. Consider that no media interviews with the survivors from Miksland—except for the very brief one I gave—ever appeared. The evidence I preserved has been 'lost'— such as the logbook of the former base commander, who conveniently died before he could be interrogated."

"Do you think this is why Grace Vatta was attacked?"

"Yes," Ky said. "And not only with poison gas in her house. Before that, one of the squad that came here seeking fugitives tried to attack her physically in her office. So I suspect that much of the legal mess

I'm facing is intended to force me into detention where I, too, can be silenced."

"That seems far-fetched," Lane said. "I see where you might think so, but in fact, by a strict interpretation of the law, you *are* in violation of the citizenship requirements. The fugitives—are you sure they are not harboring some dangerous pathogen?"

"You need to meet them, and—if she can get here—the person who witnessed the incarceration of some others."

Lane shook her head. "I can see this is going to be a long, long session. It's a good thing Howard wasn't free; he becomes quite testy when he has to work late. Better the judge in that case should deal with it than you." She pulled a voice recorder from her briefcase. "I'd like to start with you, and hear your account of all the events leading up to the death of Master Sergeant Marek." She turned the recorder on.

Ky had been over this enough, both in the recent past and in her head, to give a clear summary, from the moment she realized her electrical outlets had been sabotaged through her analysis of who might have done it, and what could be done about it, under the conditions at that time.

"I had two main problems," she said. "First, I had no way to commission a court to try Master Sergeant Marek; the only other officer there was Commander Bentik, even less attached to Slotter Key than I was. And she had been partly suborned by him—"

"How do you mean?"

"He had lied to her, and attempted to convince her that I was sexually attracted to him and wanted a relationship. She was apparently convinced that I had had sex with him one afternoon—the afternoon that I believe my outlets were sabotaged—because she saw him come out of my quarters."

"You didn't lock your quarters?"

"I did, but as we found later, he had a master key."

She nodded; Ky went on. "Commander Bentik was my second problem, both because she was foreign to Slotter Key and the procedures and traditions of Slotter Key's military, and because she was so influenced by Master Sergeant Marek. That may well have been, at least partially, the result of her unfamiliarity with our culture. At any rate, she was older than I, and had already shown herself inclined to dispute my decisions—"

"But she was staff, wasn't she? Had she combat experience?"

"None. But she was older, and felt that gave her natural seniority. I was already considering how to replace her without alienating her family—prominent politicians on Cascadia Station—when we came to Slotter Key. I had not succeeded in gaining her wholehearted support, and though she was an expert organizer, good with paperwork, she had managed to cause problems with the Moray government on an official visit there."

"I thought Cascadians were supposed to be super-polite."

"They are—or think they are." Ky huffed out a sigh. "They're polite in their own terms, but they are convinced their terms are the only terms. It has given them a homogeneous and peaceful population, on the whole, but they can get prickly with outsiders."

"So—you and she did not get along."

"I wouldn't say that, not until the very end, when she joined with Marek in opposing my command. I don't think she had anything to do with the sabotage—in fact, her electrical outlets had also been sabotaged, I found out afterward. That part was all Marek, and he was prepared to kill her as well as me, as that sabotage proved. But I found her . . ." Ky thought for a moment. "Prissy and rigid, is the best way I can put it. When we crashed, she did not—I suppose *could* not—rise to the occasion, and panicked more than once, endangering others as well as herself. It was a very scary situation, of course, but nearly all the others remained calm and tried to cope."

"She knew you disapproved of her behavior?"

"I suppose . . . though I suspect that did not bother her. She was more focused on *my* failings; she regarded the hardships of our time in the life rafts, and on the coast of Miksland, almost as insults to her personally."

"There's been nothing about that in the media," Lane said.

"I didn't notice. When I arrived back in Port Major I was plunged at once into the legalities of transferring my shares to Stella—conferences with lawyers, two court appearances—and the official interviews with Slotter Key Spaceforce about the crash and the evidence I'd managed to save. I didn't have the time—or frankly the interest—to see how the media handled it. I was, if you'll forgive me, exhausted from the survival itself."

"We can skip that now, but I must have a better idea of what the whole sequence was, in some detail. You say that evidence has gone missing?"

"So Aunt Grace—the Rector—said. Those interrogations didn't originate in her office, though she expected to be copied in on results, and wasn't. When she asked, she was told that two or three essentials had been lost. But Rafe and I were desperate for some time alone, so as soon as we could we flew to Corleigh."

Lane smiled. "I hope you had a good vacation."

Ky smiled but didn't answer. "It doesn't matter. Let me get back to the day of Marek's death." Lane nodded and Ky started in again with the next morning's accusations from Commander Bentik, her choice of the armory as a safe and private place for what had become a shocking and acrimonious conversation, and then Marek's attempt to kill her and what followed.

"And you say this Corporal Inyatta was a direct witness to this?"

"Yes."

"By your account I would say it was clearly self-defense, and—in the long run—defense of the other personnel. With a direct witness, we should be able to petition for dismissal of the murder charge, at least."

"I had Staff Sergeant Gossin—who is now in custody and under heavy sedation—collect evidence for a future legal investigation. Recordings of the place, of the deceased, of the weapons, and so on."

"Are you certain that Gossin is in custody somewhere?"

"As of yesterday, yes. Someone who actually saw Gossin in custody wanted to contact Aunt Grace, but she was in the hospital and not available. That person spoke briefly to Master Sergeant MacRobert, who sent her to me, here. The gas attack on Aunt Grace came shortly after I had met the three who escaped, and she had begun her own investigation into what happened."

"Do you think these attacks are directed at Vatta itself, or a reaction to your discoveries in Miksland?"

"The latter," Ky said. "I think we stepped right in the middle of someone's profitable activities. Though I don't know what the profit was, it was clear that both politics and money were involved. Someone had managed to get the resources to build a shuttle landing strip, and convert the part of the underground system they could reach into a base large enough to hold, at a short estimate, fifty to a hundred troops. When we flew back, I was in a Mackensee—um, mercenary company—shuttle, and we flew over the length of the continent: there was at least one open-pit mine, and some kind of settlement along the north coast."

"Do you have documentation of that?"

"Not anymore. I turned it in, just as I did the flight recorder from the shuttle, blood samples from the pilot and copilot, the base commander's log, and the evidence relating to Marek's death. Mackensee probably has the documentation of the surface data; I know their recorders were going; I bought my copy from them."

"And the communications blackout that was supposed to be keeping anyone from flying over it?"

"There was a strong magnetic field in places, but the real problem was someone putting the regular planetary surveillance satellites on a loop whenever they were overhead. My fiancé undid that."

"Well. I'd like to meet your witness . . . um . . . Corporal Inyatta now, if I could."

"Certainly," Ky said. "We'll need to go upstairs."

CHAPTER THIRTEEN

DAY 6

Inyatta, in Stella's office, was working away at her report, tongue between her teeth. She looked up when Ky opened the door. "Sorry it's taking so long, Admiral," she said.

"Sera Lane, this is Corporal Benazir Inyatta," Ky said. "Beni, this is Sera Lane. She's an attorney with Vatta Enterprises, and she's going to help us with our legal difficulties."

"You, mostly," Lane said. "You're the one who's facing murder charges."

"All of us," Ky said. "You can't separate the cases easily."

Lane grinned suddenly. "Sera Ky, you have no idea how cleverly we in the legal profession can slice and dice situations to the advantage of our clients. Sera Stella told the legal department to get you, your fiancé, and his assistant out of trouble; she said nothing about the others."

"I'm not going to throw my people to the wolves," Ky said.

"I'm not asking you to. I am saying that if Vatta wants to involve itself—its corporate self—in their problems, then it will take more than one attorney and half a legal assistant, and will put a larger crimp in the departmental budget. For which I will need the CEO's authorization. I'm not unwilling to extend my brief, but I can't do it on my own."

"Stella should be home soon," Ky said.

"Good. In the meantime, I would like to confine my activities to your situation, specifically the suspicion of murder, because its impact on your citizenship status is profound."

"All right," Ky said. Her ruffled feelings flattened again. "Beni, Sera Lane will want to record your testimony about the day Marek died. Do you also have that covered in what you've written?"

"Yes, I've just finished that part." Inyatta handed over a sheaf of papers.

"Thank you," Lane said. "I'll read these," she said to Ky, "and give you an opinion—is there a room I could use?"

"Would the dining room suit? I'll leave you alone there, and it's usually quiet."

With Lane settled into the dining room, and Inyatta continuing with the rest of her report in Stella's office, Ky took her own report into the kitchen, where Barash/Allie was once more working on the cooking. "You're showing real talent, Allie," she said. "Whatever that is smells delicious. Did your mother teach you?"

"Grandmother and aunt, mostly," Barash said. "My mother died when I was nine, in a traffic accident. My father didn't remarry. I joined Spaceforce to get away—like most people I think. I would've been the designated family cook and housekeeper after my older sisters married."

Ky nodded and went on with her writing. She heard the beep of the security system—the gates were opening for someone—the second beep of a vehicle coming into the driveway, another beep, and then— right outside the kitchen door—a crash and the sound of breaking glass.

"Barash—into cover!" Ky hit the emergency alarm and flipped on the external vid. She saw Stella's vehicle, pushed sideways into the wall between their driveway and the adjoining property, and a second vehicle, with men in dark clothes erupting from it. Stella appeared trapped in the driver's compartment. One of the men turned toward the kitchen door, aiming a weapon at it.

Ky turned back to the main house. Rafe was already on his way downstairs, sock-footed, weapon in hand. The lift hummed, coming up from below. "Rafe—Stella's car's been hit in the driveway; one hostile's targeting the kitchen door. We'll go out the back."

As they opened the French doors to the garden—still and empty in the late-afternoon light—Sera Lane spoke from the dining room. "What's going on?"

"Stay in the dining room; it's safest," Ky said. "We're under attack."

"Call the law?"

"Yes. And Vatta Security."

She had MacRobert's number in her skullphone list; she called that as she and Rafe ran across the terrace and onto the grass toward the back garden gate into the driveway. Rafe stopped suddenly, grabbing her arm. Ky whirled, scowling. "What?"

"Stella on skullphone. Don't come outside, she says. They don't want her; they want us. And the house opened. Back inside." He kept his voice low.

"No! I'm not going to leave her—"

"She's called help herself. Get inside, now."

Ky could hear another vehicle coming into the driveway, doors slamming, angry men's voices. "But—"

"Now!" He tugged; she resisted.

Then she heard the voices more clearly, from over the wall. "What are you doing to Sera Vatta? Who are you?"

"Her security detail," Rafe said to Ky. "They were only a block away. She'll be fine now; come inside."

Reluctantly, Ky went back in with him, securing the door after them.

"She's still talking to me on her skullphone," Rafe said. "Your phone was busy—you were calling the police, right?"

"No, MacRobert, in case there's an attack on Aunt Grace. Sera Lane was calling the police."

"Her security team is holding the first guys at gunpoint, and one of them hasn't put down his weapon yet—the one still pointing it at the kitchen door. She wants us to stay inside, and quiet, until she's sorted this out."

Sera Lane was standing in the dining room doorway, looking worried. "Is everything all right? Is Sera Stella—"

"She's fine," Rafe said. "I'm sorry—I should introduce myself. Rafe Dunbarger, Ky's fiancé. You're the lawyer?"

"Yes; my name's Lane. You're sure?"

"I'm speaking to her by skullphone, Sera Lane." Rafe now sounded, to Ky, the very essence of an unctuous CEO: fakey. "Her security team and whoever the other is are now at a standoff, with law enforcement on the way. Stella's in her car, not hurt but trapped by the other car; it pushed her into the wall, and she can't open the door far enough to get out. Nor can they get in, because they don't have the right equipment."

"Let's watch on the vid," Ky said. She went to the security station and switched on the screen, tilting it toward the doorway so Rafe and Sera Lane could also watch. She chose a driveway view from the others tiled across the screen, and enlarged it. "And sound," Ky said, touching that control. The voices came in clearly.

"You have no right!" A burly man in black with a smudged SECURITY label on his back waved his arms at a man in a navy jumpsuit with a Vatta logo on the front. "We're on official business; there are criminals at this address!"

"You still haven't told me your organization or your name," the Vatta man said. Two of his team pointed their weapons at three men now standing next to the wall in front of Stella's car, their arms up. The Vatta vehicle, larger than either of the others, blocked the entrance.

One of the six Vatta team members stood by the open gate, weapon in evidence but pointed down. Two more stood behind the angry man. Stella, just visible through the window of her vehicle, looked bored.

Sirens approached. Ky switched to the front-gate camera as a car marked PORT MAJOR POLICE DEPARTMENT nosed into the drive and stopped. Beyond it, across the street, a slender nattily dressed man stood behind the black palings of that yard, watching.

"What's going on here?" asked the first officer out of the car.

One of the Vatta security detail turned to face him. "Ser, I am Harmon Gothry with Vatta Enterprises Security, part of Stella Vatta's detail. That is her car, damaged and shoved into the wall. This car"—he pointed—"got between us, then ran into her purposely when she had gone through the gate, pushing her car into the wall. She is still inside. We are holding the perpetrators for you—"

"Is Sera Vatta injured?"

"She says she believes not, Officer. But she is unable to get out of her vehicle safely—the wall is too close on one side and on the other side she thinks the car that hit her is too close. Also she is afraid of these men."

The officer who got out first nodded and signaled his partners. "I will need to see your identifications and take a field statement."

"Of course, Officer."

Ky switched the view to the kitchen door camera as the police officer walked up the drive. The house system had already captured his identification as well as the license number and insignia on the car.

"Have these identified themselves?"

"No, Officer. They have said they believe Sera Vatta, or her relatives in the house, are criminals. They offered no explanation."

"You have to listen to us," shouted one of the black-clad men. "We're special agents—"

"Wait your turn," the officer said. "You can have your say at the station."

"But you can't arrest us. We're *agents*—"

"For the record," the officer said, ignoring the man who yelled and speaking to the nearest Vatta employee, "name, identification, position?"

"Harmon Gothry, D-43725904, Vatta Enterprises Security Section, assigned to Stella Vatta for her safety." He pointed to a pocket and when the officer nodded fished out an ID card and proffered it. The officer scanned it and turned to the next Vatta employee. In the meantime the other police officer moved in on the men being held against the wall.

"Did they show weapons?" he asked the Vatta men.

"Yes, Officer," Gothry said. "One—that one over there—had his pointed at the house door. Both of these had weapons pointed at Sera Vatta's car. We startled them and they did not shoot. Their weapons are behind us, near where they were standing."

"I see them." He took restraints from his belt.

"But we're agents!" one of the men said. "Call our commander!"

"I'm sure your commander—if you have one—will hear all about this," the officer said. "Best if you do what you're told and don't interrupt."

"But—"

"Like that. Not helpful." He grabbed one wrist of the leftmost man and twisted it expertly up behind him, then the other wrist and locked the hard-grabs on him. "You could've been comfortable in tangle-ties, but you just had to open your trap."

"You'll be sorry—when my commander finds out—"

"Some people never learn," Rafe said, watching this. He turned to Teague, "Anyone you recognize from Malines's warehouse?"

"No—but Mac and I killed the ones we saw."

"Point. And maybe they're not Malines but Quindlan."

"I wonder how the Vatta detail let itself be cut off," Teague said. "Isn't that what happened when Grace was attacked, too?"

"Um. Need to check with Mac if he ever found out the details of that. But it's not the same org. Grace's security was military; this is corporate."

"Still . . ."

"Right. Same tactic may mean same training, even same organization. Rodney, do you recognize any of those men, either side?"

"I haven't seen all the faces yet. Wait—that one—" He pointed at the screen, a man in Vatta Security. "—that's Manny Osuna. Before the big attack I was training under him for this kind of work. Six years ago, about."

"Where was he when the headquarters blew?" Ky asked.

"We were both out on a training run. I was driving; Manny and Ivos Stamarkos-Kellen were observing and riding shotgun. Grace Vatta was the passenger. It was going to be my promotion test. We were a little less than a kilometer from headquarters, on the way back . . . the street bucked and I hit the curb. Everything shook; glass came out of the windows of a bar across the street; and pretty soon the debris started coming down."

"What did Grace say?" Ky asked.

"'Take me home.' I turned around; Manny said, '*Rodney! Go!*' and I hit the accelerator, yanked the car around the first corner, and headed for her house. Not the one she's in now; the one on the outskirts."

"Must have been a rough test," Rafe said.

"I was in shock, I think. Manny and Ivos both looked three shades paler. I glanced in the mirror once; Sera Grace was bolt upright in the backseat, expressionless, and her eyes . . ." He shook his head. "Another thing I'll never forget. Cold fire."

Ky had kept her eyes on the screen. "So that one you know, and he's okay. Any of the other guys?"

"No."

"Police are about to gather them up and take them away," Rafe said, leaning over to see better. "But Stella's just sitting there. Should we go out now? Call someone? And who's that in the yard across the street? Bring that one up."

"I've tried to call her and ask; she's on her skullphone with someone. Not Rafe." Ky enlarged the image Rafe had selected. Expensive clothes, narrow face, disgruntled expression.

"He's recording everything," Rafe said. "Not on his implant—he's got a kit." Ky saw it, on the larger image.

"I don't know his name—Stella might." She looked at the yard and house behind him. "He looks out the upstairs window over the portico sometimes. Maybe just a common peeper. Shares Aunt Helen's taste in landscaping." Perfectly matched shrubs, trimmed to pyramids, marched up either side of the walk and along the front of the house.

Another police vehicle appeared, this one a van for transporting prisoners. Ky switched views again to focus on it. Still complaining, the four men who had been in the vehicle that rammed Stella's were shoved into it and driven away. The Vatta crew, after talking to the police, hooked a chain to the car blocking Stella's exit and dragged it a few meters away. One of them opened the passenger door and spoke to her, too low for the audio pickups to capture.

"She enabled the video from her car," Teague said. "I hadn't noticed that before. That's why she stayed in the car."

"That and not wanting to snag her suit on anything climbing out," Ky said. Rafe gave her a look. "I didn't mean that in a bad way," Ky said. "But if she's not hurt, getting dirty or ruining her suit wouldn't make as good an impression as she will now."

"Makes sense to me," Rafe said. "Penny would do the same."

By the time the remaining police officers came back up the drive to speak to Stella, the Vatta crew had pulled her car away from the wall and opened the driver's-side door.

Stella stepped out, a little awkwardly, and one of the police moved to support her.

"Well done," Rafe said. "The brave but wounded heroine. Always a good ploy."

"You think it's fake?" Ky asked.

"I saw her do the same thing years ago, when we first met."

"Is anyone home? Should you see your physician first?" The officer's voice held a note of concern.

"I'm sure they're home," Stella said. "But they may have been in another part of the house." She limped a little moving toward the kitchen door. "My ankle's a bit stiff, is all. It took me awhile to get it out from under—whatever you call that part that crumples up."

"Yes, Sera."

Ky took off for the kitchen. "Allie! Need you!"

Stella had just reached the door and pushed the buzzer when Ky dove into the pantry and Allie opened the door. Ky heard her say "Sera Stella—oh—what happened?"

"I'll tell you about it later, Allie," Stella said.

"And this is?" the officer asked, frowning at Allie.

"Our cook," Stella explained. "Allie, show the officer your ID."

"Yes, Sera," Allie said.

A moment or so of silence, then Ky heard the officer's voice. "Thank you, Sera. Sera Vatta, since you aren't alone, I believe we can leave now."

"Thank you, Officer Harwell," Stella said. Ky heard the door close, but she didn't open the pantry until Stella said, "Where's Ky and the others? Do you know if they saw the crash?"

"I'm here. We recorded it. Are you really all right?"

"Yes, though my ankle hurts. I may need to get it wrapped, but I wanted to make sure first you were all here and safe."

"Sera Lane from Legal is here," Ky said.

"I *asked* Howie Ventoven." Stella's eyes went cold. "I told him more than I would have told someone who wasn't going to be on the case."

"Sera Lane is fine," Ky said.

"But Howie should've let me know." Stella sighed. "Well. It is what it is. Here—make two copies of this—" She handed over a data cube. "Video from my car. The police will realize they forgot to ask me for it and I was too shaken up to offer it; get Rafe or Teague to duplicate the original markings, so the police can have number two. I'm going upstairs to change."

"Can I help?"

Stella shook her head. "No. Just get the duplicate made quickly, because they'll be back in a half hour if not sooner. I'm going to be stretched out elegantly on a sofa in the living room, with a cup of tea and some pastries, my ankle on a pillow." She looked at Allie. "Twenty minutes, Allie: tea and something light and sweet—in the living room. Ky, I can take the lift up; I'll be fine."

"The CEO in action," Rafe said when she'd gone up. "I'm glad the admiral's holding steady."

"Her operation, her command," Ky said, shrugging. "We can discuss who orders whom around the most later." She handed him the cubes. She'd meant to ask Stella about the man recording everything from across the street, but she could do that later.

"Ouch," Rafe said, dropping them into a pocket. "And you both order me around."

"It's Stella being my older cousin, not just CEO," Ky said. "But I need to get back to Sera Lane; we've got more to do." She turned back. "Allie, did that police officer scan your ID?"

"No, Admir—Sera. He just looked at it, nodded, and gave it back."

"Good." Ky looked into the downstairs security station; Rafe, Teague, and Rodney had crowded in together, and she recognized the distinctive sound of the data-rep machine. So Stella's recording was being dealt with. That left Sera Lane, whom she saw in the dining room, jotting down notes while reading Ky's report on Marek's death. "Stella really is fine, Sera Lane. She's upstairs now, changing clothes. Would you like some tea? Allie's making some, and if you'd like to have dinner with us—"

"Yes, thank you, to both. I have no family to worry about."

Ky let Allie know they would have a guest for dinner, then hurried upstairs. She heard Stella's shower running and poked her head into the study to find that Inyatta had finished her report and was just coming out.

"You'll have to stay out of sight when the police come to pick up Stella's video from the wreck—"

"Wreck?"

Ky explained, then went on. "Supper's set back at least an hour. I'll let everyone know about it when I know. Sera Lane is still here, and will be eating with us. I'll be monitoring the police visit from here, though we don't expect any problems."

CHAPTER FOURTEEN

DAY 6

Stella was still limping when she appeared downstairs again in soft loose slacks and a fuzzy sweater with a cowl neck that made her look fragile. A bandage around her left ankle just showed at the top of a thick sock; her other foot was in a slender felt house shoe. She'd taken the lift instead of the stairs, another sign that the ankle really hurt. Under one arm she carried two puffy bed pillows.

"It's not as bad as it looks," Stella said. "Stage dressing mostly, though it is sore, and there's a big purple bruise."

"Nothing worse? You don't need to see a doctor?"

"No." That was a very final *No*. Stella looked around the entrance hall. "Sera Lane?"

"She went to the kitchen to fetch the tea when she heard the lift motor."

"Ah. Good."

The living room glowed like a stage set now, pools of light under each lamp, or directed onto the paintings on the wall. Gentle land-scapes with quiet streams or lakes in the distance, soft colors, sug-gested peace and comfort. Stella switched on the emotional tonality her mother used most often, a combination of subtle scents and barely perceptible musical tones, all designed to put visitors in a calm, coop-erative emotional state.

Stella piled the couch's pillows against the end farthest from the front door, added one of the bed pillows, then lay back against them, sat up again, and positioned the second bed pillow under her ban-daged ankle.

"All you need is a knit throw," Ky said, grinning.

"The ground-floor linen closet," Stella said. "Green or brown."

Ky shook her head, amused at the color specification, but fetched a green throw with a brown border and laid it over Stella, with the ban-daged ankle peeking out. "Like that?"

"Perfect."

Just then Sera Lane arrived with a tray, Allie behind her with a fold-ing tray table. Allie and Ky moved one of the armchairs near the couch.

"Thank you, Allie," Stella said. "And you, Ky. We will need Rodney on the door, not Teague."

Ky looked at the arrangement: the injured party reclining on the couch, and the injured party's friend-or-attorney, depending on the way Stella wanted to play it, graciously pouring tea for them both.

By the time she'd found Rodney, and he'd put on the jacket he wore for his butler persona, she heard the doorbell ring and hurried up-stairs as Rodney moved with butlerly dignity toward the front door. In Stella's office, she turned on the video feed from the living room. Rodney opened the door at Stella's order to admit a police officer. Stella, seen from above, looked like an injured heroine in the kind of vid show Ky didn't like. Sera Lane looked appropriately older and re-spectable. The policeman looked slightly anxious.

Ky had seen Stella maneuvering people before, but never from such a safe distance or in this exact situation. She had changed some of her tactics. This time there was no overt sexuality to her calm, gentle voice; her beauty was still there, of course—it was in her bones, gene-deep, not to be lost—but the slight muting of it by her immobility, her overlarge sweater, the knitted throw over her clothes and the effect of its color, actually made her more attractive to someone whose occupation was protecting those who needed it.

Not until Stella had given her account of the attack, and handed over the duplicate recording from her vehicle, did the officer bring up any of the other things he might have brought up. "Those men who struck your vehicle—they claim to be working for Customs & Immigration."

"Do they?" Stella toyed with the border of the throw. "What does Customs & Immigration say?"

"They say there's an open case involving your cousin and her fiancé, but they deny that their people would intentionally ram your vehicle or draw weapons unless threatened. The person I spoke to—"

"Do you have a name?" Stella asked.

"Yes . . . it's a Ser Matson. His contact number is 46-7833-5."

"Thank you," Stella said. "I'm certain Vatta's legal team will want to contact him and ascertain the exact orders they were given."

"They—he—said if I could gain entrance to your house, I should search for the . . . the fugitives and take them into custody."

"They aren't fugitives," Stella said. "They live here."

"But he said they hadn't been able to gain entrance—"

Sera Lane spoke up. "Officer, their situation is being addressed by legal counsel. I am an attorney with Vatta Enterprises; my name is Lane. Excuse me for interrupting, Sera Vatta, but I believe the officer needs to know more of what's been going on. You do know that Sera Stella's cousin Ky was in a shuttle crash before she even arrived, do you not?"

"Yes, Sera. It was on all the newsvids."

"And that later it was found that she and some of the other passengers had survived in life rafts, and with difficulty made their way to shore on Miksland, and then into a formerly unknown underground base?"

"I'm not clear on all that, Sera. Isn't it just all bare rock and ice?"

"No," Sera Lane said. "It is not entirely barren. And the underground base was stocked with supplies."

Ky listened, fascinated, as Lane and Stella laid out what she had done, and how she had had no chance to follow the new procedures that had first stripped her of citizenship and then set requirements she could not meet to regain it.

"Why didn't you tell her, though, Sera?" the officer asked. "You could have prevented this problem, couldn't you?"

Ky wondered the same thing. What Stella had said didn't quite make sense; her implant should have reminded her, if nothing else. Now Stella was elaborating on what she'd told Ky.

"Frankly, I could not imagine they would apply the rule to her—it was so obvious that she couldn't have known about it, and she'd been through all that—saving those people, and before that saving all of us from that sociopath Turek. She's a hero. It just didn't occur to me. And they didn't tell *me* until my most recent arrival."

"But—the law was passed last year or the year before. They didn't send word to you? No one in your family here did?"

"When did *you* find out about it?"

"Notification to local law enforcement . . . maybe a half year ago. I mean, it wasn't a law that affected anyone I knew."

"What's happening?" Rafe appeared in the doorway of Stella's office.

"She's talking to the police guy. Gave him the tape, then he started probing about us—the ones Immigration is interested in. She's telling him she didn't know about the change in law when she first came back."

"Hmm. Why didn't Vatta Legal warn her?"

Ky blinked. "I hadn't thought of that."

"Don't they keep up with all the laws? They're an interstellar business; their legal team should be alert to any changes in customs, immigration, and tax law in every jurisdiction where they operate."

"Does ISC?"

"Yup. Of course, we used to *write* some of the laws, but certainly our legal team was aware of the different laws in different jurisdictions. ISC's legal department's huge. I wonder if Vatta's been running too lean in that regard since the attack that blew up their headquarters."

"I'll ask Stella when this is over. And of course Sera Lane."

"Didn't she say their other specialist in immigration law was in court today? That's a sign they're too lean, in my opinion. Our legal staff's divided into the experts and the litigators, the ones who actually take a matter to court."

"Thank you, Officer—" Stella's words caught Ky's attention; she'd missed several exchanges. "I appreciate your time and your courtesy—if you'll forgive me I won't see you out—"

"No, that's fine, Sera." He looked around once more. "If your cousin's not available I'm certain you can pass on what Immigration told me to tell her."

"Of course. I'll be glad to." Sera Lane stood up then and let the officer out while Stella watched with a smile. Once the door was closed and locked, Sera Lane came back and sat down again. "Does Sera Ky know that you didn't know about this until your last trip here?"

"I think I told her. Why?"

"Because she's likely to wonder why you took care of your own citizenship and didn't warn her about hers."

"What I said was the truth. I did not think they'd go after her, because she's a hero—the whole planet was excited she was coming last year, desolate when the search was called off, and excited again to find out she survived." The defensive edge in Stella's voice was clear to Ky. She expected Lane to pick up on it, too.

"But nothing much in the media."

"She didn't want a big fuss, she told me." Stella pushed her hair back and clenched her fingers in it. "Such a mess—you can fix it, can't you? It's ridiculous that they're treating her as a common criminal—"

"Not quite that," Sera Lane said, "or she'd be in prison by now, awaiting deportation. Or she might well be drugged into apparent brain damage. She's getting special treatment only because they haven't broken into the house."

"They would've tried that, if my security team hadn't shown up."

"True. I sense desperation. But you did very well; that officer was attempting surveillance, of course, but he's not the most skilled. I need to contact my office now and let the morning shift know I will be late or absent, depending on your needs. Do you think you could find out what time dinner is?"

Upstairs, Ky shut off the video feed. "Do you believe Stella really didn't think about my citizenship status?"

Rafe tipped his head to one side. "Certainly possible. She knew you were being treated as a celebrity, a hero, before you arrived. She would assume special allowances would be made, and if someone did make a fuss about it, at a level where it mattered, you would be told. She traveled back and forth several times in that half year, as you know, and it was only on the most recent arrival that Immigration tagged her. The news that you had survived, that you had led other survivors to safety—that was loud, the first days while you and she were busy with the Vatta turnover. You were ducking interviews, and the news began to die down faster than I'd have thought. We know now that someone was behind that, and the news media had already lost contact with the other survivors."

"Why, though?"

"Maybe the media were told about a possible contagion or toxin, told not to scare the population. Slotter Key's media's a lot more controlled than ours on Nexus."

"So someone set it up that way."

"Looks like. Probably not Immigration, though they might've had a mole in the hole. Or someone suddenly noticed that you weren't a great public figure anymore, and decided it was time to check into your citizenship status. And someone else said, 'Sure, go ahead, we don't need her on this planet anyway if she's not going to be a hero anymore.'"

Ky's skullphone pinged. "Yes?"

"Dinner in forty minutes. I'm lying down, downstairs. My ankle isn't broken, just bruised. Sera Lane's staying."

"I'm coming down," Ky said. She found Stella alone in the living room and told her about the man across the street.

Stella grimaced. "Oh, him. Cecil Robertson Prescott, self-appointed neighborhood watchdog, though he's really interested only in finding things to complain about. He acts like he's lived there forever, but it's really only ten or twelve years. Father used to wonder where he got the money for it."

"Why?"

"Ah. Well, according to Father, the Prescotts were one of the Founders, and chose one of the smaller land grants because of its location and the scenery. They wanted an isolated island all to themselves, because they planned to make a mint by picking up contract workers and then not paying them."

"But that's against the Founding Contract!"

"Yes, and presumably that's why they picked a remote island, and why—after a lot of stuff Father told me that I don't remember—they went broke and came straggling back to Port Landing and Port Major. This branch of the family had to do actual work up around Grinock Bay, but then Cecil managed to cobble together enough to buy that house and he's been the neighborhood grouch ever since."

"How did he get the money?"

"Father never figured out, or if he did, he didn't tell me. I was tempted to infiltrate their house and record them, but Father said let it go."

"What did Aunt Grace say?"

"I think she dug around a little, but she had other, more urgent concerns. And then the attack came."

"And this house was spared," Ky said. "I wonder why."

Stella looked at her, wide-eyed. "You don't think—"

"I know Aunt Helen thinks it's because it was a Stamarkos house to begin with. But think, Stella—how easy it is for him to keep an eye on this place."

"But why would the Prescotts want to attack Vatta? The Quindlans—"

"He could be working with them. For them. Or someone else. Aunt Grace was getting close to finding out how things connected—"

Over the course of the evening, Sera Lane interviewed all three fugitives from the military, Ky with her combination of pending murder charges and citizenship issues, and—briefly—Rafe and Teague with their visa problems. She stopped shortly before midnight. "I've got as much as I can get my head around, and I definitely need help. Sera Stella, I'd like you to assign two more attorneys and at least three more assistants to these cases—they're complicated and though I'm willing to lead, there's simply too much to do and too little time."

"I'll speak to Legal first thing tomorrow," Stella said.

"We may have to go outside Vatta," Sera Lane said. "We do not have a great deal of depth in immigration issues. It would be best to use Vatta's people on these cases, and hire outsiders for the more routine issues the company usually faces. Employees wanting to take citizenship here, for instance. I will write up my recommendations tonight—"

"Would you like to stay over?" Stella asked. "My mother's suite is unoccupied."

"No thank you. I want my own desk and my own bed; I hope that doesn't sound ungracious, but at home I have everything I need."

"You'll need an escort," Rafe said. "That police officer will have reported you're here, and someone might wish you ill. Where do you live?"

"Cantabile Gardens; I have a very pleasant unit in Section One."

"Stella?" Rafe looked at her.

"I'll call—who, though? Vatta Security?"

"I would."

Sera Lane left with a Vatta Security team driving her car, and her riding in the following car with two more. She checked in later to report that nothing untoward had happened, and she had agreed to have an escort the next morning as well.

CHAPTER FIFTEEN

DAY 7

On the way into base the next morning, Sergeant Major Morrison stopped by the vet clinic to see how Ginger was doing and bring her a treat.

"She's doing well, considering. I wish someone would invent a regen tank for dogs—but their biometrics are just too different."

Ginger whined and pushed her nose against the front of the cage. The bright-pink wrapping over the splint looked three times as big as her other legs. Morrison murmured to her and pushed a treat through the bars of the crate. Ginger gobbled it and licked Morrison's fingers.

"How's the other thing going?" Kris asked.

"Not as well as I'd like. Heard from MacRobert this morning?"

"He's over on the other side with Jo-Jo. I'll walk you through."

MacRobert, measuring rations into numbered bowls in the facility's big feed room, looked up as they entered. "Ah, Doc—how's the Red Queen this morning?"

"Doing well. Owner would like to discuss her rations with you." She took the bowl he had just filled and put it on a rolling cart with others. "I'll take these out to Jo-Jo. Owner has some special treat she'd like to incorporate in Ginger's feed."

"Sure, Doc," MacRobert said. Turning to Morrison, he said, "Sera?" as Kris rolled the cart out the door and shut it. Then he grinned. "Safe space. Here's what's I know at the moment. Someone did indeed kick Immigration into action. High-ranking military, but I don't have a name yet, or any connections other than the obvious. They've tied the citizenship thing and the murder accusation up tight. Did you hear about the attack on Stella Vatta yesterday?"

"No. What happened?"

"Supposedly Immigration, but Immigration's not confirming, rammed Stella's vehicle as she was arriving home. Ky, Stella, and Rafe agree it was probably an attempt to get into the house and grab Ky."

"They want her unable to plan a rescue of the other survivors," Morrison said.

"Exactly. Given that attack, and the near-certainty that someone in the hospital's bent, the Rector's medical team has agreed that she'll be safer somewhere else. We'll take her out under cover and with luck Dihann won't figure out she's gone for another day or so. Plenty of time to get her into a safe place. There's an apartment open in one of the towers about two blocks from where your off-base is; it's been swept for her now. She wants to see you; you'll be on the approved list."

"Why not put her in my apartment?" Morrison asked. "Then anyone following me will see me going in and out of my own apartment—irregularly, as I do. I can use the other one you've rented if she wants to be completely alone."

"She's not going to be completely alone," MacRobert said, a grim tone in his voice. "She'll have permanent in-residence security, like it or not. But that's a good idea, Sergeant Major, just for the first few days. Thank you for the offer."

"It's not that big," Morrison said, thinking of the "in-residence security."

"It's big enough," MacRobert said. "We have seen the layouts of all the apartments in that building. Since it's known your office and quarters were hacked into, doing a sweep there shouldn't arouse interest. And I'm presuming you had military-grade communications put in when you took the lease?"

"Yes." Morrison paused, then went on. "Have you found out more about the personnel who transported and guarded the survivors—or the ones who will?"

"All taken from a group that did not join the rest of the those who'd been under Greyhaus's command when that group went north for cold-weather training this past summer. Argument for using same group was possible contamination/infection. We are concerned that a flag officer arranged both their assignment and Greyhaus's 'accident.'"

"Do you know which flag officer?"

"You don't need to know that at this time, Sergeant Major." MacRobert smiled at her, an unexpectedly wistful look. "Thank you for the offer of your apartment; I'll let you know if it's feasible later today. And I can certainly adjust your dog's rations to accommodate a favorite treat. Have some with you?"

Morrison took the sack of treats from her bag, fished out the duplicate key to her city apartment, dropped it in with the treats, then handed the treat sack to MacRobert. "I meant to give you that anyway," she said. "For ease of communication."

"Been a pleasure doing business," MacRobert said. "The doc will contact you."

Morrison left through the clinic door, stopped to let Ginger lick her fingers again, and went outside, thinking hard all the way. Who—which flag officer—would have the authority to assign a subgroup of Greyhaus's command? Slotter Key's military had a command structure that was not rigidly hierarchical, as a safety feature, she'd been taught. From recruit to one of a branch's commanders, through the

Senior Command Circle to the President, it was hierarchical. But there was a side branch, established shortly after the Unification War, described to her as a workaround when there was something seriously wrong with the main command structure. As there seemed to be now. The concern had been the sudden influx of volunteers from the former anti-Unification areas, a mutiny that could lead to another war.

It hadn't happened. Both Dorland and Fulland thrived with Unification. So now, all this time later, why would it? Except, on the evidence from the three fugitives and Ky Vatta, someone had built a secret military base, trained a secret military force. It had been building up for . . . none of them knew how long. And clearly the target of the shuttle attack was the former Commandant of the Academy.

She unlocked and entered her vehicle. Started toward the base, still thinking. Her comunit chimed; she clicked on the vehicle's sound system. "Sergeant Major Morrison," she said.

"Sergeant Major, this is Major Hong. Where are you now?"

"Leaving Petsational—I dropped by to check on Ginger. I'm on the way to base."

"There's been more vandalism at your base residence, and your clerk reports that the seal we put on your office door was broken last night. Were you on base at any time last night?"

"No, I spent the night in the city."

"I need to brief you on all this; if your schedule permits, could you come to my office? Security 2-351?"

"Just a second, sir." Morrison flipped to her schedule. What she had was the work left over from two days ago, and there were no urgent requests from anyone. "Yes, sir; I'll park in my regular spot—"

"Don't. You'll be stopped at the gate; I'll have transportation for you there."

This sounded more and more serious. Even dangerous. "Yes, sir."

At the gate, she pulled into the designated parking lot just inside, and locked her vehicle. Major Hong was in the one that pulled up behind hers. He said nothing as he drove her to the headquarters complex; she followed him to his office. Once inside he turned on a scanning device first, then a jamming device, locked the door, and then waved her to a chair.

"Yes, things are this bad," he said. "It turns out that for a unified planet with no declared enemies, we seem to have a lot of spying going on. Of course, corporations spy on one another, and presumably sometimes on the military, hoping to figure out how to get us to buy their proposed weapons systems, but this is different." He unlocked and opened a drawer in his desk, and passed her a fat file in a battered green-and-black cover with EXTREME SEC on the front. "What do you know about the Unification War?"

Coincidence is a bitch, Morrison almost said. "Only what we were taught in military history classes, sir."

"Incomplete," he said. "Did you know, for instance, that the Rector was involved, as a civilian? And was later tried as a war criminal?"

"What? But that's—I mean, she's old, but she's not *that* old."

"She was very young. A teenager. On a visit to friends of her family in Esterance, on Fulland."

Morrison nodded. "I've been to Esterance several times, visiting our base."

"Yes. When she was there, she met a young man, and they started spending time together, as young people do, and he got her involved. Some street demonstrations, that kind of thing. Then she disappeared."

Morrison tried to imagine the Rector as anything but the formidable old lady with gimlet eyes and a legendary memory, but couldn't. What had she looked like as a girl? Like Ky Vatta? Surely not Stella; she was too short and too dark.

"Afterward—when the war ended—she was brought back to Port Major as a prisoner, under arrest for war crimes."

"I don't—it must have been a mistake."

"Apparently not. You will find . . . what may be evidence, or not, but was accepted as fact at her trial. Pictures. Testimony of alleged witnesses. They could have executed her. Her family petitioned to have her declared insane; she spent years locked in a hospital for the criminally insane. Then her family took custody, promising that she would never intrude into politics again, and—look where she is."

"In a hospital—*oh*. You mean she's Rector. But her family died, and the President himself asked her—"

"He didn't know. Records were sealed. But it occurs to me that her family dying opened the door for her. And there's something else. She rescued a child during that war—it was one of the things her family claimed showed remorse. Guess who that was."

"I haven't a clue," Morrison said.

"The former Commandant, Armand Esteban Burleson." Morrison had never heard anyone use the name before. "He testified at the hearing that saved her from execution—as a child, his testimony wasn't given much weight. But some years later, he testified again at the petition to have her transferred to her family's custody, when he was a military officer himself. And that *did* carry weight. They stayed in casual contact over the years. After the attack on Vatta, he assigned Master Sergeant MacRobert to liaise with her. There was speculation that she used MacRobert to persuade the Commandant to provide a suicide means to President Quindlan, because she'd lost an arm and couldn't do it herself."

"That seems far-fetched, sir," Morrison said. She had opened the folder; the first page had only the file number and a repetition of the security level. The second had the ID photo of the young Grace Vatta—Graciela Miranda Vatta was her full name. She'd had a healthy young teenage face, striking mostly for its lively, intelligent expression. She had been happy and relaxed—not that common for ID photos. Not beautiful, but pretty in the way healthy young women often were. The next photo was different—a blurry image of a thin young woman holding a long-barreled firearm—too blurry to tell much about her or the firearm—while moving through thick vegetation. Face in profile, slightly blurred; it might have been Grace or someone else. A third—obviously using the firearm, the muzzle blast clearly visible, and the face in focus. Definitely Grace. Angry, determined, expressing—could that be contempt? A fourth, of the same face as the first, but different—older, gaunt, lips tight, brows down in a scowl, eyes narrowed and—even in that still image—hostile, dangerous.

"It does. And I'm not sure the speculation has any basis beyond those who hate Grace Vatta for what she did in the past. You know, the family she took refuge with after the gas attack—the man is from Esterance. His family was active in the war."

"So—are you suggesting that he set up the gas attack?"

"No. What investigation we've had time for says he's clean. And beyond the Rector's history, there's this rogue element of our military that's been on and off Miksland for years, in a base deliberately hidden from satellite surveillance. Whose members, even with their commander dead, are surprisingly hard to talk to. They're on maneuvers, they're sick, they're . . . anything but sitting down with the right officers to explain what the farkling hells they were doing down there, and why. And who's behind it."

Major Hong, it was clear, was close to losing his temper. Morrison waited. He took a deep breath, blinked once, and said, in a calmer voice, "You visited the Rector after she was in the hospital."

"Courtesy visit, yes, sir, but I didn't get to see her. I brought some flowers and a card, and the clerk at the intake desk said she wasn't allowed visitors. I gave him the card and the flowers; he said he'd take care of it."

"But you didn't physically see her?"

"No, sir. I was told she wasn't allowed visitors."

"Ah. Your name was on the list of those who came to the hospital. It wasn't clear who actually had access to her room. There's a Colonel Dihann who should have had that list but claims he doesn't. Another break in the chain."

Morrison wasn't sure which way Hong was going with all this, and decided that asking would be the simplest way to find out. "Sir, I'm not sure what you're getting at."

He shook his head. "I'm not entirely sure myself. But that file—" He nodded toward it. "—was on your desk in your base quarters when we got the alarm and went to check it out. Right on top, out in the open, where anyone could have gotten it and read it, since the door had been broken in. I'm going to guess that you didn't leave it there."

"No, sir. I've never seen it before. I didn't know it existed, or that Rector Vatta had been involved in that war."

He nodded. "I believe you. But someone wanted to make it look like you'd left a classified file lying there out in the open. Your safe was open, with the files you'd put in it—at least I suspect those were the same, as they all refer to your recent assignments—still there."

"They broke into my *safe*? It's military-issue, approved and installed by your division; that's why I'm authorized to use it in my quarters!"

"Yes. I checked your authorization, of course. Whoever this is had an official passcoder, because they didn't actually break the safe, just opened it. Now, here's what I want you to do, because I can't. I want you to contact Ky Vatta and let her know you have important information about the Rector. I will contact the Rector. She will probably want to talk to you, after that. On my authorization, you may tell Ky Vatta anything I've told you about this entire situation. Including my difficulty in contacting Ky Vatta's fellow survivors."

"She's not . . . a member of Slotter Key military anymore, sir."

"I know that." The muscle in his jaw jumped again. "But I also know she knows what really happened in Miksland, and knows her aunt. Something needs to be done about both, and she's the link between them. Or she could be. And I'm damn sick and tired of the shilly-shallying going on here. I know what *my* duty is, and I'm going to do it whatever—*somebody*—says." He took another long breath. "So—you will meet with Ky Vatta, at your mutual convenience, and if that file should happen to travel with you, so much the better. She may know about it already."

"Yes, sir," Morrison said. "The other files that were in my quarters?"

"Here." He pulled out a stack and handed it over. "You'll want them. Your base quarters are off-limits for another ten days. I hope this time we've got enough surveillance on it to catch anyone who tries to break in again, even if they have every key in the box."

Morrison thought about telling him the Rector might be sharing her city apartment, but was he cleared to know where the Rector was?

"What's the status of my base office?"

"Closed today and tomorrow while I install better monitoring equipment in hopes that, again, we can catch whoever's getting in." He grinned. It was not a happy grin, more like Ginger showing teeth. "As you know, Sergeant Major, every department has its own internal . . . dominance disputes, you might say. I do not intend to drag you into ours, but will confess that the colonel you met at the hospital is neither my boss nor a friend of my boss. That's all I can say."

"Yes, sir," Morrison said, tucking the information into a rapidly growing mental file of things that might be useful someday.

"I'm giving you all my contact numbers—well, all the ones I can. I've already arranged for calls to your clerks to be transferred to their skullphones, so they can let you know when other things show up. Everyone in the building knows that your office was illegally entered—twice—and that your quarters on base were also entered, vandalized, and entered again. They know you're not supposed to visit your office or your quarters without my permission and an escort. The flags have all contacted me, and I've explained what I feel they need to know. So nobody expects you to be there. My advice—and this is not an order, but advice—is that you quietly go someplace you're not expected to be, read that file on the Rector, deal with the other files as you normally would, and contact me when you're done. I can have my people remove anything from your quarters you need—"

"Thank you, Major, but my city apartment's pretty well stocked. With my dog in the clinic, I don't have to worry about space for her. Though—this may be trivial, but there's an open sack of dog food in the pantry, and a box of dog treats. I could take that by the vet clinic; it's a brand they use."

"I can have it picked up now, and you can take it with you. Save everyone a trip."

And she'd have an excellent excuse to go by Petsational again, where he knew she'd been before. "Thank you, sir. That would be helpful."

Once back in her own vehicle, she contacted the clinic and told them she was bringing in some feed that had been in her quarters.

"You don't have to do that," Kris said.

"I know, but I really don't want open dog food in there. Attracts pests. Be there in a few."

She also contacted her clerks. "Where are you set up?"

"We're over in Building H, Procurement. That Major Hong brought our files and everything and there's a safe, but it's awfully cramped, Sergeant Major. There's barely room for two desks and only one of us can move in or out at a time."

"I'll be working off-base," Morrison said. "I can't get back in my quarters, either, so I'll either be downtown or with friends who live closer. Anything urgent right now?"

"No, Sergeant Major. Nothing that needs your ID, just routine. I was wondering—there's really not a lot to do—"

"If you can take turns? Yes. Half-hour overlap to change over; keep Major Hong informed who's there and where the other one is, in case he needs you. And me."

"Thanks, Sergeant Major. We'll double up the moment there's a load."

MARVIN J. PEAKE MILITARY HOSPITAL

Grace Vatta eyed the plan for her transfer from hospital to apartment with suspicion. "Why does it have to be a military ambulance?"

"Because they're in and out of here all the time," MacRobert said. "You're the only civilian patient here, and if we use a civilian ambulance it will be obvious who's inside it."

"And why are we going *there*?" She pointed at the address of Sergeant Major Morrison's apartment in the city. "I thought you'd found a place in the Towers."

"I did. Morrison will be staying there instead. She's from Esterance, Grace. So her offer for you to use her apartment is either exceptionally generous or exceptionally devious . . . and in either case gives us an opportunity to check her out. She'd been ordered to leave her quarters on base—" He shrugged.

"Ordered before or after her offer to me? By whom?"

"A Major Hong. And I'm not sure when. Ready?"

"Very," Grace said. "And I don't recognize the name Morrison from Esterance."

"That's good." MacRobert beckoned to the guard at the door.

To Grace's relief, her transport went smoothly. The only complication was the chill drizzle now falling as another front moved past, and that turned out to be an advantage. The ambulance crew pulled the retractable hood up over the gurney, and it fogged with her breath. She heard MacRobert speak to the door guard. "Sergeant Major Morrison's auntie—I believe she called?"

"Oh, yes, of course. Here—you'll want the service elevator—"

She saw and heard no one else but the two handling the gurney and MacRobert on the way to the apartment. Once inside, Mac helped her sit up and move from the gurney to a chair; she thanked the ambulance attendants as they wheeled the gurney back out to the hall. She looked around. Perfectly tidy and clean, as she'd expected, but with a few touches of comfort and color that improved on beige walls and mid-brown carpeting. The living room sofa was a pull-out bed in a pleasant blue; the chair she sat on matched it. A low bookcase ran under the long window; the daylight coming in was chill.

"Security glass," MacRobert said. "View's not great, but it's not a hospital room, either."

The bedroom had a smaller window, bed, chair, chest of drawers, dresser. Blue-and-red small-patterned bed cover; a blue blanket with a red stripe folded neatly at the foot. Grace sat on the bed. Firm, but not hard. Pillows soft but not smothering. The closet held uniforms, with polished shoes and boots racked below, a uniform coat. In the kitchen, the foods in the cooler and shelves were the only sign of luxury.

A second bedroom—or office, as it was furnished—had a desk, a bookcase, a desk chair, and a seat that also unfolded into a narrow bed.

"So I can get some work done," Grace said. "I've got to keep digging into that mess with the other Miksland survivors."

"That's why Sergeant Major Morrison wants to talk to you. At least, that's the ostensible reason. She's talked to Ky."

"How secure is this place?" Grace looked around.

"Secure as our people could make it early this morning. I had it swept. It would be better if we could use Rafe and Teague, but if they leave the house they'll be arrested."

"So Morrison and Ky are working together?"

"Not exactly. They've had only one meeting before today and it was short. Morrison can't work openly with Ky without higher authorization. And she did sign off on the committee report suggesting permanent confinement for the survivors. She felt that her own freedom of movement and even life were at risk if she didn't, and that it was more important to make it back to Port Major—and you."

"She'll be here later today?"

"Yes. And the apartment we rented for you is where she'll stay, at least for a few days. Her life may also be in danger, so she, too, will have security coverage in that building."

Grace settled herself at the desk and looked at the files MacRobert had delivered, the service records of all the personnel who had been on the shuttle, including—to her surprise—Ky's record from her entrance to the Academy to the day she resigned from it. She'd never hunted it down; she knew Ky's father hadn't asked to see it, either.

Curiosity overtook her. The picture from Ky's application misted her eyes. She had been so young, so enthusiastic, so much like Grace herself at the same age. They'd both left home hoping for adventure— and for both, that adventure had involved tragedy and loss. Well. The past didn't change. She flipped the pages quickly, past pictures of Ky as a first-year, second-year, third-year cadet, solemn and determined. Not as bad a first three years away from home as her own had been; she was glad of that. Rankings always high—first or second in every class. Honor cadet her final year, pictured with the loop of gold braid

on her shoulder. And then, at the end, her handwritten letter of resignation stapled to the back of the terse explanation for it, what she had
done. She had jumped the chain of command, gone outside it to help
a junior cadet she'd been mentoring. A political embarrassment followed.

"She's more like me than I thought," Grace said as Mac came in
with a cup of tea for her, one of the sergeant major's expensive teas.

"You didn't know the story?"

"I knew her father's version of it. Gerry—her father—was so angry.
He gave me a look and said, 'Don't ask any questions. I can only hope
she's as tough as you said she was when you advised me to let her
apply, and that she survives.'" Grace sipped the tea and set the cup
back down. "I told him she would. But since he hadn't told me the
whole story, I wasn't sure—I didn't know what had happened."

"But the press—"

"I didn't watch the media then. I didn't know what she'd supposedly
done, or if she had actually done it or been framed." She drank the rest
of the tea. "I should have asked and found out before she came back.
Our meeting—brief as it was—felt off somehow and I now see it's
because she thought I knew, and then realized I didn't, and inter-
preted my not knowing her own way."

"I covered for you," MacRobert said. "Told her what you'd been
dealing with, missing the Commandant, fighting with the various
commands to push for rescue."

"Kind of you," Grace said. "And I'll know the next time I see her.
She can't leave the house, can she?"

"No, but Stella can. And as your niece, Stella has a family reason to
see you and carry word back and forth."

"Mac, do you know everything about my past?"

"Everything?"

"You know what I mean. I know you know I was in a psychiatric
hospital for years, but—do you know all the background?"

"All of it—no. I know you were in the Unification mess, and bad things happened, and you were considered mentally unfit—with a suggestion that you had previously had, if not a breakdown, some instability."

"My defense team thought that might mitigate my sentence. And it did, eventually. Mac, somewhere in the military is the file on me. I wasn't officially military, but that's who gathered the information, and supported the charges against me. I don't know myself exactly how my father's legal team got me off—and later got me out of that mental hospital. He didn't tell me—he told my brother, who became my guardian after my father died. My brother didn't tell me, either, and I didn't ask. Then he died unexpectedly, of a fever. I asked his older son, Stavros, but he said he knew nothing about it. But what I feel now is that my crimes—and they *were* crimes—have come back to haunt the family."

"So are you going to tell me?"

Grace looked at him. No condemnation so far in his gaze; he had not shrunk from any of the things he knew she'd done to protect the family in the years since the big attack on them. He knew she'd killed. He approved of those kills. He was not going to approve of the old ones, from the Unification War.

But she had to tell him. He deserved to know. Was this the right time?

"Did the Commandant ever tell you why he asked you to liaise with me?"

"Sure. The Vatta family had been helpful to him when he was a boy, an orphan from Fulland. Brought him in, educated him, paid his entrance to the Academy. He considered you to be smart and tough, politically astute, the best contact among the Vattas but one that wouldn't be obvious to others."

"I saved his life in the war. He was just a kid. His parents . . ." She looked away, at the small window with rain smearing the glass. "His parents died in a firefight. I found him hiding. Brought him along." After a pause, she said the words. "I killed his parents." This time, when she looked at Mac's face, his eyes widened, then closed for a moment.

"Did he know?"

"No. He knew there were shots; crawled to the closet where I found him hiding. He didn't see it; it was at night. The others—the others I was with wanted to kill him, too, but I was sick—sick of the whole thing—and I—I was their commander; I said we were taking him along and the person who hurt him would die. They believed me. With reason."

MacRobert nodded. "I believe you, too." He sighed. "Well, we'd better take another look at the Vance family, and Morrison's, before you're alone with either."

"Mac . . . I'm tired of the hunt. If it takes my death to ease their pain and let everything die down—"

"You weren't the only one tried as a war criminal, on either side."

"No, but I'm still here. Most have died. I don't know how much of this mess is vengeance aimed at me, or why nothing for decades until now, but I want Ky and Stella and even that idiot Maxim to be able to live good lives. Easy choice."

"No. You never went in for easy choices, and I won't approve it now. You can still do good—you already have; the military is better off now because of you, and you're the only one who can do certain things."

Grace pulled herself up in the chair. "All right. While I can do good. But, Mac, I've had death sitting on my shoulder for days, and I don't expect to make another ten years."

"Die of poison or die of blade or gun, but don't die of self-loathing," Mac said. He squeezed her shoulder, then picked up the empty tea-cups and walked out.

Grace folded her hands and thought about it. Was it the near-death of toxins and coma that jarred loose these vivid memories? Not yet all of them; there were still holes, still sudden stabbing pain in her head when she tried to remember. But vivid enough. From the face that first brought her into it, the boy she'd met in a café, her third day in

Esterance. She'd felt so mature, shopping by herself in a strange city on another continent—another country, actually, as it was then. She'd bought her lunch, found a table, and then—he'd spoken to her. Politely, but with interest. They'd talked. They'd agreed to meet again.

And only thirteen days later he'd been killed, right beside her, dead in the street with his guts falling out of his belly, and people yelling and screaming and someone else grabbed her arm, dragged her away, made her run for safety.

Safety. Nothing had been safe from then on. Angry, frightened, disgusted, shocked—she had survived, using all the intelligence, cunning, and physical ability she possessed. She'd made it back to her parents' friends' house a few days later, hungry, scared, exhausted, hoping to find them, hoping to be rescued, but the house was a shattered ruin, with no sign of Gretchen and Portia and Miran. After that, in a city where both sides had roving gangs of supporters, she'd joined one at the point of a gun and ended up . . . standing before a court to explain how a well-brought-up daughter of a wealthy, respectable merchant family could have any excuse for what she had done.

She had no excuse. Girls like her were supposed to be immune to the seductions of handsome strangers, violent emotions, even the pressures imposed by captors. She was, according to the court, a monster who deserved death—and she'd expected it, until the day she was taken from her cell and transferred to a facility for the criminally insane, where she was drugged, probed, subjected to "reconditioning" for years. Endless years, they'd seemed. When finally the years and exhaustion quieted the turmoil inside, and suicide attempts led only to more pain, she grew numb, unresisting.

She looked at her hands. One still bore the scars—faded now—of wounds inflicted in that war. The other, almost indecently young with its smooth, unmarked skin still soft, the arm above it also young, full-sized now . . . had been lost to another attack and regrown from her own cells. Both her hands and arms had looked like that, before . . . everything. "I was beautiful," she whispered, looking at the young arm. "I *was*."

But not after. Her father, her mother had exclaimed over her, the one time they were allowed to spend a short time with her. "You look so old," her mother had said, patting her cheeks. She had flinched; her mother had looked frightened. Her father had shaken his head. "Graciela . . . I don't understand how . . . why. You were so pretty." Meaning, *You are so ugly now.* Meaning, *You ruined yourself, your value to the family.*

And somewhere a file still existed, she was sure, with pictures of her young face. When she was finally released, when she could finally get to the family homes again, after her father and uncle died, she had destroyed every one of the portraits made during her girlhood. She could not bear to see them. She could not bear to answer more questions.

She pushed herself upright again, and opened the files on her desk. Enough of that. If retribution came, she would accept it. In the meanwhile, she would do what good she could for others.

The inquiries she'd put in place before the attack had produced only partial, unsatisfactory answers. The Miksland survivors were listed as "disabled, pending disposition" in two responses, but in the most recent—two days old—their status had changed to "disabled permanently, custodial care necessary." That sounded ominous. No location was given. She had eight requests from family members and three from official sources for their location and information about them. Sergeant McLenard's wife wanted to know why he wasn't answering her mail. Sergeant Cosper's father angrily demanded to know where his son was and why he hadn't come home on leave. The family court judge dealing with the guardianship of Tech 1st Class Betange's siblings wanted to know why Betange was ignoring the legal summons to appear. A prosecutor wanted to know when and where charges would be filed in the murder of Master Sergeant Marek, because Marek's wife was considering a civil suit. Still another wanted copies of all the evidence returned to Port Major by Admiral Vatta, to see if she could be held responsible for the shuttle crash.

Still no sign of where that evidence had gone after Ky turned it in. She called her office and asked her clerk to send her Ky's debriefing statement, only to be reminded that it, like the items Ky said she'd delivered to Spaceforce, had disappeared as if it never existed.

Time to call Ky directly. She recognized Teague's voice when he answered. "Teague, is Ky there?"

"Good morning, Rector. Yes, she's here. You wish to speak with her?"

She could tell from his voice that he was in a mischievous mood, and she had no time for mischief. Mayhem, perhaps, but not mischief. "Yes," she said. "I need to ask her a question."

Ky sounded tense. "Aunt Grace? Why didn't you call my skull-phone?"

"Because I might want to talk to others in the house without a separate call," Grace said. "Do you remember who you gave your initial statement to, that first week?"

"Um . . . I'll check." A very brief pause. "My implant says it was a Colonel Vertres, in Commandant Kvannis's office. Is that missing, too?"

"Yes. We should have had a copy—I asked Spaceforce HQ for it, but they said they couldn't find it."

"I have my own recording of it. Would that help?"

"Yes. Thank you." Bless the child, she'd had the sense to do that. Even a low-density implant recording was evidence. "If you can transfer it, I can print it out here."

"Print—"

"Easier for old eyes to read, but also hardcopy to send elsewhere as evidence. What about the other items?"

"I read only part of Greyhaus's log, Aunt Grace, so my implant has a record only of those pages. I should've made another copy but—we were rushing to find a way out before the bad guys came."

"And the evidence of the shooting—do you have any independent copy of that?"

"No . . . but I have a witness."

Grace's mind blanked for a moment, as it had been doing since the gas attack, but then she remembered: the fugitives Ky had talked about, that she herself had not yet met. "One of them was there?"

"Yes. But we have to keep them hidden. The military wants them—you know that."

"Yes. Ky, I have to admit, the gas attack seems to have left some blanks in memory. The doctors said it might. I tested okay on their cognitive exams, or they wouldn't have let me out, but the questions weren't complex. I need you to tell me things again if I don't remember."

"Of course," Ky said.

"Just a hint—back up everything about your time in Miksland in some other form than your implant. I can understand if you don't want to trust it to me, but—"

"Agreed. I'll run external backups—you know that takes awhile—from leaving my flagship to the present. Duplicate backups." Ky sounded more cheerful suddenly.

"Mac says you've met Sergeant Major Morrison?"

"Yes, she was here, very briefly."

"Stella has reason to visit me, so if you have information for Morrison, or she for you, I can be the exchange point. Is Stella there?"

"No, at the office."

"Then let me speak to Rafe, please. I want to ask him some security questions."

Rafe, when he answered, sounded calmer than she'd ever heard him. "We can't get back in your house yet," he said. "Our legal situation is still serious, and we've been told by counsel to stay put. What can I help you with that doesn't involve stepping outside?"

"Ky has data on her implant that duplicates what she reported officially—in reports now missing. I need to know how far we can push an inquiry based on her data—especially who she gave the first reports to, who took custody of the physical evidence, if she knows that. She's going to be downloading her implant data and making copies; can you start working on the investigation from that?"

"Of course," Rafe said. "Even one or two names would give us something. Um—there's another possible source. The Mackensee troops that pulled her and the others out of that mountain valley may know—might have seen and even recorded—where the hard evidence she left with the others changed hands. You could contact them about it. She told me she left the recorder with the data on the shootout she had with Marek with the sergeant who was there and the tech who did the recording, when Mackensee flew her up to meet with us."

"Excellent," Grace said. "I didn't know that, and Mac has a contact with Mackensee, so he should be able to find out if anyone noticed. It's a chance, anyway."

She called Mac in and told him what Rafe had suggested. He nodded. "I'll contact Master Sergeant Pitt. It may take awhile to hear back. I doubt they're out of FTL flight on the way home."

"Whatever we can find out helps," Grace said. "Ky's downloading her implant's recording of the interview she gave a Colonel Vertres on Commandant Kvannis's staff that first week she was back here."

CHAPTER SIXTEEN

DAY 7

Sera Lane looked up from the stacks of papers she and Ky had been discussing when the call came in. "What was that about?"

"Aunt Grace. She's out of the hospital and not surprisingly full of things for other people to do." Ky grinned. "When I was little, she would visit our house and keep us all busy. We had a cook and a gardener, but she found things that she thought needed doing, and she was not tolerant of what she called 'idle hands.'" Ky sat down at the table. "Actually, we did learn things from that—aside from hiding from grown-ups with agendas—and her suggestion today is good. She wants me to download my implant's record of the interview I gave Spaceforce and make multiple copies in case of any other mishaps."

"Excellent idea," Sera Lane said. "I was going to suggest you continue writing out your memory of what transpired, but pulling data directly from your implant will be faster. Do you have the equipment here?"

"Yes," Ky said. "It'll take some time—"

"No matter. I have plenty to do and we can continue our meeting later. If I finish the petition to the court on the citizenship matter by 1500, I could get it filed today. I believe Sera Stella has spoken to our head of Legal and they're supposed to call me with the names of the additional attorneys the entire project will require."

"Will you be working from here, or going back to Vatta headquarters?"

"Here, unless you'd rather I left." She smiled at Ky. "It's not entirely because your cook is so skilled, but that does add a point in your favor."

"Stay, by all means," Ky said. "Can you function as a witness to validate the download?"

"As an officer of the court, yes," Sera Lane said, pushing back her chair. "I will need to observe the hookup—does that other Vatta employee have certification in the procedure?"

"We'll find out," Ky said.

Downstairs, Rodney was busily working through something on one of the computers. Ky explained what they needed.

"Yes, Sera," he said to Lane. He pulled out his identification and handed it to her. "I can access my personnel file for you and you can see it all, if you wish."

"Not necessary," Lane said. "Your certificate is high enough. I need to observe the hookup—any idea how long it will take?" She looked at Ky.

"No—I want to start with leaving my flagship, and then go all the way through. Hours. Maybe even another session tomorrow."

"That's too long for the storage on the media you've got," Rodney said. "We'll have to break it into chunks. These are two-hour backups." He had pulled a carton of them from one of the cabinets.

"I'll certify the hookup, and then when you break I'll take custody of the backup until copies are made," Lane said. "Perhaps break for lunch after the first session?"

"That works for me," Rodney said.

He pulled out the necessary cables and plugged into Ky's implant jack. Rafe appeared in the door. "Ky, Allie wants to know—what are you doing?"

"Downloading the record of that interview for Aunt Grace," Ky said.

"Passive download?" Rafe turned to Rodney.

"Yeah—wait—is there another kind?"

"There is at ISC," Rafe said. "It's been known to cause brain damage."

"No, it's nothing like that. Cable to the backup, backup in the machine, client specifies the file location, and the machine just sucks that location."

"Ah. Good." Rafe turned to Ky again. "Allie wants to know if baked stuffed fish is all right for dinner tonight. Grocery has a special on crabs."

"Fine with me," Ky said. "And Stella likes fish."

For the next two hours, Ky closed her eyes and watched the mental image of a glowing blue line stripping the interview file neatly into the backup cylinder. In the machine it would be broken into sound and image, separate output types for each.

It would have been restful but for her awareness that time was passing inexorably for the survivors still in custody. She had to find them, get them out of their torment, and keep them safe. Somehow. And all she had done so far was hide out in the house, accomplishing nothing. Her own and Rafe's legal problems also bore in on her. Could Lane really get her citizenship back? And if she did, then the threat of a murder prosecution still loomed, with the evidence she'd so carefully collected on the entire trip lost—or rather intentionally hidden or destroyed. And Rafe—his visa extension now exceeded—could be deported anytime he left the house.

"Want to run another right away?" Rodney asked. "Or take a break?"

"A break," Ky said. "I need to move around. Is Sera Lane still here?"

"I think so—I'll call—"

"Never mind. I'll run upstairs myself."

Ky found Sera Lane up in Stella's office, interviewing Inyatta about her statement. They both looked up as she entered. Inyatta looked tense.

"We're in the middle of something," Sera Lane said. She gave a slight nod toward the door.

"I had an idea," Ky said.

"Later," Lane said. "I need to finish with Corporal Inyatta and her statement so I can move forward on the murder charge."

Ky shut the door and turned away, more than a little disgruntled. Rafe met her at the head of the stairs. "You look like you want to hit someone," he said.

"I do. And I shouldn't. I am so tired of being cooped up in this house!"

"Better than a cell," Rafe said.

"Not enough better." Ky pushed past him, down the passage to their room. He followed. "I can't do the things I need to do to rescue my people."

"They're not really your people, Ky," Rafe said. His reasonable tone grated on her nerves. "They're Slotter Key's problem—the military's problem—and you don't have the right. Let Grace deal with it, now she's out of hospital."

"I have every right. You don't understand—" She stopped herself from what would have been insulting, and tried for a more measured response. "Rafe, even if I was wrong to take command after the crash—we can argue that later, if you want—once I did so, they became 'my people.' That's how command works. That's how I was trained; that's how I think. And clearly, Slotter Key military is treating them not as valued members of the service, but as criminals."

"I do understand your point, Ky, but be reasonable: you have no leverage. Your citizenship's been revoked, you're suspected of murder—if you involve yourself in their case, you could do them more harm."

"Or I could get them out."

"How? If you leave here you'll be arrested. You have no resources—

human or financial—to do the job. You've got to wait until you're cleared of the murder charge and a citizen again, at least."

"I've got to get serious about the mission," Ky said. "It will help keep my mind off being housebound."

Sergeant Major Morrison, in uniform, arrived at the door to her apartment building in the city to find additional security in place. The trip in, through cold rain, had not improved her mood, nor did standing in the dank breeze while someone looked down a list to find her name. Finally, he found it and let her by. Another guard was outside her door; she showed identification and he spoke into his comunit, a soft mumble. Morrison repressed an obvious sigh. She did not like this, even though she had suggested it. She should have sent someone else to pick up her clothes and move them to the other apartment, the one she hadn't seen yet.

MacRobert opened the door. "Sergeant Major," he said, with a short nod.

"Master Sergeant. I'm here to collect my clothes."

He shut the door. "The Rector is waiting for you in the office."

She went to the door of the office and stopped, startled by the change in the Rector's appearance. Always before poised and erect, she now looked a little shrunken, as old people often did. Her gray hair was lusterless, her dark skin more wrinkled. She sat slumped in the chair, eyes closed.

"Excuse me, Rector," Morrison said.

The Rector's eyes snapped open, the same silver-gray as before, and just as alive and aware.

"Sergeant Major," the Rector said. "Thank you for the loan of your apartment; I hope it will be a brief one."

"Stay as long as you like," Morrison said. "But—"

"But we have things to talk about." The Rector pulled out a security cylinder and turned it on. "Try yours as well," she added.

Morrison turned on her own. All the telltales were green.

"Have a seat." The Rector pointed to the chair. "I've been told that your quarters and your office on base suffered intrusions and security breaches. And you believe these were related to your recent TDY when you observed what you considered ill treatment of other survivors of the shuttle crash just over a half year ago."

"Yes, Rector. I'm certain of it."

"I agree. I knew nothing until my great-niece Ky Vatta called in a fury supposing I must have known about and agreed to it. I believe you saw at least one of those who escaped confinement—is that correct?"

"Yes, Rector."

"Do you also know that Ky's citizenship has been revoked and she is about to be charged with murder, as a way to get *her* into custody?"

"No—I didn't know that."

"In addition, the materials that Ky preserved through that period—evidence that might be useful in finding out who sabotaged the shuttle and the survival suits that killed all officers aboard it but Ky and her aide—have disappeared. Ky turned them over to Spaceforce personnel upon her return to Port Major. Staff Sergeant Gossin held evidence of the investigation done after Ky shot Master Sergeant Marek. It has also disappeared; presumably it was taken from Gossin when she was in custody, after Ky left Miksland."

Morrison had not known about the sabotaged suits, or the missing evidence, but all that came out of her mouth was "Why wasn't the admiral with her troops?"

"Because, fearing for her life, I had asked Mackensee Military Assistance Corporation—the mercs we hired to intervene against the Black Torch, who'd been hired to kill everyone—to have her flown directly to meet me, and then she and I traveled together to Port Major. And she is not, after all, a member of Slotter Key's military any longer."

"I see." Morrison kept her face calm with an effort. She still wanted to demand how the Rector could possibly have ignored the welfare of the other survivors, but she sensed that yelling at the Rector would not help her find out. "What did you think had happened to the others?"

"The other survivors? I was *told* that they were being interviewed and checked over medically after their ordeal and would be reunited with their families for thirty days' leave. Initially I had no reason to doubt that report. I was faced with many other issues relating to the shuttle crash, including complaints from the Moscoe Confederation about the death of their citizen Commander Bentik. The legislature opened investigations—still ongoing—into the two mercenary companies—who hired them, who permitted them to land on Slotter Key soil—and I was called to Government House repeatedly to answer questions about that. At any rate, being assured the other survivors were being taken care of, I didn't worry about them again until Ky called a few days ago. And the next night I was gassed when I came home and have been in the hospital until today."

"I did wonder . . ."

"I'll just bet you did." For an instant those old eyes were sharp as spears and just as penetrating. "You wondered if I had deliberately let them be hauled off, drugged, and imprisoned for some reason—was it a Vatta reason or a military?"

"I didn't know, ma'am."

"Ah. Well. Natural that you would worry. Natural you'd want to snap my neck if you thought I'd done it."

"And there's something else I should tell you," Morrison said. She opened her briefcase and pulled out the old file. "Someone left this in my quarters on base. It was found by the same security squad that investigated the break-in. Major Hong gave it to me with orders to keep it safe."

"What—? Oh." The Rector looked at the cover, then up at Morrison. "That's *my* file? The one from the Unification War? They never let me see it." She slipped the cover open. "Gods, I was young. And stupid."

"I read some of it," Morrison said. "It was not . . . reassuring."

"No, it wouldn't be." The Rector leaned back a little, folding her hands on top of the file. "I don't propose to read it myself; I have memories."

"Implant memories?"

"No. They took my implant, stripped it, and put it back in with their edits. The only good memories of that period I have are the ones stored in the brain itself."

"Which 'they'?" Morrison asked, fascinated in spite of herself.

"The authorities. When I was brought back here and tried—surely you read that far."

"Yes."

"Well, then. Their intent was to make it impossible for me to forget the bad things I'd done—which, if they'd had any sense, they'd have known I couldn't anyway—and make me miserable. I was already miserable. I was surprised when I finally got out of that place and back with the family, and more surprised when, after the attacks on Vatta, I was asked to become subrector and then Rector."

"Because of your family's contract?"

"Contract? No, not that I know of. Because there were still people who remembered enough to hate me. But really, it worked out fairly well. I don't look like that anymore." She glanced down at the page of images and tapped one. "Or that. And I've been functionally sane for decades."

"Your father signed a contract in which you were released to family custody on the condition that the family would not permit you to be active politically in any way," Morrison said. "You were to be kept safely confined, medicated as necessary, subject to regular inspection by a court-appointed psychiatrist until at least age fifty."

The Rector's eyes widened, then narrowed again. "Seriously? I knew nothing of that. Father told me he'd gotten me out and I should stay home, on Corleigh, in seclusion, for at least five years. Which I did. He said after that I could return to the mainland and he would provide a house and staff. Which he did. He said nothing about a permanent bar to any political involvement. I would never have taken the post otherwise, no matter what anyone said."

Morrison tapped the file. "It's in here, the official copy. The rules under which you could live outside the hospital, and the penalties if you committed any crime or became political." She watched the Rector's face, and saw nothing but astonishment and confusion.

The Rector paged through the file quickly, stopping when she found the reference, near the end. Her breath caught while she read, her eyes widened again. "He never told me. He should have told me." She looked up at Morrison. "He was—he liked to keep family business in the family. And I was a disgrace, he said, when I asked why I couldn't attend a family gathering. Then he died unexpectedly." She looked down, read the next paragraph in silence. "So—this says my brother would be my guardian after my father died, but he never said anything about this contract, either. Things did change—my husband died—"

"You were married?"

"Oh, yes. For a few years. My father insisted; he arranged it all. It would make me seem normal, he said. My husband was older, a distant relative, a widower. My father trusted him to keep family secrets in the family. He was gentle and put up with my—my nightmares and things without complaint."

Morrison tried to imagine what it had been like for the young girl, a survivor who if not convicted of war crimes would have been treated for combat trauma, not criminal insanity.

Morrison believed her. "Is your brother still alive?"

"No, he died . . . twenty years ago or so. The guardianship would have passed to either Gerry or Stavros, probably Stavros as the elder. Neither of them said anything about it. They kept me busy in the company, but that's all."

"What did you do in the company?"

"Security. Typical commercial stuff—competitors always want to know financial details they can use. Sabotage of products or production lines or other company infrastructure. We're diversified—not just a transport service anymore, and not limited to one planet. Vatta Transport alone has land, sea, and air cargo service here, and we're a major interplanetary shipper in this quadrant. We have both scheduled and chartered service. Then Gerry, Ky's father, expanded the tik plantation on Corleigh, gradually buying out others, and we moved into other products, as well. I supervised security procedures, researched new markets for possible dangers—political instability, for instance." She paused, shook her head, then went on. "They didn't want me traveling offplanet, so I had to train others when we needed someone on the ground in another system."

"Do you think your brother and your—nephews, would it be?—knew about the contract? Wouldn't your father have passed it on?"

"If he'd lived longer; if he'd foreseen his death. But if he had, I'm fairly sure my brother would have told me, and his own heir."

"Mmm." Morrison thought about that. It seemed a risky approach, but after all the family was civilian. And yet this file existed, with all the data. Where had it come from? Who had left it at her house?

"I'm wondering where this file has been all these decades," the Rector said, echoing her thought. "Someone's had it, or known where it was. If they knew what was in it, why didn't they protest when I was brought into the government? A protest would have succeeded—I'd have refused the appointment. It couldn't have been kept at Vatta headquarters; that was utterly destroyed in the explosion, and so were the libraries on Corleigh."

"I don't know," Morrison said. "But I'm willing to bet that whoever placed it in my quarters made a copy."

"Oh, obviously," the Rector said. "Of course they would. More than one. I wonder who they most wanted to get in trouble, me or you? If someone had found you reading it and told me—they might think I'd suspect you of something dire."

"Meaning you don't."

"Meaning I don't, that's right. Why would I?"

"Rector, I'm from Esterance. I might have known something about you through the family—"

"Did you?"

"No. Well before my time. Even before my parents' time. I knew very little of you at all, until you became Rector and intersected with my duties."

"Well, then. You've read it, or some of it, and you know what I was charged with—and was guilty of—so let's get to the meat. Will you work with me to get those people free of the mess they're in and back with their families, beyond harm?"

"If that's your intent, absolutely."

"Good. I don't know how long I'll remain Rector, but we need to fix this quickly, before someone else with different . . . um . . . priorities takes over. Stella Vatta, who has reasons to visit me, and lives in the house where Ky and the three who escaped are staying, can carry word from here to there. You know where they're held now, or soon will be held, I gather?"

"Yes. And we have at most ten—no, five days now—before the first of the dispersed groups is moved there. The place was full; it's taken time to move the others out quietly and without notice to make room for them." Morrison looked down at the Rector's hands, folded now on the desk; she had pushed the file aside. One old, dry, wrinkled; the other smooth, obviously young. For a moment she wondered how it felt to live with one limb so obviously younger than the others.

"Do you have any information on what they'll use for transportation or more details on the schedule?"

"My guess is they'll use vehicles that look civilian, at least part of the way, if they're worried about a rescue attempt," Morrison said. "And the committee did not define a particular schedule, only an end point. Which they might well ignore. We must hope they don't expect a rescue."

"They tried turning off the vehicles' tracking codes originally," the Rector said. "Ky's got a crew who managed to locate some of them, including Clemmander, that way. But they could use more information from you."

"I'll write them for you." Morrison reached across to the pad of paper and quickly wrote down all the names, locations, and contact codes she had. "I don't know many of the names. We were introduced

to a Lieutenant Colonel Oriondo and a Doctor Hastile at Clemmander. Oriondo was supposed to be the military watchdog for all
the rehab centers in that region; I haven't enough access through my
office to find out if he's got a history of that assignment or not. I didn't
like Doctor Hastile, if that means anything. When I asked permission
to meet with the survivors separately, he made it clear that if I did I'd
have to be quarantined for ten days or more. I took it as a threat."

"Wise," the Rector said, nodding. "Do you know their first names?"

"Only the initials that were on their badges. M. T. Oriondo and
R. J. Hastile."

"That's a big help, Sergeant Major."

"Rector, I'd be careful doing deep searches on them. If they're involved in some kind of conspiracy, they'll be watching."

The Rector grinned. "Grandmothers. Eggs."

"Sorry, Rector."

"Don't be. I appreciate warnings. But as Rector I can decide we
need to . . . oh . . . review all contracts related to military rehabilitation, starting way over on the other side of the planet and working our
way back to this continent, where of course we don't expect to find
any irregularities because it's the main one and the seat of HQ."

"I worry—they'd be so easy to kill in the state they're in now. And
if the others move up the timing . . ."

The Rector's expression sobered. "Yes. I know that. It's my intention
to probe only enough to come up with a feasible plan to get them out
before that happens, and then go after the bad guys."

"You'll need some military personnel with valid IDs to help," Morrison said. "But they must not be associated with anyone in the
conspiracy—that will take time."

"Will it?" The Rector leaned forward. "I suspect if we check with
the three survivors who got out, we can get some names of those col-
leagues who would be reliable."

"Unless they were assigned to that shuttle not as an honor but to
get rid of them," Morrison said.

"That . . . had not occurred to me." The Rector scowled at the desktop. "I wonder what kind of mind would think that up. I suppose similar to the one that decided to destroy the Vatta family to . . . accomplish something I still haven't quite figured out. Still, there's got to be some high-level person who could help us with this. Someone other than me, that is. Or you, since you've already been targeted by someone involved."

"There are the branch sergeant majors," Morrison said. "We all know each other, and—it's hard to think of any of them being involved in something like this."

"Ky found it hard to believe Master Sergeant Marek was the traitor in Miksland," the Rector said. "He nearly killed her."

"I thought *she* killed *him*. Wondered what for."

"For his second attempt to kill her. Briefly, he rewired her quarters to make using the outlets lethal. She discovered the problem. He realized she was suspicious; she anticipated that, and when he shot at her, she killed him. She can tell you more."

"How did the others take it?"

"Shocked. Horrified. Ky ordered Gossin, as senior NCO, to make a full investigation for later judicial inquiry and gave her custody of the data. That, and the fact that Marek had clearly shot first, settled things down. If we had the evidence Ky had insisted be collected, we'd know whether the Cascadian woman was killed by a ricochet or a direct hit."

"Marek wouldn't have had a weapon on the shuttle—"

"No—this was after they were underground. There was an armory, and a former commander in that secret base had also left a weapon in his desk. Marek got a junior enlisted to change the code so it could be palm-locked to Marek."

Morrison could scarcely believe a master sergeant would do that. But the Rector went on.

"Ky thinks he was threatened, sometime earlier, and that's what pushed him to it. Says she knew he was conflicted, and figures he was trying to save the others from the people who had pressured him. He might talk them into keeping a secret, but Ky—well, you don't know Ky, but—"

"I've met her," Morrison said. "She wouldn't lie."

"Not even when it's in her interest," the Rector said. "We had the hardest time pounding manners into that girl. Said what she thought. I will say, she never shirked the consequences." She shook her head, then looked at Morrison, those old gray eyes fierce. "We are going to get those people out. If you think of anything, any clue, any new bit of information, call me or come, day or night. We can't do it without you; you have the current knowledge. And none of us can do it alone."

Sera Lane was waiting outside when Ky finished the next two hours of downloading from her implant. "I'm making progress," she said. "We aren't there yet, but Immigration has at least agreed that your application for reconsideration of citizenship is not, as they originally insisted, two hundred days overdue. Also that you did not bring a warship here with intent to make war on Slotter Key, and did not keep it here for the length of time it stayed—that, on the contrary, you were unable to communicate with anyone until after it had already left, though on that I'm not entirely sure. When did you first contact someone off the continent?"

"When did the ship leave?" Ky asked. She didn't intend to tell anyone exactly when, certainly not someone who might feel obligated to pass it on to Immigration. She could imagine them deciding that she could have found out about the deadlines from Rafe—though he hadn't known—and then still insisting she should have applied sooner.

"You don't know?"

"No. It was gone when I came back. I was told it had left sometime before, but the only contact I've had was one-way: a message from my—from Space Defense headquarters—informing me that due to my long absence, my death was assumed and a successor had taken command of Space Defense Force—"

"Your fleet? The one you created?"

"Yes. That message said SDF were intending to forward back pay up through the date of change of command to my next of kin, but the Moscoe Confederation put a lock on my funds banked within that system."

"Because of their concern about your aide's death, yes. That was in your first statement." She paused. "You have no idea if you had any contact while your ship was still in Slotter Key nearspace?"

Ky tried to think back. "Just as we were going down I managed to contact them, but then communication cut off. I remember Rafe or Aunt Grace—don't remember which—didn't want the ship to know we were alive because if someone hacked that conversation they might move up their attack. But then the ship left; the next time I mentioned it they said it had gone. I know I didn't talk directly to the ship at all."

"You were, however, in contact with your great-aunt before you were rescued. She did not mention the change in law to you at any point?"

"I did not speak to her, but to Rafe; he arranged the special shielding for the skullphone link. He never said anything, but if she'd mentioned it to him, I'm sure he would have said something. I imagine she thought—"

"Please, Sera Ky, what you imagined is not useful in this context. What I need to know is exactly who said what to whom, and when. The law is very . . . practical."

The law did not seem practical to Ky. It seemed—here and in every system where she'd had to deal with it—to be formed of the whims of the lawmakers who just wanted their own notions made into walls and bars. Best not to say that to an attorney.

Sera Lane tipped her head to one side. "You think it's not practical, don't you? Young people often do. But like my supposition about what you're thinking right now, people are imperfect mind readers. What someone believes another person thinks is often wrong. That's why the law—our system of law—relies on the closest thing we can get to a fact: observed behavior, acts, and words."

COMMANDANT'S OFFICE
DAY 7

Iskin Kvannis looked at the latest iteration of the plan to move the survivors into one facility—a facility cleared of all other prisoners—and then terminate them. Finally. It should have been over by now, the sealed coffins or urns distributed to the families with due ceremony and deepest apologies for the tragic deaths of their loved ones. With a careful hint that, though of course no charges could be filed, the fault if any lay with Ky Vatta for allowing their family members to come into contact with the dread infectious agent that had killed them.

Everything had taken too long. The debate over whether to call it a plague or a toxin. The debate over where to house the survivors in the first place. Calming the panicky shock of their civilian allies, for whom the notion of planning to kill innocent soldiers, victims of happenstance, rang oddly with the same civilians' eagerness to start a civil war that would certainly kill even more innocents, civilian as well as soldiers. Trying to explain the realities of the situation, trying to persuade the media that there was no story there, just a sad aftermath. Trying to keep legislators pestered by families convinced that there was nothing else to be done but hold the personnel in quarantine. Three of the survivors had escaped before the plan was complete. True, nothing at all had been seen or heard of them since, and they might, as Stornaki kept insisting, have died of exposure. But what if they hadn't?

And now this plan, once more, had holes in it that Kvannis could see easily. Granted, the chosen rehab facility was the easiest to clear out because it had the smallest inmate population. It was remote. The locals—not very local, in fact—had shown almost no interest in it since it was built. What happened there would stay there, as the saying went, and being so remote it had its own facilities for disposing of bodies. All that was good. What was not good was how long it would take, again because of the remote area, and the specific containment needs for its present occupants. The plan proposed a 120-day period for converting the existing cells into the milder captivity suitable to the survivors, who after all did not deserve the smaller, harsher cells. He scrawled UNNECESSARY across that. They wouldn't be there long, and they'd be drugged. What difference did it make?

He marked changes on the rest of the plan, and called Stornaki in. "We need to go with this as marked," he said. "If the Rector recovers enough, if Immigration doesn't hold Ky Vatta, it will become much more difficult, if not impossible."

"Yes, Commandant," Stornaki said.

Later, on his regular afternoon drive, Kvannis stopped to buy a couple of stuffed pastries and a bottle of lemonade; the message to his co-conspirators and the receipt for the purchase both missed the trash can, but a helpful customer put the receipt in, pocketing the scrap of paper.

CHAPTER SEVENTEEN

TRANSPORT OFFICE, JOINT SERVICES HQ
DAY 7

Corporal Hector Mata looked at the information his buddy Irwin handed him and shook his head. "That's not enough. A form 431-B needs more—"

"That's all I've got. That's what the colonel gave me, that and 'Make it happen; your pal in requisitions can do it.'"

"Yes, but I need something for every one of these boxes, or *my* colonel will be on *me* about it. You can't just have transport for six people without their names, their units, and the name of the authorizing officer."

"All I know is what my colonel said—"

"I can't do it, Irwin. Give me something to put in these blanks."

"It's a classified transport, see? Nobody's supposed to know about it. So the colonel didn't tell me, and—"

"Classified? That's not a form 431-B. Classified transports are 433-R. For Restricted."

"My colonel *said,* get your friend in Requisitions to do the form 431-B. He didn't say 433-R. 431-B. C'mon, Hector, just *do* it. Keep us both out of trouble."

The last thing Hector Mata wanted was trouble, with his name up for the next promotion board. But one thing that would get him past sergeant—he hoped—was his meticulous and prompt handling of his administrative duties. Fast, accurate, honest: using the wrong form for a category wasn't. And yet it was never good to put yourself in the middle of a struggle between bosses. His own colonel was out on leave, the major had left on a TDY the day before and wouldn't be back for a week, and the lieutenant in the office was green and not likely to stand up to a colonel's request.

"He's good for it?" Mata asked.

"Of course."

"All right. At least give me some names. It'll take me a few minutes. Don't hang over my shoulder; I hate that."

Irwin handed over a list of names, minus units. Then, when Mata waved a hand at him, Irwin shrugged and went out. Mata went to work. One of the names sounded vaguely familiar, but he couldn't make a connection. Not his problem. He filled in the form as best he could, using the main database to find unit designations. Irwin would probably think he made them up. He did make one of them up, not finding it fast enough. There were a lot of Gossins in the database, several with the same initial. As it was not the correct form for classified transport, he felt smugly certain it was fine to make copies—several—to cover his butt in case something went screwy. He put the copies under his blotter, and when Irwin came back—just long enough away for a visit to the head and the coffee machine—he had the single form with its own triplicate copies attached—blue, pink, yellow—and handed it over.

"There you go. I did kind of get creative with the other boxes; hope your colonel won't mind."

"He won't. Thanks, Hector. Owe you one."

When Irwin was gone, Mata thought about it, and then dug into the database again. What was tickling his memory? It was later that day, when—after working on a half dozen other things—he remembered. Several of those names had been mentioned in the media coverage of the shuttle crash that killed the Commandant of the Academy.

It did not take long to find out that the names he'd been given were listed, just once, as survivors of that situation. Survivors, he realized, who had never been seen on the vid. Never been interviewed. Nothing had been heard of them since their return. Why would someone want the wrong form for the classified transport of those particular individuals? The same instinct that had kept him from investing in his second cousin's pyramid investment scheme, from buying a vehicle from a salesman later prosecuted for selling stolen ones as legitimate secondhand, from marrying a handsome and charming man who (it turned out) had murdered two previous spouses . . . told him this stank like week-old dead fish.

Without letting himself think further about it that afternoon, Mata quietly put the copies he'd made into an unmarked folder, went to the head where he slid the papers under his shirt and taped them flat so they wouldn't rustle, and spent the last twenty minutes of his shift doing his usual end-of-the-day filing and straightening, to leave the desk clean and ready for the next shift. On the way out of the building, he greeted the guard the same as always, indicating his plan for a beer at Shelby's before an evening watching the Port Major/Grinock Bay match in the semifinals, and then drove off-base to consider what to do next.

Shelby's was no place to sit and think clearly—the pregame crowd was there and already getting loud, but he drank his beer as usual, then went out looking for ideas. Who should he contact? Not his boss, who was away. By no means the green lieutenant, of whom he had formed no very flattering opinion. This could be serious, something bad going on that someone—someone senior to himself—should know about. He worked his way up the grade levels he knew. He wanted at least a staff sergeant, maybe a master sergeant—but none of those he thought of were exactly right. Then it hit him. Sergeant Major Morrison. Anyone could contact her, ask her advice. Known as a straight arrow, absolutely honest and as picky about doing things right as he was himself. Maybe more so. He'd been to some programs she did for junior enlisted.

And scuttlebutt had it she wasn't staying on base right now, but at her city quarters, because some idiot had broken in and messed with her quarters and her office, and her dog had been hurt. What he was worried about couldn't be the same thing—but she might be more willing to listen since she'd had trouble herself. And his skullphone had her number in it, since it had been available to anyone and he was, as well as meticulous about his work, careful to put possibly useful phone numbers in his implant.

It wasn't too late to call.

Sergeant Major Morrison packed everything in her closet in a case for delivery to her alternative housing—the apartment first rented for the Rector. When she arrived, she showed the key to the doorman, who gave her directions to the correct elevator.

She felt a certain grim amusement at the change: this building was only a few blocks away from her own, but decidedly more upscale, from the plantings out front to the stylish lobby, the carpeting in the halls, and the size of the rooms. The view from the windows here looked east and north—a corner suite—and she could see between other buildings the beginning of Government Place, where the Rector's office, the House of Laws, Government House, and the Presidential Palace sat in their wide lawns around the vast public plaza and gardens.

She had been in hotel suites of this size, years back when she'd splurged on a vacation in Makkavo with several friends. The kitchen—much larger than the kitchenette in her own apartment—would hold at least three people busily at work—staff, of course. She looked over the supplies and decided that since she couldn't put her clothes away until the case arrived, she would find a grocery and purchase a few of her favorites.

When she came back, her case had been delivered to the suite, just as it might have in a hotel. She put her clothes away in the bedroom next to the larger bath, set out the necessary toiletries on the counter in the bathroom in the same order as in her own quarters. She put the water on for tea, and anticipated a quiet evening in which no one but Kris at the vet clinic knew where she was. And the Rector, but she had looked tired and was probably headed for an early bed.

It was after duty hours now; she might as well change into civvies and relax. But even as she headed to the bedroom to change, her skullphone pinged. It was always something, she thought, as she answered.

"Sergeant Major, this is Corporal Mata, transport division. I have a—a kind of a problem and I don't quite know where to go . . ."

A young voice, so the problem was likely to be related to sex, money, or needing leave for family reasons.

"I know it's after hours, Sergeant Major, and I'm sorry, but my colonel's on leave, the major's on TDY, and the lieutenant . . ."

His voice trailed off again. Morrison recognized every tone. A competent corporal, who would have trusted his commander, but didn't trust the lieutenant, so the problem likely involved another command chain, where the lieutenant didn't have the rank to stand up to someone. It would be one of those tedious situations, where the two officers at the top of their respective commands had had a difference, and the corporal felt trapped.

"Go ahead, Corporal Mata. What's the problem?"

"It's kind of hard to explain, Sergeant Major, like this. I'm, uh, in a bar."

That didn't sound good.

"Because it's noisy and no one can hear if I murmur, but if it's at all possible, I need to see you. Tonight, if—"

Whatever it was had to be urgent. And if he really did have a problem that required a personal visit with the sergeant major, then she'd have to stay in uniform. Well. Duty called in many ways; she gave him the address.

"Thank you, Sergeant Major," he said, relief clear in his voice. "I'll be taking the tram in from here."

That was a bit odd, if he had his own vehicle. But she agreed, then looked up the schedule and realized she had twenty minutes she could spend making notes in her implant from her meeting with the Rector.

Mata, when he arrived, proved to be a short, square-built young man with the slight furrow in his brow she'd often noted with clerks in every division. His uniform was immaculate, his eyes clear with no clouding from drink or drugs, and his hand, when she shook it was firm and dry. All good signs.

"Come in," Morrison said. She led him into the dining area, where she'd laid the files she'd brought on the polished table. Grace Vatta's file was already locked in the suite's safe. She noticed the slight relaxation when he saw a table with files and a teacup, familiar territory. "Have a seat. Do you want water or anything?"

"No, Sergeant Major. I'm fine." He sat down after she did, across the table from her.

"You realize I need to record whatever you tell me that bears on official business?" He nodded. "Good. So—what's the story?" She flicked on the recorder built into the table.

The story, as he told it, brought up the gooseflesh on her arms, even before he mentioned the names.

"Do you have a copy?" she asked.

"Yes, Sergeant Major. Since it's supposed to be a classified transport I really shouldn't have, but Irwin—Corporal Irwin, that is—said his colonel insisted on a form 431-B. Classified transports are 433-R. So it's not a classified form I made copies of, only that the transport's supposed to be classified." His look now was pleading.

"Don't worry," Morrison said, even as her own worries multiplied. "Do you have a copy with you?"

"Yes—all of them. I made three: one for the file, and one for my colonel. And one for, um, if it was needed." His face flushed. "I, um, taped them together. Under my shirt."

"You're really worried," Morrison said.

"Yes—it's not *right,* Sergeant Major. It's not just the wrong form, though we have two forms for a reason. If Colonel Higgs had been there, I know he wouldn't have approved."

Morrison knew Higgs; she agreed with that assessment. Higgs was the terror of the base when it came to shady transport requests from those who thought the system should be more flexible. And was this why transport of the survivors to a single location had not been immediate: waiting for Higgs to be away on leave? Had someone sent his second, Major Vargas, on TDY to clear the way?

"How long has the lieutenant been in your office?" she asked. "Fairly new or there for . . . say, the past year?"

"Twenty-six days," Mata said, in the tone that conveyed *too long.* "He's—I shouldn't criticize an officer—"

Morrison shook her head. "We both work for a living, Mata: spit it out. With his name."

"Lieutenant Andres Marban. He graduated three years ago and missed his promotion board for O-3. He looks good enough, but he's always wandering off somewhere. I heard . . ." A pause in which it was clear Mata realized he might be accused of eavesdropping; she was pleased to note that he didn't mention it or make up some excuse. "The major ripped into him four days ago—that's Major Vargas and she's, um, easily heard—about something."

"How is he with the office staff?"

A frown. This was not someone eager to criticize officers, another good point. "He's all right. A bit fussy, but then it's important to do things the right way. Only he doesn't, himself. I had something to take to his office and there were red-tabbed files on his desk. He wasn't there."

"Mata, you were right to come to me," Morrison said. "I cannot tell you everything right now—"

"Of course not, Sergeant Major."

"But there have been concerns, at a high level, about the survivors of the shuttle crash. There's been difficulty in finding out more, obstructions. This is a very serious matter, and your information is vital. So is your silence. We may even need to protect you from any suspicion."

"Seriously?"

"Very. Down the passage to the left, there's a bathroom—get the copies out from under your shirt and bring them to me."

He returned in a few minutes, uniform correctly put back together, and handed her the copies.

They were warm from his body; she noticed that first. She was familiar with both of the forms he'd mentioned, and ran her eye down the white page of the first copy. Names, ranks, serial numbers—

"Did the other corporal—Irwin—provide you this information?" If so, the opposition was stupid—and she didn't think they were.

"Not at first, Sergeant Major, not even the names. I told him I had to have names. That's all he'd give me; he said to make up the rest, but hurry. I told him to get out for a little while, let me work. And he did. Then I looked up the names in the all-branch database. The only one I had to make things up for was Gossin—there are a lot of Gossins."

"Staff Sergeant Gossin," Morrison said.

"The database gave me the units of the others, and serial numbers and all. I still didn't have the signature of the requesting officer, but it had to be Irwin's colonel—"

She could see the name in the box: Victor Prelutsky. She'd pull his file out of the database when she and Mata were finished. "I'm going to call someone," she said to Mata. "Sit tight. Have you had supper?"

"No . . ." The uncertainty in his voice, the fear that he would bolt, stopped her for a moment.

"I have bar food," she said. "If you eat fried stuff with cheese on it, and watch the game on my big set, then you'll be able to talk game with the others later, right?"

"Yes," he said, his eyes lighting.

"Good. Turn it on. I'll bring the food in and then call."

Shortly he was settled on the deep soft couch in the suite's living room, watching the game—not as much fun as in a bar for him, she suspected, though these days she preferred being alone to having her shoulders pounded and her ears assaulted by the noise in a sports bar. The microwave made short work of heating up sausage and chicken chunks and melting the cheese. She put it all in a large bowl, on a large tray, added two kitchen towels, and set that on the table in front of the couch.

"I should warn you, I borrowed this apartment for a few days from a civilian, so we need to be careful about spillage. You would be anyway, but add another fifty percent."

"Yes, Sergeant Major."

"But don't go hungry. I'll be back shortly."

Mata turned the volume up on the vid, not too loud but loud enough to cover whatever she said; she leaned against the doorframe in the bedroom and called MacRobert's number.

"Sergeant Major."

"Yes. I have just had a most interesting conversation with someone who works on base. It may be connected."

"Yes?"

"Is Sera Vatta available?"

"I see. I will inquire."

"Sergeant Major." That was the Rector. "You have important news?"

"Yes. Not all that we need, but more names than we had before."

"Can you come now?"

"No. I'm concerned about the informant. He'll be missed if not on duty tomorrow."

"Suspected?"

"Possibly."

"We really can't stash another at Helen's." Grim amusement colored the Rector's voice. "Assessment of this individual's acting ability?"

"Moderate. He's watching the ball game and eating bar snacks."

"Well, that's normal enough. Drunk or sober?"

"Only one beer, not here. Sober enough."

"We'll call you back with a plan."

Morrison joined Mata in the living room. "Who's winning?"

"Port Major, but Grinock Bay's not far behind."

Grace had not yet been asleep—strange place, strange bed, strangeness all around—but lying eyes closed, thinking. Now, wrapped in a new robe, she sat at the kitchenette table watching Mac make coffee. "I wonder what fell out of the tree into the sergeant major's lap to make her so tense?"

"She's experienced, and she knows the problem. It won't be trivial."

"Oh, I'm sure of that. And now I'm hungry. She's got a person she wants to protect—not another of the survivors, or she'd have said, which means it's someone in the military, someone who found out something that bothered him or her and she needs . . ."

"Command," Mac said, setting a cup of coffee down beside her and handing her one of the rolls he'd bought. "She can probably think up a plan, but she wants someone to tell her so."

"It never bothered you to act independently," Grace said, eyeing him over the rim of her cup.

"It did at first. A long time, in fact. I got over it."

"Well, then, what's the best approach to help her and her informant?"

"Get the informant back to the base and duty as soon as possible, with instructions to keep his or her mouth shut and act like nothing happened. Informant should take mild precautions. No alcohol at all, no drugs other than regular prescriptions. No comments about the sergeant major and no contact with her; she will contact the informant when it's safe on her end, whenever that may be."

"I'll call her . . ."

"Eat, then call."

"How secure are her communications over there?"

"As much as here; it was set up for you, remember."

＊ ＊ ＊

Sergeant Major Morrison listened to Grace's suggestions silently, then said, "How can I get the hardcopy to you?"

"Via MacRobert. How many copies are there?"

"Three complete—that is, with the multiples intact. They'd all fit in a 25 x 33 centimeter folder. The relevant officer's name is in the right box, but not his signature; these copies were made by the clerk because he was upset by the officer's insistence that he use the wrong form. I'm thinking they should be dispersed and that I probably should not have one. The essential data's now in my implant."

"Bless finicky and honest clerks," Grace said. "I trust you. Work out your own contact protocol with him."

"Do you want his name?"

"Not at this time. Make sure you have it noted in more than one place—and perhaps that Security officer you mentioned—Major Hong?"

"Yes, Rector; I'll see to it."

"Send your informant on his way, then, and MacRobert will pick them up within the hour. Thank you, Sergeant Major; you're being extremely helpful."

"I'm also more worried about the other survivors. If they're cutting orders to transport—"

"So am I," Grace said. "Once I see the hardcopies, and dig through the other databases available to me, we should be able to get things rolling on a response."

"Thank you, Rector."

"That's it for now, then," Grace said. "MacRobert will be on his way when you've assured us your informant is gone."

"Ten minutes," Morrison said. "Not more than fifteen." She sounded, to Grace's ear, slightly less anxious but still grim.

"Marching orders," Grace said to Mac, when that call ended. "You'll be picking up copies of three complete forms, all the colored bits, and we'll want one to Ky, one to Stella for Vatta files, and one for us to pore over."

"You should get some sleep—you're still not completely recovered."

"I could not possibly sleep until I see what the forms say. Fifteen minutes, be at her door."

"Twenty. I don't want to see the individual or have the individual see me. Plausible deniability." His mouth quirked.

"Your mission; your choice." Grace looked around the kitchenette. "This place is too small to make fruitcakes and I really do feel the need to make them."

"When did you start making fruitcakes?"

"In the psychiatric prison. We made them and the prison sold them to raise money for the prisoners' canteen, little treats we could then earn good behavior points for."

Mac stared at her, appalled. The grin she sent back was pure mischief. "They let *you*—you of all people—make—"

"Fruitcakes. Yes. The last four years I was there. I was being very good and kitchen work was a reward. And of course they were *just* fruitcakes, not any of my *special* fruitcakes. And though I never did it, others in the same facility working in the kitchen did, from time to time, try to drop things into the batter and make a special design on top so some family member would buy it and they could pass things in and out. Usually got caught, but it's how I found out what you could bake at 175°C degrees and not ruin it. Including, once, poison that one of the women got hold of, to poison her family because they hadn't gotten her released. I wasn't suspected; my crimes were all violent, not sneaky. They caught her; I never saw her again."

Mac said nothing for a moment, then said, "What of yours can I stick in my briefcase, something plausible to claim was left there when we cleared it to switch with the sergeant major? My excuse for going?"

"Spare lenses. You know I have multiple pairs, and after I got up from a nap, I discovered that the blue-tinted ones with the special prescription for reading at night in dimmer light weren't with the rest." She got up and fetched them. "Here you are."

Mac made the trip to the sergeant major and back without incident. "She told him to keep quiet, and he said he would. She said he's smart and he had already figured out he had hold of dangerous information."

"Let's see what we've got." Grace looked at the first form. "Transport, Personnel, Routine Duty Station Transfer . . ."

"The sergeant major also gave me her sitrep and her assessment of the personnel she's been in contact with. She thinks several in the assessment committee—though not the chair—were part of whatever group is behind the secrecy. She's not sure about the commander who chose the committee; there could have been manipulation to make those members seem best suited."

"Does she think it all goes back to the Unification War?"

"Not exactly—it's older than that, but that may be when its focus changed from keeping Miksland's economic potential secret to involving the military. She hasn't been able to dig into the history—both lack of time and compromise of security in her office and quarters."

"But we can do that." Grace nodded. "We were on the right track, but we, too, ran out of time. Two parts to this. Immediately, we need to find those survivors before they're permanently silenced, either by the drug effects or death. We can do that, thanks to this Corporal Mata. We don't have to know the whole history until those people are safe. But then—"

"We need to know enough history so we can anticipate the source of interference with the rescue," Mac said.

"Agreed. But not the whole story until afterward." Grace tapped the form in front of her. "And we need more copies, then really secure storage options."

"You said one to Stella, one to Ky: both those should be safe enough. And we need one. Though all three copies with Vattas is risky." Mac picked up one of the copies and headed for the living room. "I'll make some."

Grace read on. The names were familiar, the same Ky had shared with her. The authorizing officer . . . she'd never heard of. In her office at the Defense Department, or in her own home before the gas attack, she had access to hardened lines to the complete military databases, direct access to all personnel records. Here, despite Mac's attempt to secure her connections, she did not completely trust them.

CHAPTER EIGHTEEN

DAY 8

Stella Vatta had never enjoyed playing courier. Now that she was officially Vatta's CEO and once more officially a Slotter Key citizen, she found it annoying that both Ky and Aunt Grace expected her to keep shuttling their correspondence back and forth just because neither could leave their respective residences. Adding the sergeant major of Slotter Key's military to the list of stops made her furious. Grace Vatta, as Rector of Defense, had plenty of personnel at her command; surely she didn't need to pick on Stella, who had, after all, an interstellar enterprise to run.

She had worked herself into a sizable fury by the time she reached her office, where a man she had not met since they were both teenagers waited in the reception area.

"Benny—Benny *Quindlan*?"

"Yes, Stella—Sera Vatta, I should say, as this is a business visit, not a social one." He looked very grown-up, in his business suit with his expensive briefcase and perfectly polished shoes. "I'm sure you didn't expect a visit from me—"

"No. No, I didn't." Why was he here? Was this about the blast that had brought down Vatta's headquarters six—seven?—years ago? About the trade rivalry that had preceded that? Or . . . what?

"I would prefer to speak privately," he said, with a frosty glance at her receptionist.

"Sera Stella, your schedule—" her receptionist said.

"Clear me fifteen minutes," Stella said. "Benny, come on. Fifteen minutes is literally all I can spare until this evening."

"Thank you," he said, without any hint of meekness, and followed her into her office. She was glad in that moment that she had sent the delicate little desk her mother had used back to storage, and found a plain, moderate-sized one instead. She had also changed out the spindly-legged chairs for solid ones that could take a man's weight without wobbling.

"Have a seat," she said, going behind her desk. "What is it?"

He sat but did not lean back, hands crossed on top of the briefcase balanced on his thighs. "I am in a difficult position," he began.

"We all are," Stella said. The vid-plate on her desk writhed as her receptionist wangled minutes out of a schedule already crowded. He flushed; he'd always had a pink face that reddened easily.

"Sorry," he said. "I know our families have been competitors and sometimes enemies for a long time. When I learned—when I heard—about the explosives—"

"You were appalled, of course. Get on with it."

"It's this." Without further verbal delay he opened the briefcase and removed a file, which he laid on Stella's desk. "I now know why our families were enemies. It's in there. That's a photographic copy of the file, and if my uncle finds out I've given it to you, he will kill me—literally—me and my wife and our twins. If he knew I had entered this building without his explicit order he would terminate my employment and all contact with the family. Luckily, he *did* order me to enter this building and give you a message from him, which I will in a moment. This"—he laid his hand on the file—"is not his message. This is my—I suppose you could say my atonement for the death of your father. I didn't know about the explosives until afterward, but I still feel . . . anyway. This is my uncle's message, to be delivered word for word."

He took a deep breath, pulled a sheet from the briefcase, and read from it in an expressionless voice. "If you think this is over, you are wrong. It will never be over until Grace Lane Vatta, that murdering traitorous bitch, is dead, and also every offspring of Stavros Vatta and Gerard Vatta. I have no quarrel with other Vattas, and intend nothing but a measured, appropriate response to what wrongs were done the Quindlan family. I had nothing to do with the offplanet attacks on Vatta; that was their own family. I may hope that Vatta Enterprises collapses, but if some distant cousin can take over, I don't care. Signed, Michael Quindlan." Benny Quindlan's hand shook slightly as he shoved the paper back in his briefcase. "I tried to talk him out of it. I couldn't. That's all. I have to go." He snapped the briefcase closed, stood up, and was almost to the door before Stella could find her voice.

"Benny—"

He stopped and turned. Face professionally blank, but she saw pain in his eyes.

"I don't hate you, Benny."

"You may after you read that."

"No. I won't. I will fight to live and save my family, but I won't hate *you*."

He nodded without saying anything, opened the door, and let himself out.

Every offspring of Gerard and Stavros. Quindlan had come close before, and killed more than that both at Vatta headquarters and on Corleigh. She and Ky and Jo's young twins had been the only survivors, and now Quindlan was still determined to kill them all. But maybe not Toby, if she could trust that—and why should she? Except that the note had sounded desperate, like someone at the end of his strength, determined to finish something he'd promised to accomplish long ago. And her job, her one job now, was to see that she and Ky and the twins stayed alive until . . . could any truce last, even if one could be negotiated? And then it dawned on her: she was not an offspring of Stavros Vatta. Would the Quindlans believe her? Not Michael, she was sure. He gave the orders others followed; his sending Benny was an unsubtle signal that the boy who'd once had a crush on her was now his uncle's obedient servant.

Her assistant pinged her. Whatever was in the file Benny had delivered would have to wait; she had a long day's work ahead of her already. She put the file into her private safe and put a serene smile on her face for her first scheduled appointment.

Midmorning she did manage to call the house and let Ky know that the Quindlans were still dangerous and after blood.

"So am I," Ky said. "If I knew whether they were involved in the military thing—"

"Never mind that. Is Sera Lane there?"

"Yes. She's frustrated that she can't get downloads from the others' implants."

"If she's not busy, ask her to come here—and bring Rodney—because I have something I want her to see that I can't talk about even over a secured line."

"Don't shut me out—"

"I'm not. She can take it back with her. Less obviously than I can send a courier."

"I'll tell her." Ky switched off.

Stella rolled her eyes and made a face at her desk before heading to the conference room for her next appointment.

Ky had spent the morning working on her own rescue plan—much of it on the organization she knew they needed. It had all been casual up to now, but the mission itself would be anything but. She used what she had learned talking to all the others—especially Teague, Rafe, and Rodney—and had just finished some organizational charts when Stella called. Ky gave Sera Lane and Rodney their orders, then went into the kitchen, where the two women were busy helping Barash with the prep for the rest of the day's cooking.

Despite their continuing peril, they looked relaxed and cheerful as they worked and chatted, each with a cutting board and knife and stack of vegetables. Chairs scraped as Ky appeared; she waved them down. "The lawyer's gone off to Vatta headquarters; she may be there all day, but she'll still be working on our problems." She pulled out a chair for herself and sat down. "Rodney's gone with her. Something's going on with the Rector and the sergeant major; I expect Rodney to come back with some useful information."

"How much longer do we have?" Kamat asked. The swelling in her face had gone down, and with a scarf wrapped around her head, her exotic beauty showed again.

"Not long. It's time for more detailed planning. When you're through here, after lunch, we'll go downstairs and get started on the next phase."

Rafe came into the kitchen, poured himself some water, and leaned on the counter. "We're discussing tactics finally?"

"About to," Ky said. "We've got the skeleton plan, all but where to take them after we've got them. And it's time"—past time; she should have done this earlier—"to compartmentalize, let each one concentrate on a particular area of responsibility. Communications, surveillance, transport, medical, assault teams, local and community support, countermeasures."

"There's not that many of us," Rafe said. "You know we need more people."

"Yes. And the sergeant major is working on that with Aunt Grace. Each subunit will have a contact person, a leader. Just one. Only the leader will know who else is in the unit. Inyatta, you have relatives in the region we're going to. You are the liaison for local support there.

Rodney has connections with local militia; he'll be the liaison for those personnel; everything they need to do will come from him. And so on: I made charts."

"Based on what?" Rafe asked.

"On what we know so far. We can't expect the charts to cover everything yet, but they'll help us analyze what else we need to know."

"I need to know how to get more ammunition," Rafe said.

"Done," Ky said. "Rodney knows a supplier; he'll arrange that. Just be sure he knows what you need." She looked at the women again. "One thing I need to know—and forgot to ask before—is how long it took you to recover from the drugs. How soon could you walk steadily across a room, or use stairs?"

The three looked at one another. "I don't know," Inyatta said after a moment. "I can't remember what it was like when we first got there, at all. I know that right after we escaped, we had trouble—our balance was off, we were shaky. If we hadn't been so scared, we couldn't have made it even a kilometer. If we hadn't found a place to hide until that wore off, we'd have been caught for sure."

"So . . . those we rescue may not be able to walk from one vehicle to another," Ky said.

"They might be unconscious," Rafe said.

"Takes more staff to ensure they don't choke," Ky said. "But basically, we can't count on any help from them—we have to be prepared to unload and load them."

"If the others are rescued, I'm sure they'll try to help," Kamat said. "But how can we possibly help them while we're stuck in this house?"

"One way or another, we aren't going to stay here," Ky said. "Even if we have to climb the back garden wall and crawl down it the way you did getting in. But I'm hoping Sera Lane will get Rafe, Teague, and me set straight with Immigration—then we can get out more easily. You three—you can't be risked; if our mission fails, you're the only ones who can testify to what happened to you, and them."

"I wonder if the media could help," Rafe said. Ky turned to stare, and he waved a hand at her. "No, listen. Right now the other side has a secret they want kept. What if rumors got out that such a secret existed—"

"They'd kill them," Ky and the others said, voices clashing with intensity.

"I don't think so," Rafe said. "That many deaths are hard to hide. What if the question came from some of the family members? They haven't been allowed to see their loved ones—even if they're in the throes of a bad plague, they should at least be allowed to see them, talk to the doctors, all that. Betange has dependent siblings—there's a tear-jerking story for you. For them. Kind of thing they love. Who's taking care of those kids now?"

"But the rules—someone has to be suppressing the news about them already—"

"It's too juicy a story," Rafe said. "After all, they were willing to buck the system to embarrass the Academy ten years ago. As long as it's from the families, not anyone here in Port Major. We can use Teague to make contact."

"You called?" Teague said from the doorway.

"We're into the detailed planning now. I'm thinking if we tickled the families of the other survivors—even yours—" Rafe looked from one face to another. "—they might be willing to complain publicly about the lack of information and contact. And that might attract media attention, and be a cover for our own fact-finding and actions."

"Have you finalized the other necessary parts of the operation while I was downstairs picking satellite images?"

"Some," Ky said. "I charted a command structure this morning, and tentative assignments for everyone. We know how many other survivors—if they're all still alive—and where they'll be taken, but I don't know even how many vehicles—trucks, vans, ambulances?—we would need, or the medical staffing. This isn't like anything I've ever done—"

"But I have," Teague reminded her, calm in the face of her temper. "If this were Gary's org, we'd want the information I was bringing, plus at least three hostage rescue teams. Rafe saw Gary's in action. We don't have those connections here, but I've been talking to Rodney about some of his friends. And since these are actual military we're planning to deal with, I will bet that some other enlisted—not part of the scheme—would be eager to help their comrades."

"Probably," Barash said, with a glance at Inyatta, "except that we're taught to follow orders. Most would just push it up the chain of command, and how do we know the top of the chain isn't corrupt?"

"Ex-military, then?" Teague asked.

"Maybe—probably," Inyatta said. "But we three—we don't know that many ex-enlisted. I don't, anyway."

"Sergeant Major Morrison does," Ky said. "She may have friends among them with the skills we need. We need to see her again."

"She's being surveilled," Teague reminded them.

"Teague, can you give me a list? Everything your employer would use for something like this?"

"Show me your charts; I can probably fill in some things."

Lunch wasn't mentioned again. They all moved downstairs to the bunker, and Teague began talking. "Pre-zero: survey the relevant locations, decide on the ideal place for the snatch. Make an educated guess—with Gary it's often certainty—about the force the other side has. Arrange for the extrication teams, post-extrication extraction from the location, and post-extraction medical and other care needs in a secure location. Slotter Key doesn't have nearly the surveillance that Nexus Two has, but in this instance we're talking about countering an official force, which is different and likely will have excellent surveillance."

"Say—three or four survivors to extricate, possibly unable to ambulate or talk."

"Mobile or static situation?"

"Mobile—we wouldn't have to break into a facility."

"Okay—you need a convincing reason for the vehicle to have to stop, something they won't immediately suspect, so they don't call for help or start shooting right away. Do you want to kill people or not?"

Ky stared a moment. She had considered Teague a neutral civilian, not a criminal. Now she wondered. "Um—would prefer not to kill anyone we don't have to."

"Then you need a knockdown drug and delivery system. Can be conventional-looking firearms, if your crew has a reason to carry them, or another method. A way of breaking into the vehicles they're using. A way of moving your survivors—if they can't walk, or if they're partially ambulatory and might struggle. Two to a survivor. Plus whoever's gaining control of the vehicle. If they're on movable gurneys, that's handy; you just unlatch them and go."

He stopped; Ky said nothing, and he started again. "The slickest of all, though I can't think how we'd coordinate that over the several holding facilities, is to replace the vehicle that's supposed to transport them with our vehicle. Would work in a vid, maybe, but probably not in practice."

"It might for one of them," Rafe said.

"Morrison says they're coming from different places, different directions. So they'll be using multiple vehicles. We know there's just one road in—" Ky scowled at the table, thinking hard. "They still want to keep this under wraps—someone still thinks it's possible to keep control of the knowledge about Miksland. For all we know they've moved their people back in."

"That's not going to work long-term," Teague said. "Both sets of mercs know about it, and I doubt either set will obey a nondisclosure agreement even if they signed one. Every soldier who trained down there knows about it. Eventually it's bound to leak out—"

"And they should know that. Someone on that side should know that; they aren't stupid or they'd have made bad mistakes before." Ky took a breath as another possibility came to her. "They *do* know it, and they don't expect the secrecy to hold forever, just long enough for—for something else. Whatever—" She paused again, then spoke as the idea came clear. "Whatever Greyhaus and those troops were training for. What do you want a secret military force for?" She looked around.

"A war," Inyatta said. "They were going to start a *war*? Why?"

"The usual reason is to overthrow the government," Rafe said. "But why?"

"And when?" Ky said. "If they're aiming to start a war and need to keep it secret until they're ready, then the survivors are definitely in their way." She pushed that issue aside. "Teague, let's get back to the actual mission planning."

"So how many people are we trying to rescue?" Teague asked.

"Fourteen, if they all survived. Seventeen should have come back, and three escaped to us."

"Do we know how many are in each place now?"

"Yes, from Morrison's report. And she's bringing more information later today."

"And where will we be transporting them? Remember, some of them, if not all, will need medical care within a few hours."

"I haven't figured that out yet."

"You forget," Stella said from the doorway, "that you have one asset you haven't mentioned yet."

Ky had not heard her come in. "You're home early."

"Aunt Grace had a message for you—here." She handed over a data-stick and a large envelope. "Sergeant Major Morrison is with me, waiting in the hall. She wants to talk to you. And—as I said—there's an asset you hadn't mentioned."

Ky blinked. "What?"

"Vatta Transport. We and our associates have a planet-wide transportation network—from way back—with trucks, vans, ships, and aircraft constantly on the move. You need to track only four vehicles to find the survivors—they'd have to track thousands of ours."

"Yes, but—"

"On this continent alone, we have warehouses in every city bigger than a hundred thousand, and in some smaller ones where it's convenient to us. At every good-sized airport, we transfer air cargo to ground transport and vice versa. The attack on Vatta concentrated on our headquarters and our space-based transport, but when I finally made it back here I discovered that our air, sea, and ground network had lost only ten percent of its capacity. And we're back to that and above now."

"But we don't have ambulances, do we?"

"No. But you don't have to have an ambulance. How about fitting out one or two of the larger trucks as a mobile clinic? Beds, if you like, or float chairs, or just comfortable furniture. Toilets. We can use regularly scheduled trucks for some of it, just claim that a particular run is oversold, and put another truck on for the deliveries. We've done that before."

Ky looked puzzled. "But I thought you felt this was all—ridiculous. I didn't think you'd want to help."

"Of course I want to help. I don't want any of you killed for lack of resources—" She looked at each in turn. "And it'll cost less than renting vehicles, won't it?" She nodded, looking satisfied at their reaction. "I can't stay—I have appointments downtown."

When Morrison joined the group, briefcase in hand, she had more than just the data in the packages Grace had sent. "I've spoken with the base commander—and here's why I felt that important."

After the first shock—like jumping into a snowbank—Ky understood her reasons.

"And you needed a way to get these personnel back into *safe* military hands," Morrison said, finishing her report. "Trying to hide them somewhere would have created legal problems for everyone involved, military and civilian. I am certain that General Molosay is not part of the conspiracy. When he realized the danger to the survivors of organizing a purely military op, he agreed I could liaise with you and granted the use of three full special ops teams."

Ky nodded. "Thank you, Sergeant Major. That will be a huge help."

Morrison turned to Inyatta. "Corporal, I have new IDs for you, Corporal Barash, and Tech Kamat. Uniforms should arrive in Rector Vatta's apartment by late afternoon, so that you can appear—if you are on the op or not—in your own identities. If you are not part of the op, General Molosay wants you to report to his office on base; transportation can be arranged." She opened her briefcase and handed out the ID packets. "Welcome home."

Ky could see the emotion on their faces; she felt a lump in her own throat. "Thank you, Sergeant Major," she said, her voice a little hoarse.

"My orders are to accompany the first group coming back to Port Major, by whatever means, so I will need to be at whatever collection point you've established. Do you have that information yet?"

"Vatta Transport will be providing transportation," Ky said. "I'd like to fly each group out from the nearest airport—that seems fastest and most secure."

"Weekes City," Rodney put in. "Vatta has regular air freight to and from a ground transport warehouse there. Frequent flights in different sizes of aircraft."

"It will be very soon—as early as tomorrow, no more than three days," Morrison said. "The Rector said she was sure you could be ready by then."

"We can," Ky said, "if we finish the planning now. You can help, if you will."

"Of course."

From there the plan moved quickly.

"Only one way in or out—we want to snatch them before that dead end," Teague said. "You want multiple exits—here's a useful branch, and here as well. Somewhere between three and ten kilometers back. We could even pick up the group coming from the east all the way back here, before they get to that last road."

"You're assuming that air transport will be safe," Morrison said, tapping her finger on that line of the plan.

"They can reach Port Major in four hours," Ky said. "And the first group, at least, will be unexpected."

"Admiral, with respect, there are two air bases between Weekes City and here, and General Molosay, in our conversation, expressed some concerns. Nothing strong enough to act on, but if you met air surveillance or interference—or an air attack on ground movement—"

"And if they figure out which plane," Ky said, nodding. "Vatta planes, like any civilian planes, are unarmed and slower than military interceptors."

"The Joint Services Headquarters has no assets to contribute for that," Morrison said.

Rodney spoke up. "Remember I told you about my friends out in that region? They're all in reserve units. Access to lots of toys that just sit around gathering dust except in summer training. Do 'em good to get some use." Morrison opened her mouth, but shut it again.

"You contact them," Ky said to Rodney. "It's your show and I hope we don't need it."

"The only problem we have left," Teague said, as the patchwork of assets grew larger and more connected, "is a way to make their transports stop long enough for us to get the prisoners—survivors, sorry—out of the vehicles without their people killing them. Faking an accident is the usual way to block a road, but that takes more personnel and vehicles. And we'd have to do it again for each group."

Inyatta held up her hand. "I can do that. Admiral Vatta's given me responsibility for local response because I have relatives in that area. They know people . . . if you'd trust me to tell them and get them involved."

"It'd be dangerous for them," Rafe said.

"They wouldn't mind that," Inyatta said. "They'll want to help. And so will their neighbors, at least some of them."

"Do you have any idea how it might work?" Teague still sounded dubious.

"It's Inyatta's call," Ky said. "You don't need to know. Our drivers will know what to expect, as soon as we have better intel on the trucks or ambulances they're using."

"The group from Clemmander will be first," Morrison said. "Then the one coming in from coastward."

Rodney and Teague moved markers around on the terrain display, each one colored for a particular group.

Hours later, tired and hungry, the group had a plan both Ky and Teague thought was workable, with branches to allow for the unexpected. Inyatta, Barash, and Kamat, with Morrison's approval and assistance, had overcome Ky's reservations about having them part of the actual rescue.

"They can return with me and the first group," Morrison said. "You'll be with them, and then I will."

"If nobody shoots at the plane," Ky said.

"You told Rodney to take care of that," Morrison said.

Ky laughed. "So I did. And he will."

Now they needed to fill all the blank slots in the personnel chart, but Morrison was sure she could find reliable medical assistance and had enough special troops. Ky looked at the terrain map again and again, zooming in and out, jotting down notes for ever more ways to react depending on what happened. She knew she could not possibly anticipate everything—but the more she did anticipate, the better their chances for getting everyone out alive.

DAY 9

Morrison spent the night in the house, and rode into town with Stella in the morning. Ky, watching from her vantage point in the front of the house, saw that the neighbor across the street was strolling around his front yard, poking a stick into flower beds, but in a perfect position to notice how many people were in each of the cars that led or followed Stella. Ky noticed several quick, upward glances toward the window where she stood. Altogether too nosy a neighbor, and she wondered again why Stella didn't seem worried about him.

She'd spoken to Stella about the coming operation—that if they had to leave suddenly, she wouldn't call at the time, for security reasons.

"Are the others going with you?" Stella'd asked.

"Probably not, but they might. I'd rather not risk them, but they want to come."

"But not tomorrow—"

"I don't think so. More likely a day or two more. We could use the time."

CHAPTER NINETEEN

DAY 9

Sera Lane had a smile on her face when she entered the house an hour later than usual. "Progress," she said.

"How much?" Rafe asked, brows raised.

"The arrest warrant for Sera Ky—the one relating to her citizenship—has been canceled. There was considerable pressure to arrest her from someone higher up, but I kept pushing until I found out the undersecretary had been told some rather inventive lies about her and her fiancé. The petition from the Tik Growers' Association in her favor didn't hurt, either."

"Tik Growers' Association?" Ky scowled. Her father had been a member, well liked because he sponsored apprenticeships, but she'd worked only one day in the packing sheds, herself.

"They had made a plaque to present to you for saving everyone from the pirate horde—that's what they called it—and brought it to the spaceport the day you were due to arrive, last spring. Apparently they were not willing to accept that you'd died, and when you returned they were planning a reception and dinner for you. When they found out you were considered an undesirable alien and a murderer, they protested to the President's Council and to Immigration." Her grin widened. "It doesn't hurt that the Tik Growers' Association is a major contributor to the majority party."

"So I can go out?"

"I'm still negotiating with the police to remove their surveillance of this house. With your citizenship in the process of being restored—you have a court date in fifteen days; I will accompany you—they're less likely to haul you in, especially as I pointed out that their prosecutor needed to have actual evidence of murder, which meant getting it from the military and interviewing witnesses. I said we had a witness of good character, competent and believable, who would testify to self-defense, and in the meantime they had no reason to arrest you or hinder your movements. They weren't ready to agree to that right away, so I've called someone else. I expect we'll hear more good news by suppertime or shortly after. You are not to talk to anyone about that until I say so, is that clear?"

"Yes, Sera," Ky said.

"On the topic of your fiancé and his associate, things are still in a knot. My understanding, from talking to both the young men and the Rector, is that she thought she had sent in a visa extension form citing a special need for their presence. That form was not received, and her poisoning meant she was not at her address—the official address of the young men—when they sent someone to look. She may or may not have sent it; what matters is it was not received. Personally, I suspect that the same person who pushed Immigration to move on your citizenship status also pushed to have them deported immediately, but since I don't know who that is, I have no proof. Right now, they are still on the list for detention and deportation."

"But—" Ky began and then stopped. Sera Lane raised her eyebrows. "Never mind," Ky said. "Thank you for all your hard work. I hope I'll be able to leave the house soon."

"Leave the house, I'm sure of. Leave the city—I would not advise that. And definitely, if you leave the planet before regularizing your citizenship status, you will lose it."

Ky looked at Rafe—he was blank-faced, and Teague the same. Sera Lane nodded and went into the dining room, where she had her temporary office set up. Ky went downstairs with Rafe and Teague, and continued working on prepping for the mission. The lists lengthened even as more items were checked off.

A few hours later, the call Sera Lane had been waiting for came through, and a Vatta courier arrived with temporary citizenship identification for Ky. "That's the most I can do for you today," Lane said. "You will not be arrested if you leave the house. You should be able to visit family members outside the city—your aunt in Corleigh, for instance—without hindrance. Your great-aunt Grace would like to see you, if you feel up to it."

"Could you give me a ride partway?"

"The whole way if you like."

They were halfway to the kitchen door when Rodney erupted from the lift with one of the maps they'd been using. "Ky, we have the time—" He stopped, seeing Sera Lane.

"I'm leaving now," she said. "Whatever it is you want to say, young man, wait until I'm out the door. Coming, Sera Ky?"

"In a moment; I want to hear what Rodney has to say."

Sera Lane nodded and went out, closing the door firmly behind her.

"It's now," Rodney said. "Morrison called. They're planning to move the group in Clemmander starting at 0340 tomorrow. We'll need to leave in an hour or two at the most, to have everyone in place. She's got the military teams moving."

"Call it," Ky said. "I'm going to see Aunt Grace. Courtesy call. I should be back in an hour."

"Tell Sera Stella?"

Ky shook her head. "Too risky, even by skullphone. She and I are the ones most likely to be monitored." She looked at Rafe. "I'll take my duffel with me, pick up more ammunition on the way. One of Rodney's friends should pick me up from Grace's."

"Meet you later."

She left the house, visualizing what would happen in the next half hour: the furniture van driving up, parking to block the view of their nosy neighbor across the street, apparently to deliver new mattresses and take away the old, while everyone now in the house slipped into the truck by the side door for the first leg of their cross-country trip. On the drive to Grace's apartment, she ran down her implant's checklist again.

"It would be unwise of your fiancé or his associate to take this opportunity to call attention to themselves," Sera Lane said.

"I'm sure that he does not intend to call attention to himself," Ky said. A few flakes of snow danced in the air; the forecast said more was coming.

"I hope not. He seems a reasonable young man, but what I've found recorded about him is troubling. It is not my place, but still: do you think your father would approve?"

"Sera Lane, I think my father's opinion would be that Rafe will be a fine addition to the family."

"But somewhat of an adventurer—"

"And so am I, Sera Lane. As have been many Vattas, including my father, when he was young."

"True." She said nothing more before they reached the apartment building. "Shall I call a ride for you to . . . the house?"

"I don't know how long Aunt Grace and I will be," Ky said.

Grace looked healthy, but moved with less energy than usual. "There you are," she said. "I have something for you. It arrived early." She pointed to a large flat box. Ky opened it to find three uniforms, complete from cap to shoes, with the correct insignia for each of the three women staying at the Vatta house.

"Sergeant Major Morrison," Ky said.

Grace nodded. "According to Sergeant Major Morrison, they should fit perfectly. She said you'd know where to send them and said the buns were in the oven."

"I just heard that from one of our research group," Ky said.

"Who's taking you to the warehouse from here?"

"One of Rodney's pals. I've met him."

"You may not save them all," Grace said, her voice somber now. "It's a complicated and dangerous operation—don't blame yourself if—"

Ky shook her head. "I can't think that way, not beforehand."

"Right. Go now. Get it done."

"Yes, Great-Aunt Grace," Ky said. Grace laughed.

Down the passage, down the lift, and there in the circular entrance drive was Kemel, one of Rodney's friends, wearing a dark jacket and a cap close enough to a chauffer's. He took the box from her. "We ready?" he asked when Ky had settled herself in the backseat.

"Better be," Ky said. "I'd hate to have wasted all those hours trying to make this plan as shaky and unworkable as possible."

Sergeant Major Morrison arrived at Grace Vatta's borrowed apartment as usual about 1900, crisply correct in uniform, a few flakes of the snow outside leaving damp patches on her cap.

"Coffee or tea?" Grace asked. "And the pastries on that tray are delicious."

Morrison smiled. "Tea, please. Snow's tailing off, but it's still a night for a hot drink." She took a security cylinder from the briefcase she carried and turned it on. Grace looked at her more closely, then poured the tea and handed over the cup.

"Something at the base?"

"Yes. I might miss tomorrow's report."

Bland and uninformative to any surveillance they hadn't found. That could be ominous—or not. Grace tried to see which, in Morrison's face, but the sergeant major had no particular expression. Grace made walking motions with her left hand across the pastry tray and raised an eyebrow. A short nod was the answer. Going somewhere. And the only likely "where" was the rescue of the other Miksland survivors.

Questions and advice roiled in Grace's mind. She hadn't been in on most of the planning; she was not used to being planned *around* instead of *with*. Not used to having someone else at the top of the decision tree. Compartmentalization, Ky and Morrison had both said. She was safer knowing less. Maybe, but safety wasn't everything. Did they have a large enough force? What about alternative plans, alternative routes, in case something went wrong? She forced herself not to ask any of the questions.

Morrison picked up a pastry and bit into it. "It's another TDY," she said. "Shouldn't be more than twenty-four hours, but you never know with these things, especially in the winter weather. Anyway, since I've been coming over here regularly, I thought I'd let you know." For Morrison, a very informal speech. "With your permission, Rector, these are especially good and I'd like to take a few with me."

"All you want," Grace said, noting that formality had returned for the moment. "They want me to gain weight but I can't eat all that without a stomachache. And there's another tray in the kitchen. Also one of those padded grocery totes to carry them in. Assuming you have something in your briefcase you'd rather not get cream cheese or fruit filling on."

Morrison laughed. Actually laughed. For a moment Grace saw excitement, eagerness, in her face, and then it vanished again behind the pleasant professional mask. "Thank you, Rector. If you'll excuse me a moment—"

"I'll come with you," Grace said. "The delivery service is excessively meticulous about putting everything away, so the location of the tote is my secret." She led the way to the kitchen. Morrison followed, without her briefcase but with her security cylinder. Grace pointed to it, and Morrison shrugged, her gaze roaming the room. So she didn't trust the security that MacRobert had cleared. Interesting. And all the lights on the cylinder were green.

"There are the pastries; I'll get the tote." Grace turned to the cabinets, opened one of the lower doors, and reached for the padded tote folded up inside. "Ooh . . ." She stumbled, grabbed for the counter for balance.

"Rector!" Morrison sounded genuinely concerned.

"It's nothing," Grace said. "It's leaning over, that's all. Bit dizzy. I think I'll sit down."

"What can I get you?"

"Nothing, nothing." Grace huffed. She leaned forward, elbows on the table, resting her head in her hands. "I'm just—so tired of not being as fit as I was—"

Morrison took the tote, set it on the table. "Will you be all right?"

"Of course." It sounded as grumpy as she intended. "I'm not going to faint or anything; I just need to rest here a minute or two."

"I'll sit with you, Rector," Morrison said. Seated, she leaned over the pastries, putting them in the tote with care. "I can't tell you everything," she murmured, still looking at the pastries. "It should work. They should all fit."

Grace realized what she was talking about. Not pastries in a tote bag. "I hope this is your last TDY for a while, Sergeant Major. And that it goes smoothly with no delays." That should be clear enough to Morrison. She saw by the glint in Morrison's eyes that it was. "Do you get winter leave like everyone else, I hope?"

"Not usually," Morrison said. "I've usually got a round of bases to visit—this year I'm scheduled for Dorland and Fulland. It'll be all day giving holiday greetings to troops at one base after another, with short-haul flights between. I take leave the week after. It is a bit of a nuisance having this TDY so close to that, but—" She shrugged and grinned. "It's my job. My career. And I like it."

"And you're good at it," Grace said. "I'm fine now; I'll see you to the door." Morrison put the cylinder in the tote with the pastries, picked up her briefcase from the living room, and they shook hands at the door. Grace felt a small datastick in her palm and used that hand on the door handle when she opened it.

"Thank you, Rector, for the pastries," Morrison said; the guard outside stared at the opposite wall, but he had ears. "They'll be a good snack on the trip, and a treat for whoever picks me up when I arrive."

"Safe travels," Grace said, then closed and locked the door.

The datastick, inserted into a machine that wasn't connected to anything else, gave her the whole plan, answered the questions she had wanted to ask. She thought of calling the Vatta house—but she hadn't yet, and that call might alert someone who should not be alerted. Stella? She could call Stella, but if Stella didn't have the same information, it would make her resent being left out. Besides, though she called Stella, and Stella visited regularly, she didn't call Stella at this time of day. That might tip someone off, especially if someone reported on Morrison's visit.

Mac arrived late, as usual; she'd half expected he would not arrive at all, would be gone on the same mission—no names had been given, just the plan's outline. "Anything interesting today?" Grace asked.

"Some. Hungry?"

"You know I eat early. The sergeant major stopped by, as usual. Didn't stay long."

"Ah. *I'm* hungry. Let's go in the kitchen."

In the passage he leaned to murmur in her ear. "They're off. The last of them moved out earlier tonight. So far no tickles from the other side."

"Good," Grace said, turning into the kitchen. "Then you can have the last cattlelope steak for dinner."

"With pleasure," Mac said.

Stella Vatta unlocked the front door of the house and checked the security indicators—though with people in the house, it wasn't really necessary. The right lights blinked in the right order. She turned around and waved at her driver before stepping inside and closing the door. She was glad to be home and out of the snow. No one was visible in the living room, but it was possible, now that her citizenship was at least nominally restored, that Ky had gone out on some errand in preparation for the coming rescue attempt. She glanced around and saw a piece of paper on the floor in front of the staircase. Ky's handwriting, firm and clear as always.

"Stay home. Find a reason to take a day off."

Take a day off? She couldn't take a day off; she had a business to run. She had left work at the office; she had put some on the transfer tray to work on here at home after supper, but not everything could be done remotely. She needed to be seen at Vatta headquarters. And no explanation. Typical of Ky, she thought, more and more annoyed.

She listened. No sound from the kitchen. No sounds upstairs. Surely someone was home; Ky had said the three fugitives would likely stay behind. She hurried up the stairs, calling for one after another. No one answered. The guest rooms were all empty, bathrooms clean, beds made, freshly vacuumed and dusted. Closets empty, drawers . . . no sign of recent occupation. Where had they put the clothes bought for them? Where was Ky's box sent down from her ship?

She checked the rest of the upstairs. Only her suite and her father's office showed signs of use. Downstairs again, past the first floor, to the basement level. Doors that had been open since the others arrived were now locked; she opened them. Everything as clean and empty as above.

The whole house was empty but for her. *Empty.* Not even a guard on duty—anything could have happened before she arrived from work. She felt the first stirring of anger. When had Ky left? How long had the house been empty, unguarded? And they had secure links from this house to her office at headquarters; Ky could have told her. Then she remembered what Ky had told her—no communication, no warning. But that wasn't supposed to be now—tomorrow, maybe. If she'd known, she'd have sent someone to—her thoughts tangled a moment. If she had sent a Vatta security detachment to the house, someone might have noticed. Probably would have noticed. Quindlans, or the government . . . but surely they'd also noticed the others leaving. She went into the kitchen. Another note lay on the table, this one from Allie. "Dinner in the warming oven, covered."

She left it there and went back upstairs to change into something more comfortable. The house was so quiet, *too* quiet. She had become used to the bustle of the others, even while telling herself she resented it. She stripped off her business suit and hung it in the 'fresher. She was about to take a knit top from her dresser drawer when she remembered she was alone in the house.

Ky had said she should wear body armor; Rafe had agreed. They had looked up the best weapons shop in the city, before they left for Corleigh, and nagged until Stella ordered a set that combined both impact protection and a chameleon function. But she hadn't worn it yet. Wearing it was an admission that she was not safe, that all her security measures might not be enough. She'd experienced a personal attack on Cascadia but . . . this was *home*. This was her childhood home, where she had always been—always felt—safe. She knew every centimeter of it, including those secret places even Ky didn't know. Even the attack in the driveway hadn't persuaded her.

She looked at the nondescript gray undershirt with its discreet buttons on the cuffs to control the chameleon function, its hood that folded down into a low turtleneck. It had cost an incredible amount for something so plain, so . . . ugly. She hadn't even been able to buy it in a color that suited her. She touched it, then shook her head.

Nothing was going to happen tonight. Whatever happened would happen where they were. And yet—if she didn't wear it and something did happen here, she would never hear the end of it. If she lived. Her thoughts veered back and forth.

Finally, with a sigh, she pulled out the shirt and put it on. Lightweight, surprisingly soft, neither warm nor chill. She left the rest of the outfit in the drawer: the long pants, the gloves, the booties that could fit over her footwear. Sensible caution was one thing, but giving in to paranoia was another.

She pulled on a pair of green wool slacks, tucking the shirt in, then one of her favorite sweaters over it. She looked in the mirror—no sign of the armor, of course. Her shoulder holster lay on the bed, another unwelcome reminder of danger. She put the harness on again, though it ruined the look of the sweater, and a short house wrap over it. Checked the pistol automatically, though she had checked it before leaving for home. Fully loaded. Spare magazine in the drawer of the bedside table, two boxes of ammunition in the cabinet below, along with her night-vision goggles and a wicked-looking knife she refused to consider, no matter what Rafe said.

Downstairs, the usual lights were on in the usual rooms, all the shielding still on as it should have been. She selected her favorite music, a string quartet playing a concerto from two centuries before that Ky had always called boring. If she had to be in the house alone, she'd play what she pleased. She took her dinner out of the warming oven and decided to take it up to the upstairs office.

She wondered, as she ate, if Ky had told Aunt Grace she was leaving and why. Surely Grace would know. Maybe she knew when it would be over. She called Grace most evenings between 2000 and 2030; a call couldn't possibly be suspect, and besides Rafe and Teague had increased the security of all the Vatta communications. When she finished the excellent little lemon tart Allie'd made, she called Grace's number.

"Stella? Where are you?"

"At home, Aunt Grace. Everything's fine. Quiet, with all of them gone—"

"Stella." Aunt Grace's tone stopped her. "Let's talk about the business."

"The business? But what about—?"

"Are you planning to open a new plant to manufacture the latest revisions of the shipboard ansible design, or can you retool?"

Clearly Grace knew the others had left—had known before she did. Probably she knew the whole plan in detail. And clearly Grace did not want to talk about it. Stella struggled to keep her voice level over the anger that rose higher. Left out again, alone again in possible danger— "Is it the link or me you don't trust, Auntie?" she asked before she could stop herself. "Never mind," she said quickly, before Grace could say anything. "No, modification in ansible design won't require a complete retooling but we'll need to move one end of the line—since I anticipated there would be future changes, the facility was built with that in mind."

"Excellent," Grace said. "Is Helen still on the Board?"

"No; she asked to be removed, so she could concentrate on the children." She did not want to talk about Helen, or the family, or the business. Before Grace could ask another deflecting question, Stella asked, "Do you have any time frame for returning to your house?"

"I'm quite safe here, Stella, for the time being. Do you find it inconvenient to visit here?"

"No—I'm just—" *Thinking of you and Mac* would not go over well. "Concerned," she chose instead.

"I'll move back to the house when I'm discharged from physiotherapy. They come by every day to make me sweat."

"That's good," Stella said. Grace wasn't going to give up a thing, that was obvious. "I'll talk to you again tomorrow, Aunt Grace."

"Good night, Stella." And Grace broke the connection.

Stella stared at the handset before setting it down with unnecessary care. She was not fooled. She was not happy. Ky hadn't had the elementary courtesy to warn her the house would be empty. Grace still treated her as an inexperienced child. She picked up the tray with care not to let the silverware rattle, and took it downstairs again. She put the dishes in the autowasher; she, unlike her cousin, never left dirty dishes lying around for someone else to clean. Ky could have left her Allie, at least.

She put that thought aside with an effort. At least she had the rest of the evening to herself, and the music Ky found boring she found pleasant. In the security office, she checked all the outdoor video feeds. The street was empty now, the tracks of earlier traffic almost covered by snow. There might be light traffic later, when theaters closed and dinner parties were over. She imagined for a moment being young again, spending an evening out, dining, attending a concert or play, laughing and chatting with friends. She had enjoyed that. But that time was over, as long as this crisis lasted.

The automatic timer turned lights off and on using its randomizing scheduler. Stella closed down the files on the office computer and opted for an early bedtime.

"Anything?" The night supervisor, Vogel, looked up from his report form when Archer took the headphones off and turned toward the desk.

"Pressure tape on the Rector's windows. Stella Vatta called, said the house was 'quiet, with all of them gone.' The Rector shut her down; Stella objected, and the conversation went elsewhere. Nothing new about the plant modifications that we didn't already know. But it sounds like the Vatta house may be empty but for Stella."

"Ah. She is usually armed, and a good shot."

"Yes, sir, but at night? The house shielding is still full on, and as reported earlier—"

"The weak bands are now fully functional, yes, Archer. I haven't forgotten. What about the garage?"

"Her car's not there, but we know it's still being repaired."

"Her ankle injury?"

"It wasn't broken, but one of the Vatta employees was overheard saying she was still limping."

"Well. Thank you. I'll pass this on." Vogel copied the recording and attached it to a report that went directly to Michael Quindlan. Aside from that it was a boring shift—no more communications in or out of Grace Vatta's borrowed apartment, nothing from Stella Vatta's house—until a half hour later he had a call from Michael Quindlan himself.

"Patch into the team leader," Quindlan said. "Call me on this link when something happens."

"Yes, ser. What—" But the link was already dead. He gave the assignment to Vogel; the other operators were monitoring other sites.

"Do you want me to run a double on the house itself?" Vogel asked.

"I wasn't told," he said. "But yes, you should if you can."

CHAPTER TWENTY

DAY 9

Stella found the empty silence less restful than she'd expected. She dozed off, woke again, dozed off, woke again. She could not help wondering where exactly the others were, what was happening, what would happen. Ky was impetuous; Rafe was decisive; Teague she still couldn't figure out. The three women fugitives would do anything Ky told them, being military. The others, the civilians and military she didn't know about, because Ky had said she didn't need to know . . . they included Vatta employees, which she felt strongly she *did* need to know about. Rodney, for instance. Shortly after midnight, still not sleeping well, she got up, pulled on her house boots, and went to the office down the passage. She called up the flight plans for Vatta. Routine cargo flights out of Port Major, delivering goods ordered for the next day, it looked like. But any of those flights might have carried up to eight passengers, some of them ten. And she knew Grace had connections with Traffic Control; passengers might or might not be listed on the manifests.

She closed that search and tried to concentrate on the work she'd put in the transfer box.

A light on the desk security display turned red. She stared at it a moment. When she didn't press the response button, the system buzzed. She touched the button. ROOF. GABLE OVER C-WING. She stared at the readout. It couldn't be. Was someone already in the house? Could they possibly get through the hull-strength protection of the main house? And she was alone. She hit the panic button on the desk, fear already rising to choke her. The direct line to Vatta HQ didn't light up. She picked up the handset anyway, entered the number. Another red readout: no connection. She tried her skullphone. Nothing.

Panic grew; her breath came short. She had her pistol, but how many intruders were there? She fumbled at the drawers, opening the one with spare magazines ready-loaded, one of her father's habits, and pocketed them before remembering that his pistol used different ammunition from hers—and his pistol had been lost in the explosion. She looked at the wall behind which the secret room lay. She could go there. She could wait it out. Unless they found the codes. Unless they blew up the house. She was up, halfway to her bedroom, before she realized it. Now what?

She linked her implant to the house internal security system—that worked, at least. Now she could see from the sensors that several people were on the roof, already entering one of the dormer windows. Others were below, near every ground-level exit. Suddenly the four near the front door disappeared as she saw the lights of a vehicle approaching along the street. It passed by; the figures reappeared as if by magic.

Chameleon suits. They had full chameleon suits. So did she, but she'd put on only the top. She kicked off her house boots, yanked off her slacks, fumbled in the drawer for the pants and pulled them up, sealed them to the shirt, pulled on her wool slacks again. Took off the sweater, shivering a bit with fear and the chill. It seemed to take hours, but the glowing clock face on the bedside table clicked the seconds off slowly. It hadn't taken even a full minute yet. Back into socks and boots. A dark close-fitting top, the shoulder holster, the dark padded jacket Rafe had insisted on, with pockets for the extra ammunition. Two and a half minutes. Only one had gone into the window so far; others were doing *something* up there but she couldn't tell what. There were ways to cut through ship hulls, if you had time and the right tools.

Where could she go? And how many would she have to deal with? She turned off the bedroom light, as if she were going back to bed, switched her implant to night-vision amplification, and made her way back down the passage toward the staircase. On the left, a door concealed in paneling let her into a storage room stacked with office supplies. She ducked under the shelving at the far end, pulled open the low door, and crawled into the passage behind it, shutting it after her. Straight ahead to the outer wall, then right.

The intruders had already entered the second attic bedroom, the one that had been Jo's. Light flared in the video pickup: they were using a torch to cut through the shielding that covered the staircase access. So they must have known about it, or hacked into the house system. It would take them minutes . . . she thought of hurrying downstairs to the security office, trying to punch a signal through somehow, but that kind of work wasn't in her skill set. If only Rafe or Teague had been there. She cursed Rafe and Ky silently, for leaving her alone with no warning. Not even Rodney, not even a day's warning to let her get someone else in. It wasn't fair!

A muffled thud from the far end of the children's wing. They were through. Shadows flowed down the staircase, opened the guest suite door. She saw them clearly now, heads covered in helmets—she didn't have one and her head felt naked, exposed, even behind the secret space's armored walls. She reached back and tugged her suit's hood out of the collar and over her hair, for all the good that would do. The finer mesh of the face shield fell down, tickling her nose on the way.

She looked through the peephole set in an elaborate piece of art-work on the other side of the wall. Two entered each of the bedrooms closer to the stairs: a fast search. If anyone spoke she couldn't hear it.

And now that group—six—were in the passage, and more were landing on the roof. Her heart pounded; her breath came short. Too many; she couldn't possibly win. And yet . . . she wanted to live. Her body felt as if it were shrinking in on itself. She forced a deep breath then another. They were to the staircase. Two started down. The other four waited, and four more came out of the guest suite.

Stella sighted on the nearest and got off two shots—both targets jerked, but did not fall—before one of the others responded with a spray of bullets that knocked chips off the carving but did no real damage to the wall or her. Of course they had armor . . . but her en-hanced sight showed the weakened hot spots where the first bullets had hit. Her next two hit the same spots; the two after that took out the faceplates on the helmets of the other two. Now the following four were flattened into the bedroom doorways, and more chips came off the carving. From below came a *whump* and her implant's icons for the house security went dead. Now she had no video contacts to know where they were.

She backed away, slid through another hidden door into the ad-joining room, opened the door into the passage, and saw one of them running toward her. She fired the rest of that magazine and the man went down hard only a meter away. She darted out, grabbed his weapon, tried to get his helmet but it wouldn't come off and it was taking too long. She jumped back into the room and closed and barred the door. Slammed her second magazine into her pistol. Back to the passage. One of them was within ten centimeters of the peep-hole, faceplate lifted. She fired directly into his face, then into the faceplate of the one behind him. Then at the two coming back up-stairs. They flinched but didn't fall. Five down, but there were more. And she had used up all her pre-loaded ammunition.

Her fingers shook as she reloaded the first magazine, slammed it home, reloaded the second. Why hadn't she followed her father's practice, kept more loaded magazines? Filling them both cut her down to one box. She had that weapon she'd taken from the man in the passage, and it had a huge magazine, but she had never used a gun like that.

Point the open end at the target; your hand will find the trigger. Her father's voice. Another deep breath; she found the comfortable place to hold it, and the trigger to pull, then set it down beside her. Then she fingered the chameleon suit's sleeve control to full concealment and saw the carpet instead of her arm—she'd forgotten to do that before— and her hands floating in the air. Gloves. She'd forgotten the gloves that extended the field. And the booties. They'd see hands and feet and intuit where her body must be.

The gloves and booties were in her bedroom. Down the passage, around the corner—too far, she was sure, to make it before one of them saw her and shot her. Could she could make it across the passage into her father's office and the secret room undetected? But then she would be trapped. It had no other exit.

The hidden passage she was in wound around to the row of bedrooms—if no one detected the void in the walls or the entrances to it. The entrance to her bedroom was through the desk in the corner; the drawer with the gloves and booties across the room, in the closet. And had she left her bedroom door open or closed? Would she come crawling out of the desk's keyhole to find them standing over her? She picked up the larger weapon and edged that way, trying not to make a sound, trying to fix her mind on practical things. Someone at Vatta headquarters should have noticed that the house was cut off from the security grid. Wouldn't they send a team to check? How long would that take?

DAY 10

After midnight, the Vatta HQ Security Watch spent most of their time checking buildings: Vatta warehouses, the headquarters building itself, the hangars and offices of Vatta Transport's space at Port Major's airport. They could do much of the work remotely, as computers at headquarters pinged the buildings' security systems and received alarms. Mobile teams then checked out any anomalies. Someone always sat in the control room, watching for any signal that one of the buildings had been broken into, fences cut, or the like.

Georg Bakli and Ferran Hallen had the watch, and Ferran had stepped out for a few minutes when one of the boards beeped. Georg punched the RECORD button and called up the incident description. The Vatta town house had failed to respond to the regular ping sent by Vatta's computers.

Such failures weren't common, but they weren't rare, either. Usually they self-repaired in a few minutes, or a branch had brought down a wire, something like that. But since the house had been broken into only eleven days before, Georg didn't wait for self-repair but queried the house's system, to interrogate its own security system. CONNECTION NOT AVAILABLE. That was unusual. The house's security system not responding on either hardwired or wireless suggested something more serious.

He looked on the log. Supposedly seven—no eight—people were staying at the house. If anything was wrong—invasion, fire, equipment failure—the backup would alert them. They would then call the security center and report it. Ferran came back in the room. "What's wrong, Georg?"

"Vatta town house—not responding and I can't get to the house system either way."

"They've had that ISC man there messing with the system—maybe he screwed something up."

"It was working fine a half hour ago." Georg pulled up the log on his screen. "Until three minutes twenty seconds ago." Had it really taken him that long to look up the residents in-house?

"I suppose we could call Sera Stella," Ferran said. "But if she's asleep she'll be annoyed."

"Better annoyed than snuck up on," Georg said. He placed a call to the Vatta house secure line. NO CONNECTION. He looked at Ferran; Ferran looked back. "This isn't good."

"We have her emergency number, her skullphone," Ferran said.

"Calling now," Georg said. "Get a supervisor; we need help." No connection on the skullphone. No connection on the house phone. It took Ferran another ten minutes to locate their shift supervisor, Philip Grayson. He had Georg on his own skullphone as he searched, and Georg reported no luck contacting the house.

"Call the police," Ferran said. "Both our watch units are out at the airport, remember?"

The police weren't that concerned until Ferran's supervisor reminded the desk sergeant that the house had been broken into before, and Sera Vatta had been attacked, her car damaged, in her own driveway. Another officer came on. "We'll send someone right out. You aren't sure there are intruders?"

"No, but we can't get *any* communication with the house."

"All right then. Keep calling them, just in case." That line cut off.

"I could call Sera Grace," Ferran said. "My grandmother's often awake in the middle of the night."

"Good idea," Grayson said. "We don't want to take chances with Sera Stella. Georg, you call. Ferran, find the nearest mobile team and tell them to go to the Vatta house immediately."

Georg made the connection to Sera Grace's phone and got a man's voice instead. "MacRobert here."

"Vatta Security at headquarters—we've dispatched a police unit to the Vatta house; the house system isn't responding and we can't get a response from Sera Stella, either. Of course, with so many people in the house it's probably not necessary, but—"

"She's there alone," MacRobert said. "Send more help. There may be an attack because she called the Rector tonight and said she was alone."

"Yes, sir. Will you inform Sera Grace?"

"Of course. *Go!*"

"I've got Cameron's unit," Ferran said.

* * *

When the police arrived, the street was empty, a clean sheet of snow pale between the pools of light at each corner, except for discreet lighting near the residences. Officers Molina and Jankin got out and saw no one at the door or near it. A light over the door illuminated the front steps. Smaller lights marked the driveway entrance and the gate's lock panel. They walked back to the drive, up it to the locked gates. A light over the kitchen door that had been kicked open before, but no sign of fresh damage. No one lurking in the drive when they flashed their lights along it. A light over the garage doors; the doors were closed. No sound came from inside, and their probes could not penetrate the house's shielding.

"Use the police master?" Molina asked.

"We could, but I don't see any reason, really. It's some electronic glitch; there's no disturbance, no sign of any intrusion." Jankin looked through the gate; the snow was unmarked.

"There's that glass door in the back, you remember? Someone might've gotten in there, and in this neighborhood nobody's going to hear anything once they're inside."

"Yeah, but—all right." Jankin used the police master passcode on the driveway gates and they opened silently, smoothly. They walked up the drive. The kitchen door had been repaired; it was closed and locked. They tried the door. No alarm came on, but the door was locked and the lock held. Farther on, the garden gate was also locked. They looked through the bars. Their light flashed on the lawn; the earlier snowfall had stopped, and what might have been footsteps marred the smooth blanket of white. To their left, the glass French doors gleamed in the light, closed. Whole. Drapes drawn across them. The very picture of a peaceful house properly closed for the night.

"She walked in the garden gate to the back door, not the kitchen?" Jankin asked.

"It's closer, if she parked in the garage." Molina looked around, swinging his light. "But there are no tracks in the driveway. If she didn't drive home, she'd have entered at the front, surely. Or the side. Not back here." He touched the master passcode to the gate lock, and it snapped open. "It won't take long; we'll just walk around to the far side. There has to be some reason the house isn't answering."

"She's not here. She went to a friend's house for the night." Jankin shrugged but followed.

"Then she would've told Vatta headquarters. That's how the rich do it. Never out of contact." Their lights flashed over windows on the ground floor, windows on the second, speared higher to the roof with its two dormers jutting out—"What is *that*?" Dark shapes that disappeared almost before they'd registered, and something lurking above that defeated the eyes' attempt to define it.

"Call—" began Molina, and then both were slammed into the snow, into a frantic battle with opponents they could not see clearly, blows coming out of nowhere. Their own blows seemed to have no effect. Only their body armor and helmets saved them—that and the sirens approaching the house. Their attackers stopped abruptly, stood, and ran for it, leaving more and fresher tracks in the snow. Molina clambered to his knees, drew his weapon, flicked his night goggles to infrared, and took aim on what he hoped was one of them, rising impossibly from the ground toward the roof. That one jerked, but did not fall; the other one was already at the roof. Molina shot again at the light blurs his goggles gave him for targets. Return fire slammed into his armor and knocked him back. Then all the blurs were inside something, and the something rose into the air, the air throbbing with the sound of a hovercraft. The backwash threw up all the snow in the yard; it was like being in a blizzard until the craft had moved away. Molina sank down, felt around for his partner. Jankin groaned. "My back—"

"They've left. Did you hear the sirens?" The sirens had now wailed to a growl.

"Yeah—help me—"

"If your back's hurt I'm not going to move you. Lie still. I'll call."

*   *   *

Stella Vatta heard the silence—not of emptiness but of determined stillness—where she crouched in her closet, easing out the drawer, fishing carefully for the gloves and booties of her armor. Someone had been outside her bedroom door—she had remembered to close it—and was undoubtedly still there, tense. Why? What had happened? The silence seemed to last forever as she pulled on the gloves, moved one leg at a time just enough to pull on the booties, hoping the intruder couldn't hear the faint rasp of wool on wool that seemed so loud to her when she changed position. The silence went on as she crouched, breathing quietly, and then, in the distance, she heard sirens. They grew louder, louder still.

Rescue? Or someone else's emergency? She heard a burst of static from outside, then the thud of boots moving fast, away from her door, back toward the middle of the house. Then shots fired outside, from the garden toward the house, toward the roof. Return fire from the roof. More boots in the distance. A voice called "Out *now*! Make sure they're dead." Shots. She eased over to her door. All the sounds distant now. Opened it a crack. Silence, except in the far end of the house. Then a muffled roar from above, directly above, a sound she recognized as a hovercraft lifting vertically. And then only a faint noise as it shifted from vertical to silenced horizontal flight.

Her skullphone pinged. She tongued the connection. Vatta, at last. She gave the countersign, a pattern of touches rather than out loud, just in case, and walked down to the main passage, leaving the larger weapon behind her. She hadn't had to use it after all.

"Sera! Are you all right? This is Vatta Security, Philip Grayson—" A name she knew. "They're all gone, we think."

"I'm alive," Stella said. "They got in from above—cut through the shielding—" She stared at the body on the floor in front of her. She could smell the blood, the death; she started shaking.

"Sera—" Grayson's voice sounded farther away. "Sera, can you open a door for us?"

"I don't know." Her own voice sounded faraway, too. "I think they . . . damaged the main . . . house controls . . ." She was sitting on the floor now, leaning on the wall. "Can you use a master?" But her head cleared, now she was sitting down. "No—I know you can't. I'll have to come downstairs and manually let you in—" What door would be safest to approach? "Where are you now?"

"Our squad leaders, Mike Wilmots and Dusty Farsich, are at the front and side doors; three of our men are also at the garden door. So any door you can reach."

Between her and the stairs—or the lift—were the bodies of more men, her kills; the smell of gunfire, blood, and death was everywhere. She pushed herself up the wall, pinched her nose shut, and edged past the body, flicking a light switch as she went. The stench was stronger at the head of the stairs: more bodies. More bodies than she remembered killing. She turned on all the switches near the head of the stairs; the colors leapt out at her. Blood on the carpet, smears of it showing clearly through her . . . her feet. The chameleon suit. She hadn't turned it off. She went down the stairs, saw the ruin of the security office to her right . . . and leaned on the newel post, transferring the pistol to her left hand so she could operate the controls and turn the suit off.

Instantly she caught sight of herself in one of the mirrored panels that flanked the front door. The soft aqua sweater was spattered with blood and dirt, ruined. The gray hood over her head, the thinner gauze over her face made her look bald and plain. She pushed them back behind her, let them hang loose over her jacket. Her face was a mess, as bad as the jacket. Tears, dust from the hiding places, all smeared together. Her eyes were wide, her expression shocky.

This would not do. She was the CEO, she had to look like the CEO, at least look calm, in control, just in need of cleaning up. Watching herself, she opened her mouth, faked a yawn, moved her head around. Her shoulders relaxed a little. She put her pistol back in its holster, took more deep breaths, shook out her hands. Chin up, shoulders down. She pulled the comb she always carried from a pocket, did what she could for her hair in a few strokes. Better still. "Look like what you want to be," her mother always said. Her mother had never fought for her life. The handkerchief her mother had also insisted on got most of the mess off her face; the lipstick in her pocket gave her a touch of color. And deep inside, something stirred she had never felt before. Now that it was over, now that she was alive and unhurt . . . could that possibly be what Ky and Rafe felt?

"Sera—?"

"I'm at the front door, Ser Grayson. Which squad leader is out there?"

"Mike Wilmots, Sera."

"Please tell him I will be opening the door after he knocks three–two–four. My sidearm is holstered."

"At once, Sera."

The knocks came. She watched herself in the mirror for another count of five, moment by moment willing herself into what she wanted to be, as calm and controlled and gracious as her mother, then opened the door. The door's manual control worked; the shielding moving aside smoothly. "Ser Wilmots, I am very glad to see you."

"Sera! May we enter?"

"Yes, do," she said, recognizing her mother's tone and phrasing. Everything was all right now. And yes, what she felt was not just the relief she'd felt other times after danger, but pride.

Wilmot's squad entered behind him; he sent them here and there with hand signals. The living room showed no damage from the invasion; he offered his arm. "Sera, perhaps you would like to rest here until we've cleared the house—"

"Yes, thank you."

He guided her to the sofa and eased her down onto it.

"And you are quite sure you have no injuries that need attention?"

"Right now I would just like to sit here," she said. "I don't think I have anything serious."

"And are all the exit doors on manual?"

"Yes."

He moved away, glancing into the security office, then back along the living room to a short passage with a closet in it. He came back with an afghan and a pillow. "Here, Sera. After such a—a situation, you will be feeling shaken."

"Thank you, Ser Wilmots."

She had the shakes again while he was out of the room, but inside she was blazing with joy. She heard the kitchen door opening, the sounds of more people spreading through the house, tramping around, muttering into their communicators, commenting to one another. One of the women brought hot tea, and introduced herself as "Marina, one of the Hautvidor Vattas. Can I get you anything else?"

Stella smiled. "No thank you. I think I'm just a little tired—I'm usually asleep at this hour."

"I should think so, Sera. We're all impressed."

"Impressed?"

"Well—you—um—killed so many of them. By yourself."

"Wasn't all my doing," Stella said, between sips of the tea, hot and almost too sweet. "They killed their wounded before they left." She didn't want to think how many she had killed. Or wounded, for that matter.

When Wilmots came back, she was calm again, and warmer. He, on the other hand, looked worried.

"Sera, you cannot stay here until the house is cleaned and made secure again. Also you must have guards here around the clock."

"I agree," Stella said. "But for the rest of the night—I'm very tired—" Her skullphone pinged. She shook her head and made the sign for "skullphone," then answered. It was MacRobert.

"Grace wants you to come here. Or there's the apartment at headquarters."

"How much do you know?"

"Grace was in touch with that night supervisor at headquarters; he's gotten reports from the mobile teams. Did you know two police were attacked in the garden?"

"No. When?"

"Vatta Security had the police send a unit out when the house didn't respond to the computer's ping. Apparently they were doing a walk-around when they were attacked by two or three men in chameleon suits. When the men ran off, the police tried to shoot them; they took fire. Our teams were out at the airport dealing with another problem."

"The house is a wreck," Stella said. "They destroyed the security office here; all the video's dead. Cut a hole in the shielding from Jo's room."

Someone started pounding on the front door; Wilmots and two of his team moved toward it. "Who is it?"

"You know perfectly well who this is," said a peevish voice. "Open this door *now*!"

"I'll call you back," Stella said to MacRobert, and to Wilmots said, "It's Ser Prescott, from across the street. Let him in."

Wilmots opened the door. Prescott looked the very image of a dapper fussbudget, from the cut of his hair to his perfectly tailored slacks and jacket and the tie with its jeweled stickpin. "Are you the person in charge here? If not I demand to speak to him or her. This is outrageous! Flashing lights! Sirens! I want you to know I'm filing a complaint with the neighborhood association *and* the city: I have already called the police and told them to cite those vehicles out front for illegal parking. And as for that aircraft—!"

"Ser Prescott, how very good to see you again. How is your dear wife?" Stella kept her voice pleasant. Ky had mentioned once that Prescott seemed too interested in this house, but her parents had shrugged it off. Maybe she shouldn't have.

His head turned. "Sera Vatta. What is the meaning of this . . . this outrage? It is the *third* time in the past tenday that unseemly noise and confusion has come to this house. If you are going to be the focus of this kind of annoyance and criminal activity you should move to a neighborhood where such things are more common. Nothing like this happened when your father was alive. You young people today—"

"Ser Prescott!" Wilmots stepped between Prescott and Stella. "Sera Vatta was attacked—she nearly died—"

"Nonsense. Some kind of costume party. And that ridiculous mess on your face, Sera Vatta—!"

Stella's initial urge to laugh was overcome by pure rage that lifted her to her feet. Not only nosy but insulting, after what she'd gone through.

"Take him upstairs," she said to Wilmots. "Show him."

"Yes, Sera," Wilmots said, and took Prescott's arm.

"Let go of me; you can't do that!"

"He can," Stella said. His face showed the beginning of fear. Good. "This is my house; you don't make the rules here." She walked toward him; he stared at her feet, and then a little behind her. She glanced down. Her feet had left bloody marks on the carpet. She hadn't noticed before.

"Your mother will be appalled," Prescott said. "When she finds out you've walked in paint and then on her expensive Eskalin carpet—"

"It's not paint," Stella said, and smiled at him. He flinched. "It's blood. Take him upstairs, Wilmots. See if he thinks it's a party then."

"No!" Prescott yanked back, but two more men closed in and pushed him, complaining loudly, up the stairs to the very top.

"That," Stella heard Wilmots say as he pointed, "is a dead man. A man who tried to kill Sera Vatta. You can see the damage he did to that sculpture."

Stella, at the foot of the stairs, put her hand on the newel post for support. She heard Prescott protesting, then saw him fold over suddenly and heard him vomit and then groan. When Wilmots looked back and raised his brows, Stella nodded. As the men brought Prescott back down the stairs, he was babbling, "I didn't know, I didn't know, it's horrible I didn't mean it I never thought it would be like this . . ."

CHAPTER TWENTY-ONE

DAY 10

Ky, taking her turn in the bed compartment of a long-haul truck, tried to relax and sink into the sleep she needed before the next phase. Her mind was too busy; she ran simulations over and over, trying to make sure she had every possibility covered, and knowing that was impossible.

She slept, finally, but not even the full two and a half hours that was her share of the time before they were at the first transfer point. Inside the big warehouse, Vatta employees moved about with loaders, transferring boxes from one cargo hold to another. The rig she'd ridden in drove off, hooked to a different trailer; Rafe and Inyatta and Teague were still in it. She and Barash climbed into a trailer loaded with twenty-kilo sacks of grain from a famous livestock feed manufacturer.

She caught another two hours of uneasy sleep during the next segment, and then, in another warehouse, climbed into the truck fitted out for the project at hand, modified hastily from the kind Vatta rented out as mobile offices. Instead of desks and cabinets, couches and reclining chairs were bolted to its floor. A complete shower/toilet fitted into the back corner, with effluent tank mounted below, and next to it a medical station.

"Med's not here yet," the warehouse supervisor told her. "On the way. We'll pick 'em up when we swing by the airport to catch the latest shipments." He winked. Ky didn't wink back. Her stomach was tight. Unlike fleet command, where she knew her entire crew and most of the ship captains, this operation was a mix of civilians and military who had never worked on something like this before. Nor had she. It felt about as stable as a stack of ball bearings.

Another truck backed up to the docks. Rafe, Inyatta, and Teague walked in with the driver. "All we need is the big guns," Rafe said.

"On the way," Ky said. He knew already; he was just tense, as she was. A military team, handpicked by Sergeant Major Morrison, should be arriving within the hour. She looked out the window in the service door; the roll-up door to the loading dock was down. This truck belonged to a Vatta affiliate, Stevens-Vatta, and had backed up to this dock many times, as had identical trucks. No one who lived in the area would think twice about it being on that road or the other places they planned to intercept the prisoner transports.

Rodney, ensconced with all the equipment he and Rafe and Teague agreed he needed in Vatta's shipping office at the Weekes City airport, pinged Rafe to signal that he had a lock on all those transports. "Given the distances," Rafe said, "we expect they'll start moving the Clemmander group any minute now. Rod's got an alarm on the system, so he can let us know when they start and where they are."

CLEMMANDER REHABILITATION CENTER
DAY 10

Staff Sergeant Gossin had hoped the sergeant major would recognize that the inmates had been drugged, but another day and another passed with nothing happening. She went through them in the same dull misery as the previous days, losing more hope every hour. A few days—she wasn't sure how many—after the committee's visit, the morning dose of medication was smaller; perhaps it was a shower day. Gossin took it obediently, but the mental fog lifted enough for her to realize that it would take time for the sergeant major to mount a rescue. And maybe, just maybe, she could do something herself to help.

The thought itself was energizing. "Shower day," said a voice from the grille in the ceiling. The cell door opened; an attendant strapped her into a float chair. Once in the tiled shower room, Gossin fumbled at her clothes and an attendant, impatient, fumbled even more because of the protective gloves. Gossin finally got herself undressed and was able to walk the meter from the float chair to the shower and stand there while the attendant turned on the water. Gossin had to admit it was easier when bald. Not that she liked it. When the water ceased, she dried as best she could with the single towel provided. The attendant left the shower room, taking Gossin's clothes. Gossin stood there naked, shivering a little, wondering what horror was coming now.

By the time the door opened again, she had rediscovered an old trick her granny had taught her, how to warm herself up without shivering. How could she have forgotten that? She'd used it in Miksland a few times. Their family had practiced some . . . training . . . she couldn't remember the name. Her implant had stored it for her but now it was gone. Something about circulation. Doing it, whatever it was, felt good. Gave her confidence.

But the trio who walked in when the door opened drove it away. All in the same protective gear, their faces blurred by the face-shields. One rolled in a cart with a tray of instruments and medications laid out on the top, and a stack of folded clothes on the lower shelf. Gossin stared at the instruments. She already had an IV port installed . . . what were they going to do to her? She wanted to ask, but she was afraid of what they'd do if she did. One of them put down a square printed with foot outlines.

"Stand here."

Gossin put her feet on the outlines. The surface was colder than the floor, and slightly rough.

"She's lost weight," one of the figures said. A female voice, Gossin thought. "Have you done a nutrient panel lately?"

"They did that at Pingats," another said. "They were fine then, and they've all been on a standard ration here."

"Draw blood for a standard panel plus nutrient history. It's got to look normal."

"Hold her." Two of them approached her and without looking at her face or speaking to her each took an arm and forced her forward so the third could uncap the IV port on her chest. She could see the hands, the syringe, her blood rising in the barrel. With swift efficiency, the one who had drawn the blood recapped her port and prepared the sample for the lab. The one who had given the orders looked at a hand unit and said, "Get her ready for transport."

Transport? Transport where? Away from the others? Her stomach clenched. One of the three turned away, left the shower room. One of the others said, "Use the toilet," and pointed to the steel toilet beside the shower. They didn't leave. They stood watching her. She knew there were scans in the cells, but she'd never had people standing in the same room watching her on the toilet.

"Come on, hurry up," said one of them.

She sat down, finished. One held out an adult-sized diaper. No. She did not want that. She remembered from the trip here, the hours strapped to a gurney, unable to move, needing to pee, and finally having to pee into the thing they'd put on her. "She doesn't understand," the other one said. "Too much drug. Get her into it."

Gossin didn't want those gloved hands touching her again. Slowly, as if unable to move faster, she reached out, took the thing and stepped into it, one foot at a time.

"That's better. Now pull it up."

She did that, too; it was better than being handled. Now the second one left the room, and the third pulled a garment off the rack. Orange, one-piece as usual, but this time with long legs ending in overlarge fabric feet. She stepped into it, couldn't get her arms into it, and the attendant grabbed her arm and yanked on the garment, shoving her arm in. Gossin took a step, and another grab on her arm stopped her even as she felt the thinness of the footed pants and realized they would be useless for walking anywhere outside.

When the attendant had secured her to the chair and opened the door, Gossin saw Cosper in a chair with an attendant behind him. The attendant pushed her back to her cell and left her there, still strapped in. Gossin used the time to explore what she could do with that trick her gran had taught her. If she could raise her temperature—or at least feel warmer—could she do anything else? Speed up blood flow, slow it down? Change anything that would clear the drugs faster? She felt more clearheaded, but then she usually did after a shower.

Gossin was the last in line as they came out the door into the open for the first time. She had expected daylight, because of the breakfast and morning meds, but it was dark, middle-of-the-night dark. Both Slotter Key's moons were up, giving just enough light to see flat lawn on either side of the wide paved walk, a wall to either side beyond it, and straight ahead a parking lot and a road leading away into the distance. She thought she could see hills there. The attendants wore headlamps on their protective suits, flicking them on only briefly as the walk changed grade down two shallow ramps.

With her head strapped firmly to the headrest, she could not see much to either side or behind; she still had no idea what the building she had been in for all that time looked like. The breeze felt cold; she hunched her shoulders, pushing her head against the strap, but there was no give to it. From behind she heard a deep sigh, and the attendant with her chair dropped a thin blanket onto her and jerked it into place. It cut the breeze a little. She reminded herself of the way she'd controlled her temperature before, and once again felt gentle warmth flow out to her feet and hands. She drew in a long breath. The cold fresh air smelled wonderful, free of the chemical smells in the clinic. With every breath, she felt a little more clearheaded.

Tires grated on the gravel parking lot. Ahead of her, the line of chairs stopped. She saw a dark shape pull up, a vehicle without headlights. Moonlight glinted from its roof; she made out the shape of a medium-sized utility truck. A light flashed at the head of the line, painting the side of the truck for a moment: green, with yellow lettering. Gossin strained to read it, but the light was gone too fast. With a clatter, someone opened the back door of the truck. Light poured out, and a lift whined. Then the light went off.

Gossin blinked, trying to regain her night vision. Another light—an attendant's headlamp—came on at the head of the line. It wavered in height and direction, but as the lift rose, she could tell an attendant and float chair were on the lift. The attendant's headlamp vanished as the float chair slid into the truck. A second lamp came on as the truck's lift whined down, and a second chair lifted into the truck. This time its attendant stayed on the ground.

The line moved forward a few meters. The third chair rode the lift up, was pulled inside. Someone called from the front of the truck, and the line stopped. The attendant at the back went forward, light still on. Now Gossin could read the lettering on the truck's side—WEST HILLS WHOLESALE SUPPLY—and also tell that it was fresh paint. Under it, in the headlamp's angled light, was another shadowy shape she could not read. But she knew it. It was a military logo. The truck had once been a military truck. The attendant came back; she got a second glimpse of the side of the truck. The chair just in front of her went up.

Her chair moved forward. Now she was too close to the truck to see anything but what was in front of her: the parking lot, the road leading away. Then it was her turn. In the light of one attendant's headlamp she could see the legs of the others. She closed her eyes. She saw a red glow as the light washed her face; someone chuckled and said, "She's finally out, then. Last little piggy goes to market." Her chair lurched as the lift rose; she didn't react. Someone inside the truck moved her chair in; clamps snicked onto its base. The doors slammed behind her; she heard the whine of the lift folding into place. Fingers touched her neck, felt her pulse. "This one's ready." A low tone came from under her chair; the seat moved under her, shifting fluid from one chamber to another. It was supposed to prevent pressure sores.

She felt the vibration as the truck moved. The attendant at her side went forward, talking softly on the way. "They're all back down; we can take turns sleeping—shall we toss for it?"

"Sure."

Gossin concentrated on her breathing. So there were only two of the attendants on the truck. Light came through her eyelids, but dimly; they must have turned on the lights inside or be using head-lamps.

"We have to check them every hour," the first voice said.

"Deliver them alive and in good order. I know." That was the second. "Wings or fish?"

"Wings." The truck lurched a moment later, turning sharply, gears grinding. "Snakes! I dropped it. Again?"

"No, I see it. Look. Fish. You bunk first."

"Hey—don't you go to sleep, too!"

"I've got a vid to watch. Wake you in four."

Silence after that. Below, tires hummed on pavement. The inside of the truck smelled like a military clinic. Gossin dared to open her eyes just a little. Dim light-strips ran along the ceiling of the cargo space. In front of her were the backs of other float chairs, two on either side of a narrow aisle. Up front, she could see a narrow bunk built into the side of the truck, and on it a shadowy form under a blanket. She couldn't see past the float chairs directly in front of her to the bunk that must be on her side, but little flashes of color on the truck wall and ceiling suggested that the attendant there was indeed watching a vid. She had no way to tell time, no way to know how long it lasted, but she did feel the increasing discomfort of a position she could not change.

She felt her body react to the truck driving around a curve, and then another, pressing on the straps harder than before. Then the truck slowed, came to a shuddering stop, and was still. Gossin closed her eyes; they might check to be sure everyone was asleep. The truck turned again and accelerated sharply; Gossin heard another vehicle passing, a short tap of the other's horn. More traffic noises outside. It had been night—but what hour of night? Had they started just after dark, at midnight, closer to dawn? They passed vehicles; vehicles passed them. She tried to interpret the sounds, figure out which were which size, anything that might help her understand where she had been and where she was being taken.

Working it out, bit by bit, with her eyes closed: they had been someplace far from a city . . . that first curvy road, the second smoother one, and now a large road with lots of traffic . . . so they were going to a city, or leaving the area entirely.

A thin beeping, a thump. Gossin peeked, saw a shape heave up in the front of the truck, then reach over to poke the one still lying on the other bunk. "Your turn."

So it had been four hours.

"Did you check them? Pulse, respiration—"

"Yup. In the log."

But Gossin knew she hadn't slept, and no one had taken her pulse. There were remote sensing methods, but—someone had checked her pulse manually after she was loaded.

"We'll do this check together."

"Oh, come on—you been sleeping; I did the other—"

"Every hour. You take that side; I'll take this."

Gossin tried to even out her heart rate, slightly cool her skin. She thought about her grandmother, lounging in the swing-chair on the porch, about what her grandmother had said. She didn't react when fingers touched her neck.

"Told you they're all okay. I'm going down."

"Can I see your vid?"

"Should have brought your own."

This attendant made the hourly checks, and even loosened the straps on Gossin's head and arms, massaged them. Shortly after the

second check, Gossin felt the truck turn, slow, turn again, and come
to a stop. A door slammed—from the cab? A triple knock on the door
behind her. The attendant came past; with the truck not moving, Gossin could feel the footsteps, then heard the clank of the door unlocking and opening a little. Daylight—a streak of sun on the floor Gossin
could see. Colder air flowed in with the light. It carried scents she
thought of as city smells.

Ky Vatta leaned forward to peek through the window into the cab.
They were parked at Bailey's Trucker Heaven, where two roads
crossed, and most of the trucks in the parking area were clearly farm
vehicles pulling utility trailers. The driver—another Stevens-Vatta, familiar with the area—had had breakfast in the café and alerted by Ky
had strolled out only minutes before. She and the team in the truck
had made do with self-heating packets of sausage rolls.

"I see it," the driver said. "Blue farm truck, one cow in the back,
followed by a green-and-yellow utility truck. There's a white van with
a brown fender behind it." Their truck was running and in gear; he
rolled out toward the road. There were two cars behind the white van,
but as it slowed to turn into the truck stop, it created a gap. Ky's driver
pulled out, directly behind their green-and-yellow target.

Ky stepped back from the window and went back to one of the
couches bolted to the floor. "Everything clear, Admiral?" the special
ops team leader asked. He'd said to call him Philo.

"We're right behind it," she said. "Clear road, weather's holding
here, though Rodney says there's a front moving in and it'll be colder
tonight. We should be gone by then." If everything worked. Supposedly everyone was in place and knew what they were doing. The lead
truck, with the cow, would take them all the way to the ambush site,
and would yield to farm traffic coming onto the road ahead. The land
would rise, and get rougher, with taller hills, as they neared the fork to
Weekes City. Her stomach churned. So many things had to go right.
She looked around. The medical trio sat in the float chairs they might

need; Rafe and Teague were beside her, and across from here were the three survivors, now in uniform.

"We'll be fine." Philo smiled. The team wore civilian clothes, farm-style—bulky jackets over stained work pants. The weaponry was obviously military-issue, but from a distance, from an aerial scan, they'd pass as farmers just like everyone else.

An hour and a half later, the driver banged on the window to the back. Ky went forward again.

"Just passed the last road," he said. "That up there might be the place. We've got the green car and the dark-blue truck behind us, like we're 'sposed to."

They were coming down a slope; ahead the road curved sharply left, just like the terrain map. Fences on both sides ran close to the road. And as brake lights flared in the vehicle ahead of them, Ky saw the cattle—a heaving mass of brown moving around restlessly, with men apparently trying to get them out of the road without much success. The first two vehicles beyond the cattle had their doors open, as if the drivers were augmenting the cattle handlers.

"Almost there," Ky said, turning around. "I can see the layout. We're still behind the target."

With a gesture, the team leader brought the team up and to the side door, ready to move out when their truck stopped. Ahead of them, someone honked a horn. Someone yelled. And with a final lurch, they stopped.

The ops team was out the door in a blur of speed, Ky and Rafe right behind them. They had the back door of the target unlocked before Ky reached it, and both attendants were down before they had time to return fire. Philo boosted Ky into the truck body. And there they were, five float chairs facing forward, five bald heads showing. Pockets on the back of each held a folder. Ky looked into the face of the rearmost, pulling out the folder. Gossin. Eyes opened, widened. "Admiral?"

* * *

When the truck finally started up, the two attendants sitting side by side eating something, it moved into heavier traffic for a while and then turned onto another, quieter road. Gossin dozed off and woke to voices both inside the truck and outside.

"Why are we stopped?"

"A traffic jam."

"Here? I thought all this was farm country."

"Driver says there's a bunch of cattle in the road—no way around it; there's a dozen vehicles ahead of us, at least one behind us."

Gossin heard a faint metallic sound from behind—perhaps a cooling grille on the truck behind them—then a hiss and a pop.

"What—?" from one of the attendants.

The door swung open; light and fresh air poured into the cargo space. Both attendants were up now, grabbing for something—and the soft *phup-phup* of a silenced weapon took them both down. Gossin felt the strap holding her to the headrest loosen; hands unfastened the straps on her arms, and someone knelt beside her, freeing her legs. She looked down into the familiar face of Admiral Vatta.

"Can you walk?" Vatta asked.

"M-maybe." Gossin felt light-headed, almost faint, with relief.

"Here—" Vatta signaled someone behind her and moved to the next float chair. "First one, quick."

Men she didn't know lifted her out of the chair and down off the back of the truck. She felt pavement through the thin fabric slippers but managed to hobble to the much larger truck behind them. She felt a steadying hand on her arm, and then a lift through the side door of that truck. This time she recognized the face—Corporal Inyatta, her hair now dark fuzz instead of the neat braid she remembered. "Staff Sergeant," Inyatta said. "Let me help you." Full-sized couches had been fastened to the bed of the cargo space here. Inyatta eased her down onto the soft cushions, then brought a stack of clothes. "You can start changing if you want. They may not fit exactly."

Uniforms. A uniform that was almost her size, just a little big, with the proper patches for her grade, her former unit. She looked around;

in the back corner of this truck were two enclosed spaces like tiny closets. Even as she picked up the clothes and stood, Chok was hoisted through the door, and with two helpers walked back to another couch.

The closet contained a toilet, a sink, a stack of washcloths and towels. Gossin felt tears on her face; she stripped, took off the hated diaper, cleaned up, used the toilet, and dressed. Proper underwear. Real shoes. A uniform jacket. She was breathless by the time she'd walked back to the couch, where someone in a medic's tunic was giving one of the two other people on it—McLenard and Kurin, Gossin saw—an injection. On a different couch, Chok sat blinking, brow furrowed. Then he shook his head.

The medic looked up at Gossin. "Antidote for the sedative load. You're looking pretty good; try this pill instead." He handed her a pill and a paper cup of water.

Gossin wanted to ask questions, but he was busy. Inyatta, at the front of the truck, was helping another—Cosper, she saw, the last of the five—to the third couch.

"You're probably hungry," the medic said. "There's food in the cooler behind that couch."

Gossin's stomach rumbled. She remembered her grandmother telling her that those exercises might make her hungry. But now others were entering the truck—none of them in military uniform. Finally Admiral Vatta, who closed the side door and looked around, her expression as grim as when she had killed Master Sergeant Marek. Then she saw Gossin looking at her, and her expression softened. She moved to the center of the truck and spoke to the medic. "How is everyone?"

"One alert; haven't done the mental status exam yet. The others in various states of sedation. What's our status overall?"

"Page nine, line seventeen."

The medic laughed. Horns started honking. "Clear?"

"Just about." Vatta turned away from the medic and came to Gossin. "You might want to sit down; we're going to move."

"Yes, sir," Gossin said, automatically, though Vatta wasn't in uniform. She sat at the end of the nearest couch; Vatta sat down as well. "What—how did you do it?"

"We haven't done it yet, Staff Sergeant," Vatta said. "Not until you're all free and able to testify in court. But in the meantime, have you eaten yet? The antidote lowers your blood sugar."

"No, sir—"

"Well, I'm hungry and you will be. Hang on."

The truck lurched forward and to the left; Gossin grabbed the couch arm, and Vatta put a hand on Gossin's shoulder, then moved quickly around the couch. "Hot or cold?" Vatta asked.

"Anything, sir."

A wrapped sandwich sailed over the back of the couch and landed beside her. Gossin unwrapped it and bit down. More flavors than she'd had since Miksland flooded her mouth; she ate rapidly until it was gone. Vatta handed her a hot-mug. "The medic said no caffeine after the antidote; that's cocoa. I told him chocolate's also got a stimulant and he said it's not the same. Hope he's right."

The truck was picking up speed now and then swerved—but less jerkily—to the right.

"Where are we going?" Gossin asked.

"To the nearest town, a warehouse where you'll transfer to another truck that'll take you to the airport. Then you'll fly directly to Port Major and then to the Joint Services Headquarters."

"All of us?"

"All of you. Not me. I'll be circling around trying to pull a similar trick on the next transport."

"What about the truck we *were* in?"

"Well . . . it's going to be towed to the next nearest town, where law enforcement will discover the driver is dead drunk, there are two dead people with no ID in the back, and the logo on the truck is a fake. That will keep them busy for a while. Especially since the tow truck will take the long way around Swallowtail Lake to get to Fordham."

Gossin nodded. "How long has it been?"

"Since we left Miksland? Four tendays. Longer than it should have been," Ky said. "I didn't know about this—that you'd all been drugged and confined—until Barash, Inyatta, and Kamat showed up at the Vatta city house. Neither did the Rector. I was mired in legal matters when I got back to Port Major, first with stuff related to a family business matter, and then with citizenship challenges."

Gossin felt her jaw drop. "*You* got caught in the new citizen and immigration law?"

"Yup. Never heard of it, family never thought to mention it. We all thought since I was born here, I was good for life. My cousin and I both had to reapply."

"But you—"

Vatta shook her head. "Even so. Immigration came knocking on my aunt's door, ready to cart me off to prison. I'd been on the planet for over a half year and never turned myself in."

Gossin couldn't help laughing. "You were stuck in a lifeboat and then on Miksland—like the rest of us."

"Yes. And finally that was accepted and I now have a court date for a final determination and the Citizens' Oath." Vatta stood up. "I need to check on the others. Another sandwich?"

The truck was moving smoothly; Gossin levered herself up, glad that she could. "I can get it—and if there's anything I can do—"

"Eat first."

Gossin retrieved a sandwich. Vatta was up in the front of the truck, talking to a man in an unmarked jumpsuit. She looked around. Kurin was awake now, sipping something from a mug and looking around. Chok came out of the makeshift bathroom, and Corporal Barash was there to offer support to a couch. Then Barash moved to McLenard, his eyes now open, but bleary, and spoke to him. With her help, he stood up and she guided him toward the bathroom. A well-run operation, as she'd have expected from Vatta.

CHAPTER TWENTY-TWO

DAY 10

By the time they reached Weekes City, all the Miksland survivors were awake and able to move around independently.

"Admiral," Staff Sergeant Gossin said. "We could be a help with the next rescue—we're up to it, at least most of us."

"Staff Sergeant, I appreciate your willingness, all of you. But we need your testimony; you'll have recorders on the plane, and Sergeant Major Morrison will help you get it all down. We're on a very tight schedule; we've got to have you all back in Port Major, in uniform, before a board that's being convened to decide your fate. We can't risk any of you on the subsequent retrievals." She could see the resistance in Gossin's face. "I know you want to help. I know you've been mistreated and you want to get back at them. But this mess is going to shake up everything—not just the military, but the government as well."

"Yes . . . I see. But I don't like it."

"Understood." Ky turned to Rafe. "I'll be back in a few." To Gossin she said, "Let's get the group together back here. Everyone should hear this."

The five just rescued and Inyatta from the first group gathered around Ky on the rearmost couch. She gave them a précis of what had been going on. "So, we have a list of names we know are implicated in concealing the existence of the base on Miksland. Some of them are high up in the government, some are high up in the business community. We think, but are not sure, that some of the same people were working with my distant and exiled cousin Osman—who's now dead—and with Gammis Turek. We know that's not all of them. But anything I say will be tainted because my family were all killed, and anything the Rector says will be tainted in much the same way." She was not about to drag in Aunt Grace's dirty past at this point.

"You people," she said, "are different. You're the innocents dropped into a situation you knew nothing about, had no connection to, and then you were abused afterward. Your testimony will have more weight than mine. Your physical condition and the medical records we grabbed—yes, they sent them along, in hardcopy, for which I'm grateful—will prove that your experiences really happened. And that's going to be in the public record. So we need to get that recorded, with both Sergeant Major Morrison, whose reputation is impeccable, and two lawyers standing by. For the fourteen of you, that's a lot of hours of recording, and the sooner it's started, the better."

Heads nodded. Ky could tell that resistance to being sent away had vanished. "Eat and drink as much as you want while you're here. The trip from the warehouse to the airport in Weekes City will be only about fifteen to twenty minutes. The flight to Port Major will be about four hours—"

"What about the others? Will they have to wait until that plane comes back? That's more than eight hours—"

"No. We have other aircraft assigned, and alternative routes by road or train if needed."

Gossin's brow furrowed. "This is really that big—as big as getting us off Miksland, isn't it?"

"Pretty much," Ky said. "And we've had to do it all with local resources. Couldn't grab a handy merc company. But then we're not up against another merc company, just a disloyal faction of Slotter Key's own military, some criminals, and a huge amount of money."

"We're glad you did it," Gossin said.

"Had to," Ky said. "And I had a lot of help."

The truck slowed; they could hear more traffic noises outside. "Coming into Weekes City," Ky said. "You'll be changing trucks soon. There'll be a couple of armed guards with you on the way to the airport."

Once in the warehouse, Ky stood by the door as the former prisoners—still bald of course, but looking more themselves in uniform—stepped down from the truck. She shook hands with each of them as they left and watched them walk across to the next truck. Then she went into the warehouse office to check on the progress of the whole mission. Three to go.

"That went well," Rafe said as the truck left the warehouse in Weekes City. "Let's hope the rest are as easy."

"Can't count on that," Ky said.

"I'm not. Just hoping. Are we on schedule?"

"Close. Rodney says the next transport stopped for an unscheduled half hour so we need to dodge about a bit. We should pick them up on 47; there's a truck stop we can use." Ky yawned. "I can't relax until they're all safe."

"You should go back with these on the plane," Rafe said. "It will give them confidence. Besides, you're tired; you hardly slept at all last night. We can handle it."

"I'll nap after we drop these off," Ky said. "I need to be here, and Morrison's on the plane. I'll go with the last load."

"If it's going to unravel, the last load is the most likely to be trouble. By then they'll know the first load and maybe the second are late, and they won't be able to raise them."

"Which is why I should be there with it," Ky said. "You can go back if you want."

"Not without you."

"And I won't leave the op until it's over," Ky said. "So keep track of your rounds."

"Have you reloaded?"

"Of course." Ky patted her own pistol, then tapped the military one slung on her shoulder. "Both."

"Let me take point next time."

"I can't. Rafe, you're used to working alone. I know you're a crack shot. I know you won't hesitate. But you're not used to working in a team, and these people haven't worked with you."

"Or you, except those on Miksland."

"I trained here. Less than sixty days shy of being the honor graduate, Rafe. I move the way they're used to, when I'm on the ground."

Stella Vatta, in the Routing Center of Vatta Transport's Port Major headquarters, watched screens depicting the location of every Vatta Transport vehicle on the continent. Trucks, vans, aircraft, railcars, the little drones that carried light packages from warehouse to destination—a screen for each type, and a huge wall panel that combined them. On her own handcomp, Rodney was transmitting from the Weekes City warehouse, and she could also see where the prisoner transports were, if his algorithm was correct.

"Ansible ping, Sera Vatta."

She left the center momentarily to step into a secured ansible booth and entered the code. No image, but Ky's voice. "One down."

"You're all right?"

"Fine. Clemmander group cleared and reported aboard final transport."

Final transport sounded ominous to Stella but she knew what it meant.

"Be careful."

"Always."

The connection closed; Stella went back out into the Routing Center. On the aircraft screen, the icon labeled 57E—eastbound flight 57—had left Weekes City and was moving toward Port Major. On the ground transport screen, icons with Vatta codes moved as they would on any weekday. The truck that had just made a delivery to Weekes City was now on the road to Green Valley.

And the truck she knew held three of the prisoners had left the truck stop and was moving east; it would reach the junction with the secondary road only a minute before the truck Ky was in, if the schedules held.

COMMANDANT'S OFFICE

"They're late," the voice on the phone said. Commandant Kvannis said nothing. "The first transport. They called in to say they were held up by a herd of cattle in the road—traffic stopped on both sides, local volunteer emergency service trying to get them back into the pasture, but they never called to say the road was cleared. I checked with that shire; the road's been clear for an hour, so they should have been here."

"Did you check satellite data?"

"Yes. The truck's not on the road anywhere. There's a branch about five kilometers from there; they might've taken the road to Weekes City, but surely they'd call."

Kvannis's stomach clenched. "What other vehicles were also stopped? Both directions?"

"I don't know. The satellite showed the blockage all right, but only fifty-five seconds of it."

"I'll put our people on it."

Kvannis stared a moment at his desk, thinking. Missing truck meant missing personnel, meant—worst case—that five more of the personnel from Miksland might contact—might already have contacted—other people. They would be at least partially disabled; they were supposed to be moderately sedated. But if someone picked them up, took them to a hospital—well, he could put someone on that. He called General Mirabeau, the Spaceforce Surgeon General.

"Why would I contact civilian hospitals in Weekes County, Commandant?"

"Personnel in quarantine have gone missing. Some kind person might find them and take them to a hospital and we need them picked up and sent to the proper military facility."

"Quarantined? For what?"

"It's—" How could he say this? Mirabeau was one of the previous Commandant's friends, and definitely not in the know, but he was someone whose rank and title would carry weight with any provincial county hospital. "It's something the ground forces have tried to keep quiet, General. Highly classified, moderately contagious, caused mental degeneration."

"Ah. I see. Well, I'll contact them."

"Tell them the military will send a secure transport and to keep the patients isolated and sedated."

"Right."

That took care of one potential problem. But—what had actually happened? What if the cattle had been a planned roadblock, so that someone could take them? But how? His skullphone pinged again.

"Commandant, I have a result on that satellite analysis you asked for. Do you want to come down or do you want a summary?"

"Summary first."

"Yes, sir. Seventeen vehicles were held up by approximately sixty cattle owned by Rock House Cattle Company. Someone came along last night, cut the fence, stole some stock that were in a pen waiting for a vet check before going to auction, and the other cattle in that field got out onto the road. The local emergency response service was there, along with ranch workers, but it took at least forty minutes to clear the cattle and get traffic moving again. All the vehicles were known to the emergency response team . . . a school bus transporting half-day students, ten private vehicles headed one way or the other, owned by residents in the area, a van owned by a large-animal veterinarian, a horse transport from Highfields Stud, a freight delivery truck—known in the area, comes that way daily—a furniture truck from Weekes City with an order of a living room suite and two beds, with mattresses, for a farmhouse recently purchased by a retired banker and his wife. Then a milk truck picking up milk from the three dairy farms. The only one not known to locals was a green truck with a yellow logo, that's your target truck, right?"

Kvannis didn't answer that. "Any ambulances?"

"No, sir. No one was injured; the first drivers saw the cattle in the road in time to stop. But the target truck—its driver passed out drunk—it had to be towed off after the traffic cleared. Informant says to Fordham, to the impound lot, because the driver was undoubtedly going to jail. He'd yelled at the crew, demanding to be let through first, and then later he was drinking something and then he passed out."

That was definitely suspicious. Drugged? But how, and by whom?

"Find out what vehicles were ahead and behind ours in line, and get back to me."

"Oh, I know what was behind. That was the regular freight delivery truck."

"Which line?"

"Stevens-Vatta, out of Stevensville, south of here. They've been around for decades. Paint their trucks yellow and red, not blue and red, even after they merged with Vatta years ago."

"I see," Kvannis said. He had no doubt in his mind that that truck and its crew had done it, whatever "it" proved to be. Worst case, scooped up all five of them—the ranking NCOs. He looked up their names, called up their records, thinking dark thoughts about Vatta as he did. Damn the woman. The Rector, the former admiral, the CEO— one of them, or more likely all three together. And was that where the first missing prisoners had shown up? He'd suspected it, but he'd had no evidence. If so, they had eight . . . eight witnesses, homegrown believable witnesses. And where were those witnesses now? First, though, he'd see that no more were taken; he had his next in command notify the other transports. He personally notified his most senior associates, those in the ruling council, advising them of the developing problem, and told them not to contact him.

Sergeant Major Morrison raged inside. What they had done to her people, what she had not been able to do when she first saw them, and what was still happening to the rest of them. Safe in Vatta's regularly scheduled cargo plane—she hoped—the five were now recording what they knew of their imprisonment. The first three, who'd given their information before, were asleep now. Morrison had not imagined, before she saw them first in the so-called rehabilitation center, that Slotter Key's military could so mistreat its own people. But they had, and that meant that someone in the command chain had planned it, authorized it, carried out those orders.

She trusted General Molosay and his aide and Major Hong. She wished she knew if Colonel Nedari was safe. He felt solid to her, but what about his senior? She was sure of Master Sergeant "Rusty" Rustowsky, her neighbor. He had been her choice to escort the second group of rescued prisoners to Port Major and waited now in the Weekes City warehouse. She hoped to be back in time to meet the third group herself, but that depended on flight times.

"Sergeant Major, would you come to the flight deck please?"

Morrison went forward, nodding to those who looked up at her. She opened the unlocked door. "Yes?"

"We've overheard a communication that's a bit troubling." The pilot's voice sounded tense. "Says it's Slotter Key AirDefense, with orders for something called Baker Flight. Change of orders, intercept a civilian aircraft and force a landing at a particular military airfield. Would you be able to tell if it's real or some idiot kids playing a game with drones?"

"Maybe."

"I recorded it—here's the playback." He handed her a tab, and she put it in her earbud's player.

The voice sounded adult, male, and professional. Not like a kid at all. She suspected the pilot had come to the same conclusion. "It's real, and isn't that this aircraft's registration number?"

"Yes. I thought it was real, too. You have any advice?"

"We don't want to land on any military airfield," Morrison said. She didn't know how much the pilot knew about their mission. "I'd better contact my command chain. Do you know how far away that Baker Flight is?"

"No—Tomas, do you have anything on radar yet?"

"No, not—wait. That might be . . . yeah. Four of 'em."

Morrison was already calling the Rector's office. Jumping the command chain was bad, but so was their situation altogether.

"Yes, Sergeant Major?"

"We're in the air; we've intercepted a signal in the clear from someone to some AirDefense interceptors to come and force us to land on a military airfield—I don't yet know where."

"Don't do that," the Rector said. "Could you tell where they were coming from?"

"Ulan, there they are!" The copilot was pointing. Faster than Morrison expected the interceptors came at them, and the cockpit communications panel came on, the speaker blaring.

"Vatta Transport Flight 57E, begin descent to three thousand meters and follow all further verbal orders. You will land at Molwarp Military Airfield following directives of Molwarp Air Traffic Control."

The interceptors roared past on either side, aircraft Morrison had seen, but never this close.

Vatta's pilot pulled his mike up and flicked it on. "Who the snarling hell are you to give *me* orders? This is a regularly scheduled cargo flight, on time and on course. You flyboys get your zippy little toys out of my airspace! You're breaking the aviation laws."

"You will land—"

"No, I will not land anywhere but at my filed destination, Port Major—what d'you think you're doing? You must be drunk out of your mind, like that twit who tried something with our flight four years ago. Who's your commanding officer? You're going to get a burn that'll have you standing up for days—"

"This is Baker Flight, AirDefense, from Molwarp Air Base, on orders from Major General Iskin Kvannis, Combined Military Command, Slotter Key Military Headquarters. You are ordered to descend to six thousand meters and change course to follow our lead aircraft immediately. Our orders allow firing on your aircraft if you do not comply."

The copilot looked at Morrison, brows raised in question.

"Kvannis *isn't* a major general, he's got no authority to order this mission, and there's no such thing as the Combined Military Command," Morrison said softly. "General Molosay commands the Joint Services Headquarters. Kvannis is the Academy Commandant." The copilot nodded.

"Firing on our aircraft!" The Vatta pilot, Morrison noted, was doing a masterful job of acting outraged and unbelieving. "Fire on an unarmed civilian aircraft that is following an approved flight plan? What the hell for? I'm reporting you to Air Traffic Control Central." He turned his head slightly. "Call it in, Tomas!"

In Morrison's earbud, the Rector said, "Iskin Kvannis . . . I did not see *that* coming. Do what you can, Sergeant Major; I'll be doing the same. Delay any way you can."

"Orders. You don't need to know more."

"I sure as hell do!" the pilot said. "It's my job to fly this plane to Port Major and unload cargo, some of it with a penalty for late delivery. If I'm late, I'll get demerits and enough of those and I get fired."

A fiery streak shot past the plane and exploded five hundred meters ahead. "That is your warning. Begin descent now."

"Well?" the pilot said. "Do we become dead heroes or—" He drew in a breath sharply.

"What the—?" the copilot said. Two streaks of light punched through the clouds just as the interceptors came into view again, ahead of them. The planes disintegrated.

"Hold your course," Morrison said to the pilots.

The plane rocked abruptly. "Turbulence from the—" the pilot began. It rocked again.

"Trailing pair gone," the copilot said, pointing to one of his screens.

"The admiral did say she had something in reserve," Morrison said.

"Those have to be military weapons," the pilot said.

"I would say so, yes," Morrison said, and went back to the survivors. Evidently Rodney had indeed taken care of it.

CHAPTER TWENTY-THREE

DAY 10

At the first delivery stop after leaving Weekes City, two hours down the road, a Stevens-Vatta employee came out and opened the rear door. "Anybody named Ky in here? Message for you in the office."

Ky went in and used the secure ansible connection to call Grace. "It's the Commandant," Grace said. "Kvannis. He called down Air-Defense on our plane. The sergeant major just reported the flight is continuing."

"Call Rodney. Tell him it's a signal change. Option 4-C."

"You have a Plan C?"

"Of course. And further down than that. Do that, Aunt Grace, and then . . . who was that good guy in Transport that Morrison knew about?"

"Major Carson and Colonel Higgs."

"Tell Higgs to contact me. Without telling anyone else. Say the sergeant major needs some help."

"What are you going to—"

"Leaving now. New schedule. Rodney can tell you."

Every plan should have branches. Aunt Grace had taught her that long ago. What if, and what if that, and what if the other thing. Rafe, looking at her plan back in Port Major, had complained that it looked like a huge tree, far too many branches to be workable. Ky had ignored him. Now, with the original plan in shreds, she was glad her first what-if had been "What if the person at the top on the other side finds out what we're doing before we get the first five to Port Major?"

"What are we going to do?" Rafe asked.

"We're going to make it work. We have the nice complicated plan. And we have sufficient armament."

"But not bodies."

"We do if we move them around."

"But the plane . . ."

"Rodney took care of it."

"But they're not at Port Major."

Ky felt her mood rising with every objection. "I know. They're nowhere near it. What they *are* near is the cache of toys Rodney's best friend Hawker placed at intervals along the plane's route."

"Toys. Like drones?"

Ky nodded. "Equipped with a nice variety of devices." Devices the sergeant major had obtained, after some persuasion, as well as those in various district armories. She checked the time on her implant. "Best get ready. We intercept in eight minutes."

"What about the sheep?"

"Not happening. Already called off. This will be . . . rougher. They know something's going on; Kvannis will have had someone warn the truck they're in, and they'll be trying to slip our tail, have us go on ahead. That's why we have the second truck behind us now."

"Possible target in behind a shopping mall," the special ops man riding shotgun in the cab said. "Parked."

"Block it," Ky said. Their truck turned at the next corner. She stood by the window, where she could see out the front of the cab. "We stop behind that angled wall. Be ready for the call when we pop their lid. Then come in right behind them."

She came out the side of the truck wide open, followed by the rest of the crew, including Rafe. The wall gave them cover for most of the way; the target vehicle was tucked in behind it, right up against some store's loading dock. That would cut its crew's visibility. She held up her hand. "We're going over," she said.

"Over!"

"Satpic from Rodney. They put themselves in a corner—listen, that's our backup team pulling across to block them in. We can land on their roof."

It was not that easy, with two team members—herself and Rafe—shorter than the others. "Could wish for low-g," Ky muttered, dragging her stomach up on the wall. But there below her was the top of the truck, pulled up close to the loading dock. The backup team had a high, distinctive truck, and one of them had already gotten out, banging on the side of the target and yelling.

"Hey! You're blocking the dock! We got a delivery! Move that thing!"

Its driver came out the off side of the cab, equally furious. "You're blocking us in! Get out of here."

"I need this dock. Delivery! Are you deaf? Move it!"

Ky let herself down on the roof of the target and flattened. Rafe dropped onto the backup truck, with a perfect angle to the inside of the target's cargo space. Another team member used his line to drop all the way to the ground between the two trucks; he looked up, and Ky dropped the door opener to him. He touched it with the charger and the lock sprang open; then he flipped the latch and pulled the door wide and continued around the side to attack the target's driver.

Rafe fired before she could move. "One. Clear." He slithered over the side of the truck he was on, and dropped to the ground. Ky swung sideways, where she could watch the parking lot. So far no one seemed to have noticed anything. Early afternoon, midweek, and the shopping mall didn't look that prosperous anyway. Most of the cars were clustered on the other side, near the entrance.

Their other truck came around the wall, turned, and reversed toward the next loading dock, blocking more view of the target. Its driver got out, climbed up on the dock, opened the back of the truck, and set four boxes on the dock. He closed the back, going through the cargo area, and opened the side door, which faced them. Then he went around, climbed into the driver's seat, and picked up a compad, like any driver reporting a delivery to his company.

Ky slid down the front of the target truck and walked around to see Rafe finish off the driver. "This vehicle—what do we do with it?"

"There's a transport nexus about six kilometers on down that road," their ally said. "Huge parking area, trucks and vans and buses coming and going all the time, but some park there for hours, waiting for a connection. It's not much worse than a car to drive, this one." He looked back and forth from Ky to Rafe.

"Let me look at the controls," Rafe said. Ky looked back at two of the ops team carrying a slack bald body in the usual prison outfit over to their truck. It seemed to take a long time; she went to the back and saw that the remaining two were far more sedated than the first load. It took even longer to get both of them into the truck. Ky had to stay with them, had to leave Rafe driving the wrong vehicle, with no legal ID and with two dead bodies in the back. If he were caught—she pushed that thought away and concentrated on the task at hand. They would switch trucks at the next warehouse, and since the Weekes City airport wasn't safe, they'd have to drive different roads to a different warehouse, switch their passengers into a different truck again. Even—if things went very wrong—split them up. She was not going to give up on trying to rescue them all.

The truck moved away from the dock, turned, backed again, then went forward. "We can pick him up at the transport nexus. How are they?"

"Inside and alive. I'll check with the medic."

The medic looked worried. "The reversal drug's not working; it may be more than a simple sedative, or not the same one they used before. Likely they were drugged again."

Ky looked at the three flaccid bodies, still in their clinic clothes. She could not recognize any of the faces, and set her implant to do an analysis. "Vital signs?"

"Two are fine on that. This one—" She pointed to one; Ky's implant suggested Yamini with a question mark beside it. "This one's got problems. Without a full diagnostic unit I can't be sure what's going on, but he's sliding in and out of irregular breathing patterns; I've put him on oxygen. There's a drug that can cause that, but there's no easy reversal; we'll have to hope his liver can get the job done in time. The records we yanked have them as Yamini, Lakhani, and Riyahn."

The truck moved on, slowed in traffic, sped up again. Ky felt chilled; the medic said, "You'd better rest while you can. We can deal with them."

When she woke from a brief nap, it was almost dark outside, and Rafe was not in the truck. She felt colder, though the cargo compartment was warm enough. They were a half hour from the next warehouse. Yamini, if it was Yamini, was still alive, but still unresponsive. The other two had roused enough to give their names and drink a little water, but could not walk or change their clothes yet.

Rodney, when Ky contacted him back at the Weekes City Vatta warehouse, was not encouraging. "Rafe had trouble at the transport nexus. He says he'll meet you later and not to contact him."

"Is he hurt?"

"He didn't say. Your first five made it to Port Major. The plane had to dodge around a bit."

They were safer, but were they really safe yet? She knew they would be taken to Joint Services Headquarters, and Morrison had assured her it would be safe, but she still worried. She wanted to know they were protected from the conspiracy determined to kill her, her family, her people. And she wanted to know where Rafe was, and what was happening.

"Your friends—" she began.

"They're fine. Set up in another location just in case." He sounded wistful. "Wish I'd been with them. Hawker said the range beam punched through the clouds so fast—they never use full power in training—"

"You had a long-range beam weapon? I thought you were using drones—"

"Well, they had drones, but Hawker said they decided not to take chances—"

Ky could imagine what it must have looked like. On full. "Do you still have a lock on the other two groups?" she asked, pushing aside the thought of any satellites in the way when the beam came on.

"Yes. One is two hours east, still coming. They stopped for a half hour several hours ago; we didn't have anyone in the area, though, for a visual ID or a communications tap. The other is closer, but it's been driving in circles for the past hour. Which backup vehicle do you want to use?"

Ky ran through the options she'd set up again. "They may be planning to convoy, or they may be just hoping we'll do something stupid. Let me talk to Blind Dog Two."

"Need to grab 'em as soon as possible, separately," that team commander told her. "Both'll likely be a hard stop. Could be injuries—"

"If those crews panic, there'll be dead prisoners," Ky said.

"Right. So we'll need that backup aircraft—" Not a Vatta scheduled flight, but Inyatta's father's friend's small plane. "—and Weekes City's emergency services will lend us one of their ambulances." That was new. Who had been talking to them? But too late to worry.

"Take whatever you need," Ky said. "I'll be jumping to another truck in about twenty minutes, heading back your way for the stragglers."

COMMANDANT'S OFFICE

Iskin Kvannis knew from the first frantic call about the missing personnel that he had been right and his associates wrong: they should have killed the survivors sooner. Just do it, he'd told them; that would be the quickest, surest way. But they had refused. He'd called Ordnay and Molwarp; they'd scrambled the interceptors. Surely that would take care of some of the survivors. As he went through his daily duties, immaculate in his white Commandant's uniform and to outward appearance untroubled and confident, his mind rehearsed all the careful plans he'd made.

But the style of the rescue bothered him. Quick—and no one was supposed to have known of the date or hour of that truck's travel except those loyal to the cause. Could the Vattas possibly have hacked his communications? He'd warned the other sites of the first interception; he trusted they would be careful. But then the second shipment had been snatched, this time not on an isolated road but in a busy town, by daylight, leaving two bodies behind and—most telling—Rafe Dunbarger's ID and money hanging over a rail-yard fence. That proved it was Ky Vatta's doing.

About the same time, he learned that the interceptor flight had vanished, and a satellite scan showed the heat signature of a beam weapon from a previously unmarked site shortly before. The Vatta flight landed safely in early afternoon, met by General Molosay's car and several others in convoy, and the nine passengers—which must include the three who'd escaped on their own and an escort—were transported to the Joint Services Headquarters without incident.

Molosay had not called him. That in itself was worrying. If the interceptor pilots had revealed the authorization, which was of course fake, then Molosay might know he was a traitor. Time to enact his own survival plan, the one he had made at the very beginning of this mess.

Safely back in the Commandant's office, all the doors closed, he unlocked his safe, took out his secured documents case, set it on the desk, and then relocked the safe. The documents case already contained the papers he wanted from the safe. To that he added all the ready cash from the cashbox in his desk drawer and a selection of papers from those filed in another drawer. He didn't care which, just that it was a big enough wad to hide the other from casual inspection.

A skullphone call pinged him: Quindlan. "Someone's identified Ky Vatta as being on one of the enemy trucks."

"Of course she is," Kvannis said, just managing not to snarl. "Where did you think she was, reading in bed?"

"You can't talk to me—"

"Yes, I can. Get to the rendezvous—"

"But this isn't what was supposed to happen! You said it would be—"

"I said we would be damned lucky if it worked. It didn't work. Now we have to deal with it." Quindlan made a loud noise and cut the connection. Kvannis took a deep breath. Quindlan had talked tough for years, pushing for action, but like too many civilians he fell apart when the time came. Well, he'd either make it to the rendezvous or not.

He himself had, he thought, at least six hours to finish up, and then two to do the final packing. He left his office on time, went to the Commandant's Residence, smiled and nodded as usual to staff, and went upstairs, claiming a headache and little appetite. In the next two hours he cleared his residence office, packed the few clothes he would take from his closet. He lingered over the presents he'd bought for his daughters, but left them. Then he went back to his main office to finish up there.

It was later than that, after all, when he left, past midnight. Too many things had needed to be burned, and burned without detection— something possible only after the Academy's document shredder and incinerator weren't likely to be heard. He'd long made a habit of wandering about in the evening when no event was scheduled, and that did make it easier.

And then . . . that last quiet descent of the stairs with his two small cases, disarming the alarm, going out to meet the waiting car, the po-

lite pause at the gate, the excuse—a family matter at his city home—
and they were off in the quiet dark for the small airfield mostly limited
to private aircraft. From there, crammed into the backseat, he stared
at the darkness below, the pattern of the lights that pierced it. By local
dawn in Port Major, he was over a thousand kilometers away, in a
roomful of fellow conspirators. He looked them over. Nervous, per-
spiration gleaming on their faces, all but the military ones. He put
aside thoughts of his family back in Port Major, and the life he had
known, and prepared to do what he could to salvage the revolution.

The rest of the day, for Ky, was a mad scramble to reposition her assets, avoid those of the opposition, and maintain contact with the rescue teams. The second group, she heard, had also made it safely to
Port Major after she left them. The third, shepherded by half the team
the sergeant major had put together, was somewhere in the northeast
now, making ground in that direction. There'd been a brief firefight;
one of the survivors had been hit, but not fatally. No names were
mentioned in these updates. She had made her interception of the
fourth group, successfully retrieving Lundin, Gurton, and Droshin-
ski. Most of the third special ops team had stayed back to delay pursuit, but Philo had come with her in case of trouble. They were now
far behind the original schedule, traveling for the moment in a farm
truck headed home from a cattle auction. The truck smelled strongly
of cattle and bounced as if it had never had springs.

A sharp turn, lurching and bouncing on gravel that crunched beneath them, and then the screech of brakes. "We're home," the driver
announced. He pulled open the side door. Ky got up, jumped down,
and helped the others out. "Mama!" she heard the driver call. "Got
folks to feed!"

Unlike farmhouses Ky had seen farther west, mostly built of stone,
this one was brick. Ky shed her muddy boots on the porch and the
others followed suit. Inside, the wood floor was polished, the walls
plastered a pale cream. The farmer, Jacob Arender, introduced them

to his wife, Anna, and the children, Barry and Luisa. "First we have supper," Arender said. "Then you can take the car and go into the city. You won't have a problem."

Ky didn't believe that last. But they were less than 150 kilometers from the city, with good communications. She took herself off to the bathroom and called Rafe on her skullphone. Still no answer. Well—he could be somewhere without coverage. She reached Rodney. "Where are you?" he asked. "I'm tracking several military search parties. And there are roadblocks on every highway into Port Major. It's been on the news—attempt to prevent dangerous contagious disease getting into the city. You'd better get a disguise."

Ky's mind went blank for a moment. They'd gone to such trouble to bring ID and uniforms for the survivors—and how could they find disguises out here, at night? Businesses would have closed in the nearest town.

"What's the word?" Arender said when she returned to the kitchen.

"Roadblocks," Ky said. "And a few chase parties trying to find where we are."

Arender frowned. "Don't want to lose my car because they spot you in those uniforms."

"They don't have to stay in those uniforms," Anna said. She grinned. "I'll go with you. Drive the car and then I can drive it back. It's almost the holidays; we can go as a group for the dance festival." She looked at Ky. "I used to go every year with my friends. I have all my old costumes."

"Anna! You can't leave the children—"

"You'll be here." Her eyes sparkled as she turned to Ky. "It will be fun, like old times. You'll see."

Arender threw up his hands. "No use arguing, I can see. When Anna makes up her mind, what's said is done."

While they ate, Anna rummaged in the storage room for costumes. Ky stared at the armloads of stripes in garish colors, ruffles, lace, ribbons that she piled on the bed. "It's a district thing, stripes," Anna said. "In those days, we all matched, but what I saw the last time I went is that some didn't. So it's all right if you don't. Here—try this one." It fit, even over her other clothes. Ky looked down at herself, trying to keep a polite smile on her face, but the green, purple, and orange combinations were almost too much for her.

Anna looked them over as they headed out the door, uniforms hidden under voluminous skirts, ruffled blouses, and shawls. She stopped Ky. "That hair—you can't have it like that." She reached up and unfastened Ky's braid, pulling her hair loose until it was a dark cloud around her face. "That's better. Means you're not married; the rest of you, with scarves and earrings, are betrothed."

The ride to Port Major, Ky crammed in the backseat with the survivors, the special ops team member now wearing the farmer's best dress shirt as well as a felt hat with a feather, and carrying a drum and three tambourines on his lap in the front beside Anna, was, as Anna had predicted, fun. They had to stop at two roadblocks—one to get on the highway, and one nearer Port Major. Both times Anna had them singing a country song she'd taught them.

The second roadblock took much longer, because a long line was ahead of them, including freight trucks. Uniformed men opened every truck and trailer; some were waved over for more complete searches. When it was finally their turn, the men in uniform asked Anna where they were going, and her confident "To Port Major, of course, for the winter dance festival. Can't you see?" Lights flashed in their faces, and one of the men said, "Can you believe it? How far back in the hills did *they* come from?" Then he gestured. "Go on, go on, don't hold us up."

Rafe hoped Ky was away safely with the three new rescues. He also wished he knew anyone on the planet but Ky's family and immediate associates. The transport center had been a near disaster. He'd parked on the wrong side, in the lot for those with season passes. The outgate had a guard checking those passes. He realized just in time, and walked off to the train station, where he'd hoped to mingle awhile and come out by another door. But the truck itself must have interested the guard—perhaps because it had no sticker in the window—because when he looked back from just inside, he saw the man walking around the truck, and then pulling at the back door.

He knew what would happen when the man looked inside and didn't wait to watch. He left the station by a side door, then went around the corner toward the tracks. A train waited; passengers crowded the platform. Could he just get on a train, pay for a ticket once aboard? But he saw a crowd of passengers, a conductor checking tickets. Ky would be furious—worried—when he wasn't waiting to be picked up, but he could call from the train. He eeled through the crowd, most of them taller than he was, aiming for the locomotive. Surely one car wouldn't have a guard—but they all did. Between cars he could see a second track, then a tall fence and then rising ground. He reached the locomotive and ducked around it. Another train was approaching—would hide him once he was across that track. A warning blast from the moving train—he was already bolting for the fence. He felt the wave of air pressure that meant he'd cut it dangerously close. But the train now blocked him from any pursuers. He leapt for the fence, pulled himself up, sacrificed his heavy outer jacket to the barbed wire at the top and rolled over, landing neatly, then bounded up the slope beyond, where coarse bushes gave some cover. And remembered that all his ID—the ID that would get him arrested and deported as an illegal alien—was still in that jacket's pocket. He couldn't go back. It took him hours to climb the hill—it felt like a mountain—as the clouds thickened, the light dimmed, and the temperature dropped. Initially he was sweating from the effort, feet slipping on the steep slope, and didn't notice the cold.

It had been full dark awhile when the slope finally eased; he stood panting there, unable to see anything but a dim glow back the way he had come. He checked his skullphone—a signal, but weak—and called Rodney. "Tell her I had a problem and not to worry. Keep right on. I don't know when I'll get back, but I will." He wondered if the opposition already knew he was on this mountain.

Surely if he just kept going down, he would come to a road or a house or something. It wasn't long before a cold drizzle chilled him and then the drizzle turned to sleet.

Any sane person would be inside a warm room eating supper. He was hungry, cold, and completely lost. He'd made it over that hill, but he didn't know where "that hill" was in relation to any road, let alone one that would lead him to shelter and reliable communications. He couldn't see any lights anywhere. He had to move slowly, careful of each step; the ground sloped mostly down but had unexpected humps and holes in it.

"This sort of thing was a lot easier on a space station," he said aloud when he'd arrived on softer ground that squished under his shoes. He was answered by a loud breathy sneeze and the sound of hooves squelching away. What made that kind of noise? He had no idea. It sounded big. Did it bite? Kick? Stick you with sharp horns? But he couldn't stand there all night, not in this weather and with his shoes leaking. He wished he'd kept his jacket. He had to keep moving. He remembered that from the books he'd read as a boy.

Eight steps later, he ran into something large and wet and hairy. Even as he reached out to feel it, understand it, something hard took him in the ribs and knocked him flat. The mystery attacker let out what sounded like a vast groan and squelched away, still groaning. He clambered up as fast as he could. Other groaning animals joined it; the noise of hooves rose around him; the ground trembled. Someone yelled in the distance, below him, and dogs barked in two different tones. He had no idea what to do, and stood there until one of the creatures knocked him down and he hit his head on a rock.

An hour later he was sitting in a warm kitchen, steam rising from his wet clothes spread on wooden chairs, and an entire family of farmers, all taller then he was, arrayed on the other side of a large table, staring at him with a mixture of curiosity and hostility.

"You were lucky I sent the dogs out and didn't just shoot into the dark," the taller man said. "I could've, ya know. Nobody 'round here'd blame me for shootin' a stranger out there messin' with the stock in the middle o' the night."

"I wasn't—" he started, and then shrugged. "I don't know this area. I came up that hill on the other side; I didn't know what was on this side; I didn't know about the livestock. I ran into one in the dark."

"You got no light?" That was the shorter man, two shades lighter than the taller one, gray eyes instead of brown.

"He's got one," the gray-haired woman said. "I found it in his pocket, put it there on the chimney ledge."

"So you got a light and didn't use it . . . skulking along like a thief, eh?"

"A fugitive, anyway," Rafe said. He was naked under the blanket the farmer had wrapped him in, and had bruises all over his torso from the monsters—cattle—that had knocked him down and—at least two legs of them—stepped on him. His feet were still cold, resting on a thin rug over a stone floor. His wet clothes were hanging on a string; his weapons had been collected and tucked into a drawer in the sideboard. His head ached savagely.

"What you done?"

"Made some people very angry," Rafe said. Killed some, but that wouldn't help his cause. He sifted through the facts to see if he could come up with a viable narrative.

"Just tell the truth," the gray-haired woman advised. "It's always best."

Rafe knew better than that, but the way his head felt he had no alternative, if he said anything. "What do you know about the Spaceforce shuttle crash last spring and Admiral Vatta's survival on Miksland?"

"This got a connection?" The taller man took a swig from his mug and set it down hard.

"Yes. Yes, it does."

"Well, then: we know the shuttle crashed in the ocean and everybody thought they were all dead until a few weeks ago. But they all caught something and are terribly sick, in quarantine; they think Admiral Vatta might die. Do you know her?"

"Yes," Rafe said. "But she's not sick, or in danger of dying from anything caught in Miksland." Except information someone wanted no one to have.

"That's not what it said on the news," the gray-haired woman said. The other woman, younger and darker with a thick head of unruly curls, was leaning against a counter and watching him over her mug. She had startling green eyes. He'd seen another pair of eyes like that, recently . . . who had it been?

He dragged his mind back to the present: what to say? In for a credit, in for a hundred. "Admiral Vatta is my . . . we're going to be married," he said.

The teenage boy burst out laughing; the tall man flicked him on the head and said, "Quit. Or go to bed now." The boy stifled the laugh with his hand, but his eyes crinkled with amusement. Rafe wanted to smack him.

"We met years ago," he said. "Then there was the war, and I was on Nexus and she was in space—"

"Wait a minute," the younger woman said. "You said *she* wasn't sick . . . what about the others? Nobody's seen or heard from them since they were rescued. Mally told me—" She stopped and glanced at the taller man.

"Mally's her cousin," the gray-haired woman said. "Married to one of them—"

"McLenard. Andrew Hugh McLenard. He's a sergeant. D'you know if he's alive?"

"Yes," Rafe said. "At least, he was when we got him out of the transport."

"You've *seen* him? Does Mally know yet? I have to call—"

The older woman stepped back and caught her hand. "No, Saneel. Not until we know more. Might not be safe."

"I don't know if your cousin knows yet," Rafe said. "I was with the admiral; she had the whole plan but I didn't, so I couldn't be made to tell it. I do know she intended everyone to know, as soon as they were all safe."

"And they aren't sick?"

"No. Did you hear about the base on Miksland?"

"Base? There was some kind of mine or something they got into, right?"

"Military base," Rafe said, saving the other part for later, if ever. "Could I have another mug please? My throat's dry."

"Be a wonder if you don't catch your death," the older woman said. She poured from a pot on the stove and handed him the mug. "Hungry?"

"I could eat—" He stopped himself from saying *a cow* and finished with "just about anything." He had been smelling the food since he came to, and his stomach wanted it immediately.

She laughed. "That's good because this stew has got just about anything in it. If you're warm enough you ought to change into real clothes; eatin' in a blanket isn't handy." She left the room and returned with a knitted pullover that looked like nothing Rafe had ever seen, a pair of rough trousers, and a pair of thick gray socks.

"That's my—" the boy started, and got another flick to the head.

"Strangers in need," the tall man said. "He sure can't wear mine or Harley's."

"Thank you," Rafe said.

"Come, Saneel," the woman said. "And you, too, lad, while he changes."

The men showed no signs of moving. Rafe stood up, let the blanket fall, stepped into the trousers, and yanked them up; they were only a little big. The shirt had only two buttons; he put that on, and then the pullover, then sat down and put the socks on.

"M'wife, she knitted that sweater," the taller man said. "Wool from our sheep. Socks, too."

"It's beautiful," Rafe said, taking a closer look at the pattern of light and dark wool. "And I'm already warmer. My feet, too."

The taller man nodded, then glanced at the shorter one. He tipped his mug up, emptying it. "Well . . . the dogs didn't eat you, and you have a story I've never heard, so I guess you can stay the night until your clothes dry and then we'll figure what to do."

"I need to find Ky—Admiral Vatta—and find out what's happened. I'm supposed to help—"

The shorter man tipped his head to one side. "What you should want most is not to be found by whoever was chasing you."

Rafe nodded. His head still hurt.

"And you got run over by at least one critter and hit your head on that rock. So you don't need to be running around in the dark getting worse hurt, and if we go down the market road on a night like this, people will talk. Some of the people who will listen may be the ones you ran from."

"You don't have any way to call anyone?"

"Not until they put in more towers, and those so-called reps we got don't want to spend money on us way out here. An' yeah, there's the ISC ansible, but that costs too much per call."

"You still haven't given us a name," the taller man said just as the two women and the boy came back into the kitchen. "You've heard some of ours. Let's hear yours."

"Rafe," he said. "Rafe Dunbarger, of Nexus Two."

"Anselmo." The tall man pointed to himself, then to the shorter man. "Enver." He pointed at the boy. "Gill. Enver's oldest."

The boy gaped at Rafe, ignoring the introductions. "You're—you *run* ISC!"

"Not anymore," Rafe said. "My sister Penny's the head of it now."

The tall man—Anselmo—had scowled at the boy, and turned back to Rafe, all the friendliness gone again. "So you're one of those rich city boys, never did a lick of real work—bring in more money a day sittin' at a desk than everyone in this sector together makes in a year."

"Not quite," Rafe said, keeping his own tone friendly. "I was thrown out on my own—family wouldn't have me. Never worked on a farm, true, but had to make my way."

"What'd you do to get shunned?"

"Killed two men who wanted to kill me and my sister, one night when my parents weren't home." He didn't want to tell the whole story again. His head hurt worse now.

"They kicked you out for that? How old were you?"

"Eleven. First they sent me for therapy, then the therapist said I needed a special school for violent offenders. A prison, essentially."

"At eleven?" The older woman set a large bowl of some steamed grain on the table, then another of stew. The younger woman went around the table, passing out plates, and put one in front of Rafe. The tall man shook his head. "If a son of mine managed that at eleven, I'd have been proud of him. Saved your sis's life, didn't you?"

"Yes." Rafe's mouth was dry again, his throat tight. "It's—it's different there. None of their friends' sons would do something like that."

"Huh. Better get some of that food down you. You still don't look too good."

He waited until everyone was seated, despite the invitation, and the older woman had handed him a spoon. "Grooly first, then the stew," she said. "That's how we do it here." Then she piled a spoonful of the grooly—whatever it was—on her plate, and used the same spoon for the stew, before passing it to the tall man. Rafe did the same, passing the spoon to the younger woman, who now sat on his left.

Memory and headache had cut off his appetite, so he took small bites until his stomach agreed he could keep going. No one talked. The grooly tasted bland; the stew was spicy, tingling in his mouth. He put his utensils down before he finished. "Thank you," he said. "It's delicious; it's just my head—" He felt nausea knot his stomach; his vision wavered.

The tall man looked across at him and pushed back from the table. "You're green. Luisa, help me."

Rafe locked his teeth, hoping not to spew at the table. Every movement hurt, and the first sour-salty taste came into his mouth. He felt them grab his arms, lift him up; someone pulled the chair away and they were half dragging him down the kitchen to a door. He tried to walk but his legs weren't cooperating. They made it to the next room before he couldn't help spewing. Someone wiped his mouth after.

"It's his head," the woman's voice said. "I shouldn't have let him eat so much."

"We can't call the doc; he doesn't want to be found."

"Sorry," Rafe said. It came out weak. He could scarcely stand, even with support.

"We'll bed him down in Chan's room. With a bucket. Think he's done?"

Rafe felt himself falling, then caught. Muttered curses, grunts of effort; he passed out then, and woke hours later to darkness and silence. His head didn't hurt until he turned it, when his neck seized, then half the muscles in his back. He lay still, teeth gritted, until the cramps let go. He didn't feel nauseated anymore, but he certainly wasn't completely well. When the neck spasm eased, his head was pounding, though less than before.

DAY 11

The next he knew, dim daylight, cold and gray, came through a gap in the curtains onto his face. He could hear noises in the distance, and the ticking of more sleet on the window. He was inside, dry and warm. A good start to any day, he told himself. His implant informed him of time, date, "no location," and "no contact" when he accessed his skull-phone. The room was square, the walls painted cream. The curtains at the window were white with a pattern of red and yellow flowers at the top. A table and chair were in the left corner across from him, and a chest with a small square mirror on top in the right corner.

A few exploratory moves in the bed made it clear he was stiff, sore, but able to move without immediate cramping. He still had on the clothes he'd been given the night before. When he tried sitting up, his head swam for a few moments, and the ache intensified, but he was sitting, socked feet on a rug made of some animal skin on the floor.

A knock came at the door to his right, and it opened before he could answer, his voice being stuck somewhere in his throat.

"Good," the gray-haired woman said. "You were too sick last night to notice, most like. My name's Luisa. How's your head?"

"It still aches, but less," Rafe said. "I'm sorry I've been so much trouble."

"We've done nothing yet we wouldn't do for anyone," she said. "There's breakfast in the kitchen, or I could bring you a tray—but I don't know what's best for you to eat."

"Little," Rafe said. "Some bread, maybe? Toast? And I should get all the way up."

She offered a hand, and he took it, unfolding painfully in sections.

"What kind of livestock ran over me?"

"Cattlelope, properly," she said, letting go his hand as he steadied. She moved out into the passage; he followed. "We mostly call them cattle. Pretty standard large herbivore for meat and milk production issued to colonies. Slotter Key has old cattle now—bovines, not the hybrids—but we've stuck to the cattlelopes because they do well here."

He'd eaten cattlelope steaks and roasts all his life but had no idea what a cattlelope looked like. He followed her down the hall to the kitchen. In daylight, the same gray daylight, he could see details that had escaped him the night before. The stone floor had a border, a ring of darker stones, about half a meter from the walls. Around the big table were children smaller than the boy the night before: five of them. Luisa had no implant, and neither had the men, he remembered. Nor the boy, nor any of the children. Were these Miznarii? His own implant was obvious . . .

Luisa smiled at him. "You're right, we don't have implants. But we're not anti-humods. I got a prosthetic eye when I lost one to a stone chip."

The food on the table smelled wonderful. Luisa set a plate in front of him and put a piece of toast on it. "Try this first. If it doesn't make you queasy there's eggs and sausage."

It didn't make him queasy. Neither did the eggs and sausage. The thunderous knocks on the door did.

"Go back to bed," Luisa said. "You're my cousin Jules. You're sleeping off a drunk. And you children, go to the schoolroom and get to work on your books."

Rafe couldn't really hurry to the room, but he made it there before Luisa opened the outside door, fell into the bed, pulled the covers over, and was asleep again before he knew it. When he woke, hours later, sun had broken through the clouds. He stayed under the covers until he heard Luisa call the children.

"Yes, come on," she said, looking down the hall. More quietly, as he came closer. "Some fellow in a military-looking uniform, said he was looking for dangerous fugitives. Described a couple of bald men. I said my cousin had a full head of black hair, a lot of bruises from stumbling and falling in the pasture in the dark, and wasn't at all dangerous when sleeping off too much liquor. He looked into the room, and there was the back of your head with black hair, and you were snoring like anything, then he left. You know any bald men?"

"Bald men and bald women," Rafe said. "They kept the survivors from Miksland shaved bald and drugged, so they'd look sick and damaged. We were getting them out." He hoped by now they were all safe in Port Major. The last interception should have been the night before. He needed to get in touch with them.

Luisa showed him the rest of the rambling, one-story house, gave him a heavy jacket, and took him outside to see what had run over him. A line of them were watching over a stone wall, ears wide, noses sniffing. They had long pointed horns curving up from their heads, and a ruff of longer hair down the neck, broad bodies covered with a thick hair coat, white lower legs and bellies, tails with a tuft of longer hair on the end. And the attitude of animals that expected feed to appear shortly. Behind them, up the slope of the hill, stones broke through the meager grass. A few of their kind grazed higher up, but turned as Luisa shut the house door and started downhill.

"Those are cattlelope. Daresay you've eaten some in your life."

"They're . . . pretty," Rafe said. Their coats were splotched and striped with dark brown and white; no two looked quite alike.

"They're extremely useful animals," she said. Then grinned. "*And* pretty, yes. Ours are considered one of the best herds in this area."

Dogs barked in the distance; the cattlelope all lifted their heads to stare toward the barking.

"Back inside," Luisa said. "That's Tag and Porro; they've found a stranger."

Inside felt much warmer. Luisa motioned Rafe back toward the room he now knew as his. The bed was a tumble of sheets and blanket; he straightened it out, went to the desk in the corner, and sat in front of it, head in his hands. It did still hurt some, though not too badly.

The stranger turned out to have been from the town, hoping to pick up news. Luisa sent him away, after questioning him. "I didn't entirely trust him," she said. "He's local enough, knew the right names, but I heard that family's had some bad eggs in their basket." She stuck her hands in her pockets and looked out the window for a moment. "He did have news you'd better know. They found your ID and money in a jacket on the rail-yard fence."

"I thought that might be trouble. I didn't realize I'd forgotten to change pockets until I was partway up the hill," he said.

"Did you kill those men in the truck?" Her gaze pinned him in place.

"One of them, yes."

She nodded. "Higgens said there was a news message about it, and about the survivors being mistreated, and some men stopped it, smashed the transmitter station. But enough got out people are riled up."

If they'd released the news about the rescue, then everyone must be back in Port Major. "Anything about Ky—Admiral Vatta?"

Her expression softened. "No, not that Higgens heard. And we'll get you to where you can call, but we'd best think how to do it, now they're looking for you in particular."

CHAPTER TWENTY-FOUR

DAY 11

Ky made it back to Port Major and the Joint Services base shortly before dawn, exhausted from two nights with hardly any sleep and a lot of hard work. She would rather have been home in bed, but General Molosay insisted that all involved in the rescue of survivors stay on base for the time being. Ky wasn't happy about being held at the base—for security reasons, they said, because of undefined unrest in the city itself. The Vatta residence had been attacked, she heard; Stella had had only minor injuries, but serious damage had been done to the house. She wasn't happy about the condition of two of the survivors. Both Hazarika and Ennisay had been overmedicated, she was told, and might have residual damage when and if they woke up. Yamini appeared to be doing well now, but was still confined to bed. All had signs of abusive treatment, and all were now in the hospital. Some already had visitors; the families were streaming in, alerted by General Molosay that their lost had been found. She'd seen Betange's siblings, escorted by a shy much older uncle, fall on him hugging and crying.

But Rafe had not reappeared, and her attempts to call his skull-phone or the cranial ansible had no response. She wanted a shower, a change of clothes, a quiet meal sitting down somewhere, but most of all she wanted to know what had happened to Rafe. Teague had arrived in Port Major shortly after midnight with the next-to-last group, driving a vehicle some relative of Rodney's had lent him, with the three survivors crammed into too small a backseat for hours, but aside from that both the survivors and he were fine. He knew no more about Rafe than she did.

"Uh—Admiral—?" A very young officer, looking embarrassed, tapped the doorframe.

"Yes, Lieutenant." Ky had explained that she wasn't an admiral anymore, but military courtesy prevailed.

"The general would like you to come to the situation room."

"Thank you," Ky said, pushing herself upright. She wished she'd managed to get clean and into her own clothes; she felt ridiculous in the stripes and ruffles and fringed shawl. Her hair, once released from the neat braid she usually wore, had reacted to freedom and the weather by forming a shapeless mass that she had to keep pushing back from her face. She followed the lieutenant down a passage.

"—and we still don't know how many units are affected, sir." A commander in Spaceforce blue looked out of the viewscreen; General Molosay waved Ky over to a seat near him.

"Have you found the lost evidence from Miksland yet?"

"No, sir. They could have destroyed it—"

"Or not. They will want to have something from there to substantiate their claim that a dangerous disease or toxin existed. Keep looking."

"Yes, sir."

The screen blanked. Molosay turned to Ky. "How much of Grey-haus's log did you read?"

"Not enough," Ky said. "I found the part that seemed to pertain directly to our situation and read that, but we were busy and I didn't read the rest. I expected someone here would, when I turned it in."

"Pity. Here's the situation as we know it now. Kvannis left the Academy after midnight last night, checked out through the gate, told the guard he was going to his family home in the city, which isn't unusual. He didn't show up there, and he never came back to the Academy. When he didn't come down to breakfast this morning, residence staff checked on him and found his quarters empty, with signs that someone—presumably Kvannis—had taken clothes, his portable comp, and all his IDs. He left no explanation with anyone at the Academy that we've been able to find. The safes in his quarters and his office have been drilled out and they're empty. Since he had access to official secrets, including personnel records and strategic planning papers affecting force organization, we have to assume he has them now, and that unauthorized persons have access to them."

"The former Commandant couldn't have known—"

"No. I never knew Kvannis well, but we've bumped into each other often enough, and I never saw that coming. But I have a question for you, Admiral Vatta." Ky waited. She'd never met Kvannis; she couldn't imagine why Molosay thought she might answer any questions about him. Molosay swallowed, looked away, looked back at her. "Will you accept the post of Academy Commandant in this crisis? We have cadets who need someone they can recognize and trust, and someone who is familiar with the Academy's routine."

Ky stared at him, unable to answer at first. He waited. Finally she managed a raspy "Why?"

"Why you? Several reasons. You would have been the top graduate in your year. The situation that resulted in your resignation was an error of youth and inexperience, as the then-Commandant recognized. Your performance since then has shown that you learned everything we had to teach, and more from others; you have experience no one else on this planet has. And the fact that you've been away for so many years means that you, alone of all the officer corps here, cannot have been part of the conspiracy. The fact that your great-aunt is

Rector of Defense is the only point against you, but it's a small one in comparison with your overall qualifications. This is not a permanent post—I can't imagine that you'd want to take on the job forever—but it would ensure competent, loyal leadership for our young cadets until we sort this mess out and can appoint someone else. So—will you take it?"

"Doesn't the Commandant's appointment also require the approval of the President and legislature?"

"Yes, but you have them, I've been assured."

"Then yes. But only if I can shower, change clothes, and contact a military tailor for a uniform. This—" She spread her arms, shook her head to move the mass of hair, and looked down at her flamboyantly striped outfit. "—is not what I call command presence."

Molosay grinned at her. "That's not a problem. The best officers' outfitter in the city has sent their senior tailor and a dress white uniform they were making for an officer near your size. There's a small suite in this building where you can clean up and he can work. We can arrange for someone to retrieve civilian clothes from the Vatta house, and the base stores have everything you'd need for a couple of days. I know you must be short of sleep, but the situation at the Academy is not entirely stable. MacRobert is over there, but he's not an officer."

Two hours later, Ky was wearing Commandant's whites with the Commandant's insignia in shiny gold on her shoulders, and its attendant layers of braid on sleeves and cap. It fit well, though the tailor promised better for the rest, and delivery of another uniform the next day. Today she had better not spill anything on it.

Her hair was back in its snug braid, and she had seen the last, she hoped, of the dance costume. She wrote its owner a thank-you note and pinned it to the blouse. She had a good black briefcase, borrowed from General Molosay, and data cubes full of information she hadn't yet loaded into her implant.

As the official car took her to the Academy, she reviewed the scant data known about the other officers serving there. Second to Kvannis was a Colonel Stornaki in the ground forces. That alone created suspicion, since Greyhaus and the troops stationed seasonally in Miks-land had to be part of whatever conspiracy this was. Stornaki's official photo showed a narrow face, gray eyes, beige skin, the usual left-sided ridge from an implant under his light-brown hair. His background had been unremarkable; the only flag at all was his distant relation-ship to one of the rebel leaders during the Unification War.

The car moved smoothly through the streets; Ky could see out, but the mirrored windows meant others could not see in. Did not mean no one else knew who the new Commandant was, of course. She knew the streets around the Academy and the amount of traffic was suspiciously low. There was the gray wall she remembered, with the Hall—the largest building in the complex—looming above it. The car turned left, then right as a gate in the wall opened and sentries came to attention. Her stomach clenched; she took a long breath and re-laxed consciously. She had left by the public entrance, those years ago; she was coming back by the Commandant's private entrance. If she had ever dreamed of a triumphal return, this was it . . . but she hadn't, and this didn't feel triumphal at all. Despite the uniform and the offi-cial car and security detail, it felt rushed and not entirely organized. She would rather have been paying a call on the Commandant who had died in the same act of sabotage she barely survived.

A man in a master sergeant's uniform came down the steps of the Commandant's Residence and stood waiting. Her driver opened the door for her. As she stepped out she recognized MacRobert. She re-turned his salute and walked up the steps into the residence.

"Cadets are assembled in the Hall, Commandant," MacRobert said. "The general called ahead. The inside route is to your right, just there. You'll meet the residence staff afterward, then an hour break and then Academy staff meeting in your residence, with refreshments."

"Good," Ky said. It was beyond strange to be addressed as Com-mandant by MacRobert. "Cadet mood?"

"Fourth-years confused, wary, trying to look professional, fairly successfully. Third-years confused and alarmed, also trying to look professional, with less success. Second-years openly worried and tense. First-years probably wish they'd never applied and look like it."

"What have they been told?"

"That Kvannis resigned without notice and is gone. That a new interim Commandant would be appointed at once, and would speak to them. Rumors are flying, but I don't know if there's a definite leak, even though you've been mentioned."

"Academy staff?"

"Harder to read, as you'd expect. I'm fairly sure some are bent in some way, but I came back only this morning, as soon as Kvannis was reported missing. Not enough data." More softly, he added. "If I may, Commandant—"

"Go ahead, Master Sergeant."

"You will be a great Commandant. Grab 'em by the throat."

She had not expected that; she felt a lift in spirits. "That was my battle plan, Master Sergeant."

Still, when she stepped out on the dais at the front of the Old Hall, once more standing under the arches of its tall nave, once more seeing the masses of cadets arrayed in their classes, memory caught *her* by the throat for an instant. By the time her second in command, Colonel Stornaki, introduced "Commandant Vatta," it was gone.

"Cadets, faculty, staff," she began. "Good morning. You may be surprised how fast an interim Commandant was appointed, but nobody wants to leave cadets to their own devices for even a day. And your instructors need someone to blame when things go wrong. That would be me." She could feel the different emotional tones in the cadets, arranged mostly as MacRobert had said, from near-professional control among the eldest to wavering on the edge of panic in some of the youngest.

"Some of you," she said, "probably came to the Academy hoping your lives would be more adventurous than that of a teacher or merchant or farmer. I came here for exactly that reason. My brothers and cousins were all satisfied with being on a tradeship crew, or working on the family farms or offices. I—" She paused for effect, and let her occasional ridicule of her younger self show on her face. "I wanted adventure. Excitement. All those adventure vid series—you know the ones—were more my speed than learning how to read profit and loss statements." Now she could feel a softening in the tension; the faces nearest hers had relaxed a little, and a few even smiled.

"Luckily for me," she said, "when I was in the Academy the only adventures we had were planned by the more senior cadets, the faculty, and the military personnel who taught us combat skills and took us on shuttle trips to experience space. Those felt like adventures to us—growing up on what we thought was a safe planet with predictable seasons and predictable politics. But those weren't *real* adventures." They were all intent now, and behind her, the rows of faculty and staff might have been focusing real lasers on her back; she felt the burn.

"Adventures are *not* predictable and moderately exciting, with predetermined outcomes. Adventures are things going wrong: situations you don't expect, friends who betray you, equipment that fails when you most need it, enemies who are stronger and even smarter than you, and the possibility—no, the certainty, at times—that you will be injured or die. And it is for the *real* adventures—the ones where your knowledge, your skills, and your strength of character are necessary to complete your assigned mission—that the carefully designed training adventures here in the Academy prepare you.

"Some of you know that I did not in fact graduate from this Academy, that I left shortly before graduation. Some of you may know why. But everything I have done since has been possible because of what I learned here. And in the time we have together, before a permanent Commandant is appointed, whether me or someone else, I will continue the traditions that shaped me, that gave me the foundation from which to take one small, slow, old tradeship and build the interstellar fleet that you've heard something about.

"I expect some of you were upset, even worried, by the sudden change in Commandants. Hear me now. Nothing else changes.

Classes, physical training, rules for correct conduct and military courtesy: the traditions do not change. The people in them may change, but the Academy will be here for you—and *I* will be here for you. And when you graduate, you *will* have the skills, the knowledge, the physical fitness, and the character to do what needs to be done."

She let her face relax into a full smile, a bit rueful she hoped. "I know from experience, some of it very hard indeed, how important this training is. I respect this place—" She lifted her gaze to the intricate vaulting of the roof, shifted it from place to place within the walls. "And I respect all it has done for so many, not just me. That is all."

Colonel Stornaki stepped forward; the cadet officers called their classes to attention. Salutes exchanged, she left the dais, somewhat surprised at how little anxiety remained. MacRobert waited to guide her back to the residence.

"Well done, Commandant," he said as they walked. "That was some masterful throat-grabbing." He guided her a different way at the first branch of the passage. "The living quarters are upstairs; you have a master suite, a separate study, and guest suites mostly used as quarters for visiting scholars. The master suite is unfortunately still under forensic lock for another hour or so; they want every hair, every fiber, every surface that will take a fingerprint gone over. They've been at it since 0730. You'll have it by this evening, at the latest. So your things, what we have, are in this guest suite." He stopped and opened the door. A small sitting room, a bedroom and attached bath. "You will have a security detail, one guard on duty in this upper hall, until the forensic team leaves. You're due downstairs in one hour to meet the household staff, and then it's the reception with the faculty and teaching staff."

Ky shook her head. "To keep the continuity for cadets, that reception should be moved to after class hours. They should be back on their usual schedule as soon as possible."

"That would be better for them, but the faculty asked for—demanded is more like it—sooner access."

"Grabbing the faculty by the throat as well as cadets is part of my plan," Ky said. "Reception fifteen minutes after the end of classes, while the cadets are out on the drill field. I doubt household staff will mind having it delayed."

He shook his head while grinning. "I said you'd be a good Commandant and you already are. I will inform the staffs, both of them."

Someone had put fresh coffee and fresh tea on a tray in the sitting room, along with a tray of cookies; the small cooler held a variety of other drinks. Ky chose tea and—having missed both breakfast and lunch by this time—a couple of cookies. The bathroom held a reasonable array of toilet articles; she looked at herself in the mirror and retied her braid into the shape that best suited her new uniform cap. She wished she'd asked MacRobert if the communications lines in and out of the residence were as secure as those from the headquarters building.

Ky put her feet up on a convenient stool and leaned back in the chair. The new shoes that had come with her new uniform were still stiff. When her implant pinged, giving her ten minutes to check the details and get downstairs to meet the house staff, she needed only a quick glance in the mirror to know that her braid was still secure.

CHAPTER TWENTY-FIVE

DAY 11

She met Mac coming up at the head of the stairs. "Minor problem, Commandant," he said. "Two of the former military on the house staff are missing, presumed to have left sometime earlier this morning. One was supposedly on a supply run; the vehicle has been found, but the supplier says he never showed up. The other simply walked out; the guard at the gate assumed he was off-shift. Both were kitchen staff; both had done prep work on the refreshments for the faculty reception. Chef says nothing could be wrong . . ."

"Dump it anyway," Ky said. "We can get cookies and pastries at any large grocery—"

"We shouldn't." MacRobert stopped two steps down. "First, it's bad practice to go outside the military supply chain. Second, Chef won't be pleased."

"Chef will be less pleased if half the faculty start writhing in agony, or drop dead six hours later."

"You need to talk to him. His name's Ilan Volud. Ask him to take care of it and not poison your guests or you."

Ky counted to ten, silently, then nodded. "All right. Right after this."

The meeting with house staff did not take long: introductions, shaking hands, showing appreciation. She'd done that in many meetings on many planets by now. Everyone looked worried and tense at first, and less so when she had worked through the line, inputting faces and names into her implant, along with any personal information they shared. Somewhat over half were former military themselves.

When it was done, she noticed that Ilan Volud, the chef, sent his kitchen staff on and stayed behind. "Commandant—you will have heard two of my people are missing."

"Yes. Are you concerned that they might have a reason to tamper with supplies?"

"I wasn't thinking about that until MacRobert asked me. I can't believe that Cerise or Eran would . . . but after they found the van and he wasn't there—" He shook his head. "I don't think they did. I can't imagine why they would."

"Remember, my family was nearly wiped out six or seven years ago," Ky said. "People tried to assassinate me in more than one system. My aunt, the Rector, has been attacked, and so has my remaining cousin."

"I knew about the bombings," Volud said. "But not that you'd been targeted other places. Come see—"

The kitchen reminded her of the kitchen in Miksland—spacious, spare, industrial. Volud showed her around, introduced her to the remaining kitchen staff again. "This is what I chose for the reception." He handed her a menu. Cookies, finger sandwiches, small pastries, trays of raw vegetables. "A dozen of each kind; two dozen of those that are favorites."

"When did the missing two leave?" Ky asked.

"About five minutes into the morning shift, Colonel Stornaki called to cancel the breakfast order for the Commandant—I mean, General

Kvannis—and prepare for a reception for the faculty. He was sure the department would send an interim replacement today, and even if they didn't, the faculty would have to meet and decide what to do. So I started at once on the pastry and cookie dough, and started the juniors prepping the vegetable platters."

She hadn't been asked until after that, so Stornaki could not have known who it would be. "When did you find out who the new person would be?"

"About nine, nine thirty. Cerise left for the supply run about then, as usual, and Eran checked out through the gate at nine forty-five."

Ky nodded. "Then I think the food's probably safe, Chef. You'd made the dough before anyone knew who was coming, and—if those two are bent—they left as soon as they heard."

"Probably isn't good enough," Volud said, frowning. "I don't want to take chances. Would you authorize a onetime use of commercial sources?"

"You mean like using prebaked items from a grocery store bakery or specialty bakery?"

"Yes, Commandant," Volud said. "There's simply not time to run everything through a full analysis and have it ready for the reception. Modern poisons are too numerous and complex—"

"I think that's a good idea," Ky said judiciously. "And if you can store the foods that might have been contaminated, you can send samples for analysis. If they're fine they can be used later."

"Yes, Commandant. That's exactly what I propose." His face had relaxed a little. "I don't suppose the Commandant has a favorite store—?"

"As a matter of fact," Ky said, "my aunt and cousin swear by Minelli & Krimp on Pickamble Street, and I can attest to the quality of their bakery."

His eyes lit up. "I know that store. I will contact them immediately. And—while you're here—your orders for dinner this evening? And your preferences for breakfast?"

It took only a few minutes to answer his questions, then, as Ky confessed she had missed breakfast and lunch except for the snacks in the guest suite, she escaped upstairs to her temporary quarters with a ham sandwich, having refused soup on the grounds it might make her more sleepy. Staff were in the process of moving her things to what had been Kvannis's suite, now that forensics was through with it. They were skilled, and it wasn't long before she was able to shut the door on everyone outside and allow herself to flop into one of the big leather club chairs around a low round table and set the mug down. "I could sleep in this," she muttered aloud. "But I'd better not." She looked at the desk off to one side. On it were three color-coded comunits: green, yellow, and red. She willed them not to ring, but got up again, sandwich in hand, and went to explore the other rooms in the suite.

In the bedroom, she faced a huge bed with a massive carved-wood frame; the headboard included the seals of all the branches in the Defense Department, in high relief, in the same left-to-right order as on the Commandant's insignia on her shoulders. The pointy end of the old-fashioned spaceship in the Spaceforce logo stuck out at least five centimeters. From the rub-marks on the other side, generations of Commandants had decided to sleep on the other side of the bed— the carved waves under the Sea Forces ship had blurred just a little— rather than risk spiking themselves on the head. She shouldn't—but she lay down, just for a moment.

The yellow comunit on the bedside table let out a loud buzz before her eyes could close.

"At least it wasn't the red one," Ky muttered, heaving herself out of the bed before she answered.

"Commandant, this is Major Osinery, in the Academy's Public Affairs office. I was at your address to the cadets—excellent job—but didn't meet you as I was supervising the recording."

Recording? They'd been recording it? Of course they would, she realized after a moment of shock.

"The thing is, Commandant, something has come up that—that the Commandant needs to be aware of. I don't suppose you're watching the midafternoon news break—"

"No, I wasn't," Ky said, just barely managing not to say *It's my first day I just found out this morning I'd have this job do you really think I have time to sit around watching the midafternoon news* all in one breath.

"There's something on now, if you could just spare ten minutes or so, that has generated requests for an interview with you, and we will need at least a half hour to brief you—"

"Perhaps you could just tell me what it is," Ky said.

"I'm not sure that's—could you just come to our office in Old Main for a conference?"

"No, that's impossible," Ky said. "As you can imagine, the sudden and unexpected departure of the previous Commandant has left a lot of loose ends, which I'm busy dealing with. Also, I don't have a full uniform set yet; that's supposed to be delivered tomorrow."

"But you had on a uniform at the—"

"Yes, but it was hastily altered from an AirDefense dress uniform at the base. For any formal interview, I should be wearing a uniform that is perfect in every detail, don't you think?"

"Oh. Yes. Yes, of course, Commandant. I thought they would have told you sooner—"

"Kvannis only ran off last night," Ky said. "No one expected that. I didn't know about this assignment until this morning. I suggest you offer a written statement from your office, to the effect that because of the suddenness of the former Commandant's departure, and the un-expected nature of the appointment, Commandant Vatta is extremely busy sorting out—I suppose we shouldn't say *the mess Kvannis left* but that's what the statement should mean, in whatever tactful language you want to use. Commandant Vatta is committed to the Academy and its mission, and to the welfare of all cadets in training."

"Oh . . . yes, Commandant. Uh—may we use a clip from today's re-cording?"

"Very brief, and I hope you spent some time capturing the audi-ence reaction. Come by my office here in the residence so I can see it when you've got it together."

"Yes, Commandant."

She finished the sandwich and thought longingly of a few hours' sleep. She peered into the bathroom, the walk-in closets—one empty, one with her few clothes hung neatly at one end of the pole. Back to the sitting room. Its window overlooked a small paved area apparently off the kitchen and one end of the Science Complex. She sat down in one of the club chairs. Quiet. Solitude. Where was Rafe? All the others had reported in long ago. She dragged her mind back to the faculty reception, reviewing the names she knew, and checked the time. Her supposed rest period was dwindling; she should freshen up for the reception.

"Commandant?" A tap on the door. "Major Osinery, from Public Affairs—"

"Come in."

Her first thought was, *Oh, not another one,* because Major Osinery could have been Jen Bentik's not-quite-twin sister: older, pretty, perfect in every way. But not, she realized at once, the same attitude, despite what she'd sounded like on the phone.

"Commandant Vatta, I am so pleased to meet you—I never thought I'd get the chance." Osinery flushed. "Sorry—I mean, since we didn't know you'd be the next Commandant until an hour before you arrived. I had heard of you, of course, but didn't think—Sorry, I'm babbling. Here's the press release; we can view the video on your desk—"

"Let's go down to the briefing room; it's almost time for me to head for the faculty/staff reception, anyway."

Downstairs, she reviewed and approved the brief press release; the video clip Osinery had chosen should play well, she thought. Osinery left. By then MacRobert had shown up, to brief her on the reception; they walked together into the residence's dining room, where the kitchen staff had laid out refreshments.

Ky complimented the chef and staff, and then the faculty began to straggle in and introduce themselves. She let her implant record it all. In case some of the faculty were part of the conspiracy—though she doubted it—any detail of expression or posture might reveal it. Later, she circulated through the room. The instructors she'd had seemed glad to see her again; others were simply curious. They all left promptly at the end of the hour, excusing themselves politely, all according to military courtesy, and she looked at the ravaged platters of food ruefully. She hadn't had time to eat even one pastry.

Chef Volud reappeared. "If you would like, those could be sent to your suite for snacking. And your dinner will be ready in forty minutes, if that suits. Will you eat down here, or in your suite?"

"Let me just check before you go up," MacRobert said, before she could answer.

"I'm taking one of those pastries *now*," Ky said. The sandwich had not been enough. "And I'm sitting down." She snagged a pastry off one of the platters and sat in the nearest chair.

"I'll bring your dinner here, then," Chef Volud said. "You are tired and hungry; *that* is something I understand."

One of the staff poured her a cup of tea and asked if she would prefer coffee instead.

"Tea is fine, thank you," Ky said. "I just haven't slept much the past two—three—nights." Her feet were throbbing. She wanted her other boots, not these new ones.

"It must be difficult," said one of the staff, a young woman whose name tag read LORIN.

"It's been a surprising day," Ky said. "A good night's sleep should take care of it." Only she wasn't going to have a good night's sleep because Rafe was somewhere far out in the country and she didn't know if he was safe or in jail or something. Rodney's report was many hours old. And she had to sleep in an unfamiliar bed with what looked like the perfect way to get a headache built into the headboard.

Sooner than expected, her dinner appeared; it smelled delicious. MacRobert came in with his own plate, two sandwiches made with leftover cold cuts from the reception. "May I?"

"Certainly."

He sat across the big table from her; they ate in silence until she was through. The little dessert plate of cheese and grapes and one chocolate truffle had finished it perfectly. "So," Ky said, "any other useful tips?"

"You haven't had time to meet your security detail; you should do that before you go to bed, if you can."

"Of course."

"They won't be permanent, most likely—"

"Neither will I," Ky said. "I'm interim."

"Not as interim as some of these are. You don't have Kvannis's detail, but most are still from the Academy list. I haven't combed them deeply yet."

"Let's go, then," Ky said. "And—I need to arrange transport for Rafe when he calls in."

"Yes. It sounds like something Stella could arrange. Have you called her?"

"No. No time, really."

"It will come better from you, after last night. It was a very near thing." When she just looked at him, Mac went on. "You hadn't heard? The house was attacked after you left—all communications cut off first. That's what alerted Vatta Security, though it took them awhile to respond. The attackers broke in from above. Stella was alone; she fought them off until help arrived."

"Is she all right?" Ky knew Stella would be furious, would connect this to every time Stella had felt unprotected.

"Yes, but the house isn't. A lot of damage upstairs, the security office wrecked . . ."

"Security detail first, then I'll call her."

When she had met the security detail, she went upstairs and hoped for an early night. No one interrupted her during her shower, or while she dressed again in her own clothes and put her Commandant's uniform and her personal armor in the 'fresher, but she knew they could. She called Stella's skullphone.

"Ky? You could at least have told me—"

So Stella was comfortable enough now to complain. "I'm sorry. We thought you'd be safer if no one knew; we were wrong."

"Yes, you were. I'm at Grace's house; home is unlivable for now."
She sounded amazingly cheerful about that. Ky tried to think what to
say, but Stella went right on. "I'm fine, but for a few scratches and
bruises. You know that annoying Mr. Prescott across the street?"

"Yes . . ."

"Well, he was working for Quindlan, and that's how he afforded the
house. Spying on us. You were right about that. He's under arrest
now." Stella actually chuckled; the hair stood up on Ky's neck. Was this
the same Stella? "He came storming over to complain about the noise
and claimed I was having a wild party; once he saw the bodies he
nearly passed out and started gibbering."

"The bodies—?"

"I killed them, Ky. Or most of them. But I had to, and I did, and it
was *different*. I was afraid—not just of them, but of being a killer like
my father, like Osman. I'm not afraid now. I'm not like him. Not 'that
idiot Stella,' either. I can kill when I have to, and stop when I don't
have to. It's a good feeling."

"I'm . . . happy for you," Ky said.

"Have you heard more about Rafe?"

"Not since Rodney's report yesterday. He drove one of their trucks,
to dump it, then didn't show up at the pickup site. He called Rodney,
said he was on the run but fine. A local station in the west reported
that a man had killed three men, stuffed their bodies in a truck, and
fled over the fence at a train station. His ID was found in clothing on
the fence."

"He's very capable," Stella said. "Maybe he's hiding out where he
can't get a signal."

"I hope so."

"You sound tired—where are you?"

"At the Academy." The incongruity of the situation hit her suddenly,
exhaustion and worry making it suddenly funny. "I'm the—" She
couldn't stop the laughter. "I'm the new—the new Commandant!"

"You're *what*? Are you serious?"

The urge to laugh vanished as fast as it had appeared. "Yes. I'm just very, very tired and it's been a long busy two days. And I'm worried. Stella, I'm sorry I was wrong and you were attacked. And I'm so tired—I really need sleep."

"Talk to me tomorrow," Stella said. She sounded calm, reasonable, no undertones of resentment at all.

"I will."

Ky lay back on the bed and hoped for sleep so deep nothing could wake her. She suspected something would. Sure enough, the moment she had turned out the light, one of the coms beside the bed rang. Yellow again.

"Commandant? This is Major Hemins. We have a situation in the second-years."

"Define *situation*." She fought back a yawn.

"A fight. Three cadets. About . . . um . . . you. Your selection. Whether it was legal."

"What is the protocol for handling fights among cadets these days?" Ky asked. "In my day, cadets fighting would have been confined to quarters overnight and lined up in front of the Commandant's desk the next day."

"It's . . . well, that's it, but I thought you should know."

"Of course I should know, if I'm going to be ripping them a new one tomorrow morning. I want them in my office at 0700. And I want a complete report on the fight on my desk within the hour."

"Yes, Commandant. By complete you mean—"

"Complete. Start to finish. Witness names, names of staff in that barracks, full dossier on all three cadets. You can cut and paste, for the background, but I want it all."

"Yes, Commandant. Within the hour." He sounded tired, as she was, and not completely convinced.

"Major, if you think I'm on the wrong tack, spit it out."

"Not wrong, Commandant; it's your choice. But—it's not characteristic, and all this is sudden—"

As if wars weren't. Ky swallowed another yawn. "And?"

"This class started with the Old Man—before Kvannis. And then the shuttle crashed and Kvannis took over. Yes, the Old Man had been grooming him for it, but it wasn't the same, couldn't be. And now Kvannis is out and you're the third Commandant they've had in a year and a half. And to these cadets it doesn't matter whether Kvannis ran or was booted, it's still another sudden switch. They knew Kvannis; he'd been second in command when they arrived; the senior classes all knew him, too. They don't know you except by reputation."

Ky said nothing, waiting him out. Somewhere in there was something he thought important.

"That's no excuse, of course. The fight was wrong; they have to be disciplined . . ."

"Do you have a suggestion, Major?"

"The whole class is upset and they've been talking it over, arguing. Only three of them actually mixed it up before their cadet officer got there, at least that she saw."

"Um. Do you know *why* they think my appointment wasn't legal? Just the change or something specifically about me?"

"That I don't know. But I know since the Old Man died the tone has changed. You were here; you remember how in the second year a class really begins to come together."

She did remember, though she'd paid little attention to her memories of her class. "Yes—for some of us it was earlier, but most—second year."

"Well, it hasn't happened in this class. There are little groups, but not any real unity."

"That . . . puts a slightly different light on it, Major. So you noticed a preexisting disunity, not connected to me because I wasn't here."

"Yes, Commandant. And I think whatever you choose to do, it needs to be something that will meld them together, at least get that started."

"Something that will affect the entire class—ideas?"

"I can't really think of anything, Commandant."

"All right. I'll sleep on it. Tell them they'll be seeing me in the morning; don't specify a time. Confine them *all* to quarters until then, skip breakfast, mention 'inspection' and 'classwork' and let them sweat some. I'll contact you in the morning, let you know if I've thought of something more than I planned at first."

"Yes, Commandant. Thank you."

"I need an idea fairy," Ky said to the silence in her bedroom. And went to sleep.

CHAPTER TWENTY-SIX

DAY 12

The great hall was cold in the early-morning light, and the mass of second-year cadets standing in their ranks looked both hungry—they had not had breakfast—and sullen. Ky could feel the mood, as well as see it in their faces. Resentment, not just apprehension. Well . . . that was unity of a sort, however negative and transitory; all she had to do was make it positive and permanent. Major Hemins, beside her and a step behind, radiated determination, if not confidence in her.

"I was informed late last night that a new disturbance had broken out among the second-year class." Ky paused to let that sink in. More apprehension, less resentment, for the moment. They didn't know how much she knew. Good. "I was also informed that this is not the first disturbance among you, not the first sign you have not learned the importance of bonding among military officers. Why this was not handled promptly and effectively before, I neither know nor care. What I will tell you is that on *my* watch, your lack of ability and willingness to trust your classmates—and to be worthy of their trust—will not be tolerated."

A vague stir among the cadets.

"By this time in second year, you should have shown more growth in character. No doubt there are individuals among you who have done better than the rest, and no doubt you are proud of yourselves. But excellence in your own accomplishments is not enough for an officer, and your excellence has not transferred to your classmates. You have not brought them up to your standard.

"And *that* is a vital part of leadership: to inspire, enforce, and enable excellence of character and skills in everyone who serves beside or under you. That is what your Academy training is for, not merely personal advancement." She paused again, seeing chagrin on some faces, stubborn resentment on others, surprise on a few. What had Kvannis been doing, that these youngsters didn't already know this?

"Now," she said, "as far as the cause of various disturbances, it seems that some of you feel qualified to critique the actions of officers who are far senior to you. And you feel it appropriate to incite or take part in arguments and . . . disturbances . . . related to your opinions. I remind you of Section Fourteen, paragraph one, in the *Joint Services Manual of Courts-Martial,* as well as Section Three, paragraph one-f, in the Code of Conduct for this Academy: 'Cadets are not to engage in discussions of politics outside those classes in which it is relevant.' Inciting disturbances is an article within the *Joint Services Code of Military Justice,* an article that, if it appears in someone's service record, whether a court-martial finds them guilty or not, permanently excludes that individual from having a security clearance above Basic Two. And thus, since officers must all possess a Senior Two or above, it excludes any person awaiting commissioning from being commissioned."

Now the anxiety was more obvious. "It would be not be beyond the reach of the Code, on the basis of reports I have received as to your conduct in your second year so far, to consider the entire second-year class as guilty of willful incitement." She let that sink in; and let the fourth-year cadet officers deal with the shifting and a few murmurs. "It would, however, be excessive to apply that standard immediately. It is your good fortune that last night's incident did not rise to the level of physical violence, because I would have had to conduct a formal inquiry and very likely propose a formal court. Consider this your final warning. Future incidents—disturbances—will not be tolerated."

Almost, but not quite, a universal sigh of relief. Too soon, too soon. "I expect immediate improvement, and a commitment to the spirit as well as the letter of the Code. By *immediate* I mean starting this moment. Though you will not face a formal court, you will face administrative punishment, also starting now.

"For the next thirty days, there will be no personal time, no Midwinter leave, and no communication outside the campus except in cases of serious illness or injury that require notification of families. Your formerly free periods will be spent on punishment details, including more physical training because *some* of you seem clumsy enough to walk into doors and damage yourselves." She looked directly at the three arrayed in front of the group.

"You will have more supervision and more inspections. I have reminded the faculty and fourth-year cadet officers of their responsibility to ensure that all articles of the Code are strictly enforced. At the end of thirty days, you will either have begun an acceptable rate of improvement or other measures will be taken. Those who wish to withdraw from the Academy are reminded that doing so transfers them to a Basic class in one of the enlisted recruit centers and they will still be obligated for two years' active service past Basic Training." She turned. "Major Hemins, you have your class." And walked off.

Colonel Stornaki waited for her outside. "You were pretty rough on them, Commandant."

"You approve of fighting in the barracks?"

"No, but they're young—"

"Major Hemins tells me they're not where they should be, and they started backsliding after the Old Man's death . . . are you arguing with that assessment?"

"Well, it was a shock to all the cadets."

"And yet the fights have been confined to the second year. Tell me, Colonel, how would you have handled it?"

"Brought in the ones who actually fought, and reamed them out—punishment details for them, to be sure, but not the whole class."

"And was that done for the previous incidents?"

"Well . . . that's what Commandant Kvannis did."

"And how has that worked? With multiple incidents reported, from loud arguments to at least two incidents of hazing, and three actual fights, including the one last night?"

Stornaki chewed his lower lip, clearly surprised to be confronted so firmly. Was he, as Ky half suspected, one of Kvannis's accomplices?

"The issue of bonding is critical, as I'm sure you know," Ky said. "A class is supposed to cohere on the basis of the behaviors and attitudes the service needs. A divisive class bodes ill for cooperation and trust among fellow officers later on. This class is divided, and divided along both political and religious lines—yes, I have read the reports on all the previous incidents, and reviewed the records of all the cadets involved."

His brows went up. "When?"

"Very early this morning," Ky said. "Did you think I wouldn't?"

"Apologies, Commandant. No, I did not think you were negligent—no one who's won the battles you won could be that."

Flattery or sincerity? She wasn't sure. He had not chatted with her at the reception the day before or provided any useful information.

"It's just that Commandant Kvannis—well, you didn't know him. A fine officer, I always thought. I still think he may have been abducted—it just isn't like him to abscond in the night."

"You will excuse me," Ky said, "but I have other appointments this morning. We'll have to discuss Kvannis another time."

And she would have to find a new second in command for the Academy.

Grace Vatta looked at President Hester Saranife across the wide presidential desk, waiting for her response. Saranife, elected only two years before, had been, in Grace's opinion, a competent, if reserved, head of state. Nothing had gone badly wrong until the shuttle crash, and no one had blamed the President or the Saranife administration for it. Now, however, the President sighed, shifted in her seat, and did not meet Grace's gaze. That, Grace thought, was not promising. "It's difficult," she said. "This whole situation. My predecessor—"

"Did not know about the terms of the release. Neither did I."

"So you said. I find that difficult to believe. Surely you'd have been told."

"I was still considered incompetent, under medical supervision. I was given orders, not explanations."

"Even at home?"

"Yes. Confined to the house and grounds, with a nurse-companion for the first years, until I was married off and my husband took over the supervisory duties."

"And the others in the family didn't know?"

"Not the details. It was to be a secret, you see. The government at the time—over fifty years ago—would have found it embarrassing to admit I had been freed. I was supposed to disappear into the family as thoroughly as I had disappeared into the psychiatric ward of the prison. The other adults knew only that they were responsible for my staying 'out of trouble.' The children knew only that I'd been in some kind of hospital—they didn't know about the war crimes trial at all. When the government decided to downplay the war in the interests of unity, it wasn't discussed in any detail in schools."

"But why wasn't *someone* told—?"

"I believe my father expected to tell his heir, and that heir would tell his, and so on. But through accident and sudden illness, two generations of family leaders died without passing the information on. I had begun doing some work for the family from home—an idea of my husband's, before his death—so when Gerard and Stavros took over, they saw no reason why they shouldn't use me in a more active role." She shrugged. "It was pretty clear that I wasn't crazy anymore; even the nightmares had worn themselves out, at least until the big attack on our family."

"And then?"

"And then the nightmares came back."

"Did you kill the President?" That was stark enough; Grace was glad she could answer honestly.

"No. Wanted to, yes, because I'd learned he'd allowed the attack on Vatta in return for, supposedly, no attack elsewhere on the planet, but I'd lost an arm to an assassin trying to kill Stavros's grandchildren."

"What? I heard you'd lost the arm in an accident."

"That attack wasn't publicized, for safety's sake. It nearly succeeded. The twins had run out to sneak an early-morning pony ride. I heard shots—screams—one of the ponies was down. There were two assassins. I shot the first; the second shot me, and was coming for us—Shar and I were both on the ground, easy prey—when a nearby fisherman, who'd heard the noise, came up behind the assassin and killed him." No need to say who that was. MacRobert's part had always been kept dark. "At any rate, when the President died, I was flat on my back in a trauma ward."

"Did you tell the Commandant to offer him a suicide pill?"

"No."

"But you knew the Commandant well. Why else would he have done it?"

"Possibly because he also recognized the danger to Slotter Key from a head of state who was in league with outside powers. I had shared information with him because I did not know who else to trust in the military system. If the President was corrupt, so also might be the Rector of Defense, or any of the officers that I knew very slightly."

"And just how did you know the Commandant?"

"I saved his life when he was a boy. Got him out of a bad situation. Our family took care of him—not me, because I was in prison. When I was released, he wrote me a note, and we corresponded at least twice a year from then on."

"About?"

"Personal things: his promotions in Spaceforce, the girl he was interested in at the time, his family life when he married—his wife was killed in a traffic accident while he was in space; she was pregnant at the time. He never married again. I told him about birthday parties, marriages, children born. He corresponded with other family members, too. He knew them better than he knew me, but I was the one who had stood between him and those who wanted to kill him. And the rest of the family was willing to let me take over the correspondence, for the most part."

"Did he visit your family?"

"While he was still a junior officer, yes. Less as he advanced, and not after he was appointed Commandant. He needed other connections; everyone understood that."

"What I'm trying to get at, Rector Vatta, is why your niece was accepted into the Academy—if you or he influenced that decision—"

Grace laughed. "Like at least half the other cadets who used influence to get in? Did you think it was all about the entrance exams? Ky topped them that year, but she was also—is—a member of a wealthy family, daughter of the CFO at that time and niece of the CEO. Merchanter's brat or not, she'd have been accepted, but the family reputation certainly helped, and the Commandant's notice got her put in the most competitive of the entering units. I didn't do anything but push back against her desire enough to make her stubborn and even more determined."

"Why that?"

Grace shrugged. "I'd been in a war. Ky was intelligent, spirited, stubborn by nature, but also warmhearted. She was always getting into scrapes trying to rescue others, take care of someone weaker. I didn't want her hurt the way I had been, and I knew how bad it could be. So I wanted to be sure that if she went, it was a genuine desire, not one of her juvenile rescue fantasies."

"Hmmm." The President looked grave, then nodded; Grace felt like poking her with a pin. That was such a pose of noble public-servanthood. No politician was that noble. When the President's expression changed, as if a switch had been flicked, Grace felt vindicated. It was all an act. "Well, then," she said. "Back to you and this problem. You admit that if you had known, you would not have taken the post of Rector—"

"I would not have taken the post of *Assistant* Rector," Grace said. "*Or* the promotion to Rector. I was certainly as qualified as the man who held it before me . . . except for the fact that I was never supposed to become involved in politics at all. I would not have risked the situation we're in now, where my past is doing damage to the entire government."

"But here we are," the President said. "And so far I don't see the damage."

"Someone will release that file publicly," Grace said. "That's why it's surfaced again. Whoever put it in official hands may wait a short time, but you know they'll push the issue, and soon. When they do, I won't be the only target of their chosen revenge. I'm old; it doesn't matter much what happens to me. But the fallout will affect my family and your government as well."

"Did you appoint your niece Ky to be Commandant?"

"No. I had nothing to do with that; I was informed of it after the fact. General Molosay, commanding Port Major Joint Command HQ base, was faced with an emergency—Kvannis's clandestine departure—and asked Ky to take the Commandant's position as an interim post since he did not know what other officers in the Academy might be part of whatever conspiracy Kvannis was in."

"But didn't he know she killed Master Sergeant Marek?"

"Of course he knew. And he knew why. He had the testimony of the three survivors who had escaped from isolation, one of whom had witnessed the incident and been wounded by Marek."

"I haven't heard any of the details."

"I'm sure you'll be briefed as soon as the other survivors—only just rescued from the same confinement—have been interviewed."

"Do you think it means there's any serious disaffection within the military?"

Grace managed not to snort in disgust and did her best to keep her expression neutral. How could the woman—reputed to be brilliant about many things—be that stupid? And why were so many people in positions of power that stupid? She picked her words carefully. "The existence of a military base on Miksland kept a closely held secret for so long suggests it. The use of military personnel to fox the satellite data suggests it. The treatment of those survivors—trying to keep them permanently isolated from everyone, with a plan to gradually kill them off under cover of a dangerous communicable disease—suggests it."

The President glared, huffed, and jerked forward in her chair, which squealed in protest. "But how could there be a conspiracy that big without anyone knowing? Someone—"

"The people in it knew it. The evidence so far—"

"All derived from *your* family's activities—"

"The evidence," Grace repeated in a flat voice that startled the President enough to keep her still, "is that the family first discovering Miksland's potential, via a family member who explored the north coast in his personal yacht, chose to keep it a secret, aided by a decade of particularly harsh winters. That discoverer died unexpectedly; his privately published journal of that voyage, and the map he drew, were suppressed. Master Sergeant MacRobert found them in the special collections of a university library. The family opened small-scale mining operations there for another forty or fifty years, but had difficulty selling the product when it was known no such deposits lay in their recorded holdings. They made the error of working through a less legitimate partner—"

"Who?"

"It will be in the report. A criminal enterprise. They sold the refined mining products offplanet. Cargoes Vatta refused, by the way. Vatta didn't have a clue where it really came from, but we didn't want anything we couldn't provide full provenance for. We were beginning to compete in the interstellar transport market and needed a clean reputation. And we suspect that was one reason for the attack on Vatta, since one of our own was involved."

"Osman," the President said, nodding. "Trouble early on, right?"

"Yes. Stavros evicted him from the family business, so he stole one of our ships and used it for piracy."

"He died in the war?"

Grace considered. Was the President likely to know the truth? Maybe. "He attacked Ky and Stella in deep space; he had a larger, faster, heavily armed ship. He attempted a hostile boarding; Ky fought and killed him."

"Hand-to-hand?"

"Yes."

"She likes to kill?"

Irritation got past her guard. "He was trying to kill *her*. What do you think she should have done?"

"But she killed that sergeant."

"Master Sergeant Marek," Grace said. "Yes. He was trying to kill her and her aide both."

"But violence—she could have negotiated with him—"

"You were never in combat, were you?"

The President flushed. "No. But—"

Grace overrode her. "It's different. That's all I can say. You can't possibly understand. It's not about liking to kill or not liking to kill; it's about survival, and—in Ky's case—protecting those that depend on you." Though, as she knew well, she and Ky both *had* enjoyed killing. Ky, as far as she knew, had never misused it, as she herself had. "And anyway, Ky is not the current problem. *I* am. I can resign from the Defense Department—"

"No! We need you, at least until this mess with the survivors and this, this—whatever it is—in the military is straightened out."

"You need someone, but I may be making things worse."

"Grace, I trust you even when I don't agree with you." The President had large, dark, slightly protuberant eyes that seemed to plead for understanding.

"But others don't," Grace said. "That's the problem. And even if I resigned, it's not enough. What matters is that I broke a legal contract my family had with the government. That contract stated that if I became involved in the government in any way, with or without the knowledge of my family, the agreement to terminate my confinement would lapse and I would be returned to custody, to be adjudicated by a court."

"I don't even know what court that would be—"

"Neither do I, but I know that's what's called for, and I know some court will take it on."

"But you can't—I mean, at your age, going back to prison, or a psychiatric hospital—it's a risk to your life."

Grace shrugged. "Many things have been risks to my life, including the recent assassination attempt, and yet here I am. Besides, I'm old. Old even by the standards of modern medicine. I'm not afraid of death, and I know from experience that I can survive in confinement. I'm not afraid of that, either."

"It's not fair—you spent decades without causing any trouble—"

"Except being a thorn in the side of those who never forgave my family for letting me have as much freedom as they did. And possibly, because of that, giving encouragement to those still unsatisfied with the results of the Unification War."

The President stared at her, clearly unwilling to countenance the decision that seemed so obvious. She herself was the problem; she was guilty of those deaths she had dealt; she had broken a contract and thus dishonored her family.

"You need to call a Council meeting and have me explain it to them, then start proceedings to determine the correct legal actions," Grace said.

"So who would you recommend as your replacement?"

"I can't make any recommendation. It would taint the process. If I'm ineligible to serve, then I'm ineligible to advise, as well."

"I can't—I can't make a decision now," Saranife said. "And I don't want changes in the administration with a possible crisis coming. What if they just kill you?"

"Then I'll be dead," Grace said. She could not resist the temptation to poke the woman again. "You do realize, don't you, that everyone does die? Of something? I'm going to die; you're going to die; everyone dies."

The President actually shivered, visibly. Well, she was only forty-seven, and her children were still in school. Grace softened her voice. "It's been the human condition since long before we left Old Earth. And keep in mind that it doesn't bother me. Hasn't for a long time. So even if the court decrees an execution, I won't be making a spectacle about it."

"Do you have any feelings? Anything you enjoy, that you'd miss?" Saranife was looking at her again. "A reason to stay alive?"

She had not expected that. But then, people still surprised her, and she knew she surprised them. "Yes," she said, making sure her voice softened. "I love my relatives. The twins—well, they're at one of the difficult ages right now, but they'll grow out of it, if assassins don't get them. I'm fond of my friends. I like cooking, the process of it. I used to like gardening—the colors of flowers and leaves, the fragrance of soil and healthy plants—but these days my knees hurt."

"So if you hadn't accepted my predecessor's invitation, you'd be perfectly safe enjoying your family, cooking, gardening—it's not your fault, dammit!"

"True. But now that I know, continuing on a course that will inevitably harm my family and my planet would be my fault. And your letting me do so, now that you know, will be your fault. Don't wait too long to make your decision. Let's limit the harm as much as we can." Grace stood up without a dismissal and walked toward the door.

"Grace." The tone of the President's voice made her turn around. "I promise you I will do my best to make the right decision at the right time. For everyone."

Grace bowed, her mismatched hands together. "Thank you," she said. "I will await your word."

CHAPTER TWENTY-SEVEN

DAY 12

Grace arrived at the Joint Services Headquarters base still thinking about the implications of her own history. Arriving as Rector of Defense for a press conference, with a security escort to protect her from danger, not others from her, was a stark contrast with her first sight of the place as a prisoner in chains. It had been hot that day, humid, with thunderclouds looming.

Now a few snowflakes danced in the air, but none survived on the ground and the flurry dissipated quickly. Her little cavalcade passed quickly through the gates, driving past the various buildings and parking lots to deliver her directly to the base hospital where the survivors were being treated and reunited with their families. Grace made her way in with her two guards to find an official reception committee inside the foyer: the base commander, General Molosay, the hospital commander, Colonel Byers, and Sergeant Major Morrison. Grace shook hands with them all.

"The survivors are doing better this morning," Byers said. "All but two are ambulatory, and having their families has eased the burden on our staff as well as raising their morale."

"Good," Grace said. "Do we have time for me to meet them before the press conference?"

"Yes, Rector," General Molosay said, giving Byers a sharp look. "If you'll come this way—"

This way meant into an elevator to the fifth floor, given over for the moment to the survivors and their families. The noise when the elevator doors opened included not just a crowd of adults, but children down to toddler size as well. The survivors, in casual clothes, were notable only for being bald, though many of them wore a hospital robe over their clothes. A cluster of family members surrounded each one.

Colonel Byers took Grace first to the two who had been injured in the rescue. "Gunshot wound to the leg," he said of Ennisay as he led Grace down the hall. "He's still too affected by the drugs to tank him for the leg, but he's much better today." He pushed the door wide, and said, "Here's the Rector of Defense come to check on you, Ennisay."

He looked even younger than he was, and his mother, sitting beside him, glared at Grace like an angry hen. "You!" she said. "You let this happen to him."

"No," Ennisay said, his voice just audible. "Not the Rector, Mama. It's her and the admiral who got me out."

His mother huffed, arms crossed. "I want him home for good," she said. "None of your nonsense about regulations and service commitment."

"Mama!"

"We want to get his leg fixed, Sera Ennisay," Colonel Byers said to her. "Time enough after that for him to make a decision."

"Half a year with no word at all and then nothing for four tendays after he's supposed to be home—!"

"Mama!"

"Sera Ennisay," Grace said, stepping forward. "I do understand—

it's been a terrible time for you and your son's family. And you're welcome to stay here with him until he's recovered completely."

Sera Ennisay looked at her, and her face softened. "You—you have children—grandchildren—"

"No, I couldn't have children—but I have nieces and nephews I loved as my own, and their children are like my own grandchildren." Not entirely true, but not entirely false, either. She had taken the entire Vatta family as hers, after the disaster, and Shar and Justin definitely thought of her as a grandmother type. "It's always hard when you don't know where they are, if they're all right."

"Then you do know." Sera Ennisay burst into tears and came forward, reaching for Grace's hands. "Thank you! Thank you for bringing him home!"

"I'm sorry it took so long," Grace said, giving the other woman's hands a strong squeeze, then releasing them. "And I'm sorry I must leave you now, and see the others."

"Oh—oh, of course, I'm sorry—"

"Just stay here and cheer him up," Grace said, turning toward the door. A stupid thing to say to the woman, but maybe she'd stop crying and actually smile at the boy.

Next was Lakhani, who'd suffered a broken arm and a strained back in the melee that occurred during the third group rescue attempt. He, too, had family in the room: father, mother, and two brothers. They were undemonstrative people, taciturn but not unfriendly. "I brought a fruitcake," Sera Lakhani said. "His favorite. There's a little left." She pushed a small piece onto a place and offered it to Grace with a fork.

"Thank you," Grace said. "Is it your own recipe? I make fruitcake, too, and I'm always looking for new recipes."

"Not really. I got it off the package of dried fruits years ago, when he was little." Sera Lakhani pointed her own fork at Corporal Lakhani. "But since our orchard's grown up, we dry some of our own fruit. I think it's mostly the same."

"Tastes the same," Lakhani said.

"It's very good," Grace said after an exploratory nibble. "Is that— just a hint of cocoa powder in it?"

Sera Lakhani beamed. "It is, indeed. And no, it wasn't in the original recipe. And we use our own honey for the sweetener. Citrus honey."

"I will have to try that," Grace said. "Corporal, I wish you a swift recovery."

"Thank you, Rector," Lakhani said. "They told me they'll tank me to heal faster after the press conference." He paused. "Is the admiral coming today?"

"I think not," Grace said. "She was asked to take over the Academy as Commandant after Kvannis fled."

"Good," Lakhani said. "She'll be good at that."

The rest of the survivors and their families were milling about, going from room to room, stopping to exchange stories in doorways, blocking traffic. Families introduced themselves to other families. It was chaotic, but Colonel Byers led her from one to another of the survivors and helped her extricate herself from the family members. She had met almost all of them when the elevator doors opened again and General Molosay's aide came up to her. "Rector, the general's asking everyone to get ready for the press conference. The media vans are here."

"Where exactly will we be?"

"In the lecture hall downstairs; there's room for all the ambulatory survivors on the stage, and for families to be seated. Hookups for all the equipment, as well."

Ky Vatta finally had time to sit down in the Commandant's office, the one she had last seen the day she'd been ordered to resign from the Academy. The carpet had changed, she noted; it had been a deep green and now it was blue, with a thin gold border. The office had three doors, not something she'd noticed back then. There was the one she'd come through before, opening onto the passage. She investigated the others: the one on the left as she entered opened into the Commandant's secretary's office. An older woman with short gray hair looked up from a desk and stood up. She wore a neat blue suit, not a uniform.

"Commandant Vatta—I wasn't sure you would be in today. Colonel Stornaki couldn't tell me when I asked. I'm Sera Vonderlane. Perhaps you'd like to see the usual schedule? There are queries from some faculty and staff—and Commandant—er, former Commandant Kvannis—did not finish all the tasks he had said he would before he left." Her singsong accent defined her origin, Hautvidor on Arland.

Ky smiled. "Sera, I need a few hours just to settle in and familiarize myself with the layout of the offices here. If you could send an ordinary day's schedule to my desk display, we can go over it later today. Do you have a direct link to my office in the residence?"

"Yes, Commandant, certainly."

"Then if you could arrange items in order of urgency, and send the less urgent to the residence office, I'll work on those after dinner tonight. Unless there are too many urgent ones."

"I have eleven red-flagged ones now, Commandant."

Ky repressed a sigh and stepped over to Vonderlane's desk. "Let's see them."

First up was the initial report from the night before of a disturbance in the second class. "That's taken care of," Ky said. "Those three"—calls from the Rector, General Molosay, and Public Affairs—"if they call me before I reach them, put the calls through. These four items I'll need more background on; please send that to my desk display also, or if it's classified, have the files ready. And the last three . . . I may need you to make courtesy calls and explain, but I'll try to get through all of them."

Vonderlane's expression brightened. "You don't waste time, do you, Commandant?"

"Not if I can help it," Ky said. "And excuse me, now—I'm going to be walking around opening doors. For all I know something's moved in the last eight years."

She went back across the Commandant's office, reminding herself it was now hers, and opened the door on the other side. She found a small room that could clearly serve as a break room for the Commandant—it held a small cooler, low table, small sofa, and two upholstered chairs; a half bath opened off it. Its narrow window overlooked the front court and main gate.

In the next half hour she found Stornaki's office, the Communications office, the general Administration office where most of the clerical and accounting functions were carried out, and the Security office. She spoke briefly to everyone she saw, from Major Palnuss, the duty officer in Security, to Corporal Galyan, a file clerk coming down the passage from Admin with a rack of data cubes. Everyone knew she was aboard and in charge, and that, she hoped, would hold things steady until she really understood this assignment.

One door opened into the Commandant's private library, where she had sat that day, struggling to find the right words for her resignation. Where she had waited until Master Sergeant MacRobert came to escort her to the gate, and had spent part of that time looking at shelves of logbooks, fascinated.

She looked, but did not find them on the shelf where they had been. Instead that shelf was filled with video racks full of entertainment titles. She could not imagine the Commandant of her day replacing those handwritten logbooks with entertainment.

Finally she went back to the Commandant's office, walked around the desk, and sat down. Here she was. Not just in the Commandant's office, but in the Commandant's chair, behind the Commandant's broad empty desktop and a hastily manufactured nameplate in polished wood. Wearing a Commandant's uniform, with the gold braid and insignia. And incidentally missing the press conference out at the base, at which all the rescued survivors would be on display and Aunt Grace would give a speech.

This desk was not the same dark desktop she remembered; this one was a yellowish wood grained in gray. Had Kvannis brought in his own desk, or had the previous Commandant chosen a new one for some reason? She leaned over and looked at the dark-blue carpet. Yes . . . she could just see a faint depression where another piece of heavy furniture had been, not quite matching the footprint of this one.

On the desk's empty surface, the display plate almost reproduced the desk's grain. Ky tapped it; the display shifted to a menu. She ran through it: her secretary's grid for a daily schedule, now blank, the list of action items, a quick-call list, a faculty list, a staff list, a submenu of cadets arranged by class. She picked one off the cadet list at random, and found Arls Galonton's complete record laid out for her perusal. Class (third year), his home (Fairmeadow, on Fulland) and family history, entry test scores, all complete to his performance on the mid-quarter exams (modestly above the mean).

She went back to the quick-call list. Heads of departments, of course. Rector of Defense. Some names she didn't recognize. And one she did: Quindlan. That family, involved in the destruction of Vatta's previous headquarters and the deaths of all within it that day, connected—she was sure—to the Malines crime family. She had no idea how many Quindlans there were, or which Quindlan was the one Kvannis had on his quick-call list. Something to find out later.

The shallow center drawer of the desk held a couple of erasers, rubber bands, paper clips, a stapler and a half-empty box of staples, a stylus for the desk's screen, half a roll of mints. Well, Kvannis would've had time to clean this out. She was surprised that there was anything left. In the top drawer of the left-hand side, she found a box of notepaper embossed with the Academy's name and logo, and the title COMMANDANT, and another box of envelopes. Behind them, shoved to the back of the drawer, was an empty pistol case similar to the one Greyhaus had left in his desk in Miksland and an empty metal box that reminded Ky of a cashbox. She sniffed it; it smelled of money.

The drawer below held hanging files, most empty. The labels meant nothing to Ky—cryptic combinations of letters and numbers. She pulled out one of the few papers, part of a spreadsheet printout that looked like it might refer to financials, and put it back in its folder. She moved the files back and forth, to see what was under them. At the back of the drawer, someone had created a pocket; Ky fished in it and brought out a small orange envelope. Empty? No. A tiny key.

Ky put the key on the desk and took another look at the bottom of the drawer. There was a discontinuity in the grain. She lifted out all the file folders and tapped, then looked at the front of the drawer. False bottom? Surely Kvannis would have emptied any secret compartments; if the key opened anything in this office, he'd have left it, but not the contents of the secret places. Or the key might be to some lockbox of his own, at his city home. She looked at the wall where the drilled-out safe gaped open. No way to tell now if this key would have opened it.

She shrugged, put the key in her own pocket for later consideration, put the files back in the drawer, and moved to the drawers on her right. The upper one held bound books, mostly of regulations. She was surprised: Kvannis had worked for the previous Commandant; surely he knew the relevant regulations by heart, or could have consulted them in the Commandant's library. *Manual of Courts-Martial,* 13th Edition, looked as she remembered it from her classes, and so did *Slotter Key Joint Services Training Standards,* but *On Conspiracy, Treason, and Sedition,* though bound in the same gray cloth with black lettering on the cover . . . held sheets with lists of names and places, contact numbers, and timetables.

Ky stared at it. Why had Kvannis left *that* here? Had he thought someone else would clear it away? Was this a copy left behind for someone who would collect it? She closed the cover, moved it to the shallow middle drawer, and moved the books to see what was underneath. As she did, a knock came at the door, and immediately the door opened.

"Commandant, excuse me—" It was Colonel Stornaki. "I was just wondering—" His gaze wandered across the desk to the open drawer. Ky saw the momentary check, heard the hesitation in his voice, then the renewed pace as he went on, "if you knew where Master Sergeant MacRobert was."

"I'm not certain," Ky said, "but he may have gone out to the base with the Rector."

"Oh. Well, he had certain files; I wonder if he put them in the—in your—in that desk."

"I doubt he would, Colonel," Ky said. "If they were files he knew you needed, he would leave them in your office, don't you think?"

"He may not have known," Stornaki said. He could not keep his eyes away for long from that open drawer. "Were you looking for something yourself, Commandant? Perhaps I could help."

"Perhaps you could," Ky said. "If I knew exactly what I was looking for. Mostly I just wanted to know where things were—markers, stylus, paper, clips, and file folders. I still wonder why Kvannis fled in such haste—"

"I still think it may have been an abduction."

"Between here and his family home? That seems most unlikely. And no trace of him found, or of his driver, or of the car, or of the two kitchen staff who disappeared a little later? Even more unlikely. I believe he was fleeing some trouble, and I have been looking for clues."

"In—in his desk?"

"Yes. The forensic team was looking for indications of what might have been destroyed. I know they found evidence that the shredder and incinerator had both been used late in the evening before he left."

Stornaki was sweating now.

"I found a small key in a hidden pocket of the bottom drawer on the other side," Ky said, keeping her voice casual. "Obviously not to the safe—do you know what it was for?"

"Perhaps a lockbox at home? His wife had some expensive jewelry. He might keep the spare here."

"Perhaps," Ky said. "Though I would expect that to be in the Commandant's quarters, not here. But no matter. I found disarray in the files, some things clearly missing, others disordered. And in this drawer—" She touched the top volume, tapped it. "Books of regulations. Did he have a particular interest in court-martial procedures? Was some cadet about to be indicted for a court-martial offense?"

"Not that I know of, Commandant." Stornaki jerked his head, as if his collar were suddenly too tight. "Of course, something might have come up that . . . uh . . . he had not yet told me. Or perhaps he'd been asked to serve on a court by General Molosay, out at the base."

Ky nodded, as if that made sense. "And this other volume, *Joint Services Training Standards:* are you aware of any problems here with satisfying the standards of a particular branch? Is interbranch rivalry a problem these days? I don't remember problems with it, from my time . . ."

"No . . . not that I know of." Sweat rolled down his face now, darkening his high collar.

"Um." Ky looked down, deliberately, to see what he'd do, freed of her intent gaze. He slumped a little and took a step nearer. "There was another volume in that drawer I found somewhat . . . surprising." She opened the middle drawer and with her left hand slid out the one she'd just put away, laying it flat on the desk as she pulled her pistol from the quick-draw she'd found. "Was it *this* you were looking for, Colonel Stornaki? This supposed text on conspiracy, treason, and sedition? With all the examples?"

He turned even paler, and staggered. Ky had the pistol out and pointing at him. "Sit down in that chair behind you, hands on your head, Colonel."

"But I—but I didn't do—but I didn't—don't—know—" The whites of his eyes gleamed.

"I'm certain that you do know," Ky said, riding the bubble of anger she felt. She tapped the desktop without taking her gaze from him, though he looked to be a shivering wreck. The menu came up, and she tapped Security.

"Yes, Commandant?" It was Major Palnuss; she was glad she'd met him within the past hour.

"There's a situation in my office. I need the duty officer and two armsmen to take a prisoner into custody."

"Wha—Yes, Commandant." Almost no hesitation.

"I am armed and holding the prisoner at gunpoint. Inform your people that shooting me is not a good idea."

"Er . . . yes, Commandant."

In seconds Ky heard feet in the passage. Stornaki drew himself up, trying, she could tell, to look unafraid and innocent of all wrongdoing, but the patchy red and pale of his face betrayed him. A knock came first: "Commandant. This is Major Palnuss, Security duty officer."

"Thank you, Major. Come in. The prisoner will be to your left, seated, arms on head." Stornaki jerked, as if to move his arms, but then held rigidly still. The door opened; Major Palnuss entered with two armsmen. His eyes widened a little when he spotted Stornaki but he said nothing.

"It's not me!" Stornaki said. "It's her—she's—she's crazy or something—"

"Commandant, do you have a charge to prefer?" Palnuss's voice was calm.

"Yes," Ky said. "I have evidence that Colonel Stornaki has been part of a conspiracy to commit treason, in concert with former Commandant Kvannis."

"That's ridiculous—you can't possibly believe her!" Stornaki squirmed back in the chair as one of the armsmen pulled out a set of cuffs.

Palnuss nodded to Ky. "You will be convening a court?"

"Indeed," Ky said. "In the meantime, I want him confined, and interrogated by another officer with the skill set, to whom I will transfer the evidence I have."

Palnuss nodded again, then turned to the passage. "Everts, Matsuko, take Colonel Stornaki into custody and confine him in an empty cell for the time being."

"You can't—!"

Palnuss interrupted him. "Former Commandant Kvannis arrested a colonel, as I'm sure you recall, Colonel Stornaki. Held him three nights in the Academy lockup before letting him contact his family. Inasmuch as Commandant Vatta is the Commandant, I'm certain she has just as much authority."

Stornaki clamped his jaw, glared at Ky and Palnuss alternately, then, shaking his head, stood and allowed himself to be cuffed and led away.

Everts and Matsuko handled Stornaki efficiently, warily. Ky holstered her pistol as they took him away. Palnuss stayed behind. "For your information, Commandant, our facilities are not really suited for long-term confinement of senior officers. They're fine for the drunk enlisted who needs to sleep it off, but—"

"What other facilities are available to us?" Ky asked. "This is only my second day and I'm just learning my way around."

He smiled. "Yes, Commandant, I know that. May I ask how much threat you think Stornaki poses? Flight risk? Violent attacks?"

"Flight risk, definitely. A risk to any investigation, as well. Likely to communicate with others in the conspiracy if he gets a chance." She pushed the book toward him. "*This* is what he came to the office for this morning—he was surprised to find me here, and more surprised when I confronted him with what I'd learned. I'd assumed Kvannis would have taken anything incriminating with him—"

"He destroyed documents the night he left," Palnuss said, walking up to the desk. "Documents Destruction was locked up as usual when one of my people left at 1800, but Kvannis had a master key. Like all the master keys, it was numbered and recorded, so when he used it after 2030 to open the room, the automatic surveillance recorded his visit. I don't know what he shredded and then burned, but I know it was about a tenth of a cubic meter."

"This book contains names, contact information, and timetables: some handwritten, some printed off a device." Ky opened it to show the pages. "You will notice it's bound like other books printed by Legal Services . . . that suggests to me that someone in the printing office is involved in this, too. I found it in the top drawer, right-hand side, of this desk, along with two other similarly bound books I haven't yet examined fully. I had already found a key carefully hidden in the bottom drawer on the left-hand side." Ky paused while Palnuss picked up the book, opened it, and looked at several of the pages. "I'm surprised Stornaki didn't take it yesterday, before I arrived."

"I had a team in here all day, drilling out the safe and trying to understand what Kvannis was up to," Palnuss said. "Then after you arrived I imagine the colonel had other worries." He cocked his head. "You were looking because you thought you'd find something incriminating?" he asked, setting the book back down and pushing it toward her.

"Kvannis fled in the night, after—" Ky paused. "You do know about the fate of the other survivors of the shuttle crash?"

He shook his head. "Not all the details, but we got a bulletin from the base yesterday evening. They'd been illegally detained, mistreated, and were being freed and transported to the Joint Services Headquarters. There's supposed to be a big press conference today, I heard."

"Going on about now," Ky said. "I would be there if this weren't my second day as Commandant. I didn't get back from the rescue until early yesterday morning."

"You were out there? I guess you would be, but—how dangerous was it?"

"Moderately," Ky said. "Shots were fired. Our side had more people and more firepower." Some of which—Rodney's militia and reserve friends with their "borrowed" armaments—would not ever be publicized. "A few nonfatal injuries on our side; a mix of fatal and nonfatal on the other."

"And you think Kvannis directed attacks on the rescue—"

"Yes. There's evidence that he specifically called out an AirDefense interceptor flight to attack the civilian aircraft in which personnel were being transported back to Port Major. I think he directed the entire operation. And when that was unsuccessful, he fled; he hasn't been found yet. Since he was destroying documents before he left, I wonder why he didn't destroy this." She patted the book. "Unless he meant it to be found and rescued by his assistant. Stornaki caught my attention yesterday by what he said about Kvannis. When he appeared this morning, was surprised to find me, and then showed such interest in the open drawer and what I'd found . . . I knew."

"Commandant, I hope you're right about this, because I'm going to cooperate without reservation. May I speak freely?"

"Go ahead."

"I would like to transfer Colonel Stornaki immediately to the Joint Services Headquarters, but I do not know if all the security staff there are reliable. Do you?"

"I know some of it is not. Sergeant Major Morrison is aware, and has officers she is sure are loyal—"

"Morrison was involved in this?"

"Yes. She arranged specialist troops for the rescue. It's too long a story for now, but she found out what was going on, and helped us on the rescue. General Molosay is fully briefed on this issue as well. Would you like me to contact the general?"

"Yes, I would. And I would advise that this book be copied immediately, with witnesses to swear to its provenance and the methods of copying, then sent to the forensic division at the headquarters."

"All good ideas," Ky said. "I'll call the general now; would you like to be on the call?"

"Yes, as a witness."

"Take a seat, then. If you have orders to give your staff, do that now; we may be busy awhile." She looked at the time. "Right in the middle of the media event out there . . . General Molosay may be unavailable, and so may the sergeant major and the Rector." She touched her control screen. "Let's see. It's on open voice now."

"General Molosay's office, Captain Gunsey speaking."

"This is Commandant Vatta at the Academy, Captain. Is the general available for an urgent matter?"

"Commandant, he is still in the press conference. Can I be of assistance?"

"I need to speak with the general at his earliest convenience," Ky said. "In fact, the matter concerns the Rector and the sergeant major as well. I have discovered documents in the former Commandant Kvannis's desk that bear on military security; we have a prisoner, Colonel Stornaki, who was involved in the conspiracy, in custody as well. I will be presenting a charge of treason."

"I see. Let me just check—"

Ky raised her brows at Palnuss. Gunsey was speaking again before she could say anything.

"Commandant, General Molosay can speak with you in five minutes; I have not yet ascertained if the Rector and sergeant major are available but I'm sure they will be. That gives time to set up a secured link for a conference call."

"Excellent," Ky said. "I will be waiting."

She closed the connection, picked up the book on the desk, and stood. "I suggest, Major, that you check on Stornaki—make sure he has nothing on him for suicide. This is telling you your business, but I lost a prisoner that way once."

"Yes, Commandant. I will be back within five minutes."

CHAPTER TWENTY-EIGHT

DAY 12

When the signal came, Ky and Palnuss were both in her office. "Commandant Vatta," Ky said. "Major Palnuss, the Security duty officer, is also present."

"General Molosay," he said. "At your request, Rector Vatta and Sergeant Major Morrison are also present, along with Major Hong of Base Security, and Captain Gunsey, my aide, who will be recording this discussion. What's happened?"

"Colonel Stornaki, Kvannis's second in command, is in custody, on my orders, for evidence of conspiracy. I found an intentionally mislabeled bound book in Kvannis's desk containing information of operational significance: names, contact lists, dates, and at least one outlined plan of action for a mutiny within the military."

"Is it the only copy?"

"I don't know, General, but I doubt it. I believe Kvannis left this one for Colonel Stornaki to retrieve. We are concerned that this facility is not ideal for holding Colonel Stornaki; nor do we have the forensic and interrogation expertise."

"You want to send him here?"

"Yes, General, if you have the facilities."

A pause. "We have the facilities, technically, but we, too, have discovered disturbing problems in personnel. Major Hong?"

"Yes, General. Commandant, we also have identified a few individuals who appear to be involved with the same conspiracy to mutiny, but we are by no means certain we have found all of them. We've been working on this problem, as it regards this base, since the sergeant major returned from TDY—"

"I know about that," Ky said.

"Yes, Commandant. That's why I'm not at all certain we've found all the conspirators—we still don't know how many there are, and we're having to rely on self-reporting far more than is safe. Some of those we've detained have managed to suicide."

"Do you have another suggestion for Colonel Stornaki?" Ky asked.

"No, Commandant. Just giving you the latest facts. I can arrange transportation by a team I trust, if that is your decision. What about the book? Do you want the forensic team here to go over it?"

"Yes. We will make plain copies here, then send the original to you. The Academy does not have multiband scanners and other forensic tools."

"Understood. We don't actually have much in the way of documentary evidence here, so it can go to the top of the stack at once. From your brief examination, is there immediate threat status in it?"

"I'm not sure," Ky said. "I've looked at only a few of the pages. Though the header is in clear, dates appear to be encrypted."

"Definitely an urgent concern. It will take me about an hour and a half to arrange for the prisoner transport."

"We will make copies of the book—"

"Two witnesses, if you can, from separate organizations—"

"Understood, Major. If there's nothing else—?"

"Not from me, Commandant. Sir?" Hong turned to General Molosay.

"We have a plan," Molosay said, with a tight smile. "Rector?"

"I will contact the Commandant later," Grace said.

"Then I'll get my people busy on those copies and continue a detailed search of this room," Ky said. "And of course Stornaki's quarters."

When she disconnected, Major Palnuss said, "There's a copier on this floor, Commandant, just down the hall. We can snag a Student Services clerk on the way."

The copying went smoothly and the clerk prepared affidavits for them all to sign and thumb-stamp. Back in the Commandant's office, Major Palnuss did a quick search of the desk, finding another hidden compartment in the bottom drawer on the right. Both, when opened, held slim folders full of more information. The right-hand drawer's compartment also held the little book Ky had last seen in Miksland, Colonel Greyhaus's logbook.

"We won't have time to copy all that," Palnuss said when she showed it to him. "We could send it along—"

"I turned it in to the military once," Ky said, "and it disappeared, along with the other evidence I'd brought."

"What other evidence?"

"IDs from the pilots of the shuttle and everyone who died. Bio samples from those poisoned—"

"Poisoned! I didn't hear anything about that."

"No. Well, the pilots' emergency suits—and the Commandant's and his aide's—were all sabotaged to inject poison when they closed the faceplate. I collected samples of foam—saliva—from their lips. And the shuttle's black box. Carried all that everywhere we went, handed it over to the military on my return to Port Major."

"So we should be looking for that, too?"

"If you see something like a flight recorder—it was in an orange case, by the way—it could prove that the shuttle itself was also sabotaged."

"Right. And ID packets?"

"Yes. I imagine the samples taken from the dead were simply incinerated, but then here's Greyhaus's logbook."

"And he's dead, too . . ."

"Yes, so I was told."

"I think I should go along and make sure that Colonel Stornaki and the other items reach someone reliable."

"I was about to ask you to do just that, Major. I should not leave the Academy until things have settled out."

"Agreed."

After he left, Ky opened the door to her secretary's office. "Sera, that disturbance you heard was Colonel Stornaki showing himself to be a conspirator; he is now under arrest."

She looked frightened. "Am I—"

"You are not under arrest, Sera, but I do need some answers. Did you ever suspect Kvannis or Stornaki of wrongdoing?"

"N-no. Commandant—former Commandant—Kvannis hired me; he is—was—such a nice man. I was actually his wife's social secretary for years. I thought they had only military personnel out here, but he knew I needed a job and said the military pay plus a little more from him would be better. And he said he'd be more comfortable with me than with the former Commandant's secretary, who was—well, I gather they did not get along. Of course he would prefer someone who didn't argue all the time."

Ky nodded, to keep her going.

"It wasn't a very taxing job, Commandant. Much the same as working for his wife—actually *less* stressful because I didn't have to arrange parties or redecorating or anything. Of course he never gave me anything classified to work with—he did all that himself, he and Colonel Stornaki. Are you—are you sure that Colonel Stornaki did something bad?" She looked worried.

Ky said, "Even though you've been very helpful today—"

"Oh, please!" Sera Vonderlane looked ready to cry. "Please don't fire me! My daughter—I mean, I'm sure I can please you, just give me a chance."

"Sera, you have not given me cause to fire you." Ky kept her voice soft with an effort. "But the situation is such that I must have you checked out before you continue, because the person who hired you is absent without leave—and in the military that presupposes an ill intent. Before you become my permanent secretary, for however long I'm here, I must be sure that you are not secretly passing information outside this office."

"I wouldn't! That would be wrong!" Vonderlane's eyes were wide open.

"Yes," Ky said. "It would be. And that's why you need to pass a security check." She paused. The woman was trembling and a tear ran down her cheek. Genuine fear of losing a job or good acting? "Tell me—what is it about your daughter?"

That brought on a flood of tears and a narrative broken by gasps and sobs. "She—she was out with her children—for a break—the train to Falls Park and this car—it derailed—and they died—and she can't—can't work—and has no one—the house—her pension—"

"I see," Ky said. "I understand; I'm so sorry. Listen carefully now. I am not firing you. Your salary will continue—though not the subsidy Kvannis was providing. But you cannot be working for me, in this office, until you have been cleared by security. I will do my best to find you a place to work in the meantime, but you will still get your salary regardless. Do you understand?"

"I—I will be paid?"

"Yes. Now, I want you to stay right there while I make a few calls. Can you do that?"

She wiped her eyes. "Yes, Commandant."

"I will talk to you again shortly."

"Yes, Commandant."

Ky went back to her desk, leaving the door open. Sera Vonderlane was crying again, but softly. Now what? The woman was older than her own mother would have been. What could she do? Secretarial work, obviously. But where? It was irregular for her to be the Commandant's secretary, and Ky would have preferred a military appointment for that post. But she could not toss the woman out to deal with a disabled adult daughter on her own, either. And she doubted Kvannis's wife would take her back as a social secretary.

Vonderlane's employment record was available to her: she could look up any of the staff. Sure enough, the woman had not undergone a background check when Kvannis hired her as his secretary. That was a breach of security and standard protocol. Her prior employment, as his wife's social secretary, was on the record, but her references were all civilian women listed as "longtime family friends." No credit check had been reported, no check of political connections or conflicts of interest. Clearly both Kvannis and his wife had counted on his rank and appointment to cover this breach. Which meant that someone in security was bent; she hoped it was not here at the Academy. Not, for instance, Palnuss, who now had the Greyhaus diary.

She used her skullphone to call the Rector again. Grace listened to Ky's report. "Obviously she can't stay as your secretary," Grace said. "If she passes the security check, I'll see if we can find her another place in the department. Do you think Kvannis is the one who hid all the evidence you brought back?"

"I suspect so, since we found Greyhaus's log in his desk. Why he kept that I don't know. My guess is that he incinerated the samples I hoped would help determine what poison was used. But we didn't find the flight recorder, and those things won't burn."

"Someone's got it, or threw it into the ocean," Grace said. "Maybe it's somewhere around the Academy. You should look for it."

Ky closed her eyes briefly and shook her head. "This place is a warren," she said. "There are far too many hiding places. But I'll see what I can do."

"Put the students on it. A reward to the one who finds it."

"Aunt Grace, I'm not going to tell a bunch of young people to go poking around when some of them may have families who are part of the conspiracy. Besides, they're on strict schedules. Military academy, remember?"

"Oh. Well, do your best."

Next Ky called back to the Academy security team. "I need an escort to take Sera Vonderlane home," she said. "And start a background check on her—no background check was done at the time she was hired. And do you know who a Colonel Dihann is? Was he ever on staff here?"

"Commandant, there's only me and Corporal Metis here right now; Major Palnuss took the others with him out to the base because they'd been witnesses to making those copies. We're not supposed to have fewer than two here in the Academy at any time . . ." His voice trailed away.

"Then who do you suggest I have escort her home? Any spare bodies around? She's upset and worried, and I want her to get home safely."

"Yes, Commandant, I can find someone, easy. Maybe ten minutes?"

"That will do. You can start running a proper background check on her. Her only former employment listed in her file here is working for Kvannis's wife. And—Colonel Dihann?"

"Yes, Commandant. Colonel Dihann—no, he wasn't ever assigned here. He came to talk to the former Commandant or Colonel Stornaki. Him and the major didn't see eye-to-eye sometimes. The major thought there was something wrong about him, but we didn't dig anything up."

"Dihann signed off Vonderlane's employment application," Ky said. "On Kvannis's word." She glanced at the file again. Vonderlane had started at the Academy as soon as Kvannis took over . . . immediately after the shuttle went down.

"That'd be because he and Kvannis were buddies. He told the major they'd worked together in Dorland, at Joint Services Headquarters South."

Dorland. Capital Makkavo. Had Aunt Grace been there, or at Esterance, when the Unification War started? "I'll get back to you later;

I need to speak to Sera Vonderlane again, make sure she understands she cannot take anything out of the Academy."

Sera Vonderlane looked slightly better; she wasn't actually crying and she remained calm while Ky explained what she would need to do. "You'll have an escort to your residence; your pay can be sent there, or deposited automatically, as you prefer."

"It goes to my bank now, Commandant. The military pay, I mean. Commandant Kvannis gave me the extra himself, in cash."

So—under the table, what could easily be construed as a bribe for her silence. "It will be a few days before I talk to you again," Ky said. "I have a lot to do, and I'm sure you deserve some days off. And you must not take anything from here—your keys to this room and the files, for instance. I have begun a background investigation, but I don't expect to find anything amiss. Please do not leave the city, however."

"I wouldn't!"

"Good. I—" She paused as a tap came on the secretary's door to the passage. "Come."

It was her own assigned driver; she wished she'd thought of that herself. "Ah—Corporal, Sera Vonderlane wasn't feeling well and will be taking a few days off. Take her to her residence and see her to the door."

"Yes, Commandant."

Sera Vonderlane looked at Ky, her expression pleading, but Ky had already given her what she could. "Take care of your daughter," Ky said. "This will all work out, one way or another." Vonderlane nodded and followed the driver out. Ky picked up the keys from the desk and locked both doors to the secretary's office. She would need a new secretary, but before that the office would have to be searched. She was tempted to do it herself, but she needed a witness.

Stella Vatta stared at the surface of her desk, having finally cleared the morning's items, and wondered whether the change she felt would last or fade away. For now, it was still vivid in her mind—the attack, her fear, her determination to survive, her realization that she had to walk on blood and broken glass past men she had killed, through the destruction the intruders had wrought inside the house, and finally the moment when she saw herself in the mirrors flanking the door— the mirrors her mother had made her check every time to be sure she was fit to be leave the house—and had seen herself whole, real, for the first time.

Grimy, bloodstained, disheveled, her good clothes fouled past cleaning, everything she had been brought up to avoid—what should have completed her dismay—but still herself. Out of the dirt and blood and fear she had found a new self emerging, familiar and new at the same time. Stella Vatta, CEO of Vatta Enterprises, a woman whose strength was not her beauty, whose elegance was not her wardrobe, who could enjoy beauty and clothes and a fine house, but did not need them.

And that, she was sure after another brief consideration, was not going away. She didn't want to be attacked—no sane person did. She would rather be clean, well groomed, wearing comfortable and attractive clothes—any sane person would. But never again would she feel incomplete without them. Never again would she feel guilty just because something had dirtied her face. She had earned that internal stability, not just by surviving the attack, but by all the years she'd lived, all the challenges met—even the ones she'd met badly. She had no mirrors in her office, but she didn't need them. She knew who she was, and being a bastard, adopted, daughter of a monster—was not her identity. She thought of Osman, this time without shame or horror. "I'm not you," she said quietly. "And you can't define me."

She took a deep breath, glanced at the time—three whole minutes?—and looked at the latest security analysis that had just popped up on her screen: threats detected, threats averted, threats reported to authorities. On Cascadia six incidents against the Vatta factory making shipboard ansibles, four of them traceable to the Bentik extended family. Jen's relatives blaming Ky—and then Vatta—for her death. Somewhat to her surprise, Stella saw that although local law enforcement went warily on the first two, the next incidents had brought the usual swift and efficient response, senatorial family or not. Two family members were under arrest, and the family had been assessed a fine and a financial hold. Only two Vatta employees had been injured, and both were now in stable condition.

Stella sent personal notes to their families and commendations to her security staff and the Cascadian law enforcement. The other two threats hadn't been traced yet.

Here on Slotter Key, other attacks had continued, at least partly in response to the rescue of the Miksland survivors. Besides the attack on the Vatta aircraft the day of the rescue, Vatta trucks had had tires slashed, resulting in one wreck. The home of a Vatta senior manager in Dorland was broken into and vandalized, with substantial property damage, but the family had been on vacation. She contacted Bry Skinner and promised that he and his family would be getting a Vatta Security detail as soon as possible. They were staying in a remote forest lodge.

"I'd like to send the family to live with my parents in Arland for a while," he said. "If this gets worse—"

"Absolutely," Stella said. "Have you been in contact with your parents?"

"Yes, Sera. They have a large house—it was on the market but they'll be just as glad to stay there as long as it's not just the two of them. They're in Arsinine."

"When can you get to a transport hub?"

"I'm not sure. I'm leery of hiring private transport in an area I don't know well; ideal would be a VTOL of some sort, but the resort lists only local operators."

"We'll send info with the security team."

She realized, in the midst of making calls to charter a VTOL craft with the range to extract them, arranging a charter flight for the family to Arsinine, letting Bry know that help was on the way, and ensuring ground transportation from the Arsinine airport to his parents' house—that this was much like what Ky had done. That her care for

Vatta employees was like Ky's for her soldiers. Well. Another new idea, and one she would have to share with Ky when the Commandant had time.

Ky and Corporal Metis began searching Sera Vonderlane's office. "Tech Coston will call if he needs us," Metis said. "Did you turn out her purse?"

"Had her do it. I'm sure I have all the keys but the one she said opened her apartment. Also two datacards, the probe with the access built in, a couple of letters. Nothing in her pockets but lint."

"She seemed like a nice lady," Metis said. "Of course, I saw her only occasionally."

"I think she is a nice lady," Ky said. "But she's been economically dependent on Kvannis for years. As his wife's social secretary, she apparently did him some favors, too. And he was paying her another twenty-five percent on top of her salary."

"That's . . . illegal, isn't it?"

"Yes, but I don't think she knew. She'd started working for his wife because of her daughter's injuries; he already knew about her medical expenses from that. She'd be doing him a favor to come to the Academy; he wouldn't let her income suffer. That kind of thing."

"I wonder what he wanted her to do," Metis asked. They had found nothing in the center desk drawer but what should be there: styluses, pencils, notepads, some with notes and some not. A printed list of the Academy faculty and staff, faculty with blue checks beside their names and staff with orange. Metis opened the left-hand drawer. "Well. Here's something."

Ky looked over. He held up a small machine. "What's that?"

"Something she shouldn't have had. A fully programmable franking printer. She could make something look like it came from any government agency." He pulled a pad from the center drawer, fiddled with the controls, and inserted a sheet; the machine emitted a beep and then the image of a Slotter Key stamp imposed on the Department of Defense logo. Another sheet; he changed the controls and that one printed out OFFICE OF THE PRESIDENT. "These are coded, supposed to be strictly controlled." He put it into the trolley he'd brought along for evidence.

Also in the drawer were preprinted envelopes with the return addresses of a dozen or more governmental agencies and offices in the military.

"Look at this," Metis said. On the point of each envelope flap was a small irregular spot, a smudge as if it had been touched by a soiled finger. "A signal that these envelopes weren't what they seemed?"

"Could be," Ky said. Her drawer had produced a box of stationery, completely blank, a box of pens printed with the Commandant's name and title—Kvannis, not Vatta, of course—and at the very back, a small envelope attached to the back of the drawer. "Bet this has a key in it," she said.

"Let me, Commandant," Metis said, as she reached for the envelope. He pulled a set of tongs out of his kit and tugged gently at the envelope. It ripped and a cloud of white powder flew out. He dropped the tongs and turned away, scrabbling at his pocket; Ky slapped her own emergency mask on and a second on him before he got his own out.

"Hurry," she said, pulling him toward her office. Eyes wide, he followed her, but stopped at the door, pointing to his shirt front, speckled with white. "I'll call," Ky said. Tech Coston answered from the security office. She told him what had happened, what they needed.

"Closest tox scanner is city emergency response," he said, sounding worried. "There's a team out at the base, of course, but that's twice as far—"

"Call the closest. Corporal Metis has visible powder on his uniform. I'm at my desk and will answer any questions."

"Yes, Commandant."

This was going to take hours, even if it turned out to be face powder. "Call's going in to the city team," she said to Metis, still standing at the doorway. He looked fine, though worried, as well he might be. "I'm going to check for emergency supplies in this office."

There was, in fact, an emergency box mounted on the wall of the little sitting room, and another in the toilet. More emergency masks, a fire hood and mask, fire-resistant gloves, in both places. She put on the fire hood and brought the other one to Metis. He shook his head. "Even with tongs, my hands might be contaminated. I'm better off with the one I'm wearing."

"I can put it on you without touching you," Ky said. "It'll protect your face better. Turn around."

She had put these things on in drills—on herself, on someone else—and in seconds his face was protected. She went to the window of her office and looked out. Flashing lights approached.

"That was fast," she said. "Something's coming."

"Maybe we don't need them," he said. "I don't feel anything. It's probably nothing. And you slapped that mask on me really fast."

"I certainly hope so. But you're going to be checked over and the stuff analyzed, anyway." She went back to the window. A single vehicle, not any larger than a personal car, had pulled up below. Her desk com chimed. She answered. "Commandant Vatta."

"This is Port Major Emergency Response. Please state your name, address, and the nature of your emergency."

"This is Commandant Vatta. I'm in my office in the headquarters building of the Academy, and one of your vehicles just pulled up to the door. The nature of the emergency is possible exposure to a dangerous substance unknown at this time."

"Oh . . . this is the actual Commandant? Not a secretary?"

"Yes, this is Commandant Vatta. Two persons were exposed; one of them has particles of a white powder on his uniform. I was in the room but not immediately adjacent to the release of the powder."

"What was it released from?"

"An envelope. We need—"

"We understand your needs, Sera; please calm down." She hadn't raised her voice; she had an urge to raise it now, when the voice added, in the same tone, "Why were we called? The Academy is outside our jurisdiction."

"You are the nearest emergency service with the ability to handle toxic materials," Ky said. "Although you are not military, you are listed as first response anywhere in the city. The Joint Services base is west of the city, and it would take much longer for them to arrive. That is why Tech Coston called you."

"Is he breathing?"

"Tech Coston? He was not exposed."

"The person who was exposed. Is he breathing?"

"Yes. But if the powder is any of several things I can think of, it's imperative that he be decontaminated and taken to hospital quickly."

"It's just—a moment, my supervisor wants to speak with you."

Ky heard voices in the background of the call. She punched her controls for video, but it was blocked.

"Commandant Vatta?" A deeper voice this time.

"Yes," Ky said.

"We have a problem. You—well, not you personally but the Commandant before you—ordered Port Major law enforcement off the premises, threatened us if we ever intruded again. We'd had an emergency call and sent an ambulance—"

"Surely you've heard that former Commandant Kvannis is now a fugitive—"

"I knew he was gone—"

"Yes. And I'm the Commandant for the interim—no dates set yet—and we need you as quickly as you can get here. That Corporal Metis hasn't fallen over yet is reassuring, but not conclusive proof that he, or even I, haven't had exposure to a dangerous toxin or disease."

"A crew's on the way, Commandant; we just had to check that we weren't walking into a trap."

A trap? What kind of nonsense had Kvannis been pulling?

"No trap on my end," Ky said. "Just a need for emergency response; glad you've dispatched one."

Thanks to the city crew's delay, the military response team arrived first, by two minutes. Ky made sure its commander was cleared by Major Hong as having no part in the conspiracy before letting them treat Metis—swathing him in a bubble half the size of the room, vacuuming his clothes and mask, and then taking him, in a tented gurney, off to the military hospital. When the civilian team arrived, Ky asked them to proceed with the analysis and search of that office; they also took samples from her.

"I don't think it's toxic," one of them said finally. "I think it's a marker of some kind. Intended to catch thieves or snoopers, not kill them. It's been how long since you saw it puff out? Not an hour yet? If it's what I think it might be, and if it got on your white uniform, you may have speckles—green or blue, usually—where it landed."

"So I can take this mask off?"

"Yes, Commandant."

"Why the delay? Why not an instant marker?"

"So the thief doesn't know they've been marked right away. It reacts with protein slowly, creating an indelible mark that can't be washed off."

Ky looked at her sleeve. "You mean—it could ruin this uniform permanently?"

"If it's an animal fiber, like wool. Mostly it marks skin. May I ask what you were searching for?"

"Evidence I had turned in to the military upon my return from Miksland. Former Commandant Kvannis claimed it had been misplaced or lost. We found some in my office, and another piece in that one. I think Kvannis was hiding it in various places; we think it will reveal who was responsible for the shuttle crash."

"Why would Kvannis do that?"

Ky considered the risks and benefits of opening another gap in the conspiracy of silence and went ahead. "Miksland's mineral resources and utility have been kept secret for several hundred years, exploited by the few who knew the secret. When we survived to land on it, and found one of the installations there, we—all the survivors—became targets for those who wanted the secret kept. I didn't know that at the time, of course, so I had collected evidence I thought might be useful later. Kvannis was part of that conspiracy, so of course he suppressed it."

"Why didn't he just destroy it?"

"I have no idea. Maybe someone else told him to keep it, or maybe he had a use for it later. He absconded from here when he realized that the other survivors had been rescued from their imprisonment—"

"Imprisonment? What had they done?"

"Nothing. Supposedly they had some contagious disease that required them to be quarantined. Surely you've seen the newsvids about that in the last couple of days? The plan was to kill them and dispose of the bodies in sealed coffins."

"You weren't flying the shuttle, were you?"

"No. Nor did I sabotage it, or poison the pilots."

"The pilots were poisoned?"

"The pilots, the Commandant, his aide—all the officers aboard, by a mechanism in their survival suits. If I hadn't insisted on bringing my own suit with me from my flagship, I'd have died before the crash. I brought back samples of the poison and also saliva from the pilots, hoping it could be analyzed to find out who was responsible, but that's part of the evidence that disappeared after I turned it in." The officer opened his mouth but Ky went on before he could speak. "That investigation properly belongs to the military, and now that I've located some of the missing evidence I'm sure an inquiry will go ahead."

"Well—the crime didn't take place here in Port Major, so I don't suppose anyone will ask for our help in it."

Ky didn't comment on that.

"But we are concerned with crimes within the city. You know about the Vatta house—?"

"The attack night before last? Yes, Stella and I have been in contact."

"It was a near thing—damage inside the house, from the firefight. Sera Vatta did a fine job defending herself."

"Firefight! She didn't tell me about that." She had cut Stella short, accepting her brief reassurance.

"Yeah. Vatta HQ called us to check when they lost contact with the house and couldn't raise Sera Vatta. Our first people were attacked, but got off a call for backup. Vatta had a couple of crews on the way, but they'd been all the way out at the airport. In the end Sera Vatta was alive with only minor injuries, all the intruders on the scene were dead, and we captured some familiar faces from the Malines cartel downtown."

Ky felt another stab of guilt for not warning Stella they'd be leaving the house empty, and remembered she'd agreed to call Stella herself sometime today.

"Sir—there's a box here with a lock that might fit this key."

"Try it," Ky said when one of the officers glanced at her. She watched from across the room. No puff of powder, nothing threatening at all until the lid came up and she saw what was inside: the samples she'd taken in the shuttle that first day.

"That looks like biological waste," the officer said. "It's got numbers on it—important, Commandant?"

Her voice caught for a moment, then she cleared her throat. "Yes. Those are the samples I collected. Let me see—I labeled them, and when I handed them over they were stamped with a number—"

"Pilot Hansen? Copil . . . that must mean copilot?" Another glance at Ky.

"The shuttle was rocking around on the waves," Ky said. "I didn't have time for more."

"Sunyavarta," the officer said. "And these tissues had their saliva? You collected it?"

"Yes—they had foam at their lips. We had a med tech aboard, she drew blood samples—those tubes."

"We have a competent forensic lab—you still think all this should go back to the military—?" *Who "lost" it in the first place,* was the clear unspoken message.

"I do," Ky said. "Since the survivors have been freed, and their stories are going public—and the military isn't all bent, after all—these things need to be investigated there. They have the data on personnel that you don't, and it's someone on the inside who sabotaged the shuttle and the survival suits. For all we know it was someone up on the station."

"All right—but I'll want to observe a clean chain of possession to retain the evidentiary value of this evidence."

"Absolutely," Ky said. "I would prefer that your personnel remain here until my security officer gets back from the base to take possession of it, and then we'll certify that your people didn't tamper with anything."

"Fine. How long will that be?"

"Several hours—I'm sorry, but this office didn't have a large security staff, and they were transporting a prisoner. I'll call and see if they can cut him loose earlier."

He left her in her office, and she called the officer's outfitter to find out what to do about her uniform.

"*That* powder? Can you change immediately? We were about to deliver your second uniform."

"Yes," Ky said. "I hope you can save this one."

"Do not put it into the 'fresher; that could set the stain. And avoid daylight."

Which meant cutting through the inside corridors above ground level. Circuitous, and added almost ten minutes to the usual time.

She left word that she was going back to the residence to change and wash off any residual marking powder. By the time she had arrived there, the tailor she had first seen at the base was there to deliver her second uniform and take away the first. Ky cleaned up, dressed in her new uniform—it fit even better—and called Major Palnuss from her quarters.

CHAPTER TWENTY-NINE

DAY 12

"I'll come back right away," Palnuss said when Ky told him about the evidence she'd found. "Major Hong's taken over the investigation, reporting to General Molosay. Everything I brought out has been logged and is as secure as they can make it. Stornaki's not going anywhere; he's been screened for suicide and is presently sedated and prepped for interrogation. They don't need me, really."

"Good," Ky said. "I hate to keep the police here too long but we want that chain of custody—"

"Of course. An hour at most, depending on traffic."

Ky offered the police refreshments—it seemed the decent thing to do—and went on dealing with the items on her desk that needed work. Her driver came back after delivering Sera Vonderlane to her home and seeing her to the door. About a half hour later, her skull-phone pinged.

"I'm safe," Rafe said. Ky felt her shoulders relax, tension she hadn't recognized in the midst of everything else. "I'm exhausted, hungry, dirty, and wearing the clothes of a mountainous thirteen-year-old farm kid. I'm being driven from place to place by friends of the first farmer. Can't take other transport without ID. Just got in range for calling again. Where is everybody? Where are you?"

"In the Commandant's Residence at the Academy," Ky said, over the pounding of her pulse.

"Why?" Rafe demanded. "Are you in trouble?"

"Haven't you heard?" Ky said, in the most honeyed tone she could manage. "I'm the new Commandant."

Silence for a moment, then a snort of laughter. "You. The new Commandant. What happened to the old one?"

"Ran away in the nighttime," Ky said. "Where were you?"

"Running from trouble up and over a small mountain. Then it got dark. Not just dark: cold, wet, and full of big hairy monsters with horns and hard hooves, and I did battle with them. Outnumbered, I fell, was trampled, and rescued by heroes—"

"In other words you stumbled into a pasture and bumped into some cattle and the farmer drove them away."

"No, I drove them away, but they chose to run over me first. Also, it was a total dead zone for communications. Some of these farms don't even have electricity. Right now I need a faster way home than from farmhouse to farmhouse, and a change of clothes. But when I finally get to Port Major, I can come over there and rescue you."

"I don't need rescue," Ky said. "I'm fine—new uniform and all."

"You really are the Commandant of the Academy?"

"Yes. With a full schedule and add-on excitement. Police, military security, attempted assassinations, traps—"

"Gods. Any chance you can arrange a free ride on a Vatta truck for me? I'm a few kilometers outside some town called Stone Crossing."

"May be much later, but yes. I'll call you. Or Stella will. Stay where you can catch a ping."

"Yes, Commandant." Lilting, sweet.

Relief felt like the bubbles in wine. All the people from Miksland had been rescued. And now Rafe was safe. Or would be, when she'd found him transport. She called Stella.

"Rafe's called; he's stuck out on a farm near . . . uh . . . Stone Crossing. With no ID, and his visa status still not fixed. Does Vatta have anything nearby he could hitch a ride on?"

"Let me look—Stone Bay, Stone Center, Stone . . . there it is. We don't have a warehouse there, and the daily eastbound truck went through there two hours ago; the next truck is westbound, in an hour. He could connect to an eastbound at . . . um . . . that's another four hours and then more hours back. Stone Crossing has a small general-aviation field, no commercial flights. It would take one of the little planes. Is that safe? I heard one of our long-haul planes was threatened."

"It should be safe; they don't have any checks on passengers there, do they?"

"Not in their listing. It's only Rafe? Just one passenger?"

"Yes . . ."

"I'll send the Pug. Two-seater, no Vatta logos on it. It'll be . . . a two-hour flight or more depending on weather, plus prefight prep. Dark there when it arrives. Can he be there in three hours?"

"I'm sure. But does the field have anyone there at night?"

"Probably not. Morning, 0900. It'll be light by then. Still the Pug. Let him know."

"Thank you," Ky said. "Where can he go when he gets here? Not the Vatta house, obviously."

"Aunt Grace's. Rafe can stay there if he can get in undetected. Ummm—he should come here, to Vatta headquarters, the freight entrance. I'll let the airfield know to have someone drive him in."

"Thank you," Ky said.

"Got an appointment," Stella said. "Talk to you later."

Ky shook her head. Stella sounded different—none of the usual edge in her voice. She called Rafe back; he assured her he could find a safe place to stay overnight and make it to the airfield on time.

* * *

When Major Palnuss arrived, he took custody of the other items, and after a discussion between Palnuss and the senior police officer, the police departed.

"Tell me what other searches you think we need to do. Stornaki's office—?" Ky still felt energized by hearing from Rafe.

"A more thorough search, yes. And his clerk. What are you doing about Sera Vonderlane? You need some kind of assistant—"

"Military, but I don't know how previous clerks were selected." Ky glanced at the paperwork already stacking up.

"Kvannis insisted on her," Palnuss said. "Said we didn't need to do a full security screen; she was part of his household and he vouched for her."

"Yes, she told me that. I may find her a job over at Vatta, depending on the results of a security screen. She's got a disabled daughter, and is disposed to be loyal to anyone who pays her. At least, that's my interpretation. You?"

"Not much initiative, not too bright, worshipped the ground Kvannis walked on. I can find you a decent clerk pretty quickly—say a day or so."

"That'll do," Ky said. She nibbled on a cookie on the tray she'd had sent up for the police. "You know . . . Kvannis could've destroyed the evidence we found. Whatever his reasoning was, maybe he saved all of it. Want to go looking for the flight recorder?"

"Would you mind if I grabbed something to eat first?"

Ky blinked. She hadn't had anything but the cookie since—a scant and hurried breakfast. "Good idea. First food, then search."

"And that list of things you had to do?"

"It's only my second day. How far behind can I get? And if I'm seen stalking around and peering into things, everyone will know I'm here and working." She watched his reaction: surprise, then humor, then appreciation. "Now—that food you mentioned. I don't suppose you can nudge the kitchen into producing some quick, sustaining food, preferably with protein?"

* * *

"So where do we start?" Palnuss asked, after they had demolished a tray of sandwiches and Ky had dealt with four calls.

"It's about this big," Ky said, demonstrating with her hands. "Bright orange, with a striped design in a band around it. Not too heavy; I carried it around in the chest pocket of my survival suit for ages."

"About twenty by twenty-five centimeters, then? Not quite as thick as that briefcase? Looks like a part of something mechanical?"

"I guess. It's a box, basically."

"So it would look out of place in an office, unless it was inside a safe or something like that. And the safe here was drilled out—and the one in the residence, too, right?"

"Right."

"So I think we should look in places where something like that would fit in."

"Machine shop?"

"And every other place here that has boxes about that size."

"And where things aren't inventoried on a regular basis," Ky said, thinking of various stores units she'd seen. "Maybe where flight recorder spares are, or things waiting repairs . . ."

They set off through the Academy. Despite her desire to find the flight recorder, Ky paused to look into one classroom after another—not to search, but to show herself present and interested. Finally they reached the labs where cadets learned to maintain and repair those machines they would use later—a large lab for each branch—and the shops where skilled technicians maintained all the military equipment and machines the Academy used, from firearms to robots. They prowled through one after another, almost as if they were an IG team.

Palnuss called attention to several surveillance modules that were not working properly in a passage that connected two storage rooms in the Land Forces lab and suggested to Ky that a complete inventory of that stockroom might be a good idea. The tech 2 behind the counter of the first started sweating. Ky nodded. "Best call in your team, perhaps."

When they passed on to the actual shops, they found most moderately busy, tools in use, technicians willing to describe what they were doing, seemingly quite at ease. Ky entered each one, glanced around, asked a few questions. The technicians opened cabinets and closets happily, showing off how neatly arranged they were. As they neared the end of the row, Ky said, "I'm wondering about something that was on an inventory list in Commandant Kvannis's office—but it's not there. Do you have any idea where I'd look for number 238–665–9817?"

"What size, Commandant?"

Ky outlined the box with her hands. An assistant looked up sharply. "I remember—it was an orange-striped thing, kind of like a flight recorder?"

"The list didn't give a description."

"I'm sure of it. It'll be down in room one-twelve-C. That's the Air Safety Investigation and Research Unit, and they have a pile of those things. Their staff isn't there right now—they've been off investigating a crash since yesterday—but I can let you in."

Indeed, the shelves along one side were stacked with flight recorders. Their guide rattled on. "They said some of these are really old—sixty years or more—from all kinds of aircraft. They do some kind of testing—lots of kinds, I guess. But they're not here all the time, like today."

"How long has this unit been here?" Ky asked. "It wasn't here when I was a cadet."

"Oh—not that long. I think it came in sometime last spring." He stepped to the door. "Hey, Louie—Commandant wants to know when this unit came in!"

"Before or after the shuttle crash?" Ky asked, without waiting for an answer.

"Oh, just after, I guess."

Ky looked at Palnuss and he looked back. "Well," he said. "The

Commandant may want to look around some more. I don't think either of us has ever seen this many flight recorders in one place. You can return to your work."

Ky added a nod to that, and the guide wandered out. Palnuss shut the door behind him. "Now what? We look at every one?"

"If we have to," Ky said. "But just let me prowl for a minute or two. If he's hidden it in here, it'll be where someone who finds it will be marked in some way. So where is something especially dirty, or balanced where dusty or dirty ones will fall, something like that?"

"Not just behind a stack?"

"The shelves aren't that deep. They're not hung on the wall; they're freestanding racks. I think they were moved from wherever this unit was before, and were purpose-sized to the more modern recorders. If I'm reading his thought processes right, he'll assume a searcher will expect it to be at the back, or under something . . . hidden." She turned around, eyeing all the shelves.

Major Palnuss, following her gaze, looked along each shelf in turn. "I don't see—"

"There," Ky said. She went toward the door, to the narrower rack beside it, with a clipboard hanging from a string and a battered pencil thrust into the clip.

"Why that?"

"Because every shop I've ever seen had the formal, official list of what was there—on some kind of tablet or computer—and then it had the real list, usually on actual paper. A clipboard or a spiral notebook, kept where it is handy to the techs but could pass for a sign-in/sign-out sheet if the brass comes by."

"You think it will be listed?"

"Yes. Even if Kvannis told them not to put it in the official catalog for some reason, they'll have it here." She took the clipboard down; Palnuss craned his neck to see the top page. SIGN IN/SIGN OUT.

"I'll be—is there something like this in the other shops?"

"Yes—I noticed them when we were there. Just like other stores and shops I've been in, civilian, merc, military alike."

She flipped up the pages until she came to something different. "Aha. This is their personal stack map. With initials, how handy. D for drop-offs, CI for currently investigating, R for removals. Item's accession number. And a column for who dropped it off or picked it up, conveniently labeled WHO. And date. And this at the end is where it is."

"And you can figure out that code?"

"I think so. The most recent item dropped off was six days ago, by RG, whoever that is. If L2-T means top of the stack on the second shelf of the left-hand set of shelves . . . now, is that coming in, or going out?" She was facing the back of the room. "I'll take the one on my left, you take the one over there."

"What's the accession number?"

"For this entry? XRM-VTOL-2914M8." Ky looked at the second shelf on her side without success. Three stacks and the top item in all three had the wrong number.

"Three stacks on this shelf," Palnuss reported. "Aha!"

"So they mapped facing the door," Ky said. "Now, how long would it have taken for that item to get here, after I turned it in?" She worked backward through the scribbled notes until she saw IK in the WHO column. Two days after she'd handed the flight recorder in, Kvannis had turned it in here. "Accession number correct, Kvannis's initials correct, but—no map code. Wait. They put it in and he must have made them erase it."

"That I can fix," Palnuss said. "We're good at forgeries, invisible inks, and the impressions left by pencils. Let me see it." He dusted it with powder, blew softly, and said, "B. Back, that should be. L . . . lower or left. Three T. Let's try the third shelf near the left end, on top. Or, if Kvannis made them move it, somewhere nearby."

"If he annoyed them enough, they probably put it back where they wanted it," Ky said. Ky recognized the right flight recorder as soon as she was close enough, on top of the end stack on the third shelf. It had snagged a thread in the pocket of her survival suit, and the short

length of orange thread was still there. She checked the number anyway.

"Where do you want it now?" Palnuss asked. "The safes won't lock."

"Do you have one in your office that will?"

"Yes, but all my personnel have the combination."

"And do you trust them?"

"Yes."

"Then keep it there. It won't be long, I think, before you or I will be
asked where it is. We should know that."

CHAPTER THIRTY

DAY 13

Rafe woke finally and listened to the house. Silence. Was he alone here? It took him several minutes to remember that Teague and the others were out at the base, that the Vatta house had been damaged and he was at Grace's. His implant told him it was 1600 local time, afternoon of the same day he'd flown in from Stone Crossing. He showered, raising his eyebrows at the bruises the cattlelopes had left on him, but glad the headache had gone. Dressed in slacks and a sweater, he tucked his usual weapons into their places and padded downstairs to investigate.

He found MacRobert in the kitchen giving instructions to a pair of men in uniform. MacRobert looked up sharply, then nodded at Rafe. "I was thinking we should call a physician, Ser Dunbarger." Formality in front of the guard; MacRobert had been calling him Rafe. "You slept a long time."

"Being run over by large animals with hooves and horns will do that to you," Rafe said. "Is there anything to eat?"

"Can you cook?" MacRobert asked. "I've got to go back to Grace, and these gentlemen are here as guards, not servants."

"Well enough for a quick meal. Eggs still in the cooler?"

"Fairly well stocked. Enjoy yourself. The Commandant will be glad to know you're awake."

The Commandant—that was Ky, now. "What else has been happening while we were gone?"

"Too many attacks on Vatta," MacRobert said. "There's a little brushfire out in the Southwest and a frank attempt at a revolution got started about twelve hours ago in Makkavo—that's on Dorland. Last we heard something probably related was also popping in Fulland."

"Heard that yesterday—if it was yesterday. That knock on the head messed up my time sense. Ky and Stella both all right, though?"

"Yes. Ky's supposed to be interviewed on the news later."

Rafe rummaged in the cooler, coming out with eggs and a chunk of ham. He put Grace's smaller frying pan on the stove, added a knob of butter, and took a slice off the ham and diced it. The two guards hitched up their weapons harnesses and left the kitchen, one to the front of the house and one to the back.

"The Vatta legal staff and Grace are both working on your visa status," MacRobert said, relaxing now that the guards were gone. "It's too bad you lost your ID jumping a fence. Teague's safe at the base. Immigration can't get at him there, and the guards here have been told to say nothing."

Rafe found the drawer with the whisks in it, and beat up three eggs and poured them into the frying pan. He reached for the diced ham.

"If you added an egg to that, I wouldn't say no to some," MacRobert said.

Rafe cracked three more eggs, gave them a brief mix with the whisk, and poured them in, along with the diced ham. "Easier to divide in half," he said. "And if you don't want that much, I can manage to get around it."

MacRobert chuckled. "Always did appreciate a partner who could cook."

"So we're partners now?"

"Only in that we're both working for Ky at the moment. And Grace, of course, though she's gone odd since the gas attack."

"Odd how?"

"Blaming herself for not knowing about the deal her father made to get her out of prison, and accepting a political post. She thinks that's what set the Quindlans off. Which it isn't; the attack on all the Vattas came before that."

Rafe dumped a heap of stirred eggs and ham onto one plate and the rest on another, turned off the stove, and carried the plates to the table. "I thought that attack was mostly Osman."

"Osman wanted Vatta taken down, but so did Quindlan." MacRobert shoveled in a mouthful of eggs and after a moment went on. "After all, why put in a secret access to your customer's basement if you're not planning to harm them? We don't know when the charges were actually placed, but my guess is that they'd been there a long time."

Rafe nodded. "And Vatta had refused to carry Quindlan's cargo that they couldn't give provenance for—that was long before, wasn't it?"

"Right."

"That time in the psych prison Ky told me about—did Grace ever get any treatment for combat trauma?"

"Apparently not."

"She should," Rafe said. "It helped Ky a lot."

MacRobert looked at him and shook his head. "Rafe . . . you're too young to understand some things, never mind what you've been through."

Rafe bowed slightly. "My apologies."

"Accepted. That Vatta lawyer's stopping by later to talk to you about the progress on your own legal problems."

*   *   *

Midmorning, Ky gave a brief press interview, at Joint Services Headquarters, along with General Molosay, Sergeant Major Morrison, and
a representative from the Assembly. She let the others explain how the
rescue plan had developed.

"But then you were rewarded by being named Commandant of the
Academy," said one journalist. "Isn't that so? And is that not unusual,
that someone not actually a graduate should be offered such a post?
Or did you ask for it?"

"I will answer that," General Molosay said, "since I made the decision."

"I asked Commandant Vatta," the journalist said.

"It was not a reward," Ky said, "nor did I ask, or imagine it, until the
general asked me to accept the post. When the former Commandant
left secretly, it was understandable that the higher command would
be concerned someone else at the Academy—the next in line for promotion, for instance—might be part of the same conspiracy, the one
that kept the survivors isolated and in captivity."

"But you—"

"But she had no connection with any of them," Molosay said. "And
she had combat experience, which most of our officers do not have.
Plus familiarity with the Academy and its procedures. So for an interim
appointment—and I stressed that it was an *interim* appointment—my
staff and the government all agreed that she was both qualified in terms
of military knowledge and stature, and completely unconnected with
the current group of senior officers."

"I see," the journalist said.

"Next question," Molosay said before the man could ask more.

Afterward, Molosay complimented her on her responses.

"The Public Affairs officer at the Academy coached me," Ky said. "I
could have used such coaching in the past—I know I ruffled feathers
best undisturbed."

"On another matter," Molosay said, nodding toward the corridor that led to his office. "You have been busy over there, ferreting out bent officers and discovering most of the missing evidence. But have you had time to go over the items I sent with you that first day?"

"Frankly no, sir, I have not. Is there something that you want to brief me on?"

"Yes. Come on in—" He opened the door, then spoke to his aide. "Jerry, we'll want something to drink and sandwiches; this may take awhile. Be sure the screening's on max." He waved Ky to a seat. "Do you have any information on the size of the conspiracy? Who else is behind it besides the former Commandant and this Colonel Stornaki you sent us?"

"I would bet on the Quindlan family, or some part of it," Ky said. "While I was on Miksland, the Rector discovered some evidence that they had known about Miksland very early and had originated—or cooperated with—the plan to keep it secret. I'd always known our families were rivals in trade; what I didn't know was that one of my ancestors refused to help one of theirs transport raw materials from Miksland and sell them—illegally—offplanet."

"I'm more concerned about the military conspirators," Molosay said. "You told us about Greyhaus; his logbook reveals that he was training military personnel chosen for their political bias and attachment to the Separatists, preparing for an insurrection funded in large part by those valuable ores being mined in the northern part of the continent. But such a conspiracy has to be bigger than a few officers and a few hundred disaffected soldiers. Even a large corporation like Quindlan, or a criminal organization like Malines—that's not enough to pull off a successful revolt. Controlling the surveillance satellites so that in several hundred years they never reported what the surface was really like—?"

"The data could've been intercepted and falsified elsewhere," Ky said.

"Not reliably for that long. And there's this: you, as Commandant of the Academy, have other military duties that—worst case—might show up."

"What's that?" She hadn't signed up for anything but running a military academy, definitely a full-time job. The sudden realization that though her word might be final in the Academy, she had someone above her in the command chain put a chill down her spine.

Molosay handed over a folder with the title of EMERGENCY ORDERS LOCAL. "The Academy is part of the Central Command's Table of Organization. Normally that means nothing much. But in the event of an attack on Port Major, or any major emergency situation involving the capital, the Academy is tasked with protecting the seat of government. The ceremonial honor guard, though armed, may not be sufficient in the case of attack."

Ky opened the folder and scanned the first few pages. "Has the Academy ever been called on?"

"Once or twice for urban riot situations, when the request for help came from the police. Never for protection from military attack. Even at the height of the Unification War, conflict never made it to this continent." He looked at her as if expecting an answer.

"But now, since Kvannis hasn't been captured, you're worried. Any idea what troops he might turn up with?"

"Greyhaus's bunch, for sure. They'd been moved to a northern base, but then dispersed, and now a number of them are AWOL. Right now it looks like somewhere between five hundred and a thousand, which isn't anywhere near enough to win a war. Kvannis must know that. And I don't know how many more there might be—two thousand? Three? Surely not more than that, at least not on this continent. But if they decided to hold the President hostage, occupy the Palace or Government House—"

"So . . . it's my job to protect them with the ceremonial guard and cadets and staff? Is there an actual operational plan in here?" Ky tapped the folder.

"That's a copy of what was written originally, with an update from maybe a hundred and fifty years ago. Not worth the paper it's printed on, but you needed a copy. I know ground warfare isn't your thing, and you were right to get your people out ahead of the trouble in

Miksland, but I don't have a spare thousand or so troops to lend you."

"Any idea when this mysterious possible attack might take place?"

"No. But my gut tells me it's coming. Not today or tomorrow, but if he's got powerful and most of all wealthy allies in Port Major, it could be within a few tendays. There are riots in both Makkavo and Esterance; word is some ground troops have broken into the armory at Fort Jahren and marched toward Makkavo's portside."

"If we're in your command, then how do we get more supplies?"

"Ask me, or my aide. We're well supplied at the moment, so I can release ammunition, firearms—"

"Transport?" Ky asked. Molosay looked confused. "If there's already an element of this conspiracy in the city, it would be stupid to march the entire cadet corps on foot across town to the government complex. They've had no training in urban maneuvers."

"I'll connect you with someone," Molosay said. "I'm sure we have vehicles, but . . . do you have room to park them over there?"

"Some, certainly. I don't know how many it would take. No Land Force background."

"I'll see that you get that information in the next two days."

DAY 16

It was three days before a Colonel Hatch called her and explained that the only transportation available for the Academy was a unit of four buses usually reserved for transporting dependents. "And we need a week's advance notice to reserve them," Colonel Hatch said. "The forms for reservations are here in the transport division office—"

"That won't do," Ky said. In those three days she had reviewed all the information she had and conferred with the senior Land Forces instructor on urban tactics. He had not been encouraging about what she could hope to accomplish, and she was not in the mood for procedural nonsense from Transport. "Transportation is needed pursuant to Emergency Orders Local—"

"Emergency? What emergency? Why haven't I been told?" Hatch sounded completely rattled.

"Emergency Orders Local states that, in case of attack, the Academy is tasked with supporting the honor guard at the Presidential Palace and Government House," Ky said. "General Molosay has told me to develop a new plan for doing so, and that involves arranging transport from the Academy to those locations. As an attack would be without warning, that transportation must be immediately available."

"But—but what if it's scheduled for another—what if it's full of dependents—"

"That's why your initial option won't do. The Academy needs a permanent installation of enough vehicles—armored, preferably—sufficient to transport cadets—"

"Cadets! You'd be taking cadets into—"

"A combat zone, yes. Because that's what Emergency Orders Local says to do. So let's start over. I need transport for the three upper classes of cadets and another fifty to sixty—"

"But that's over a thousand—"

"Major." Ky's tone cut him off. "If you like, I can have this conversation with your commander. It's true I do not have a Land Forces background, as you probably know. That's why I'm not simply telling you what models and numbers I need. This is supposed to be your area of expertise."

"We don't have enough," Hatch said, in a calmer voice. "A third of our transports are either off on remote assignment or in maintenance. Those four buses are all I have to spare, and they're spoken for through eight days from now."

Ky thought longingly of Vatta Transport and Stella's ability to move trucks seemingly at an instant's notice. But a convoy of Vatta freight haulers would be just as obvious and less secure for her cadets. She wondered, though, about Hatch and his reluctance to cooperate. "I'll see if I can knock something loose for you," she said, and ended the call. She was shaking her head when her new clerk came in.

"Something wrong, Commandant?" Bik Kamat, a corporal from Joint Services Headquarters, had brought a completely different feel to the former secretary's office.

"Major Hatch of Transport," Ky said. "What have you got there?"

"Major Hemins's latest assessment of the second years' performance, and Colonel Laurent's notes on the defense of Government House. With annotated plats, as you requested."

"Thank you," Ky said. "Anything urgent in the next hour?"

"No, Commandant. Do you want your lunch sent in from the Academy mess or Commandant's Residence?"

"Residence. I've annoyed Chef already by skipping too many meals." Ky grinned at Bik, who grinned back. "Tell him to make that two lunches, unless you want what the mess has."

"Thank you, Commandant; I'll eat at my desk, too. That way the calls won't interrupt you."

According to Hemins, the second year was already improving, though still far from the goals Ky had set for it. But better was better. She turned to Laurent's plats and comments. He had come to the same conclusion she had, that the complex of government buildings surrounding the Presidential Palace and Government House would be impossible to defend from a serious attack with twice the troops the Academy could supply:

"It would be better to remove the President and her staff, and the senior legislators, to a safe place—not that such a place exists at this time. The Academy itself would be easier to defend from ground attack, but not from the air. The only substantial bunker-like areas are under the oldest buildings. I do have a file of previous plans other than the one you sent me—I would have expected them to be in the Commandant's office somewhere unless they were removed by the previous occupant."

Ky felt a chill go down her back. Kvannis had taken the plans, of course, and that meant he was up to date on the most recent. She read further.

"My senior Land Force students participated in the updating of the plan every year, as well. I've shipped the copies to your desktop. However, I believe we need to talk about this."

"Indeed we do." Ky looked at her schedule and then his, then touched the button that connected to his office. "Colonel Laurent, this is the Commandant. I agree with your assessment. Do you have anyone scheduled for your office hours today?"

"No—are you free then?"

"Yes," Ky said. "I will be scaring the second-years again today, but then I will come by your office on my way to the gym."

"Thank you, Commandant."

Ky looked quickly at the plans he'd forwarded. All brief, not much change from year to year. Starting back in the days when a ditch had encircled the future "government place" for drainage, the plan had been to place a cordon of troops around that margin—first using the ditch and the little mound on the inside as cover. Later, when the ditch was eradicated during the construction of Ring Street, the plan developed two concentric rings of "protection"—the outer being a ring of "checkpoints" where a small number of troops would supposedly control entry, and the inner being the perimeter of each building. At no point was defense of the government complex moved out across Ring Street to make use of the cover of other buildings.

"Insane," Ky muttered.

CHAPTER THIRTY-ONE

DAY 16

A few hours later, in Colonel Laurent's office, Ky laid the plans on his desk. "These haven't changed much in four hundred years."

"True. And regrettable. I asked repeatedly for permission to expand the parameters, but was told there would never be an attack, that this was all theoretical. It would be a training exercise only and students could be told why it wouldn't work."

Ky shook her head. "Frustrating, I'm sure. Do you know who was behind the lack of planning?"

"Pure laziness and cost-cutting, I believe. We could use an engineering section, with appropriate machinery. But no. 'Oh, no, we can't have you making ruts in the roads or digging up the beautiful gardens.' We could use a way to emplace anti-aircraft, but again, the sacred gardens. I'm not the first chair of the Land Force department to be told no, and I want to make clear that we all fought for better planning, but . . . this is what we have. Once a year, in the spring—the same date every year to avoid alarming civilians—we reserve some transport from the base, bus the two upper classes of Land Force cadets over there, and have them parade around the perimeter with empty weapons and practice peeking around the corners of the buildings. It's Drill Day."

"Not even the entire cadet corps?" It made no sense at all to Ky.

"No. Because the others will never need to know about land warfare, at least not until they attend Staff College later." Laurent grimaced. "You would think the Unification War had been a little disagreement settled with shouting and sign-waving, something that could never happen again."

"What is the presumed enemy for the drill?"

"Farmers upset about the price of fuel and a drop in the price of produce, played by senior school students from two private schools. They were always intimidated by the cadet troops and dispersed without actual contact."

"I had no idea . . ."

"You wouldn't. You were Spaceforce-designated. You were on your shuttle training flight."

"And Kvannis knows these plans?"

"To the centimeter. He knows how far ahead you have to reserve the buses. He knows the exact coordinates of every room in every building." Laurent looked at her quizzically.

"Do you think Kvannis expects these plans to be followed? In general or in detail?"

"Commandant, I must admit Iskin Kvannis and I were not particularly close. We had had . . . disagreements. His intent, he had told me, was to get rid of me for being, in his words, insufficiently respectful of his position once he became Commandant. Because I did not like him, it is possible that I have not fully understood his thought processes. And I have no idea what insight he had into *your* thought processes, or if he thought Colonel Stornaki would take over the Academy after he left."

"Points taken," Ky said. "Conclusion?"

"I think he expected Stornaki would be named interim, and Stornaki would do what Kvannis told him. Surrender the Academy, even. I'm sure he knows you're the new Commandant. He knows you were trained for Spaceforce, and your experience was entirely in space warfare. He may expect you to follow the plan because you have no expertise in land warfare, or he might think you will do something different but equally inept." Laurent tipped his head a little.

Ky nodded. "Then I think I should surprise him by doing something different and effective. Don't you?"

He smiled at her. "Yes. Did you have something in mind?"

"Indeed. But if you have any ideas, I'd rather hear yours first."

"The plan as it is could be improved by adding that engineer brigade and moving some dirt around, to the consternation of the Port Major Garden Club. Adding some artillery, air defense emplacements, surveillance drones . . . do we have any hope of getting such resources from the Joint Services HQ?"

"In other words, augment the current plan? With resources we almost certainly could not get within a tenday, let alone create real defensive positions?"

"That's true. If we expect an attack that soon, about all we can do is evacuate the likely targets—the President, the senior legislators, the heads of departments—but we can't. I raised that possibility and everyone acted as if I wanted to kidnap them and put them in prison—"

"Everyone is going to have to accept the necessity," Ky said. "We don't have the troops, equipment, or time to make that area really defensible, though we don't know the actual time of attack. We know the other side has subverted part of AirDefense: they were able to send planes up from Ordnay to intercept an aircraft carrying rescued personnel."

"What happened?"

"Better planning," Ky said. "I regret the deaths of those pilots, but we got the survivors safely to Port Major." He nodded and she went on. "We don't know whether Sea Force has been subverted as well, so attacks from ships at sea, or troops transported by sea, could be involved, as well as Land Force units moving into the city. We would need much longer—and we don't have it, because the other side has to move quickly; they can't easily hide out for a half year. Now that they've started, speed is their ally."

"So—how are you going to convince the government officials to leave—and where will you take them? And what about the damage the attackers will do to the buildings?"

"The buildings are less important than the people and the data—data transfer needs to start today. I need to talk to the President and the Council today without telling them more than they need to know. And we need to convince Kvannis that our plan is his plan because I— the idiot from outer space—can't think of anything else. So we're going to act as if that plan *is* our plan. There will be drills. We'll get those buses, load 'em up, drive over there, and have cadets march around. We've got two small airfields—who's reliable in AirDefense, do you think?"

"Well . . . there's Basil Orniakos, but your aunt the Rector had a feud with him last spring. I've heard rumors he's gone over to the rebels, but I don't believe it. He was in my class here, and it's my belief he's rock-solid loyal, but could be pretending to defect."

"AirDefense faculty here?"

Laurent looked down, frowning. "I can't be sure. I don't want to accuse anyone unfairly—"

Ky let out an exasperated hiss. "Colonel, I have to trust someone, and I've decided to trust you. So let's deal with the loyalty due fellow officers as subordinate to the loyalty due Slotter Key as a whole. Is there anyone on the AirDefense track here that you trust unequivocally?"

"No," he said, meeting her gaze. "Commander Vinima made . . . comments during the time you were in Miksland that indicated his lack of respect for former Commandant Burleson and his adherence to Kvannis. His second, I believe, transferred to the Academy when Vinima became chair of the department."

"Then I will get in touch with Orniakos, through proper channels."

"And the rest of your plan?"

"Remove the human and data targets, and appear to be following the old plan, in order to lure the opposing force into a trap."

"There'll be damage . . ."

"To structures. Which can be rebuilt. If we have the right combination of weaponry, damage will be confined to the government corridor, but evacuating the closest buildings would be a good idea."

"That might actually work," Laurent said. "But you still need to find a secure place for the President and the others."

"I need staff," Ky said. The plan was crystallizing now, and she could almost see how the parts would mesh. "We'll need three different groups to pull this off. Command structure for each." She felt the familiar excitement, energizing. "I'll want your recommendations for the main group, and your support when I tackle Joint Services HQ."

"It'll take me the rest of the day—"

"Fine. I'll see the President and the Rector. Keep in mind that this new plan is not for anyone else. No one, as this point, but you and me."

"Yes, Commandant. But what about General Molosay?"

"I will inform him in person, but not via any communications device." And not yet, she thought. They would be lucky if they had ten days, extremely lucky if something delayed Kvannis twenty days. She wished every meteorological and mechanical disaster on him and his forces.

By midnight, when she finally got to bed, Ky had talked to President Saranife, the Rector of Defense, and the few others she felt she must inform. She had a list for the next day's calls as well. Colonel Laurent had prepared an organizational chart for the operation she'd outlined and they'd spent a couple of hours after supper refining it.

DAY 17

The next day Ky informed the entire faculty that the Academy's traditional duty of protecting the seat of government might be called on, and advised them to be ready for sudden schedule changes.

"You mean someone might actually invade the city? Who?"

"Dissident elements of the military," Ky said. "Possibly led by the former Commandant—"

"Are you sure he wasn't abducted?"

"Yes," Ky said. "We have evidence that he was plotting to overthrow the government and dissolve the union, restoring at least one southern continent to political independence."

"That's ridiculous; they can't possibly expect to win."

"Be that as it may," Ky said, "General Molosay told me that in his opinion an attack is possible, and that the Academy would be expected to follow Emergency Orders Local and protect at least the two most important government buildings, Government House and the Presidential Palace. The Joint Services Headquarters expects to be fully engaged as well, so this is our problem, like it or not. Plans for this have been drawn up, as you know, and yearly drills held—"

"But nobody ever seriously expected an invasion to come—those plans were just an exercise for the seniors in Land Forces to learn from," Major Parker said. "If it's really an attack—" He glanced at Colonel Laurent.

"Colonel Laurent has already explained the plan's shortcomings," Ky said. "General Molosay has agreed to transfer a unit of combat engineers and their equipment; the President has agreed—reluctantly— that we can create some defensive barriers in the public gardens. That will start tomorrow; it will take most of the day to move the equipment into the city. I expect you to prepare the upper-division cadets for this, and avoid panic."

"Do you know when the attack might come?" asked Colonel Dagon, chair of the AirDefense department.

"Not yet," Ky said. "General Molosay's assessment has been forwarded to your desks." An assessment she had edited, with his permission, to mislead those faculty members who were part of the conspiracy. "It's proving difficult to detect suspicious troop movements and concentrations due to the winter weather." That much was true.

"I still think it's a stupid plan," said Commander Seagle, chair of Spaceforce division. "It's a rectangle of relatively low buildings and open ground, and you're proposing to build earthworks? The only sensible thing to do is evacuate the government—to space, for example, where these rebels can't get at them—and wipe 'em out when they show up. One or two drone-mounted smart bombs would do it." Seagle leaned back in his seat with the air of someone who had just said the obvious to a roomful of idiots and expected admiring applause.

"The President will not agree to that," Ky said. "She feels that abandoning the Palace will be seen as abdication."

"Well, she's—" He stopped himself with obvious effort, and subsided, scowling.

"We're going to have to go with what we already have. Colonel Laurent and I are working on more detailed plans. All cadets will participate in some of the drills we'll be holding, but only the two upper classes will be part of the defense force should an attack come. I realize this will disrupt the usual class schedule, but our orders take precedence. At this time, cadets will be informed of the possibility of attack, and that drills will occur, but nothing more."

DAYS 17-37

Over the next ten days, Ky dealt with the Port Major city council and its agencies, none of whom were thrilled to have large construction machinery making dents in city streets and inconveniencing traffic . . . with the Port Authority, which resisted military "interference" tagging communications with incoming and departing ships . . . with the commanders of both the small AirDefense bases nearest the city . . . with a steady stream of questions, orders, revisions of orders, from the Joint Services Headquarters . . . and with the usual work of a Commandant.

She had seen Rafe only three times since his return, and Stella not at all, though she had talked to both of them daily, mostly about business. Rafe, Rodney, and Teague had moved back into the Vatta house, ostensibly to supervise the repairs. Ky trusted their intel reports more than those from Molosay's office.

On the tenth day, Rafe contacted her with new information. "Rodney's been following the shipping news at all major ports. A Quindlan freighter, *Xonsulat,* that had just loaded cargo at Makkavo dumped it back on the dock, then filed a new route to a Quindlan-owned facility—a private port, basically. No idea what they took on, but the ship then filed for Green Harbor—south coast here—and ultimately Port Major. We have it on satellite; it'll be eight days to Green Harbor, minimum. Six to eight days more to Port Major, depending on how long they're at Green Harbor. *Xonsulor* also diverted, and is due at Sunhome Bay on Cape Harmon in ten days."

Ky tried to remember where Green Harbor and Sunhome Bay were, but Rafe went on talking. "Both those ports could be easily reached by troops from anywhere on the south coast. Kvannis could have started people moving in small groups—"

"Ship capacity?"

"We're trying to find out, but I haven't a clue how to convert gross tonnage and dimensions into passenger capacity."

"Neither do I, but I know who does, roughly. Get Rodney to ask someone in Vatta's sea freight division—"

"Got it. I'd have thought Kvannis would just use trucks, or fly them in—"

"It's a possibility he'll use all three. Ships can carry heavy equipment less obviously than trucks or trains."

"So we don't quit looking for more transports—"

"No. Any transport originating from any military facility—those can be cross-checked with orders from Joint Services Command HQ."

Ky passed this information to General Molosay. Twelve to fourteen more days to prepare before the ships arrived—at least. Already the long park in the government complex had been dug up and reshaped by the combat engineer units, using their massive machines to create trenches, dugouts, and what the Port Major media insisted was a huge unnecessary mess. On the excuse that some of the necessary drills would involve live ammunition, government buildings across the streets that ringed the complex were told to evacuate rooms facing those streets, and the windows were covered with shields.

As the days passed, tension in the city oscillated between worry that a real attack might come, and annoyance that since nothing had happened, citizens endured traffic delays and detours for no reason. Ky kept the Academy running, insisting on classes being taught even if the schedule changed. Some faculty seemed to enjoy the challenge; others grumbled if asked to move a class a half hour, let alone from day to night. The second-year class, somewhat to Ky's surprise, improved faster.

And day by day, the two Quindlan ships came nearer and nearer to Port Major. Each had spent two days in its intermediate port, and now they were in tandem, obviously intending to reach Port Major on the same day.

DAY 38

"I think it's because they see the other classes also having hardships now," Major Hemins told her one afternoon when she had stopped by to check on the second-years' progress. "Also, the heavier schedule means their extra work isn't punishment. The overall attitude has changed a lot since you chewed them out. Definitely class cohesion. I'm quite pleased with them now."

"Good," Ky said. "Because I have an assignment for them that they must not know yet, but you can."

"Commandant?"

"The ships we think are bringing insurgent troops to Port Major are only four or five days away now, but this still remains a secret. Is that understood?"

"Yes, Commandant."

"All right. Tonight, the President and her staff will leave the Palace and move to temporary quarters. Tomorrow, one-third of the legislature and their staffs will evacuate Government House, followed by another drill that explains the evacuation. Critical data have already been shifted to other servers; all the servers in the Palace and Government House will be wiped. The two senior classes, as in the plan, will engage the invasion force we expect, but the second class will be assigned to assist the honor guard in protection of the persons of the President, her second, her staff, and those seniors in the legislature whose positions might draw enough attention to attack their homes. I have looked at your assessments carefully; by tonight, I want your advice on choosing specific personnel for each assignment." She handed him a data cube.

"You're—you're moving the President? Like Major Seagle said?"

"Yes, but it was important not to let potential traitors in the faculty know. You must not discuss it with anyone."

Ky had just settled back in the chair at her desk when her skullphone pinged. Grace.

"Ky, I know you're busy, but I wanted to warn you about what's going on in the legislature."

"The legislature?" The only thing she knew about the legislature was that they refused to leave the chambers "until the bombs are falling," as one of them put it.

"It affects you slightly, but mostly me, for being Rector. The President and Council are planning to throw the situation with the Miksland personnel to the standing committee on military affairs. Did you know your survivors came from every continent but Miksland?"

"Yes," Ky said.

"Well, it's a mess. Continental legislatures are furious about what happened, as well they might be, but some of them are also divided. My neck is on the block, as far as some are concerned, and I can't blame them."

"You couldn't have known," Ky said.

"I should have known. I should never have taken this post. That's tearing them apart, Ky."

"It's not all that's coming apart. Nothing you did would spark something this big. Hiding the truth about Miksland began long before you were born." Ky spoke harshly; Grace needed to get over her guilt trip and start thinking clearly about the present mess.

"You're right about that," Grace said. Ky could hear her sigh. "Right now what matters is spiking this incipient civil war, because that's not going to help anyone, whoever wins it."

"Good. Start with that. Admit that you didn't know, it was a mistake and can be dealt with later, but right now—we've got the murders and the mistreatment of military personnel to cope with, and the conspiracy behind them. Start fast and keep going. Don't let them talk over you."

"You sound like me," Grace said. Her voice was stronger now.

"No, *you* sound like you. They can cut you in pieces and fry you later, but right now they need to save the government and the security of the whole planet. Put that way, they'll fall in line."

"Unless they're involved," Grace said.

"And then you'll know," Ky said. "And so will everyone else." She felt peculiar, giving advice to Grace, who had given so much advice to all the Vatta children.

"All right. I'll do my best."

"Do you want me to be there? As Commandant?"

"No, I don't think so. The Commandant has always stayed away from the Grand Council unless invited. If you're invited, though, I'd say come."

Grace Vatta sat staring at the wall for a moment, thinking about Ky's advice. Why hadn't she thought of that herself? A tap on the door interrupted her.

"Rector, you have a visitor—in uniform—Commander Basil Orniakos."

Grace just managed not to gasp. Orniakos, Region VII AirDefense, with whom she'd had that disastrous argument when the shuttle went down. Orniakos . . . she could not remember all the things she'd found out about him . . . why was he here? He was stationed on the far side of the planet.

"I'll see him," she said. She left the papers she'd been studying on top of the desk, and made sure her personal weapon was in reach.

The door opened; she recognized him from his image, loaded into her implant more than a half year ago.

"Rector Vatta," he said; he stood stiffly.

"Please sit down," she said, waving to a chair. "And forgive me for not rising to welcome you; this is my first day back in the office."

"I was appalled when I heard you'd been poisoned," he said, pulling a chair a little closer to the desk before sitting down. "Have you found out who stole the toxin from the military?"

"Not yet, though I suspect the instigator was Michael Quindlan. According to my great-niece, who had the message fairly directly, he intends to kill us all—me, my great-nieces still alive, and my other great-niece's two children."

"Rector, you may be wondering why I am here, and not contacting you in a more . . . conventional way."

"I assume you have a good reason," Grace said. "Besides showing that you, as well as I, could jump the chain of command. A mistake, in my case."

A glint of humor flashed in his face, then vanished. "I hope this will not prove to be one. I believe I have information that should go immediately to this office." He opened the briefcase he carried. "This is a letter I received shortly after our previous . . . encounter . . . from someone who believed I was ripe for recruitment to their faction. Their research was inadequate; though I was angry with you on that day, and sore about it for a week or so, in the long run nothing could turn me from a loyal officer to a traitor. However—I let them think I was tempted. And this is what I found." He laid the letter and a data cube on her desk. "I have the names of what I believe are ringleaders in an attempt to restore Separatist territories. Miksland was to be the first. I did not know that until after the breakout there."

Grace picked up the letter, looked at the signature, and looked back up at Orniakos. "Greyhaus?"

"Yes. I—one of the reasons I hadn't contacted you, Rector, following that . . . disagreement we had was that I'd had subtle signals that if I was in your doghouse, someone else might turn it into a mansion. I waited, to see what would happen. And this came. Interesting, I thought, that it came from someone of the same rank, in another branch."

"And it came as an actual letter, not electronically?"

"Yes. This is, as you see, a copy; the original self-destructed after an hour. So no fingerprints or other biological evidence, except—" Orniakos grinned, a feral grin, and laid down a photographic enlargement of fingerprints. "I had anticipated that real conspirators would take precautions. So there was ample time to copy this letter photographically under several filters. Now that Greyhaus is dead, it might be useful to compare the fingerprints that were not his and not mine with the military database."

"It might indeed," Grace said.

"The data cube has lists and dossiers on all the personnel I found whom I believe are associated with the plot. The further communication between us—Greyhaus was supposedly my handler—" Again, the feral grin. "—is also in that data cube, composed on a machine that has never been connected to any other. You will have to take my word for it, however, because I never received paper communication once they became sure of my allegiance."

"Interesting, that they thought they had such secure electronic links."

"Yes, I thought so. They disappeared about the time the second mercenaries were heading down to Miksland. What I did get then was word of a fire on a server farm somewhere on Dorland and another on Fulland." He lifted one eyebrow.

Grace nodded. "Yes, such fires did occur. A less-than-perfectly-successful effort to disrupt communications between Pingat Base and the Black Torch mercenary company."

"Rector, I can leave this information with you—or, if you wish, give you my summary."

"Please do give me your summary. Are you willing to have another person—to whom I'd pass it on anyway, I must tell you—hear it as well?"

"Certainly. That would be Master Sergeant MacRobert, would it not?"

"I was thinking also of General Molosay."

"Fine, if he can come here. I would rather not be seen on the base right now."

"Where does your command think you are?"

"Somewhere else." His look challenged her to figure it out.

"Give me a one-minute pitch while I contact them," Grace said. For Mac she need only ping him and tap twice.

"Three families, eight organizations within the military, two possible choke points to prevent this thing blowing up too big. It's going to blow—can't stop it—but we can, if we move fast, have a controlled explosion in a confined area."

By the end of the one-minute pitch, Grace had both MacRobert and General Molosay on conference mode. Several hours later, the conference mode had expanded, and Grace had agreed with Molosay that Orniakos should command the government's forces on Dorland.

"There will be casualties," Orniakos warned. "I'll try to keep it confined to the actual traitors—the civilian population down there doesn't want another war—but the butcher's bill may be expensive."

"If you can save the planet, I'll pay the bills out of my own pocket," Grace said. "Were you far enough up the chain that they showed you my file?"

He flushed a little. "Part of it, yes, Rector. In fact it's the reason I trusted you enough to come to you instead of to the general. I understand combat trauma; easy to see how a youngster without training, caught in that mess, would be messed up for years. And how some things would rub you wrong later. But that's beside the point. What we've discussed will hold the carnage to a minimum, although—in my day the Academy was supposed to protect the government centers. Your niece Ky—brilliant commander in space—does she know anything about surface warfare?"

"She has advisers," Molosay said before Grace could reply. "And she is heeding them."

Orniakos gave a half shrug. "Good. I have nothing against her." He turned to Grace. "Quindlan really hates you, Rector—not only you, but all Vattas. And so do several others."

CHAPTER THIRTY-TWO

PORT MAJOR
DAY 44

Michael Quindlan had waited impatiently for this day, and now at last it was happening. Quindlan ships had brought the troops; Quindlan influence and Quindlan money had finally—*finally*—resulted in his being given a position in the upper echelons of the resistance. He would rather, he told himself, have been out there leading a squad or platoon or whatever they called it of Greyhaus's soldiers, but Kvannis wouldn't allow it. Ridiculous, the way the military pretended civilians knew nothing. He'd watched the movies and vid shows.

In lieu of that, he'd taken action within his own family. His niece Linny had done the second-level check on Benny that he'd ordered her to perform—her first official duty, one she knew might get her promoted. Those two had been antagonists since childhood, so if there was a dirty spot on Benny's apparently perfect character, she'd find it. And she had.

Benny had betrayed him. Linny had befriended Benny's idiot

wife—well on the way to alcoholic if not there already—and pried out of her the fact that Benny had handed over a secret file to Stella Vatta. The boy had had a crush on Stella back when he was eleven or so, but supposedly his father had beaten it out of him. Not hard enough. Well, Benny would find out what happened to Quindlans who disobeyed the head of the family. He would find out in stages, starting with a tragedy he would not, initially lay at Michael's feet. With luck, he might even blame the Vattas for the vicious attack on his wife that left her alive, but permanently damaged, and his children dead. He should be hearing about it any time now.

"Weather looks difficult," Molosay's meteorologist said. "This is a serious snowstorm moving in—"

"It won't bother them," Ky said. "They trained both on Miksland's southern half and up north."

"But dark and snow—"

"They'll be more used to it than our troops," Ky said. "This may be why they hung around an extra day or so before heading into port. They want the dark and snow; they figure it will hurt us."

On the way back to the Academy, Ky watched the shelf of high clouds as it closed in the sky, horizon-to-horizon. Beneath it, the first softer clouds moved out of the northwest like rolls of fluff. Sleet rattled on the roof of the car as it turned into the Academy gates to the Commandant's Residence. It had stopped by the time she walked to the door.

She was halfway to her office when Rafe pinged her. "We lost visual satellite surveillance with the clouds, but the ships are not stealthed or silenced. Both ships picked up pilots; *Xonsulat* is within the harbor and will dock on the north side, near the foot of Ertanya Street. There's an open berth behind that I'd bet *Xonsulor* will take."

"As we expected. Weather says snow starting after dark, with mixed sleet, rain, and freezing rain until then."

"That'll make the streets slippery," Rafe said.

"No problem for them with their tracked vehicles. I need to make calls now."

In her office, she found messages from Joint Services Command, Neese Base, Harbor Point Base, and the President, who wanted to know if her removal from the Palace was really necessary since nothing had happened since she'd moved out.

"It's happening *now*," Ky said. "The suspect vessels are docking as we speak."

"Oh. Then I suppose you won't let me go home—"

"No—your home address is too well known and just about indefensible. Please stay where you are and do not contact me. Your security troops will be with you very soon now."

Molosay, at Joint Services Command, knew about the ships and wondered if Ky had put any surveillance drones up.

"No, General; we would rather they were less suspicious than more. It's still too light—" Though the light was dimming as the lower clouds thickened. A snowflake danced by the window, followed by a shower of sleet.

"You expect them tonight."

"Yes, General. Why would they wait? They've come in under cloud cover and it's almost full dark now; what better time to surprise us? How are things at the base?"

"Trouble at Ordnay—fighting between the loyalists and the insurgents. We expect to be attacked here—" On a sprawling headquarters base that, like the government complex, had never been designed for defense in a serious war.

Ky reminded herself not to give advice that hadn't been asked for and ended the call. She called a meeting of the faculty and staff who had passed MacRobert's deep screening—they'd run out of time to screen them all—and gave them a heads-up. The engineer group reported all vehicles fueled and ready to position; that would begin within the hour.

She looked in on the cadet mess hall. No way—since the cadets had no implants—to give them four hours or so of good sleep before the action she expected this night. How long would it take the invaders to get all their equipment off the ships? How long to form up? She went back to the residence, changed into the base layers of her combat gear, and set her implant for four hours, with an override if her skullphone pinged earlier.

Ky's skullphone pinged, and her implant informed her it was a half hour to midnight. Even as she rolled over and sat up, the red line's light came on. "Commandant—Unit One. Cattle arriving at stockyard."

"Enough for that Academy banquet?"

"Would think so. Send them on to processing?"

"Go ahead."

Ky alerted her local commanders without using the main alarm system. Someone in the Academy was almost certainly on the conspiracist side and in contact with Kvannis. She went to the window: silence outside, and snowflakes dancing in the light from the room. In the distance, soft blurs of light; the forecast had predicted snowfall starting around midnight and becoming heavier toward the morning.

The red com beside the bed buzzed louder. In rapid succession she fielded calls from General Molosay, the two small airfields, and Rafe. She dressed quickly, including the chameleon suit, and made sure she could reach its controls.

Then she checked her weapons, ammunition, gas mask, and communications before heading for the Old Hall. Her combat helmet, pre-loaded with com codes, connected her to the Command Center at the base, to the Rector, and to her subordinate commanders; she ran through the checks to be sure all channels were live.

The long passage between the residence and the Old Hall, dim under emergency lighting, lay before her, empty and silent, any sound from the Old Hall baffled by the angles in the passage. Another skullphone ping. "Cattle arriving at entrance . . . route Mixer three-two. Alt route Prom two-nine." So advance patrols were using the Military

Avenue route from the harbor to the government complex, just now passing 32nd Street, and another group was coming up Promenade but had reached only 29th. Almost time to call the alarm, because the city police should have noticed troops in the street by now. Ky checked the elapsed time and switched to the general alarm channel.

"This is the Commandant. This is not a drill. Emergency Orders Local Zodiac; Emergency Orders Local Zodiac. All cadets, fatigue dress, with emergency kit, to the Old Hall immediately. Armsmaster and techs to the Armory. Faculty to the Old Hall, fatigue dress."

"Commandant—is this a drill?" Someone always asked. She didn't recognize the rather squeaky voice.

"This is not a drill. I expect all personnel to comply quickly and without panic."

"Commandant, Armsmaster Tilley reporting on station at Armory."

"We will need to arm those cadets who have qualified, Armsmaster."

"For a riot or something? What is the Zodiac suffix, Commandant?"

She had not been certain of Tilley until MacRobert had cleared him late the previous afternoon. "There's an attack on the city. Police report unauthorized troops in the city, including armored cars. Confirmation from the Joint Services Command base. Command believes it's Kvannis and his allies."

"They came *here*?"

"Apparently. As per Emergency Orders Local: issue helmets, vests, weapons, and ammunition; I'll be sending the fourth-years first."

"Yes, Commandant." He sounded solid enough, and nothing had shown up on MacRobert's search of his records.

She turned a corner in the passage. Ahead, only dim emergency lights showed, with the dark maw of the stairway to the dais of the Old Hall on the left and the closed door to the assembly level on the right. If someone had been pre-warned, if she herself was considered a danger, attack would come here. Ky slowed, slipped her pistol out, and thumbed the safety off. She eased to the corner, and around it. Before she reached the steps, she saw a darker shadow move; shots rang out—her own and the other's. Ky felt a hard blow to the chest; a wave of heat washed over her as her armor reacted. Behind her another several rounds ricocheted off the stone walls of the corridor. She heard the clatter of a weapon hitting the stone steps, the sound of someone falling. A breath, another breath, as her implant reacted to the adrenaline burst, as no more shots were fired. Whoever it was hadn't had the weapon on auto override.

Voices from above . . . no one would miss the parallel to the situation with Marek. She walked forward, still poised to shoot again. The light on the stairs came on, revealing the fallen shooter: Colonel Bohannon, chair of the history department. Blood still oozed from the holes in his chest, staining his uniform, pooling on the floor. The exultation that had followed previous killings lasted only a moment, washed away by grief. She'd thought he was one of the loyalists.

"Colonel Bohannon? What's happened?" came from above. She wasn't sure of the voice.

"Stay back," she said. "Don't come this way; I'm armed and checking for more shooters." They would know *her* voice. She heard someone's shocked exclamation: "The Commandant!" but did not answer. She picked up Bohannon's weapon, which turned out to be palm-locked to him. She took it anyway, and emerged at the top of the stairs to find Major Palnuss and Captain Ramos, standing well back and blocking the others' approach to the stairs. Nobody had a weapon aimed at her, which proved only that they had good sense. Her gaze scanned the group: all the department chairs but Bohannon, the rest of the faculty, faces still expressing shock or concern.

"What happened?" Colonel Shin asked.

"Colonel Bohannon shot at me; I returned fire and killed him. I was hit, but my armor protected me." She watched their reactions: shock, concern, and reasonably quick return to control.

"He said he was going to look for you—that he was worried you might have run into trouble."

Ky didn't say the obvious, that he had been the trouble. She needed them focused on the greater danger. "An enemy force has landed from two ships in the harbor, and is now beginning to move toward the government center. Those of you who've been specially briefed know what our plan is. For the rest, our orders have been modified by the Zodiac suffix; if you have not previously been briefed, remember that you are under the command of those who have. I'm assigning Major Palnuss to take over here, commanding the skeleton force to protect the youngest class; they have not yet had enough training to be of use in the field. As per the Orders, I will command the force that protects the government complex. Class advisers will stay with their classes."

"But they're not—"

"We have our orders," Ky said. "Our more senior cadets are quite capable of doing what is required." She looked at Palnuss. "Major, when the first-year class has arrived, you will take them to shelter and proceed to secure the Academy."

"Yes, Commandant."

She heard the clatter of boots in motion and turned to see the first cadets entering the Hall. As expected, these were the seniors, a half year away from graduation, lining up quickly in their usual formation.

"As other faculty arrive, Major Palnuss, you will check their credentials and—ah, Major Osinery—"

Osinery, white-faced, had come past Bohannon's body on the way up the steps. "Commandant, there's a bulletin—"

"I'm sure. You will take over as my communications aide. Record and relay as I tell you. Major Palnuss, on the basis of investigations so far, ensure that persons we have discussed do not have access to weapons."

"Yes, Commandant."

She turned to the cadets ranked below her. "The capital is under attack; you know from recent drills what is expected of you: obey all orders, hold your fire until ordered to shoot. These orders may vary from what you drilled on; we have received supplemental instructions. Do what you're told and things should go well." The fourth-years looked back at her with resolution. "Major Massoudian, take your class to the Armory now."

"Yes, Commandant."

"Third-years—" They had moved forward in order as the fourth-years left; the second-years were filling in behind them. "Major Leonidze will take you to the Armory next. Your class and the fourth-years are an essential part of this defensive plan. I expect you will do as well as they do—there'll be a prize for the best class." A few grins among them now, quickly smothered. Ky looked beyond them to the second-years. They certainly looked better than before. Her implant ticked. "Major Leonidze, take your class to the Armory." He gave the order and she waited until they were gone. She imagined the progress of the enemy, the last of them just coming onto the decks of the ships that had delivered them, climbing into the armored cars, and starting off to the north, to the government complex.

"Second-years—" No grins here, but a sense of determination and unity the class had not had before. They wanted her approval now, wanted to succeed. "You will not be in the same action as the upper classes." They didn't like that; she could feel it. "You have a different assignment—because you have earned the right to it. You will be guarding important members of the government. You will be issued weapons and be transported to several different locations: Major Hemins will divide the class appropriately. You will be under the command of experienced combat veterans. We know there are criminal elements, allies of the conspirators seeking to take over the government. We know they will try to find and capture the President and other senior members of government. You must not let that happen."

"Shots fired," came a voice on the police channel. "Shots fired, police falling back as ordered."

"Major Hemins, take your class to the Armory," Ky said. She turned to the faculty, some of whom looked much less steady than others. "Major D'Albini, take your class to the bunker. Those whose names I call will report to Major Palnuss in the basement, with the first-years. You can assist there." She read the list, skipping over Colonel Bohannon, and sent them on their way. "The rest of you received the supplementary orders; you know your assignments and your resources. Those with me—let's go."

CHAPTER THIRTY-THREE

DAY 44

Outside, the snow fell more heavily; lights glowed through the falling snow, but visibility was limited. Another ping of her skullphone, this time from General Molosay's staff at the base. "Air strike here; your guys IDed a ground force on the way—we're ready. Good luck to you."

"Going now," Ky said. Her combat helmet gave her its interpretation of what she looked at, mixing multiple bands to provide a faux-sharp image that wiggled uneasily as thicker and thinner strands of snow crossed it. Another screen gave her a view from one of the drones poised above the government complex: looking down through falling snow dizzied her for a moment. The former gardens now looked like textbook earthworks, as they should, with rows of hot dots on the infrared view that the oncoming troops should assume were cadets.

"Commandant? We're ready." The command transport had pulled up beside her.

INTO THE FIRE 433

"Right." Ky accepted a hand up the step and into an interior that reminded her a little of the ships she'd commanded: the glowing screens, the banks of instruments. Osinery followed her, looking nervous, the light on her recorder blinking. Once inside, Ky had a view of the two columns of personnel carriers ahead of them. One had already split off to the north. The other moved east.

"We're on the tick," said a familiar voice; she looked over and saw Corporal Inyatta grinning at her. "Column one is almost to the north end, well ahead of the attackers." Seven of the survivors had argued their way onto this op, including the first three to escape plus Staff Sergeant Gossin, Sergeant Cosper, Corporal Lakhani, and Corporal Yamini.

Ky switched channels and contacted Neese, the northern base. "Cattle entering processing. Light the fires."

She could hear nothing over the sound of the vehicle she was in, but imagined the big drones starting engines, the low *whoomp-rumble* rising to a high whine. Snow should muffle the sound; she hoped it would be enough.

"First enemy troops past the Defense HQ . . . President's Guard and police opening sporadic fire." Just enough to convince the enemy the defenders were there, but confused. Ahead of her command car, personnel carriers full of third-year cadets, and troops borrowed from the base moved out. At the head of each line was a squad of combat engineers with the armored earthmovers they'd used to rearrange the formal gardens into something resembling military earthworks. "Twenty percent past Defense HQ, coming up on Government House. Permission to launch—"

Here the attacking force would expect stiff resistance from the guard units normally stationed there.

"Launch defensive weapons," Ky said. On both sides of the government complex, the buildings one street away from the original rectangle housed offices, not residences. Now the robotic batteries implanted in slightly hardened positions spouted fire at the attackers, fire they returned. The attack force's movement slowed a little but did not halt. More and more of them poured out of the constriction of the business district onto the wider avenues that ringed the government district.

As expected, the attackers had personnel carriers, mounting both beam and missile racks, as well as dismounted troops in full battle gear. And with the first launch of missiles against the Presidential Palace, the battle was joined in earnest. As Ky had hoped, all those preparations in the great public gardens around the Palace had focused the enemy's attention and convinced Kvannis—or whoever was commanding—that the defense plan hadn't changed that much.

But it had. The robotic batteries simulated fire by actual troops—irregular and, though effective, less than what the batteries could produce. More and more of the enemy moved into the area, focused on resistance from the supposed defenders, pouring heavy fire at the trenches. The heads of their columns were now even with the Palace. Would they see what awaited them, through the snow now blowing out of the north into their faces? The big earthmovers had traveled dark, pushed by the vehicles behind them. Even infrared sensing might not spot them.

"In position," Massoudian said finally. "Both routes blocked to the north. East still unsecured."

"Set," Ky said, and contacted the air base again. She felt the mix of alertness and calm so familiar from space combat. Once an engagement began, once forces were committed, the stomach-clenching wait was over. She watched the screens, the icons marking movement. Just as the attacking infantry overran the trenches and climbed up to the level beyond, the first flight of drones arrived, raining cluster bombs down on what had been the broad central walk. Debris clouded the sensors. Attackers still mounted in their carriers spun their beam weapons, trying to hit the drones, but those were long gone, heading for the harbor and the ships that had brought the attackers. The concussion and flare of that explosion traveled through the snow; for an instant all movement seemed to stop.

As if in answer, the snow thickened. Some of the attackers turned, tried to flee back across the broad avenues to the cover of buildings, but the cadets, stiffened by a few experienced troops, mowed them down. Belatedly, the personnel carriers turned their guns to the other side, but by then the smaller drones had locked in on them. Only two on this side, three on the other, were able to return fire before they blew, one after another, debris shattering windows across the street as effectively as their weapons.

"Timing is everything," Ky murmured. Several people in the car gave her a startled look. "Old military axiom," she said.

At both ends, attackers tried to get out of the now-obvious killzone. To the south, they ran into their own still-arriving troops; to the north they met the cadets and troops behind the earthmovers with their impervious blades.

"Should've brought real artillery," Major Oslik said.

"Glad they didn't," Ky said. Some of the attackers now ran for the Presidential Palace, encountering the minefield that would've been obvious in daylight or clear moonlight. Compared with space battles, this one seemed faster in some ways, slower in others. In space, ships might have only a second or two to attack a target before it was out of range; here, stuck in almost two-dimensional space, troops could pound each other again and again. But the weirdest thing to Ky was the way all the debris fell onto the planet's surface and stayed there, instead of expanding in a lethal sphere.

She shoved that thought away. The surviving enemy had better armor and more experience than her cadets—they were still very dangerous, more effective one-to-one. And they weren't about to surrender yet. They could endure a higher percentage of loss before breaking than her green troops.

Those in the main plaza had regrouped and moved cautiously, using every bit of cover, toward Government House. Presumably they knew about the tunnel between that and the Palace. Not that it would do them much good. She called in another drone strike. This time they heard the drones coming and dove for the trenches on that side of the plaza, but the bombs targeted the trenches. The drones themselves went on south, to finish the attack on the two ships.

"It's just . . . killing," someone murmured. "They don't have a chance."

"It's not a game," Ky said. "They intended to kill the defenders, including our cadets, and seize the President and other government leaders, if not kill them. And there are plenty still alive."

"If they surrendered—"

"If they surrendered, we'd put them under guard. I don't expect they will; the media's been savage ever since the Miksland survivors had a chance to tell their stories. They know they're not popular. Even in Dorland and Fulland." Her skullphone pinged; she held up a finger for silence.

"Academy's now under attack—a small force, maybe six hundred, mix of uniforms and civvie. We're handling it. Any change in engagement orders?"

"No," Ky said. "Lethal force authorized."

"Lethal force, understood."

What she could now see in the screens showed the first real fragmentation and disorganization of the attacking force. And in that moment she felt for the first time a wrenching sense that these, too, were her people, on her home planet, some of whom she might have known if she'd stayed here. She knew, she *felt*, what they were feeling and thinking as their plans unraveled around them. She had felt that same confusion and uncertainty herself—and gone on to win engagements, or at least escape destruction. And where were their commanders? Here, or out at the base, or safely hidden somewhere else? She had a sudden urge to leave the command carrier and knew it for folly.

Instead, she reached for the link to Major Massoudian. "Put some pressure on them, advance fifty meters."

"Fifty meters, understood."

A new heat signature bloomed in the infrared feed as the earthmovers' engines spun up. Behind them, the troops advanced firing steadily. Ky watched closely. If the attackers had any ace in the hole, now would be the time to play it.

"Ky—air strike on the way!" That was Rafe in her skullphone. "Under two minutes."

Nothing showed on the screens. That meant nothing; the suspect air base had a squadron of stealth aircraft. She opened the all-units channel. "Air strike—pull back now."

"Commandant?"

"Now! With luck they'll hit their own troops instead."

She signaled to the command car driver, who immediately started backing down the street. "We need to clear this route for those ahead of us. If that were me, in those planes, I'd hit the buildings on Promenade and Military and the street behind. Try to catch all the defense in one or two passes. This weather—"

A roar in the distance broke through the soundproofing of the vehicle.

"What if they attack the Academy?" asked Osinery.

"They certainly could. All the cadets there should be safe enough in the underground. But since Kvannis knows it will be mostly empty, attacking it would be a waste of his resources. He's not stupid." Her helmet picked up the infrared signatures of the four aircraft coming in low and fast. What were they carrying? Missiles, bombs? And what were they targeting?

In seconds they knew: the Palace, Government House, Defense, and Treasury. When the debris and smoke cleared enough to see, the infamous pink dome of the Palace was gone and the walls just east of it were piles of rubble. Government House had also taken a direct hit. But up in the clouds, blurry flashes of light revealed an aerial battle going on.

Ky concentrated on the ground fighting, concerned that her inexperienced troops would get into trouble, but the professionals were doing a good job of leading the cadets where they needed to be.

"Ships sunk," Rafe reported on her skullphone. "Direct hits on both, and they're now flickering hulks."

"You're getting poetic," Ky said. "But glad to know they won't be reinforced from there. Any word from Grace and company?"

"All fine so far. I expect some trouble here, but Stella's safe where she is."

President Saranife sat in a comfortable overstuffed chair in the living room of the house where she'd stayed since the evacuation. At her feet, a large, furry tan dog leaned on her legs, its heavy head on her knee, pinning her down.

"All right, Hester?" asked the Second President, Joram Cassidy, from a similar chair across the room. "You're looking strained."

"There's a war starting," Saranife said. "I should be strained." She was not particularly fond of her Second President, a stiff man who rarely smiled and who had told her once he was more competent than she. She started to stand up and pace, but the dog leaned harder and put a big furry paw on her other knee.

"It's more comfortable here than at the Palace," Cassidy said. "You won't find—" A loud *whomp* in the distance rattled windows. "What was that?"

"An explosion," said one of their hosts, the tall rangy woman called Kris. "Somebody's lobbing something at the base."

"Should we . . . uh . . . find shelter or something?" Cassidy asked. Now *he* looked strained.

"Not yet," Kris said. "Irene—let's bring them all inside."

Saranife heard a door open and the scrabble of many dogs bounding up the back steps, across the porch, and into the kitchen. Two of the dogs came right through into the living room. One was a reddish dog with a splint on one hind leg—Ginger, belonging to Sergeant Major Morrison. Suzy was the dog now leaning on her, and Billy, a match for Suzy, had now pinned Cassidy just as efficiently.

"I don't really care for—" *Whomp!* "—this dog sitting on my feet."

"Therapy dog," Irene said, coming in with a tray of mugs and pastries. "They know when people are nervy."

"I'm not nervy!" Cassidy protested.

Irene, a little shorter than Kris but radiating equal authority, raised her brows and said nothing, offering the tray instead. He took a mug in both hands, as did Saranife.

"You didn't put anything in it—"

"No sedatives. You want to be clearheaded, I know. We have a storm shelter; we'll move there if there's need."

"Do you know what's going on?"

"A little. The ships unloaded troops into the city; the battle has started there."

"I should be there," Saranife said. "I should be in contact—"

"Safer this way," Kris said. "They don't know where you are, and you'll still be here when it's over, able to take charge of the civilian side. I know it's frustrating."

Kris was a veteran, Saranife knew. "Do you wish you were back in at times like this?"

The dark eyebrows went up. "'Times like this'? This is the first armed conflict since the Unification War. Yes and no, is the honest answer. I never wanted to see combat—and didn't—but I know people who are active now, and I'd like to be with them, helping them. But the best thing I can do is keep the two of you safe."

"The two of you and that squad of cadets who think this is a great break from class and are chowing down on doughnuts," Irene said. She sipped from her own mug. A series of smaller *whoomp*s in rapid succession startled Saranife enough that her warm drink sloshed on her hand. The dog leaned even harder on her leg.

"Anti-aircraft," Kris said.

"Shouldn't we be watching the news? Surely someone—"

"Power's out in the city," Kris said. "We'll probably lose power here, too."

Saranife had never experienced a full power outage; Port Major had been built with redundancy in mind. Both the Palace and Government House had emergency generators as well. A night without streetlights? Without lights and heat in the house? She opened her mouth to ask and shut it again. She had never felt so inadequate.

"This is ridiculous!" Cassidy pushed Billy aside and lunged to his feet. "I'm not going to sit here helplessly like a baby in a crib."

Irene opened her mouth; he shook his finger at her. "You're just a dog doctor; what do *you* know? Hester, if you're too scared to take charge, I'm not. I'm going out there, and back to the city, where I can do some good."

Hester tried to sit up straighter, but Suzy now had half her furry body across the President's lap. Cassidy strode across the living room, out to the front porch, and slammed the door. "Men," Irene said, with feeling. "I suppose we should—"

"Let him go, is what we should do," Kris said. She smiled at Saranife. "Now that he's gone, would you like to come down to the bunker? Suzy, go easy."

The dog slid off Saranife's lap and stood with waving tail as Saranife clambered up, a little stiff. Kris led the way to a concealed door, and then down a stairway into a basement lined with wine racks and shelves of supplies. Another door, a shorter stairway, another door, and they entered a large room, very quiet. Bunks were built in on one side; a door at one end led to a shower, toilet, and sink. "You'll be safe here with the dogs," Kris said. When Saranife looked back, Irene was coming down slowly with Ginger, helping the dog navigate the stairs.

"Do I have to be alone?"

"No—I'm going back up to fetch your guard detail."

"What about Joram—Cassidy?"

"He won't make it to the city." Kris's look chilled Saranife to the bone. "He's on the other side," Kris said gently. "Your guard will take care of him."

Grace Vatta watched the battle from the clubhouse of her residence tower, though the blowing snow obscured it almost completely. The

sound of explosions carried through, muted by snow and the double-
glazing. Nearly all the inhabitants of the tower crowded in, like scared
cattle Grace thought. Her excuse was more reasonable.

After the streetlights below went out, some residents followed the
emergency instructions to return to their apartments. Corridors had
emergency lighting and every apartment had at least two, but the
clubhouse had gone dark. Those who did not obey clustered near the
windows, not sure what they were looking for. Then a column lit by
chemlights appeared first as a long blue-green glow, then as individual lights making their way toward the tower.

"Rector—get away from the window. Uh . . . please?" Cadet Price
had not developed any command voice yet.

"They can't see me," Grace said. "With the snow, they're going to
have trouble counting floors."

"Yes, Sera—Rector—but we want you down in the basement level
for your own safety."

Grace gave him a look that had withered stronger men, but realized
it didn't do any good in the dark. "I need to go by my apartment first."

"I'm supposed to take you directly—"

They were in the hall now and she gave him the look; sure enough
he wilted a little. "Apartment first; I have classified materials there. In
case they scale the back side of the building and break in through the
windows." Unlikely, but war was war. In her apartment, Grace picked
up her two light bags and handed the one with clothes and snacks in
it to him. "Don't drop that; it's important." She had the classified bag
herself. The elevators weren't working of course. They took the stairs—
she more slowly, because she still did not have her full strength back.
Cadet Price galloped ahead, pausing at each landing to wait for her.

When the exit door at ground level opened just as Price reached
the landing above it, Grace had no time to say more than "Look—"
before two armed men in the wrong uniform barged in and fired on
Price, who fell. Grace had paused on the landing above him, trying to
get her breath. She opened the door beside her and found herself in
the building's administration section. The keys she'd insisted on hav-

ing from day one let her lock the door and she moved quickly down the passage, past Accounting, Maintenance, and Service to lock the service stair door as well. Then she called the guard unit in the basement.

"Rector?"

"Enemy is in the building, ground level, and has access to the stairs. I'm on level two, Building Administration. I've locked two staircases into this level; I'm heading for the others. Cadet Price was shot and killed below me on the stairs." She ended the call and headed for the far end of the building, where another bank of nonworking elevators and two staircases were. This level had few windows, which was good, but she knew it was a trap if they got in. Maybe resistance elsewhere would keep them busy.

She was able to lock the other two staircases before any intrusion, so she found a convenient office that provided multiple hiding places, opened her case of classified materials and devices, and considered trying to find a shredder. Every office had a shredder. But even if she could bypass the lockouts to emergency power, a shredder would make noise, and data cubes and sticks merely jammed shredders. She picked up the shielded communicator Rafe had given her and called him.

"I'll get help," he said.

"Not you," Grace said. "But if you could get word to Ky . . ."

"Stay alive," he said, "or I'll never hear the end of it from your niece." And that was that.

Michael Quindlan had heard nothing from Benny. Had Benny not gone home? He wasn't in the Quindlan headquarters; he wasn't at the Quindlan warehouse. Though in either case the downtown power outage might be to blame. Frustrating that the progress of the battle wasn't available on the vidscreen. He peered out the window of his elegant three-story home, seeing nothing now but heavy snowfall.

When his skullphone pinged, he tongued it open.

"Michael—get out!" That was Derrin Malines, his counterpart in the Malines family and his ally in everything.

"What's wrong?" Ally or not, Derrin did have a tendency to over-react to problems.

"It's all over. They're all dead."

"Who?"

"I don't know where that bitch got the troops, but our people—I have hundreds dead in the street. Caught in crossfire. There were drones—planes—I thought *we* had the planes! Isn't that what Kvannis told you?"

"We did—we do." Michael tried to sort it out. Something had gone wrong but surely not everything. "Ordnay air base—ours, I'm sure of it. Lots of planes—where are these other planes coming from?"

"How should I know? The whole center of the city is dark, my people are pushed back into the warehouse district, the ships just blew up and sank—"

"What? What do you mean the ships blew up?"

"Michael, they're just hulks in the water, and the other dockies are ambushing my people—they have *weapons*, Michael. I didn't know they had weapons!"

The phone on the desk rang. Michael muted the sound in his skull-phone and picked up the handset. "Yeah?"

"Kvannis here. The landing was unsuccessful. Be advised I can get you on a flight to Makkavo if you can reach Ordnay in the next ninety minutes—"

"It's a two-hour drive—"

"The flight leaves in ninety minutes; take it or leave it."

"I've got my own damn plane—where do we meet?"

The line went dead. Fine. Malines was shouting into his skullphone when he turned up the volume. "Calm down, Derrin. Kvannis called me. He's pulling out of Ordnay—"

"What about us? What about me? I've got—"

"Can your people get around the harbor to the south docks? We have a ship there, ready to go. *Zazdotlyn*."

"Is that where you're going?"

"No, I'm going inland. But I'll call the ship. Captain's name is Mohardhri." It might just be time to sever the old connection with Malines, if enough Malines—the ones who knew where the bodies were buried—didn't make it out. "I'll call him but here's an ID code for you: Better Days." He ended that call, made the call to the *Zazdotlyn's* captain, and gave his instructions. Most Quindlan aircraft were somewhere else, as usual—their air freight service was much smaller than Vatta's, though just as widespread. But the executive craft were always available . . . if he could get to the small airport south of the city and if the weather allowed a flight. He called the staff he wanted, picked up his overnight bag, and left his wife asleep in her suite.

CHAPTER THIRTY-FOUR

DAY 45

Ky had lost track of time, focused as she was on the fighting. The attack on the Academy itself had been easily repelled, mounted mostly by civilians—Quindlans or Malines, she assumed—and only two Academy staff had been injured, not seriously. The attack on the condominium tower where Grace lived had been partly successful—a hundred of the enemy had made it inside—but they had been defeated, finally, by the unit assigned to protect the Rector, the General Secretary of the legislature, and the heads of the three major parties. Eight casualties there, including two fatalities, one of them Cadet Price.

The main fighting, concentrated around the government center, had been more sustained, as expected. Some of the enemy troops had made it into both the Palace and Government House, but the majority had been repulsed, again and again, along both sides of the central plaza. Snow continued to fall, making the fight even harder when the power went out and the lights failed. This gave the enemy a chance to withdraw without effective pursuit, though by then they had lost well over half their number. And a better chance to penetrate into the city singly or in small groups. She checked with General Molosay's staff.

"We're doing well. With the help of AirDefense and our limited artillery, we've halted the advance of the column approaching from the west. We're mostly in the mopping-up phase."

"What about Ordnay?"

"Ordnay is still not secured, but Jesek and both the bases near Port Major are, and Ordnay's lost its air traffic control and two of its three runways, plus a number of aircraft. Do you need additional troops in the city?"

"Yes," Ky said. "Power's out, and though we cut the numbers down, we still have individuals and small groups that escaped the cordon and got out into the city. We don't have enough, even if we used every single cadet, to do the necessary sweeps."

"Reinforcements will arrive within the hour." A code contact string followed.

Dawn came late, under the clouds and on one of the shortest days of winter. "No firing in the last forty-five minutes," MacRobert reported. Troops from the Joint Services base had swept the city within a kilometer of Ky's command vehicle. Snow had lightened to occasional thin skeins lasting only a minute or so. Ambulances were rolling, carrying wounded from both sides back to Marvin J. Peake Military Hospital.

"I'm going to see what kind of peace we have," Ky said. She stood up, feeling stiff in hips and back. "Osinery, you're with me. It's likely to be gruesome."

Ky made it to the line the cadets were still holding, with the help of seasoned troops, and met with their class advisers. "Major Leonidze, Major Massoudian, your classes have done extremely well. I understand you both have casualties—have all your wounded been evacuated now?"

"Yes, Commandant. The—the dead are over here, if you—"

"Of course." Ky looked at the row of bodies laid out neatly. She had known they would lose some; each deserved recognition and respect. "I'll call for transport." She leaned over each, naming the cadet and murmuring a Modulan prayer for their soul's passage. "I'm relieving all the cadet units; get them back to the Academy and we'll hold a brief assembly first of all. I know they're tired and hungry, but they need to know their effort is recognized and their sacrifices honored. I will need a list of all your casualties to read out to the assembled cadets."

By noon, she had spoken to the assembly, naming each of the dead and wounded. Looking out at the solemn faces—now edged with a maturity they had not shown before—she thought how different their experience was from her own first encounter with violent death. "And all of you—every class—showed that you are in fact qualified to be future officers. I am honored to be your Commandant." When dismissed, they marched out heads high, but she knew there would be a backlash in the next day or so. Well, she had resources for them that she'd lacked for herself.

In the meantime, she had the evidence she needed to report certain faculty members to General Molosay as conspirators, and she had the report on Colonel Bohannon's attack and death to file. Eventually there'd be an official investigation. Writing and filing reports took up the rest of her day.

Over at the government center, workers were still digging bodies out of the snow—none of her force, at least—and the regular troops reported sporadic firing and resistance in the business district. All the buildings had damage. But none of the government officials had been hurt—a fair trade, Ky thought.

At the harbor, a Quindlan ship had sailed from the south docks before dawn, and was making good time eastward, apparently bound for the west coast of Voruksland. By report it was carrying farm machinery and other manufactured goods; the manifest and course had been certified the day before. Ky suspected that was a lie, but Voruksland had been notified; they would deal with it when it arrived. Other ships had left even earlier, their captains declaring it was safer at sea in a blizzard than in a harbor under attack, so the Quindlan ship's departure didn't raise any questions.

Stella, Rafe, and Grace all reported in by midafternoon, to Ky's relief, though she had little time to talk to them. The Academy needed all her attention now that Molosay had officially relieved her of her task of protecting the government.

DAY 49

Four days later, it was certain that a general uprising had been avoided. The survivors from Miksland had been interviewed repeatedly as they recovered, and they had expressed such anger at the treatment they'd received from those trying to keep Miksland secret that public sympathy turned hard against the insurgents. Fighting in the cities of Dorland and Fulland had lasted a couple of days, but it was clear that the Unionists outnumbered the Separatists. Traitors, they were now called. The governors of every continent and province declared full confidence in the planetary government and allegiance to it. Dorland's pointed out that they'd prospered much more after the Unification than before it. Sporadic raids by Separatists over the next day had been met with blunt words and gunfire by the rural population, and on the fourth day, the last Separatist group surrendered to the chief of a fishing village.

One immediate effect of the new stability was Immigration immediately crediting Ky with the required half-year residency for her time on Miksland, expediting all her paperwork, and converting Rafe's visa to permanent residence as long as Ky vouched for him. Teague's visa was extended for another half year.

Rafe called with that news and asked if she would be coming to the Vatta house anytime soon.

"Not yet," Ky said. "The cadet corps is still unsettled—" The aftermath of combat had caught up with several of the cadets. "They need me." She paused; the silence on the com deepened. "And I need you. The Commandant's Residence isn't as big or fancy as that house, but it's bigger than a spaceship."

"Won't that cause a problem?"

"I won't let it," Ky said.

"I love it when you sound commanding," Rafe said. "Two hours?"

"I'll notify the gate. You'll be escorted to the guest suite. I'll be on the drill field then, discussing the condition of the turf and how it's going to be fixed by graduation."

"What's wrong with it?"

"Those tracked earthmovers we borrowed from the Joint Services base. Frozen ground or no, they claim the gouges are so deep the turf can't possibly be repaired by graduation. I suspect it can, but the groundsmen want me to be amazed when they accomplish it."

That night, Rafe and Ky relaxed in the office adjoining her bedroom, talking as they had not since returning from Corleigh. When no interruptions had come for a full hour and a half, Ky led the way into her suite. Rafe stopped short, staring at the bed. "What in the world?"

"The insignia of each branch. Hand-carved, not molded. It's old, from when the Academy was founded. It's considered irreplaceable, so we'd best not damage it."

"And all those coms on the bedside—that's the side you sleep on?"

"Yes. The three colors are important. And it's almost certain that at least one of them will ring every night."

He walked to the other side of the bed, where the Spaceforce insignia's spiky nose protruded. "Did anyone ever sleep on this side? This thing looks like it's designed to puncture someone's skull."

"I have no idea." Ky was grinning at his expression. "Maybe they had lots of pillows."

Rafe felt the tip of the carving and shook his head. "I wouldn't trust pillows. That would poke through anything less than three centimeters of solid wood. Perhaps it was intended to ensure a Commandant's celibacy."

"Too late," Ky said. "Maybe the intent was to move the Commandant to this side of the bed, where the com connections were."

"Whatever," Rafe said. "I think we'd be more comfortable somewhere else." He waggled his eyebrows. "Surely you'd like to see the interesting etchings in my guest suite, Admiral."

"I'll have to switch the coms over to that room. Commandants are on call all the time."

"Fine with me. Better than being stabbed by a spaceship."

No call came that night.

DAY 50

Ky's first call the next day was from General Molosay. "You'll be hearing from President Saranife sometime today; she has an offer to make and I hope you will consider it favorably."

"You can't give me a hint?"

"No, I can't. I can tell you that the heads of all the branches were consulted and agreed, as did the Council."

"Thank you for letting me know, General," Ky said as possibilities bubbled up. None of them things she wanted to do.

Her next call was from Stella. "Did I tell you about the attacks on Vatta property back on Cascadia?"

"No . . ."

"Anger over Jen Bentik's death, by a Bentik relative. Same as the reason for their putting a hold on your financials and mine. Well—their court decided that the Bentik family had breached the courtesy laws by not informing us—individually—of their grievance and giving us a chance to ask for arbitration prior to trial. The attack on my employees and property damage without prior reference to legal proceedings meant *they* were in the wrong, so they unfroze our accounts. Now I can finally pay you for your shares—and you've got your severance pay. If I were you, I'd transfer it fast."

"Won't that make them angry?"

"The money's with Crown & Spears, and Crown & Spears doesn't talk."

"I'll have to go personally," Ky said. "I'll try to do that today."

"Aunt Grace is still determined to resign," Stella said.

"I know. I think she's right."

"Yes, but—she wants to do it publicly."

"It won't hurt Vatta's business," Ky said. "It may help if we go quiet the way the family used to be."

"I suppose. The Vatta house is secure enough now and almost refurbished. I'm moving back in but with some live-in staff. Mother's keeping the children on Corleigh to the end of this school year and I don't want to be alone."

Ky's call to Crown & Spears, the interstellar banking giant, went smoothly—but yes, they did need her to appear in person, with her current Slotter Key ID, and provide a bio sample. "Just in case. I mean, Admiral—Commandant—we know who you are, but our auditors—"

"That's fine," Ky said. "I'll be there in an hour or so."

"Anytime, Commandant. At your convenience."

Her official car, the one with the little flag displayed in front, took her to the Crown & Spears offices downtown. The street had a row of track marks down it from the invading force's personnel carriers, but otherwise traffic was back to normal and she saw no damage from the fighting. The invaders had been so eager to get to the government buildings they'd bypassed other targets.

"Luckily," said the manager who greeted her, "there was only one incident, over on Promenade, the Hassel & Sons hattery, but it was only one broken window, no other loss. Let me just check you in. Retinal scan, fingerprints, and do you have DNA mods of any kind?"

"No," Ky said. She put her hands on the plate and looked into the hood.

"We're comparing with both your previous information provided here and that on Cascadia—it will be just a few minutes. Perhaps you'd like tea? And did you need any information about local investment opportunities?"

Very shortly her identification scans cleared, and she had transferred her balance on Cascadia to the local branch here on Slotter Key. While she was still there, the transfer from Vatta for her shares came in. And her skullphone pinged. It was her clerk at the Academy.

"Commandant, the President would like to see you; I told her you were away from the Academy, and she asked if you could stop by the Palace on your way back."

The bank manager slid a message to her—the total now in her account. Half a spaceship? Maybe. Ky held up a finger and answered. "Yes, please tell the President I will be on my way there shortly."

The bank manager smiled, as if having a bank client sending messages to the President was a credit to the bank. Maybe it was, Ky thought, as she turned to him. "Excuse me—I need to leave now, but I will discuss my plans with you later." When she knew what they were.

The government center was an ugly mess, glassless windows staring darkly at furrowed ground, dirty snow, and men in uniform poking through the piles for weapons and bodies. Rows of trucks lined the margins of the plaza, some for equipment and some for bodies. The towerless Palace looked completely different from before. Better, Ky thought. But inside, the halls had been swept and Ky walked on carpets—stained but still in place—to the President's office.

There she found President Saranife, General Molosay, and several other officers, along with the Chair of the Council.

"I must thank you," the President said, coming forward to shake hands. "I admit to being worried—even scared at times—but you were right. Dispersing the members of government to different private homes was safer than staying here, even in the basement."

"I'm glad it worked," Ky said.

"The reason we asked you here," Saranife said, with a glance around at the others, "is that we wanted to thank you and offer you a permanent position. Everyone agrees that you're the right person for the job, a fitting successor to the great men who have held it before you. You don't have to answer today, though we would be thrilled if you accepted right away." Nods from the others. "We would like to make your appointment as Commandant permanent. It's not just the defense of the government during the recent conflict, but the work you have done with the cadets—"

Ky had a moment of panic. They wanted her to stay on as Commandant permanently? "I'm honored you thought of me," she said, "but you have many qualified officers who are actually graduates of the Academy, officers of more experience and seniority. I was appointed in an emergency; the emergency is over—"

"You're not—you can't leave now!"

"I can't stay forever, either. I don't feel I have the qualifications I would need to be a good long-term Commandant." Not to mention having the wrong personality and the wrong ambitions.

"But—you'll surely finish out the semester—if you won't accept, it will take us time to choose someone in a more deliberate fashion."

Despite their words, Ky felt a relaxation in the room. They had wound themselves up to offer it—everyone had agreed because they felt they had to—but in fact they were relieved, even if they didn't know it yet. "Tell you what," she said. "Suppose I stay through graduation this year, a bit longer if you can't find someone right away, but no longer than three years beyond that. And I'd prefer that you find someone sooner."

"Well." Molosay's gaze swept around the group of officers again. He gave a slight shrug. "I guess we'll have to find someone, then."

"The sooner the better," Ky said. "And if you'll allow—though I admired Commandant Burleson enormously, I suggest setting a firm limit to anyone's tenure as Commandant. Six or eight or ten years, perhaps. Their experience with troops will be more recent. And the opportunity—the temptation—to become involved in politics will be much less." To arrange the suicide of a President, for instance, which must surely be on everyone's mind.

"You disapprove of Burleson's action?"

"I wasn't here," Ky said. "It may have been the correct thing to do under the circumstances. But his being Commandant so long raised suspicions about the military, didn't it?"

"Yes . . ."

"And for some people, both in and out of the military, it gave support to the disaffection that erupted recently. Some knew of the connection between Burleson and my family—and took that as proof we were trying to manipulate the military and government."

Two of the officers, though not Molosay, nodded.

"You know your aunt is determined to resign as Rector of Defense," Saranife said.

"Yes, and I think she's right to do so. She did not know about the conditions of her release from prison—but once she found out, her resignation was imperative."

"So I have to find a new Rector *and* a new Commandant," Saranife said. She shrugged. "Well, nobody said this job would be easy." She turned to Ky. "To celebrate your recent actions and your new—we hoped—post, we have refreshments set out in the next room. Do you have time—?"

"Sera, I always have time for pastries."

The group moved into the next room, but the meeting broke up quickly. "What will you do?" Saranife asked Ky as she was leaving. "You're not in the family business now—have you a plan?"

"Get the cadets through this semester and the graduating class through graduation. Later—well, something will come up. It always does."

CHAPTER THIRTY-FIVE

DAY 70

Benny Quindlan fingered the weapon he carried, checking again that it was loaded, charged, ready to use. He had returned to Port Major only the day before, tracking his uncle Michael from a distance. He had paid for a temporary DNA assist the day after his wife died in the hospital—a blend that came under the heading "cosmetic enhancement" rather than "identity replacement"—and so far had been able to travel unrecognized just by changing his clothes and putting a small lift in one shoe.

He had never believed himself capable of this sort of thing, until the evening he came home to find his wife mutilated, barely conscious, posed in the foyer of his home with their two children dead beside her. He knew at once who had done it, and knew that Michael believed "soft Benny" wouldn't dare retaliate. Now that Michael had returned to Port Major, he must, Benny knew, be planning the vengeance he'd sworn on the Vatta family. He would be looking for an opportunity to kill Grace, Stella, and Ky, and if he succeeded in those, he would then seek out the last two survivors of the line he'd chosen, Stavros Vatta's grandchildren.

Today's meeting of the Grand Council, at which all three of Michael's targets would be recognized for their service to the planet, was a perfect opportunity, Benny knew. And he himself would have to stop Michael, because no one else could, or would believe what he told them. He'd tried to tell the police when he found his family that his uncle had done it, but Michael had explained that Benny was the family dullard, harmless but clueless. Benny had tried again when he heard about this ceremony, calling the anonymous tip line, but could tell from the bored tone of the woman he spoke to that she didn't believe him. He tried calling Stella Vatta, but her com lines were all under a security wrap, requiring a code he didn't know for access. So coming here was his only hope.

It was colder than it had been, but the clouds were high and thin, the air under them clear. Benny, along with others, picked his way along what had been broad walks on either side of gardens in the plaza south of the Presidential Palace. Now, though clear of snow, they were pitted by the tracks of heavy machinery and bomb damage. Scaffolding covered the worst of the damage to the Palace and Government House.

Visitors, Benny among them, went up the steps of the Palace, weaving around the gaps. Inside, the rotunda under the former dome had been cleared of debris, and the mosaic maps of Slotter Key were whole again, forming a ring around a new globe in the center. The ceremony would be held here, and around the margin tables were covered with refreshments. Some of the visitors were already accepting tidbits from the trays. Benny couldn't see the Vattas yet, but he spotted his uncle, staring across at a corridor entrance on the other side of the rotunda. He turned away casually, picking up a pastry from a tray, and moved on.

Michael would be carrying multiple weapons. And he would probably have several of his goons with him—or would he? Benny moved closer, along the wall with the others grazing at the tables, keeping people between himself and Michael, and pausing and moving as the others did. He heard the clatter of feet on stone coming along the corridor Michael had been watching, and—looking that way as well—moved even closer.

Four ceremonial guards, in their bright uniforms. Four others, less obvious, in business suits. The President led the way, today in formal dress, her height emphasized by the lines of her dress and cape. Behind her were the Grand Council members, with their ceremonial capes and chains of office, and behind them, those being honored: not just the Vattas, but several others Benny didn't know. Ky wore the white uniform of the Commandant; Stella wore a green suit; Grace wore plain black, her white hair bright against it. The others in that group included both military and civilian, dressed accordingly. Benny dared a glance at his uncle. Michael was staring at the Vattas. Which one would he attack first?

President Saranife began her introductions; Council members nodded when their names were called, and the small crowd automatically formed into an arc in front of them. Michael Quindlan stayed on one end of the arc; Benny had maneuvered toward the other end, but found himself stuck only partway to the ideal spot. He was, however, closer to the cluster of Vattas and he had an excuse to look back toward the President, and beyond.

One by one, President Saranife announced and handed out awards: to Port Major's mayor, heads of city emergency agencies, the commanders of both small air bases near Port Major, the harbormaster, several private citizens who—it turned out—had given shelter to senior government officials during the attack. The Vattas, apparently, were to be last. Benny glanced again to the right; Michael was moving, as if heading for the nearest refreshments, apparently. Benny knew that was a ruse. A person just in front of him, who had applauded someone who had sheltered a functionary Benny'd never heard of, turned to go, obviously having come just for that one award. Benny moved into the gap, now just across from Stella Vatta. She wasn't looking at him.

"And now it is time to thank Sera Graciela Vatta for her service as Rector of Defense, on her last day in that position. Sera Vatta has resigned and issued a statement to the press, which will be available after this ceremony. Sera Vatta took this post in a time of emergency, at a risk to her own safety, and stayed on at my request when I was elected to the presidency. But she says the more recent attacks on her, the poisoning she suffered, have weakened her enough that she is not able to continue—and as well, she feels she should not have accepted the position in the first place. I for one am grateful for her service, and hereby award her the Presidential Service Medal." Saranife lifted the medal, on its ribbon, from the box an assistant held for her, and moved behind Grace as another assistant stepped in front, to steady the medal until Saranife had closed the clasp.

The little crowd clapped and cheered; Grace looked down, then turned to thank Saranife. Benny glanced around again for his uncle. Who was standing immediately behind him.

"Well, you made it," Michael said. "Isn't that *nice*, Benny?"

Shock held him for an instant, long enough for Michael to lean close and murmur: "This is perfect. I'll get the Vattas, one–two–three, and then you . . . your girlfriend first, I think."

Shock and panic vanished in a burst of fury; Benny felt no fear, not even anxiety as he whirled, crouching, and slammed into Michael, snarling, "Not again!" Michael staggered back, one arm flailing for balance, the other reaching into his coat. Someone else yelled "Gun! Gun!" Benny charged on, trying to grab Michael's arm even as Michael squeezed off a shot that went wild, up into the scaffolding and tarps. Two more shots were fired, close by—someone else. Michael stumbled, started to fall, as other hands and arms grabbed him. Benny ignored the hands that now grabbed at him, trying to pull him back as he landed on Michael, beating on his face, unaware of what he was saying, the tears running down his face. "Not her too! Not her too! Never again! No more of this!"

Finally he was hauled off, roughly, and handcuffed by the honor guard. His uncle lay motionless, blood spreading from beneath him.

Michael's face was a bloody mess; his own hands were bloodstained, raw, hurting now. "Ser—Ser—you must calm down, ser. The man is dead. He was shot." He tried to breathe; his throat was raw. Hands patted him down, found his holstered weapon, found his ID packet.

"He tried to kill them," he managed at last. "Michael Quindlan. My uncle. He killed my wife . . . my children . . . and I couldn't let him kill anyone else."

Others crowded around him, curious; he looked over and saw President Saranife still on the dais with the honorees, surrounded by more guards. All of them alive, unhurt. Whatever happened now, it was worth it.

"You're Benjamin Arnold Quindlan?" asked the guard in front of him, looking at his open ID packet.

"Yes," Benny said. "Who—who shot him?"

"I did." Benny looked at the speaker. A shortish man, black haired, dark-eyed, well-dressed.

"I'm Rafael Dunbarger. He's dead, and *you* didn't kill him. I did. Thank you for that lunge you made, by the way. I couldn't get a clear shot at him, when I first saw what he was up to. Your shoving him opened a gap."

"Ser, you're injured—" one of the guards said.

Benny's hands fell apart, released. His left arm hurt suddenly; he could feel the tickle of something hot moving down his arm. When he looked, blood had soaked his jacket sleeve and his hand was bloody. He felt sick.

"Let me see," the short man—Dunbarger—said. "Ah—you need to sit down. Yes, right down on the floor." To the others "An aid kit, a medic. Quickly." He took a handkerchief from his impeccable jacket and pushed it into the wound. "You'll be all right. I've seen worse."

"Benny—" Stella was there, kneeling beside him, looking at him— and in her face he saw no anger, no contempt. "You saved our lives."

"He did," Benny said, nodding toward Rafe.

"You," she said, and laid her hand on his bloody one. "I won't for-get."

* * *

President Saranife shook her head at her guests. "I was going to talk about how individuals and families—including the Vattas—had through their recent efforts brought us peace again," she said. "I was going to use your family as an example: Vatta's peace. And then, right here in the Palace, this brawl. Almost an assassination."

"It could have been a lot worse," the Chair of the Grand Council said. "We could have had another all-out civil war." The other guests nodded.

Ky, watching Rafe care for a Quindlan who apparently wasn't an enemy, felt a rush of warmth and mischief together. "Well, let that be our motto then," she said. "Vatta's peace may not be perfect, but it could have been worse."

ACKNOWLEDGMENTS

This book was written under difficult circumstances, mostly physical, and could not have been written without the help of many. This includes those who took other loads off my schedule, those who helped with specific tasks I could not complete, those who kept my spirits up when I was struggling. I could not name them all, because some were brief encounters when someone was just more patient with my slowness or clumsiness than I expected. Things are improving.

Special thanks to Ruta and Ferris Duhon for the constant friendship since college days, Ellen and John McLean for just as constant friendship over the last thirty-eight years: old friends help in many ways, including necessary corrections at times. To John Hemry for invaluable help with a scene in the fictional Slotter Key Military Academy. To Karen Shull for reading and commenting on innumerable draft sections and a keen awareness of when a character slipped out of focus. To the entire Thanksgiving Day crowd, who pitched in to help make it great when I was overtired again and then talked books later, and the Usual Suspects among my fans who read the blogs and help me locate details I've misplaced. Karen Meschke for encouraging words and good advice. Laura Domitz (who came two days before Thanksgiving to help with prep). Bill Fawcett (always an idea fountain), Jody Lynn Nye, Lee Martindale, many others who were there for me at the 2016 WorldCon and at DragonCon this year. David Stevens, choir director, who told me to take all the time I needed.

Anne Groell, my editor, Joshua Bilmes, my agent, were both invaluable on this one, and copy editor Laura Jorstad was a hero: to be blunt, saved the book. Likewise, Senior Production Editor Nancy Delia, who has done great work on not just this but all my books here. And finally, the ultimate helper: Richard, love of my life, who talked me down from the ceiling repeatedly, brought food, insisted on my getting prescribed rest, and could always get me laughing when things were grimmest.

ABOUT THE TYPE

This book was set in Minion, a 1990 Adobe Originals typeface by Robert Slimbach (b. 1956). Minion is inspired by classical, old-style typefaces of the late Renaissance, a period of elegant, beautiful, and highly readable type designs. Created primarily for text setting, Minion combines the aesthetic and functional qualities that make text type highly readable with the versatility of digital technology.

extras

www.orbitbooks.net

about the author

Elizabeth Moon served in the US Marine Corps, reaching the rank of 1st Lieutenant during active duty. She has also earned degrees in history and biology, run for public office and been a columnist on her local newspaper. She lives near Austin, Texas, with her husband and their son. Twenty-six of her books are in print, and she won the Nebula Award with her science fiction novel *Speed of Dark* (also shortlisted for the Clarke Award), and was a finalist for the Hugo in 1997.

Find out more about James Islington and other Orbit authors by registering for the free monthly newsletter at www.orbitbooks.net.

if you enjoyed
INTO THE FIRE

look out for

PROVENANCE

by

Ann Leckie

Following her record-breaking debut trilogy, Ann Leckie, winner of the Hugo, Nebula, Arthur C. Clarke and Locus awards, returns with a thrilling new story of power, theft, privilege and birthright.

A power-driven young woman has just one chance to secure the status she craves and regain priceless lost artefacts prized by her people. She must free their thief from a prison planet from which no one has ever returned.

Ingray and her charge will return to their home world to find their planet in political turmoil, at the heart of an escalating interstellar conflict. Together, they must make a new plan to salvage Ingray's future, her family and her world before they are lost to her for good.

1

"There were unexpected difficulties," said the dark gray blur. That blur sat in a pale blue cushioned chair, no more than a meter away from where Ingray herself sat, facing, in an identical chair.

Or apparently so, anyway. Ingray knew that if she reached much more than a meter past her knees, she would touch smooth, solid wall. The same to her left, where apparently the Facilitator sat, bony frame draped in brown, gold, and purple silk, hair braided sleekly back, dark eyes expressionless, watching the conversation. Listening. Only the beige walls behind and to the right of Ingray were really as they appeared. The table beside Ingray's chair with the gilded decanter of serbat and the delicate glass tray of tiny rose-petaled cakes was certainly real—the Facilitator had invited her to try them. She had been too nervous to even consider eating one.

"Unexpected difficulties," continued the dark gray blur, "that led to unanticipated expenses. We will require a larger payment than previously agreed."

That other anonymous party could not see Ingray where she sat—saw her as the same sort of dark gray blur she herself faced. Sat in an identical small room, somewhere else on this station. Could not see Ingray's expression, if she let her dismay and despair show itself on her face. But the Facilitator could see them both. E wouldn't betray having seen even Ingray's smallest reaction, she was sure. Still. "Unexpected difficulties are not my concern," she said, calmly and smoothly as she could manage. "The price was agreed beforehand." The price was everything she owned, not counting the clothes she wore, or passage home—already paid.

"The unexpected expenses were considerable, and must be met somehow," said the dark gray blur. "The package will not be delivered unless the payment is increased."

"Then do not deliver it," replied Ingray, trying to sound careless. Holding her hands very still in her lap. She wanted to clutch the green and blue silk of her full skirts, to have some feeling that she could hold on to something solid and safe, a childish habit she thought she'd lost years ago. "You will not receive any payment at all, as a result. Certainly your expenses must be met regardless, but that is no concern of mine."

She waited. The Facilitator said nothing. Ingray reminded herself that the gray blur had more to lose than she did if this deal didn't happen. She could take what was left of the payment she'd brought, after the Facilitator's commission—payable no matter what happened, at this stage. She could go home, back to Hwae. She'd have a good deal less than she'd started with, true, and maybe she would have to settle for that, invest what she had left. If she lost her job she could probably use what connections remained to her to find another one. She imagined her foster-mother's cold disappointment; Netano Aughskold did not waste time or energy on unambitious or unsuccessful children.

And Ingray imagined her foster-brother Danach's smug triumph. Even if all Ingray's plans succeeded, she would never replace Danach as Netano's favorite, but she could walk away from the Aughskolds knowing she'd humiliated her arrogant brother, and made all of them, Netano included, take notice. And plenty of other people with power and influence would take notice as well. If this deal didn't go through, she wouldn't have that, wouldn't have even the smallest of victories over her brother.

Silence still from the gray blur, from the Facilitator. The spicy smell of the serbat from the decanter turned her stomach. It wasn't going to happen.

And maybe that would be all right. What was she trying to do anyway? This plan was ridiculous. It was impossible. The chances of her succeeding, even if this trade went ahead, were next to nothing. What was she even doing here? For an instant she felt as though she had stepped off the edge of a precipice, and this was that barest moment before she plunged downward.

Ingray could end it now. Announce that the deal was off, give the Facilitator eir fee, and go home with what she had left.

The blur across from Ingray gave a dissatisfied sigh. "Very well, then. The deal goes forward. But now we know what to think of the much-vaunted impartiality and equitable practice of the Tyr."

"The terms were plain from the start," said the Facilitator in an even tone. "The payment was accurately described to you, and if you did not consider it adequate, you had only to demand more at the time of the offer, or refuse the sale outright. This is our inflexible rule in order to prevent misunderstandings and acrimony at just this stage of the proceedings. I explained this to you at the time. Had you not expressed your understanding of and agreement to that policy, I would not have allowed the exchange to go forward. To do otherwise would damage our reputation for impartiality and fair dealing." The gray blur did not reply. "I have examined the payment and the merchandise," said the Facilitator, still calm and even. "They are both as promised."

Now was Ingray's chance. She should escape this while she still could. She opened her mouth. "Very well," she said.

Oh, almighty powers, what had she just done?

The assigned pickup location was a small room walled in orchids growing on what looked like a maze of tree roots. A woman in a brown-and-purple jacket and sarong stood beside a scuffed gray shipping crate two meters long and one high, jarringly out of place in such carefully tended, soft-colored luxury. "There is some misunderstanding, excellency," Ingray suggested. "This is supposed to be a person." Looking at the size and the shape of the crate, it occurred to her that it might hold a body.

Utter failure. The dread Ingray had felt since the gray blur had demanded extra payment intensified.

Not moving from her place at the far end of the crate, not looking at it, not even blinking, the woman said, primly, "We do not involve ourselves in kidnappings or in slave trading, excellency."

Ingray blinked. Took a breath, unsure of how to continue. "May I open the crate?" she asked, finally.

"It is yours," said the woman. "You may do whatever you wish with it." She did not otherwise move.

It took Ingray a few moments to find all the latches on the crate lid. Each came apart with a dull snap, and she carefully shoved over one end of the heavy lid, wary of sending it crashing over the back of the crate. Light glinted off something smooth and dark inside. A suspension pod. She pushed the lid a few centimeters farther over. Reached in to pull back the cover over the pod's indicator panel. Blue and green lights on the panel told her the pod was in operation, and its occupant alive. She could not help a very small exhalation of relief.

And maybe it was better this way. She could delay any awkward explanations, could bring this person to the ship she'd booked passage on without anyone knowing what she was doing. She pushed and tugged the crate lid back into place, relatched it.

"Your pardon," she said to the woman in the brown-and-purple sarong. "I didn't anticipate that…my purchase would arrive packaged this way. I don't think I can move this on my own. Is there a cart I can borrow?" How she would get it onto a cart by herself, she didn't know. And if they charged for the cart's use, well, she had nothing left to pay for that. She might have to open that pod, right here and now, and hope its occupant was willing and able to walk. "Or can it be delivered to my ship?"

With no change of expression, the woman touched the side of the crate, and there was a click and it shifted toward Ingray, just a bit. "Once you have claimed your purchase," the woman said, "it is no longer in our custody and we will not take any responsibility for it. This may occasionally seem inconvenient, but we find it prevents misunderstandings. You should be able to move this on your own. When you are clear of our premises and have reenabled your communications you'll be shown the most efficient passable route for objects of this size."

There must have been some kind of assist on the crate, because although it had to be quite heavy it slid easily, though it swung wildly until Ingray got the trick of moving it forward without also sending it sideways. And she almost lost control of it entirely when, coming out of a nondescript doorway into a broad, brightly lit black-and-red-tiled corridor, she blinked her communications back on and a long list of alerts and news items suddenly appeared in her vision. A surprising lot of news items, when Ingray had set her feed to winnow out local news, all but the most urgent. Though the largest and brightest of them—large enough that she couldn't help reading it even as she desperately swung the shipping crate away from crashing into a wall—was definitely of more than local interest. GECK DIPLOMATIC MISSION ARRIVES IN TYR, it read, and smaller, beneath that, TYR SIILAS COUNCIL APPROVES REQUEST FOR PROVISIONS, FUEL, AND REPAIRS. Well, of course they had approved it. The Geck were signatories to the treaty with the dangerous and enigmatic Presger, and whatever anyone felt about who had made that treaty and how, no one was fool enough to want to break it.

Her attention to the headline brought up a cloud of more detailed information, and opinion pieces. CONCLAVE A BLATANT RADCHAAI POWER GRAB shouted one, and CONSCIOUS AI MAKES ITS MOVE AT LAST—IS THIS THE BEGINNING OF THE END FOR HUMANITY? asked another. A quiet voice whispered in her ear that a noodle shop she'd eaten at six times since she'd arrived here was open and nearby, with a relatively short queue—a personal alert Ingray had set days ago and forgotten to turn off. She hadn't eaten breakfast, or the cakes the Facilitator had offered her. But suddenly noodles sounded very good.

There wasn't time. The ship she'd bought passage on departed in three hours, which meant she had to be aboard in less time than that. And even if she'd had time—and any money at all—she could hardly queue for noodles with this body-size crate in tow that she could barely steer. She thought away every message except the route to her ship, and kept going. She could eat on board.

The route she'd been given kept her mostly out of the station's busiest areas, though on Tyr Siilas "less busy" was still quite crowded. At first she was self-conscious, afraid she'd attract unwelcome curiosity pushing a suspension-pod-size crate through the station's thoroughfares, but the crowds split and streamed around her without contact or comment. And she was hardly the only person pushing an awkward load. She had to swerve carefully around a stack of crates full of onions, apparently trundling along under its own power, and then found herself stuck for a few frustrating seconds behind what at first she took to be a puzzlingly tall mech, but when it finally moved she realized it was actually a human in an environmental support suit, someone from a low-gravity habitat, to judge from their height and need to wear the suit.

At one point she had to wait a half hour for a freight lift, and then spent the ride pinned against the lift's grimy back wall. She regretted wearing her stiff, formal sandals and the silk jacket and long, full skirts that she'd kept when she'd sold the rest of her clothes, with the intention of looking as seriously businesslike as possible. Very probably pointless—the Facilitator likely didn't care so long as her money was good, and whoever was on the other side of the deal she'd made couldn't see her anyway.

As soon as she was off the lift she girded up her skirts, and took off her sandals and set them on the crate along with the small bag that held everything else she owned now—her identity tabula and a few small toiletries—and then set out on the long stop-and-start trek through the docks, swerving around inattentive travelers when she could, the time display in her vision reassuring her, at least, that she still had plenty of time to reach her ship, which was, predictably, in the section of the docks farthest from where she'd entered.

She arrived at the bay tired, frustrated, and anxious. The bay was much smaller than she'd expected, but then she had only ever taken the big passenger liners between systems. Had taken one here, but she could not afford even the cheapest available return fare home on such a ship. She'd known this ship was small, a cargo ship with a few extra berths for passengers, known that her trip home would be cramped and unluxurious, but she hadn't stopped to consider what that would mean now that she was bringing this crate with her. If this had been a passenger liner, there would have been someone here she could turn the crate over to, who would make sure it got to Ingray's berth, or to cargo. But the bay was empty. And she didn't think she could get both herself and the crate into the airlock.

While she stood thinking, a man came out of the airlock. Short and solid-bodied, and there was something undefinably odd about his squarish face—something off about the shape of his nose, or the size of his mouth. His hair was pulled back behind his head, to hang behind him in dozens of tiny braids. He wore a gray-and-green-striped lungi and a dark gray jacket, and he was barefoot—less formal than what nearly everyone here wore for business dealings or important meetings, but still perfectly respectable. "You are Ingray Aughskold?"

"You must be Captain Uisine." Ingray had booked this berth through the Tyr Siilas dock office, days ago, before this ship had arrived here. "Or is it Captain Tic?" Somewhere like this, where you met people from all over, it was difficult to know what order anyone's name was in, or which one they preferred to be addressed by.

"Either one," said Captain Uisine. "You didn't say anything about oversize luggage, excellency."

"No," Ingray said. "I didn't. I wasn't expecting it myself."

Captain Uisine was silent a moment. Waiting, Ingray supposed. Then, "It's too large for the passenger compartments, excellency. It will need to be loaded into cargo. That's accessed on the lower level. But it's sealed up at the moment. And I'm not opening it before I see a duly registered Statement of Contents."

She didn't even know there was such a thing, or that she might need it. Then again, she'd never expected to have to deal with cargo at all. "I can't..." She really ought to have eaten something that morning. "I can't leave it behind. Is there time to open the cargo access?" She thought she was standing quite still, but she must have moved the hand that rested on the crate, because now it slid forward. She grabbed for it.

Captain Uisine laid a hand on it to stop and steady it. "Plenty of time. Departure's delayed. Have you not checked your notifications? We're here another two days."

"Two days!" It didn't seem possible. She summoned her notifications to her vision, and saw what she would have seen immediately if she'd checked her personal messages—a brief, bare note about the delay, from

Captain Tic Uisine. *Unavoidable delay*, the note called it, *due to current events*.

Current events. Of course. Ingray pulled up the news, looked closer at the information about the Geck diplomatic mission. Which mentioned, quite clearly but further in than she'd bothered to look, that arrivals and departures were being rearranged to fit the Geck in as quickly and safely as possible.

There was no arguing with that, no recourse. Even if Ingray had been traveling with Netano Aughskold, who had herself not infrequently demanded (and received) such priority, it wouldn't have done any good, and not just because this wasn't Netano's home system. The Geck were aliens, not human. They almost never left their homeworld, or so Ingray understood, and had done so now only to attend to urgent matters regarding the treaty with the alien Presger. Before the treaty, the Presger would tear apart human ships and stations—and their passengers and residents—seemingly at a whim. Nothing could stop them, nothing except the treaty, which the Radchaai ruler Anaander Mianaai had signed in the name of all humanity; the Presger apparently did not understand or care about whether there might be different sorts of humans, with different authorities. But no matter how anyone felt about the Radchaai taking on that authority, no one wanted the Presger to start killing people again.

Eventually the Geck had also become signatories, and much more recently the Rrrrrr. And now there was a potential third new nonhuman signatory to the treaty, and a conclave, called by the Presger, to decide the issue. Probably everyone anywhere in the unthinkably vast reaches of human-inhabited space was aware of it, had opinions, wanted to know more, wanted to know how this conclave would affect their futures.

Ingray couldn't bring herself to care just now. "I can't wait two days," she said. Captain Uisine said nothing, didn't make the obvious comment—there was no avoiding the wait, and he had no control over it. Didn't take his hand off the end of the crate. Probably wise—Ingray didn't know how to turn off the assist. "I just can't."

"Why not?" he asked. Serious, but not, it seemed, terribly invested in Ingray's particular problems.

Ingray closed her eyes. She would not cry. Opened her eyes again, took a breath, and said, "I spent everything I had settling up at my lodgings this morning."

"You're broke." Captain Uisine's eyes flicked to Ingray's bag and jacket and sandals still perched on top of the crate.

"I can't not eat for two days." She should have had breakfast that morning. She should have eaten some cakes, when she was dealing with the Facilitator.

"Well, you can," said Captain Uisine. "As long as you have water. But what about your friend?"

Ingray frowned. "My friend?"

"The person you're traveling with. Can they help you out?"

"Um."

Captain Uisine waited, still noncommittal. It occurred to Ingray that even if Captain Uisine charged for carrying the crate in cargo, it would likely be less than a passenger fare. Maybe she'd have enough to at least buy a meal or two between now and when the ship finally left. "And while you're thinking about that," the captain added before Ingray could speak, "you can show me the Statement of Contents for the crate."

For a panicked moment, Ingray tried to think of some way to argue that she shouldn't have to show one. Then she remembered that so far the Facilitator seemed to have anticipated what she would need to bring the crate away with her. She pulled her personal messages into her vision again, and there it was. "I've just sent it to you," she said.

Captain Uisine blinked, and gazed off into the distance. "Miscellaneous biologicals," he said after a few moments, focusing again on Ingray. "In a crate this size and shape? I'm sorry, excellency, but I didn't hatch this morning. I'll be exercising my right to examine the contents myself, as outlined in the fare agreement. Otherwise that crate is not coming aboard."

Damn. "So," said Ingray, "the person I'm traveling with is in here."

"In the crate?" He seemed entirely unsurprised.

"In a suspension pod in the crate, yes," Ingray replied. "I didn't expect em to come this way, I thought I would just, you know, meet em and bring em here, and..." She trailed off, at a loss how to explain any further.

"Do you have authorizations permitting you to remove this person from Tyr Siilas? And before you mention it, I am aware that such authorizations aren't always legally necessary here. I, however, do always require them."

"An authorization to take someone on your ship?" Ingray frowned, bewildered. "You didn't need one for me. You didn't ask me for one, for...my friend."

Still not changing expression, Captain Uisine said, "I don't transport anyone against their will. I say that specifically in the fare agreement." Which Ingray had read, of course; she was no fool. But obviously she hadn't remembered that. Hadn't thought, at that point, that it would be an issue. "I can ask you right now, do you want to leave Tyr Siilas and go to Hwae..."

"I do!" Ingray interjected.

"...and you can tell me that." His voice was still serious and even. "This person cannot tell me if e wants to go where you are taking em. I don't doubt there's some very compelling reason you are bringing em aboard in a suspension pod. I would like to be sure that compelling reason is eirs, and not just yours."

"But..." But he'd already said that this wasn't a matter of Tyr Siilas law. And if he refunded her money, she might be able to find another ship for the same fare, but if she went through the dock office again she'd have to pay another fee, which she didn't have. She might be able to find passage on her own, but that would take time. Maybe a lot of time. She sighed. "I don't know why e's in a suspension pod." Well, actually, she had some idea. But that wasn't going to help her cause with Captain Uisine, plainly. "I went to pick em up, and this is how I found em."

"Is there some medical reason this person is traveling in a suspension pod?"

"Not that I know of," she said, quite honestly.

"E didn't leave you any message, or any instruction?"

"No."

"Well, excellency," said Captain Uisine after a few moments, "I suggest we open the pod and ask em. We can always put em back in if e prefers that."

"What, right here?" The bay wasn't really closed off, not at the moment, and coming out of a suspension pod was uncomfortable and undignified. Or so Ingray understood. And in the time it had taken to push the crate here, she had decided that maybe she preferred things this way, preferred to delay introducing herself to this person and explaining just why she'd brought em here.

"I don't have oversize luggage regulations for amusement's sake. The only way that crate is coming on board is through cargo access. And for what I hope are obvious reasons I'm not going to agree to that happening."

If Ingray's mother Netano were doing this, she'd have somehow obtained whatever authorizations she would need to satisfy this ship captain. Or she'd have bought passage on some ship where the captain or other crew owed her favors, or were in her power for some reason. Danach—Ingray's foster-brother Danach would probably find some way to threaten Captain Uisine, or charm or bribe him into doing what he wanted. Maybe she could bluff her way through this. Maybe tears would do it; they would certainly be easy to produce right now. But judging from the captain's reaction on hearing that she wouldn't be able to afford to eat for two days, she didn't think that would work.

She had to do something. She had to get herself—and the person in this suspension pod—onto that ship. She had no other option, no other available course, beyond staying on this station, broke and starving, for the rest of her life.

She was *not* going to cry. "Look," she said, "I need to explain." Captain Uisine had already put the worst possible construction on the situation. It wasn't going to look any better once the suspension pod was opened. She looked behind her, through the entrance to the bay, but no one was passing in the corridor beyond. Looked back at Captain Uisine. Sighed again. "I paid to have this person brought out of Compassionate Removal." No glimmer of recognition on Captain Uisine's face. She'd used the name most Bantia speakers would have used, on Hwae; maybe he didn't recognize that. She tried to think what the word might be in Yiir, which she had been using here, had used in all her brief dealings with Captain Uisine so far. She didn't think there was one—here on Tyr Siilas nearly every crime was punishable by a fine. All the language lessons and news items she'd run across discussed crime and its consequences in those terms. She called up a dictionary, tried searching through it, without success. "You know, when someone breaks a law, and either they've done it over and over again and you know they're just going to keep doing it, or what they did was so terrible they're not going to get another chance to do it again. So they get sent to Compassionate Removal."

"You're talking about a prison," said Captain Uisine.

In the corner of Ingray's vision, her dictionary confirmed and defined the word. "No, it's not a *prison*! We don't have prisons. It's a *place*. Where they can be away from regular people. They can do whatever they want, go wherever they like, you know, so long as they stay there. And they have to stay there. Once you go in you don't come out. You're legally dead. It's just, it would be wrong to *kill* them."

"So you paid everything you had—which to judge from the clothes you're wearing, and your manner, was quite a lot—to have your friend broken out of a high-security prison with a name that sounds like a euphemism for killing vermin. What did e do?"

"E's not my friend! I've never even met em. Well, I was at an event e was at once. A couple of times. But we never met in person."

"What did e do?" Captain Uisine asked again.

"This is Pahlad Budrakim." Winced, after she said it. Had she really done this? But there hadn't been any other choice.

After an endless moment, Captain Uisine said, "Am I supposed to recognize the name?"

"You don't?" asked Ingray, surprised. "Not at all?"

"Not at all."

"Pahlad's father, Ethiat Budrakim, is Prolocutor of the Third Assembly, on Hwae." No reaction from Captain Uisine. "A prolocutor is..."

"Yes," put in Captain Uisine, evenly. "A prolocutor presides over an Assembly, and represents that Assembly to the Overassembly. I've been to Hwae Station quite a few times, and I pay attention to station news. I know who Prolocutor Dicat is, e's Prolocutor of the First Assembly. Eir name is on all sorts of regulations I have to follow when I'm docked there. But I don't know anything about the Third Assembly."

That made sense. Hwae Station and the several Hwaean outstations—and the intersystem gates, for that matter—were all under the authority of the First Assembly. It made sense that Captain Uisine would pay attention to First Assembly affairs and not to the Assemblies based on Hwae itself. Ingray blinked. Took a breath. "Well, Prolocutor Budrakim has held his seat for decades. There was an election just a few years ago. It was very dramatic. He almost lost. Which is how… Pahlad is…well, *was* one of his foster-children. Ethiat Budrakim is part Garseddai."

"Him and a billion other people who think it's tragic and romantic to be Garseddai." Captain Uisine's voice was disdainful. "It's only the most notorious out of a long list of Radchaai atrocities. The only system to resist invasion so effectively that the Radchaai destroyed every last one of them for it and left the entire system burned and lifeless. People like your Prolocutor Budrakim can claim ancestors who are either especially valorous or especially deserving of sympathy, whichever suits them better at the moment. Lucky for them there's no way to prove it one way or the other. Let me guess; he's descended from an Elector who managed to secretly flee the system before the Radchaai burned everything."

"But he is!" insisted Ingray. "He has proof. He's got

part of a panel from inside the shuttle his ancestor fled in, and a shirt with blood on it. And a lot of other things, jewelry and a half dozen of those little pentagonal tokens stamped with flowers that I think were from some kind of game. Or, he used to have those things. They were stolen. You really didn't hear about this?"

"I really didn't." Captain Uisine sounded half sarcastic, as though the idea that he might have heard about something that had consumed the attention of everyone Ingray had known, and pretty much every major news service in Hwae System, struck him as ridiculous.

"It was an inside job. Pahlad had grown up in Ethiat Budrakim's household, and e had been given a post overseeing the lareum where the Garseddai vestiges were kept." There had been a lot of comment about how, while it was of course generous of prominent citizens to raise foster-children from less advantaged circumstances, or even the public crèches, it had been foolish of Ethiat Budrakim to trust Pahlad so implicitly. No one was as close or loyal as your own acknowledged heirs, everyone knew that. Thinking of it still made Ingray, herself a foster-child out of a public crèche, cringe unhappily. "Nobody could have done it except Pahlad."

"And for this e is cast permanently into an inescapable prison, what did you call it, Compassionate Removal? And declared dead?" He took his hand off the crate. Put it back, when the crate shifted again, even though Ingray still held her end.

"E had betrayed eir parent! It was a huge scandal. And e showed no signs of remorse at what e had done. The whole thing had been very elaborate and cold-blooded. E managed to make copies of the things and put them in the lareum in place of the real ones, and there was Prolocutor Budrakim showing people around, you know, thinking they were the real ones, and no one knowing they were fake the whole time. And his foster-child Pahlad standing right there nearly every time, just as cool as anything, as though nothing was wrong." And after all, it wasn't as though e was being executed. "The copies were nearly perfect."

Captain Uisine thought about that a moment. "And your interest in this?"

"They never found the originals," Ingray said. "Pahlad wouldn't say what had happened to them. E insisted e had stolen nothing, and done nothing wrong. But of course e must have done it, no one else could have. So e must know where they are."

"Ah." Captain Uisine seemed to relax, and leaned back against the airlock frame, folded his arms. "You think this Pahlad Budrakim can lead you to the originals, which you can then, what, sell? Hold hostage? Restore heroically to their proper place?"

Any of them would serve Ingray's purpose, really. But what she wanted more than anything was to be able to bring them to Netano. "My mother is a district representative in the Third Assembly. She wants to be Third Prolocutor—she tried, last election, but in the end the votes tipped Budrakim's way." And Netano had never been friendly with Ethiat Budrakim, an enmity that couldn't be explained by differences of faction. After all, plenty of other Assembly representatives managed to get along quite amicably whatever their differing positions on tariffs or fishing limits. "Right now I'm one of three..." Not three. Vaor had gone last year. Gone because e'd wanted to, e'd insisted, not because Netano had sent em away, but e had wept the whole time e'd packed, wept walking out the door, and e hadn't answered any of Ingray's messages since. "Two foster-children in my mother's household. One of us will get to be Netano eventually."

"And this is how you intend to distinguish yourself in your mother's eyes," Captain Uisine guessed.

"I didn't expect Pahlad to come all packaged up like this!" She couldn't resist the impulse anymore—she grabbed a handful of soft silk skirt. "I went to, you know, the usual sort of broker here, and made an offer, to whoever could discreetly bring Pahlad Budrakim out of Compassionate Removal." Honestly, she hadn't really expected that anyone would take that offer up. The plan had been desperate from the start.

"Slavery and human trafficking are among the very few things that aren't legal here," Captain Uisine observed. "Technically, anyway. Of *course* they would deliver this person to you all packaged up. It gives them deniability. And I must say, excellency, the fact that that didn't occur to you, or that you weren't at least prepared for the possibility, suggests to me that you're not best suited to follow in the footsteps of your apparently political mother." Ingray frowned. She was *not* going to cry. Captain Uisine continued speaking. "I mean no offense. We all have our particular talents. What happens if you aren't selected to be your mother's heir?"

Possibly not much. Possibly she would just continue in her job, in the family, as she had. But Netano had always said that in anything worth doing, the stakes were all or nothing. Most families on Hwae had sent one or more children out for fosterage, or were fostering children from other households, some in temporary arrangements, some in permanent adoptions. Danach, for instance, was a foster from one of Netano's supporters. But there were always some children in every district whose parents were unwilling or unable to care for them, and had no one willing or able to foster them, who ended up as wards of the state in one of the district's public crèches. Ingray, like Pahlad Budrakim, had been one of these. "I don't really have a chance to be Mama's heir. I never really did." But if she left the Aughskold household, or was sent away, she had no other family to turn to. She would be entirely on her own. "Mama likes it when we take initiative, and she likes schemes, but she doesn't like it when we fail. If I fail badly enough I'll probably have to leave the household. Worse, I'll be in debt. I borrowed against my future allowance, to get enough for the payment. So even if I don't lose my job—which I probably will—I'll be broke. For years." For decades. "I know it wasn't exactly a prudent use of my resources," she admitted. Willed herself to open her hand, raised it to lay on the crate but instead clasped it with her other hand, a perfectly acceptable pose with no danger of anxiously clutching at things. "If I was going to borrow like that, I ought to have just invested it some-where safe. Then if Netano sent me away, I'd have at least had enough to keep myself with. I just..." She just couldn't stand the thought of Danach sneering openly at her. Of losing any chance at all of Netano Aughskold's regard.

Captain Uisine stared at her over the crate. "I am on the very edge," he said, finally, "of refunding your passage—both of the berths you've paid for—and ask-ing you to leave this bay. I haven't made up my mind yet. But I'll tell you one thing, there's no way you're bringing that person—Pahlad Budrakim, you said?—aboard my ship still in that suspension pod. And considering you expected to meet em awake and unfrozen, you won't have any objection to thawing em out now, I presume?"

"Will you take us aboard then?"

"I'll *consider* taking *you* aboard then. Pahlad Budra-kim can do as e likes." A moment's thought. "If e doesn't want to come aboard, I'll refund you eir fare."

It could have been worse, Ingray supposed. It was *some* sort of chance, anyway. Captain Uisine put his other hand on the crate. "Step back, excellency, you don't want your foot caught under this." Ingray stepped back and the crate settled to the floor with a *thunk*. "Do you know if this person has ever been in suspension before?"

Ingray picked up her jacket and bag and sandals off the crate lid. "No, why?"

Captain Uisine touched the crate's latches and care-fully slid the lid aside. "E might panic if e doesn't know what to expect. A little help would be nice."

Ingray dropped her sandals and bag, pulled her jacket on, and then helped brace the lid as Captain Uisine tilted it and let it slide down to rest against the crate.

Captain Uisine looked for a moment at the smooth, black surface of the pod, then slid open the pod's control panel. "Everything looks good," he said, as a giant black spider scuttled out of the airlock, nearly a meter high, a rolled-up blanket clutched in one hairy appendage. Weirdly, disturbingly graceful, it skittered up to Captain Uisine and stopped, turned one of its far too many stalked eyes toward Ingray. No, it wasn't a spider. It was…something else.

"Um," said Ingray. "That's…is that a spider?" She didn't know why the back of her neck was prickling. She didn't mind spiders. But this…thing was so unsettling. Its legs were jointed wrong, she realized, and its eyestalks sprouted right out of its blob of a body. There was no waist, no head. And something else was wrong, though she couldn't quite say what.

"Of course it's not a spider," replied Captain Uisine, still frowning at the suspension pod. "You don't get spiders with half-meter bodies, or two-meter leg spans. Or, you know, not unaugmented ones. But this isn't a spider." He looked up. "But it's *kind* of like a spider, I'll grant you that. Do you have a problem with spiders, excellency?" The not-spider's body trembled gelatinously, stretched to become oblong rather than round, and four extra legs slid out to touch the bay floor. "Does that help?"

Seeing the thing change shape was somehow even more disturbing, but she refused to step back, even though she wanted to. "Not really. And I don't mind spiders at all. It's just, this looks so...so organic." Except in a wrong, squishy, itchy sort of way.

"Well, yes," said Captain Uisine, standing square and stolid by the open crate. Entirely unbothered by the spidery thing beside him. "A lot of it is. Some people find it unsettling, and apparently you're one of them, but it's just a bio mech. You'll get used to it after a few days, or if you don't I'll keep it out of your way." He touched the control panel and the smooth surface of the pod broke open with a click and slid aside. For just an instant Ingray saw a person lying naked and motionless, submerged in a pool of blue fluid, unevenly cut hair a tangled mass over half of eir sharp-featured face, thin—thinner than she remembered pictures of Pahlad Budrakim—the long welt of a scar along eir right flank.

Then the smooth, glassy surface of the preserving medium rippled and billowed as the person opened eir eyes and sat convulsively up, choking, one outthrust arm smacking hard into Ingray. Captain Uisine grabbed eir other arm. "It's all right," he said, voice still calm and serious. The person continued to choke as blue fluid poured out of eir mouth and nose, sheeted away from eir body back into the pod. "It's all right. Everything's fine. You're all right."

The last of the fluid drained away from the person's mouth and nose, and e gave a breathy, shaking moan.

"First time?" asked Captain Uisine, reaching down for the blanket the spider mech still proffered.

The naked person in the pod closed eir eyes. Gasped a few times, and then eir breathing settled.

"Are you all right?" asked Ingray. In Bantia this time, the most commonly spoken language in Hwae System, though she was fairly sure Pahlad Budrakim would have understood Yiir, which Captain Uisine had used.

Captain Uisine shook the blanket out and laid it around the naked person's shoulders.

"Where am I?" e asked, in Bantia, voice rough with cold or fear or something else.

"We're on Tyr Siilas Station, in Tyr System," said Ingray, and then, to Captain Uisine, "E asked where e is, and I told em we are on Tyr Siilas."

"How did I get here?" asked the person sitting in the suspension pod, in Bantia. By now the blue fluid had all drained away to some reservoir in the pod itself.

"I paid someone to bring you out," said Ingray. "I'm Ingray Aughskold."

The person opened eir eyes then. "Who?"

Well, Ingray had never really met Pahlad Budrakim in person. And e was ten or more years older than she was, and not likely to have noticed a very young Aughskold foster-daughter, not likely to have known her name when she had still been a child, let alone her adult name, which she'd taken only months before e'd gone into Compassionate Removal. "I'm one of Netano Aughskold's children," said Ingray.

"Why," e asked, eir voice gaining strength, "would one of Representative Aughskold's children bring me anywhere?"

Ingray tried to think of a simple way to explain, and settled, finally, for, "You're Pahlad Budrakim."

E gave a little shake of eir head, a frown. "Who?"

Ingray suppressed a start as another spider mech came skittering out of the airlock. This one held a large cup of steaming liquid, which it passed to Captain Uisine before it spun and returned to the ship. "Here, excellency," he said, in Yiir, offering it to the person still sitting in the pod. "Can you hold this?"

"Here," said the first spider mech, in a thin, thready voice, in Bantia. "Can you hold this?"

"Aren't you Pahlad Budrakim?" asked Ingray, feeling strangely numb, except maybe for an unpleasant sensation in her gut, as though she was not capable of feeling any more despair or fear than she already had today. The Facilitator had said this was Pahlad. No, e'd said e'd examined the payment and the merchandise and both were what they should have been. But surely that was the same thing.

"No," said the person sitting in the suspension pod. "I don't even know who that is." E noticed the cup Captain Uisine was proffering. "Thank you," e said, and took it, cupped it in eir hands as Captain Uisine stopped the blanket from sliding off eir shoulders.

"Drink some," said Captain Uisine, still in Yiir. "It's serbat—it'll do you good."

"Drink it," said the spider mech, in Bantia. "It's serbat—it's good and nutritious."

What if there had been a mistake? This person looked like Pahlad Budrakim. But also, in a way, e didn't. E was thinner, certainly, and Ingray had only seen em in person once or twice, and that was years ago. "You're not Pahlad Budrakim?"

"No," said the person who was not Pahlad Budrakim. "I already said that." E took a drink of the serbat. "Oh, that's good."

Really, it didn't matter. Even if this person was Pahlad, if e was lying to her, it made no difference. She couldn't compel em to go with her back to Hwae, and not just because Captain Uisine would refuse to take em unless e wanted to go. Her plan had always depended on Pahlad being willing to go along. "You look a lot like Pahlad Budrakim," Ingray said. Still hoping.

"Do I?" e asked, and took another drink of serbat. "I guess someone made a mistake." E looked straight at Ingray then, and said, "So, when a Budrakim goes to Compassionate Removal it's only for show, is it? They send someone to fish them out, behind the scenes?" Eir expression didn't change, but eir voice was bitter.

Ingray drew breath to say, indignantly, *No of course not*, but found herself struck speechless by the fact that she had herself gotten a Budrakim out of Compassionate Removal. "No," she managed, finally. "No, I...you're really not Pahlad Budrakim?"

"I'm really not," e said.

"Then who are you?" asked the spider mech, though Captain Uisine hadn't said anything aloud.

The person sitting in the suspension pod took another drink of serbat, then said, "You said we're on Tyr Siilas?"

"Yes," said the spider mech. Ingray found she couldn't speak at all.

"I think I'd rather not tell you who I am." E looked around, at the suspension pod e sat in, the crate still surrounding it, at Captain Uisine, at the spider mech beside the captain, around at the bay. "I think I'd like to visit the Incomers Office."

"Why?" asked Ingray, almost a cry, unable to keep her confusion and her despair out of her voice.

"Unless you have financial resources we're unaware of," said the spider mech, "you won't be able to do more than apply for an indenture. You may or may not get one, and unless you have contacts here you very probably won't like what you get if you do."

"I'll like it better than Compassionate Removal." E drained the last of eir beverage.

"Look on the bright side," Captain Uisine said himself, to Ingray, in Yiir, as he took the cup from not-Pahlad. "I'll refund you eir passage, and you'll be able to eat actual food for the next couple of days."